PRAISE FOR M. L. BUCHMAN

Tom Clancy fans open to a strong female lead will clamor for more.

— *DRONE*, PUBLISHERS WEEKLY

Superb! Miranda is utterly compelling!

— *BOOKLIST*, STARRED REVIEW

Miranda Chase continues to astound and charm.

— BARB M.

Escape Rating: A. Five Stars! OMG just start with *Drone* and be prepared for a fantastic binge-read!

— READING REALITY

The best military thriller I've read in a very long time. Love the female characters.

— *DRONE*, SHELDON MCARTHUR, FOUNDER OF THE MYSTERY BOOKSTORE, LA

A fabulous soaring thriller.

— *TAKE OVER AT MIDNIGHT*, MIDWEST BOOK REVIEW

Meticulously researched, hard-hitting, and suspenseful.

— *PURE HEAT,* PUBLISHERS WEEKLY,
STARRED REVIEW

Expert technical details abound, as do realistic military missions with superb imagery that will have readers feeling as if they are right there in the midst and on the edges of their seats.

— *LIGHT UP THE NIGHT,* RT REVIEWS, 4 1/2
STARS

Buchman has catapulted his way to the top tier of my favorite authors.

— FRESH FICTION

Nonstop action that will keep readers on the edge of their seats.

— *TAKE OVER AT MIDNIGHT,* LIBRARY
JOURNAL

M L. Buchman's ability to keep the reader right in the middle of the action is amazing.

— LONG AND SHORT REVIEWS

The only thing you'll ask yourself is, "When does the next one come out?"

— *WAIT UNTIL MIDNIGHT,* RT REVIEWS, 4
STARS

The first...of (a) stellar, long-running (military) romantic suspense series.

I knew the books would be good, but I didn't realize how good.

Buchman mixes adrenalin-spiking battles and brusque military jargon with a sensitive approach.

13 times "Top Pick of the Month"

LIGHTNING

A MIRANDA CHASE POLITICAL
TECHNOTHRILLER

M. L. BUCHMAN

Receive a free book and discover more by this author at: www. mlbuchman.com

SIGN UP FOR M. L. BUCHMAN'S NEWSLETTER TODAY

and receive:
Release News
Free Short Stories
a Free Book

Get your free book today. Do it now.
free-book.mlbuchman.com

Other works by M. L. Buchman: (* - also in audio)

Action-Adventure Thrillers

Dead Chef
One Chef!
Two Chef!

Miranda Chase
*Drone**
*Thunderbolt**
*Condor**
*Ghostrider**
*Raider**
*Chinook**
*Havoc**
*White Top**
*Start the Chase**
*Lightning**

Science Fiction / Fantasy

Deities Anonymous
Cookbook from Hell: Reheated
Saviors 101

Single Titles
Monk's Maze
the Me and Elsie Chronicles

Contemporary Romance

Eagle Cove
Return to Eagle Cove
Recipe for Eagle Cove
Longing for Eagle Cove
Keepsake for Eagle Cove

Love Abroad
Heart of the Cotswolds: England
Path of Love: Cinque Terre, Italy

Where Dreams
Where Dreams are Born
Where Dreams Reside
*Where Dreams Are of Christmas**
Where Dreams Unfold
Where Dreams Are Written
Where Dreams Continue

Non-Fiction

Strategies for Success
Managing Your Inner Artist/Writer
*Estate Planning for Authors**
Character Voice
*Narrate and Record Your Own Audiobook**

Short Story Series by M. L. Buchman:

Action-Adventure Thrillers

Dead Chef

Miranda Chase Origin Stories

Romantic Suspense

Antarctic Ice Fliers

US Coast Guard

Contemporary Romance

Eagle Cove

Other

Deities Anonymous (fantasy)

Single Titles

The Emily Beale Universe
(military romantic suspense)

The Night Stalkers
MAIN FLIGHT
The Night Is Mine
I Own the Dawn
Wait Until Dark
Take Over at Midnight
Light Up the Night
Bring On the Dusk
By Break of Day
Target of the Heart
Target Lock on Love
Target of Mine
Target of One's Own
NIGHT STALKERS HOLIDAYS
*Daniel's Christmas**
*Frank's Independence Day**
*Peter's Christmas**
Christmas at Steel Beach
*Zachary's Christmas**
*Roy's Independence Day**
*Damien's Christmas**
Christmas at Peleliu Cove

Henderson's Ranch
*Nathan's Big Sky**
*Big Sky, Loyal Heart**
*Big Sky Dog Whisperer**
*Tales of Henderson's Ranch**

Shadow Force: Psi
*At the Slightest Sound**
*At the Quietest Word**
*At the Merest Glance**
*At the Clearest Sensation**

White House Protection Force
*Off the Leash**
*On Your Mark**
*In the Weeds**

Firehawks
Pure Heat
Full Blaze
*Hot Point**
*Flash of Fire**
Wild Fire
SMOKEJUMPERS
*Wildfire at Dawn**
*Wildfire at Larch Creek**
*Wildfire on the Skagit**

Delta Force
*Target Engaged**
*Heart Strike**
*Wild Justice**
*Midnight Trust**

Emily Beale Universe Short Story Series

The Night Stalkers
The Night Stalkers Stories
The Night Stalkers CSAR
The Night Stalkers Wedding Stories
The Future Night Stalkers

Delta Force
Th Delta Force Shooters
The Delta Force Warriors

Firehawks
The Firehawks Lookouts
The Firehawks Hotshots
The Firebirds

White House Protection Force
Stories

Future Night Stalkers
Stories (Science Fiction)

ABOUT THIS BOOK

Miranda Chase—the autistic heroine you didn't expect. Fighting the battles no one else could win.

Revenge? A terrorist attack? Or a declaration of war?

The head of the Senate Armed Services Committee lies dead. The murder weapon? An Air Force jet deliberately crashed into his DC hotel room.

Half a world away in the South China Sea, an F-35C Lightning II crashes during landing. It cripples the aircraft supercarrier USS Theodore Roosevelt. An accident? Or China's next move toward world domination?

Miranda Chase and her NTSB air-crash investigation team are spread thin as they struggle to unravel two horrific crashes at once — and halt a global firestorm before it burns them all.

Worse, the next target could be Miranda herself.

PROLOGUE

Friday evening of Memorial Day Weekend
Joint Base Andrews
Washington, DC

"Two to go," US Air Force Captain Beth Johnston told her C-20C Gulfstream III bizjet as she brushed a hand on the high-polish paint. It wore the distinctive *United States of America* blue-and-white of a VIP transport for the 89th Airlift Wing. One of three identical birds kept in this auxiliary hangar at Andrews Air Force Base, but this sweet 20C was hers.

Tonight's VIP lift mission was a flight to Georgia to return the Secretary of the Treasury to DC after a four-day vacation. Most people were headed out of DC for Memorial Day weekend, the secretary was headed in.

Beth would take her pilot's job over any other. She didn't care crap about glory or power or politics—she wanted to fly.

This flight would leave her with only the Secretaries of Interior and Veteran Affairs who she hadn't transported yet. She had every other cabinet secretary's signature in her log book.

Of course it would be nice to snag a VP or even Presidential lift, but that wasn't likely. She'd followed their big planes any number of times for emergency coverage, but had not been needed. And as much as she'd like to snag their signatures, she'd rather not have the scale of emergency that would call for the Commander in Chief to climb aboard her little ten-passenger jet.

At 2007 hours, Captain Justin O'Dowd strode into the hangar and waved as he walked toward *his* usual 20C. She didn't recall there being a second lift mission tonight, but it was Friday before a three-day weekend so anything was possible. Odd that his copilot wasn't with him. It was easy to fly the plane solo, but it wasn't certified for it.

"How's your mother holding up?" she called out.

"Still mad for each other, they are," he replied in a ridiculously overblown Irish accent. One of Justin's running jokes was about his quiet Lebanese mother surviving his boisterous Irish father. His looks belonged to his mother, his sense of humor to his father, and his piloting skills to the US Air Force. He flew at least as well as she did.

She returned to her preflight inspection. Her copilot Reggie was following behind her so that everything was double-checked. She'd always loved the peaceful process of checking over her plane from fan blades in the engines to tire pressure—before they went out and ripped a hole in the sky.

"Hey, Reg, could you come take a look at this?" Justin's accentless voice was overloud in the quiet hangar.

Reggie glanced at her for permission, then circled around to the other side of Justin's plane.

Like her, Justin was always pure business when it came to flying. Another reason to like him, but she never quite felt that *snap* of attraction. She knew he was single and interested, but there was always something that had her keeping their relationship strictly professional.

Moments later, a shout of surprise echoed about the hangar.

Beth ducked low to look under the fuselage of her plane toward Justin's plane—as Reggie's body slumped limply to the scrubbed concrete floor.

She sprinted around the nose of both planes, then around the long wing to where Reggie lay crumpled by the open rear baggage access.

"What happened?" Beth knelt over him and reached for his pulse, but there was no need. His eyes were shot wide and his mouth was fixed in a rigid O of surprise. "What happened?"

Kneeling beside her, Justin rested a hand on her shoulder to keep her steady.

Then she saw his other hand. He held a needle-thin stiletto —with a blood-red blade.

He shifted his hand from her shoulder to clamp it over her mouth. With the other, he slid the blade into her chest, angling up below her left ribcage. A scorching agony overwhelmed any sense of fear as he plunged the blade into her heart and then circled the tip with a quick twist of his wrist. Minimal hole. Minimal blood.

She looked down in time to see the small stain of red on Reggie's shirt where the blade had severed his heart inside his chest exactly as it severed hers.

"I'm sorry, Beth. But I need your flight clearance tonight."

Captain Beth Johnston's last thought ever as her head hit the concrete was that her look of surprise was going to exactly match Reggie's.

―――

"Pull to the curb here!"

CIA Director Clarissa Reese's driver obeyed and slid out of the thick Friday evening traffic pushing into Columbus Circle.

The congestion was worse than ever as everyone tried to escape the already sweltering city for the Memorial Day weekend. He eased into a crosswalk at the corner of North Capitol and E Streets, a half-block shy of the Kimpton George Hotel to her left. In a token gesture to the pedestrians, he backed up three feet to clear a slice of it, as if they mattered.

Behind her, the US Capitol Building glowed orange in the May sunset; the sun still touched the dark bronze Statue of Freedom atop the dome so that it shone brighter than anything else in Washington, DC. Clarissa could feel her bronze glare like a simmering heat at the back of Clarissa's head.

She wished she could light the statue like a fuse on a dome-sized bomb. Or at least a missile-sized one dropped on the head of each member of the House Permanent Select Committee on Intelligence.

The fact that she knew she was overreacting did little to ease the knot that had built in her stomach throughout today's excruciating meetings, though she'd been careful to keep that off her face. Hadn't she?

Ahead, the columned facade of Union Station, stained dull orange by the setting sun, dared her to leave town. For the first time in her career, that actually sounded tempting.

She didn't want to face...anything.

"You can do this, Clarissa." Her self-instruction wasn't helping. She'd been muttering some version of it over and over for the last twenty-three days with minimal effect. Twenty-four days ago she'd had a dozen plans all running fast on a clear and open rail. Then her world had changed and she couldn't force a single one of those plans ahead.

Her driver studiously ignored her. She'd long since made it clear that the last thing she needed was to interact with any agent who'd never be more than a security peon. By the time she was his age, she'd been at a CIA black site extracting information from the worst dregs of humanity involved in the Afghan madness.

There'd been an art to that—one she'd thoroughly mastered.

This? This was hard. In the last month, she'd lost everything.

With her husband's death, her path to the White House had been blocked. Vice Presidents were *supposed* to be well protected. But not Clark. His Marine Two helicopter had gone down in flames, the bastard.

Now, the goddamn President was elevating his National Security Advisor Sarah Feldman to become Vice President rather than herself. The announcement was tomorrow and Congress was going to approve her nomination so fast that Feldman might suffer whiplash. She was the perfect mix of pro-America yet not rabid, which fit both parties well. She was, Clarissa hated to admit, incredibly well qualified as well.

Clark's death had also put Clarissa on the street. The grand Queen Anne Victorian at One Observatory Circle was for the Vice President, not his widow.

She never should have sold her prime condo in Foggy Bottom, but Clark had been such an obvious choice to next occupy the Oval Office that she'd been assured of her future residence for years to come.

The long stretch of E Street ran past the George to the White House, where now she'd never rule from the Oval Office.

And at the rate the housing market was exploding in DC, even the sale of Clark's *country* place out in Poolesville, Maryland—a place no one had heard of who didn't actually live there—wouldn't make up the difference.

For the moment she had a crap townhouse rental out in Langley.

And she'd had *no* part in the biggest political initiative since Bretton Woods and the Cold War.

The President's new MERP—Middle East Realignment Plan—had captured the imagination of everyone but the most hard-core contrarians who hated any idea that wasn't theirs. Even marginal allies were flocking to the call.

The flocks of people scowling at her driver as they squeezed past the front bumper were probably all talking about how wonderful it was. This was DC after all, and the disavowal of several long-term but terrorist-harboring *allies*, and a lifting of several Iranian sanctions had the entire city abuzz. If President Cole could run for a third term, they'd probably cheer down to the last secretary and dog walker.

Worse, President Cole had made sure that the bulk of the credit had gone to her dead husband and NSA Sarah Feldman. If the woman didn't screw up, she had the next election, eighteen months out, in the bag.

Of course, when Sarah ran, she *would* need a Vice President...

Clarissa couldn't even find the energy to snarl at yet another closed door. If she couldn't be President, she wouldn't be able to pass for VP either.

The hidden scandals—thankfully, all classified Top Secret but littered with Clarissa's name—had guaranteed her shut-out from any future chance at the Oval Office. It was clear that *certain parties* would release everything if she tried to run. The House Intelligence Committee—that was damn well supposed to be on her side—had made that painfully clear all through today's meetings.

She had enough dirt to ruin half the committee and have the other half burned at the stake for the evil witchcraft they'd perpetrated during their careers. But their idea of a united front was, if they went down, they'd take her down with them.

Bush's route from CIA Director to Vice President to the Oval was lost to her, and it was time she accepted it. Time to move on...but in what direction?

Clarissa sat in the back of her SUV and stared at the cubic brick edifice of the George and did her best to discover some shred of composure. It had become harder and harder in the weeks since Clark's death as she identified more pieces of herself that she'd lost. Beyond her home and her path to the White House, there was the surprising revelation that she missed Clark himself. Immensely.

Her fortieth birthday was in three days, and Clark had promised her a big Memorial Day celebration. She'd planned one for herself. Before it all came apart, she'd intended to inform him of her own place as Vice President on his ticket for the next election if that wasn't his surprise. But his unrevealed plans—probably some romantic getaway, knowing Clark—had followed him to the grave.

Another issue had become crystal clear during today's meetings beneath the Capitol Dome. For once, she'd misjudged all of their power plays completely. She did that very rarely—and never before so badly.

At the White House's request, she'd had the CIA draw up a master list of every known terrorist action against the US. She'd done so for every nation from Afghanistan to Zimbabwe—actually to Yemen as both Zambia and Zimbabwe were too busy wallowing in their own shit to bother the US in any notable way.

And she'd listed every CIA counterstroke, the good and the bad. She'd left out any true black ops performed by the CIA's Special Activities Division—as well as anything patently illegal done by the Special Operations Group—but included everything else.

It was supposed to be a strictly internal document, but it had predictably leaked. Clarissa had expected that and planned accordingly. The disastrous 1974 leak of the dreaded *Family Jewels* memos had chronicled the hundreds of times that the CIA had overstepped their charter. The public and

Congressional retribution, which had nearly led to the breakup of the CIA, were not going to happen on her watch.

And they hadn't.

Instead, against all projections, the opposite had occurred.

Clarissa had carefully laid all of the questionable activities at Clark's feet as he'd been the CIA Director before her. Finally, having a dead Vice President for a predecessor and a husband came in handy.

It was always better to blame a dead man.

Except, instead of the leaked summary wreaking domestic havoc this time, it had become a key document in the President's proposed MERP. It had justified massive realignments and the disavowal of several long-term Middle East allies caught with their fingers deep in terrorism.

It had also elevated Clark's posthumous popularity, for laying the groundwork to the realignment, to far past anything it deserved. She knew that for a fact as she'd spent years engineering his image during his ascendency. Now it was impossible to take back the credit, even for her own operations, that she had so publicly given away. The House Intelligence Committee had made that abundantly clear this afternoon.

This committee will protect our nation and Vice President Clark Winston's legacy—despite knowing damn well how much of that was hers—*against all comers.* The silence that followed had echoed about the meeting room until it hurt her ears. They'd *gladly* shred her reputation if they thought they could survive doing so.

Grinding on past woes achieved nothing. She needed a way forward.

Clarissa sighed and checked her watch. The committee had kept her until she'd been fifteen minutes late, now she was twenty. Senator Hunter and Rose Ramson would be waiting in the George's penthouse suite where they always held their monthly dinner meeting.

She didn't need the influence of the Chairman of the Senate Armed Services Committee, not anymore. Hunter had lost much of his power in his efforts to block the President's Middle East Realignment Plan. MERP had voided billions of dollars of foreign arms sales for Hunter's pet defense contractors and dropped his lobbying power to near zero.

To say that the contractors and the Saudis, among others, were livid about his inability to quash MERP, was a significant understatement. They'd all become much less friendly over these same three weeks since Clark's death.

No, she hadn't needed anything from Hunter since long before his fall from grace. Now there was a growing doubt that he'd manage to retain his Senate seat for a fifth six-year term at the next election. There were rumors—that she knew to be true —that *both* parties were vetting new candidates to replace the suddenly vulnerable Hunter Ramson. No longer the favored son.

What Clarissa needed tonight was the sharp mind of Washington's top socialite, Rose Ramson, the so-called *First Lady of DC*. Perhaps so powerful in her own right that she could weather the storm of her husband's fall.

Clarissa had once promised Rose the future Vice Presidency but, as hard as it was to accept, that was gone and they both knew it. The question now? Could Rose help her consolidate what power she did have? Clarissa would leave it up to Rose to name her price.

Sadly, Clarissa suspected that her scattered thoughts wouldn't become any more coherent than they were at this moment.

"Let's get this done already," she finally told the driver.

Pedestrians had stopped in the narrow slice of crosswalk at the front of the car. They were gawking and pointing at something behind her.

The driver checked his side mirror—ducking low to look upward. He didn't look away.

Clarissa turned to look out the rear window.

Instead of a big truck blocking the lane, she spotted a jet, a black blot on an achingly deep blue evening sky. Weaving around the Capitol Dome as if the Statue of Freedom was the marker post for Turn Four in a horse race. It sped toward them—where no planes were ever supposed to be.

Downtown DC was the most protected no-fly zone in the country.

An idiot, hoping to be in tomorrow's headlines for buzzing DC, had swooped between the Capitol and the Supreme Court Building, and was now carving a hard turn at Columbus Circle above Union Station.

Heading for the White House? If both President Cole and future-VP Feldman were there, and it all went wrong... Well, the Speaker of the House, who was next in line, was a ridiculous progressive and had no love for the CIA, making him hard to leverage.

It was a sleek C-20C Gulfstream III painted in *United States of America* blue-and-white.

"Damn, they're low," her driver spoke for the first time since leaving the Capitol Building.

They were.

In fact, they were so low that—

The plane passed close overhead as it flew into the narrow slot of E Street Northwest, which was barely wider than its wingspan.

Below the tops of the buildings.

Was the pilot out to kill himself?

The sonic lash of its jet engines reverberated along the brick-and-glass canyon. The wind of its passage slammed into them hard enough to shake her Cadillac Escalade SUV despite the extra weight of the Class VI up-armor and thick bulletproof glass.

Rather than racing along E Street for the mile and a half to the White House, the jet banked right with an abrupt twist—and flew into the side of a building.

The moment was so unreal she couldn't blink or turn away. It looked like a Hollywood film without any slo-mo or alternate angle shots.

The plane disappeared through the wall of the top floor.

For a moment...nothing.

Only a dark hole where the outer windows and red brick no longer reflected the sunset sky.

Then a massive plume of fire roiled out gap.

Two seconds later, all of the glass and much of the brick on that floor blew outward as the fuel spilled by the shattered plane exploded deep inside the building.

Half a block away, the shock wave slammed her SUV hard enough that the shoulder belt was all that kept her in her seat.

A cloud of debris rained down on the heavy traffic. Her car rattled in the thick hailstorm of debris peppering the metal body. A chunk of bricks the size of a footstool slammed off the center of the hood with a bang of bending steel louder than a gunshot, making both her and the driver jump. It tumbled into the crowd of gawking pedestrians.

Screams of the injured added to the mayhem of car alarms and blasting horns. The hard crunch of fender benders as drivers lost control. The cries when they crushed an unwary pedestrian in the process.

While the last of the debris still pattered down upon them —a pair of *alert* fighter jets raced low over the city. Not a sonic boom, but so loud that Clarissa ducked despite knowing they were far above her and in better control than the first jet had been. They disappeared to the west, circled hard, and made another roaring pass over the unfolding disaster.

Too little, too late.

When she looked up again, she finally noticed which building had been struck.

The George.

The top floor.

The point of entry...

The southeast corner suite—

Clarissa barely flinched as a car slammed into the passenger door close by her elbow. Numb with shock, she couldn't move a single muscle.

She was used to looking *out* that window, not locating it from the outside.

The Gulfstream *hadn't* been out of control.

It had impacted the hotel *precisely* where, at this very moment, she was supposed to be having her monthly dinner with the Ramsons. The couple stayed there on the last Friday of every month to enjoy the Presidential Suite's luxury—or rather the luxury of its bed—preceded by a fine dinner and an off-the-books meeting with Clarissa, the Director of the CIA.

Either the defense contractors or the Saudis had tired of Senator Ramson failing them.

Or both.

Or, Clarissa couldn't swallow against a throat gone dry, had the House Intelligence Committee decided it was time to erase her?

———

Jeremy hated moving days.

He lay on the condo's charcoal-gray carpet, staring up at the blank white ceiling.

"Who invented the idea of moving?" No answer was scribed upon the white walls, but the deep carpet was soft against his back, so that was nice. If he discovered what caused *moving* to happen, maybe Taz could do something about never letting it happen again—ever.

For now, he lay in the middle of a sea of cardboard-beige boxes. Some were covered with dull-green-and-orange graphics that he assumed were meant to be reassuring—but weren't. Others bore the IKEA logo, none of them assembled. Like they were waiting to explode in a thousand little bits and pieces that would consume him at the slightest provocation.

Taz was, of course, being her usual whirlwind. The three eighteen-hour days of the cross-country drive in a rental truck hadn't fazed her in the slightest. Only on arrival had he discovered that she was one of those unpack-right-away sorts; he was more of an I'd-rather-die-first sort. It was the fifth move of his entire life: college at MIT when he was sixteen, grad school at Princeton at nineteen, the NTSB Academy in Virginia (all three of which he'd lived in dorm rooms), Miranda's NTSB team house in Washington State, and now the *other* Washington—DC.

How had this happened to him?

Three weeks ago, he'd been investigating the horrific crash of the Marine Two White Top helicopter that had killed the Vice President, his security detail, several guests, and the three Marines aboard, along with three hundred and fifty-seven Walmart shoppers and employees.

Happily a member of Miranda's team.

Never wanting more.

Now he was drowning in a sea of boxes.

What had he been thinking? He'd *liked* being Miranda's right-hand assistant. The mind games that Mike played. Holly teasing him about which Bond film he was in this time and calling him Q. She thought it was an insult but he thought it sounded like the best job in the world. Though she did play rough, he wouldn't miss that...unless he was warped enough to actually miss it when she rapped her knuckles on his skull?

"And two bosses? What's up with that?"

"We'll find out soon enough, won't we?" Taz paused long enough to look down at him with either pity or annoyance. Or maybe both. Her long dark hair draped over her shoulders. She looked...softer. Taz was still the four-eleven of hyper-fit Latina with years of Air Force Service, but she was actually smiling. She was the half of their couple that was always serious.

"When did you become the optimist and me the cynic?"

She tipped her head one way, then the other before shrugging. With a kick against the bottom of his sneaker, she was off again.

He ignored the hint to get his ass in gear.

Jeremy had come to DC to take an opening in the National Transportation Safety Board's headquarters on the lab team. But, with Taz re-enlisting into the Air Force, he'd also been seconded to—

His phone rang. Please let it be the cable guy. He needed to get online, for even an hour, simply to clear his head.

"Are you going to answer that?" Taz swept by with an armful of Air Force blue-and-gold towels, off to make their condo bathroom perfect.

Really, really done with her rootless life to date, she'd picked out the townhouse and was busy making it into a home...for them.

Which itself was too weird for words.

Jeremy had always assumed that he'd find someone someday. But he'd never thought seriously about being a *them* until Colonel Taz Cortez had slammed into his life. *Someday* had become very real and very now.

"No," he hoped he was referring to the phone call and not the future. Then answered it to prove that he was completely onboard, even if he could barely move from his position lying prostrate on the floor. "Jeremy here."

"Good evening, Jeremy."

"Hi, General Macy." He didn't need a call from their other new boss at this moment. General Macy ran the US Air Force's AIB—Accident Investigation Board.

"Did you make it to DC yet?"

"We're fully out of the truck and living in a cardboard ocean. Or maybe it's a jungle." He liked that metaphor better. Someone else had already chopped down the trees and helpfully corrugated into boxes. Totally climbable.

"Yep, moving sucks, son. Trust me, after thirty years in the Air Force, I can attest that it doesn't get any easier. Jeremy, I know that you and Taz aren't technically starting until Tuesday after Memorial Day weekend, but are you available for a launch?" There was heavy chatter in the background on the general's end and it sounded urgent.

It might be only a temporary reprieve, but being called out to a crash investigation *would* save him from drowning in a cardboard sea *or* climbing a corrugated forest. Kill two metaphors for the price of one. "Where?"

"E Street NW. Off Columbus Circle," the general was echoing someone else's words.

Jeremy jolted upright. "In *downtown?*"

Taz, already returning from the bathroom, stopped in mid-whirling dervish. In keeping with Newton's law of the conservation of momentum, his guilt at not helping increased by precisely the same amount as the reduction of his relief when she'd stopped.

"Yes. We even have the crash on camera from the Air Force alert fighters that were chasing the jet. It impacted the top story of a downtown hotel."

"We're on our way."

"Good man." When General Jack Macy said that in his *command* voice, it was very motivating.

Jeremy pushed to his feet.

Another burst of someone talking rapidly to the general,

though Jeremy couldn't catch any of the words. Then General Jack Macy proved that neither the Army nor the Navy had any advantage over the Air Force when it came to swearing. When Macy spoke again his voice was deathly calm.

"We need to know *fast* whether this was a terrorist act. Foreign or domestic. Or merely some damn idiot on a joyride. And Jeremy?"

"Yes sir."

"I don't want to bias the investigation, but it looks like it was one of ours."

"Ours? Oh, the Air Force's." He'd only ever been a member of the unaligned NTSB. Now he worked for both the NTSB lab and the US Air Force Accident Investigation Board as a consultant. "Really?"

"Really." General Macy hung up without another word.

"Holy afterburners, Batman."

"What's up, Boy Wonder?" Taz's hands were still full of bed frame parts, the longest she'd been still since the last box had come off the truck.

"We've got a launch. Here in DC. Air Force plane ran into a hotel. We need to find out if it was an accident or a terrorist act —fast!" He struggled to his feet and began pushing around the boxes, desperately scanning scribbled labels. He couldn't read half of them, and they were mostly in his own handwriting. How did they get so much stuff?

Mom and Dad, Miranda, and the other members of the team had made sure that he and Taz had beds and couches and everything to outfit a kitchen and office, within hours of their decision to move East. But then they'd needed a truck to haul it all and ended up towing the car they would have fit into before.

He shook a box and it sounded like a cement mixer. No idea what that was. There was a bright *tink* of something breaking. He could only pray that Taz didn't hear that. The next—

"What are you looking for?" Level-headed Taz wasn't

flustered for a single second, calmer than General Macy. Despite all of their time together, it was still easy to underestimate slim Taz. He constantly had to remind himself that she had spent nineteen years in the Pentagon and, due to her immense skills, had worked her way up to being a full colonel three years faster than should be possible. She'd turned being steady into an art form.

"My field pack!"

Taking a single step, Taz tapped a finger on a box—size large, four-point-five cubic feet, one-eighth cubic meter—that had bright red tape instead of the standard brown. It was the only one like that in either the sea or the forest, whichever this was. Red algae or fall-maple-leaf red? Nope, still no clue if he was in a sea or forest.

He vaguely remembered that Taz had said something about why it was red, but couldn't recall what.

She flipped out her Phaeton fighting knife, slit the tape, then slid it once more out of sight along her wrist in that smooth move he'd never been able to follow. She folded open the flaps. Inside were their vests and crash-site investigation packs.

He scooped her against him, rested his cheek atop her hair, and held her tight.

Taz snuggled in close. "This had better work, Jeremy, or I'm going to be super pissed."

"The crash investigation? Why wouldn't it?"

"No, you doofus. Us."

"As long as we're in this together, nothing else matters."

Taz sniffled. "Aw shit, Jeremy. You know you shouldn't say stuff like that to me."

"Why?"

"Because if you keep doing it, I might start believing it."

"Good." He smiled as he kissed the top of her head.

She held him a moment longer, then poked him in his

ticklish spot, making him jump away. Freed, Taz grabbed her pack from the box. She also pulled out the Taser that had earned her the nickname and strapped its belt and holster on so that it hung at her hip.

He fished out his own pack, then peeked into the corrugated depths. Empty. No murky ocean depths in sight. No unmapped root systems either. One down, eighty-three billion four hundred million and fifty-four boxes to go.

"Come on, lazybones. There's a crash, get a move on." And his personal whirlwind was out the door before he'd taken a breath.

1

Elmendorf Air Force Base
Anchorage, Alaska

"JEREMY LOOK AT HOW..." FOR THE SEVENTEENTH TIME TODAY, Miranda Chase turned and discovered that Jeremy wasn't there.

A light dusting of snow, probably the last of the year, was holding on beneath late afternoon gray skies. At three degrees below freezing, atypically chilly for late May, a bare centimeter had fallen. It made the site of the air-crash look safe and clean, masking the disaster underneath. But the weak sunlight was already melting it into blotchy patches. It looked like a skin disease.

Turning quickly away from where Jeremy wasn't, she inspected the sprawl of the shattered KC-46 Pegasus aerial tanker spread down Runway 06 at Elmendorf Air Force Base.

JBER—Joint Base Elmendorf-Richardson—had a T-placed pair of runways. The main buildings and all current air traffic were along the shorter top stroke. The KC-46 had splattered itself over the first one thousand and ninety-two meters of the long vertical of the T, closing the main runway.

This was limiting Air Force operations. Already two super-heavy flights were on hold, awaiting her permission for the Air Force to clear and reopen of this runway. That at least was familiar, they were always pressuring her to cut short an investigation to clear a field for operation before she was done. It was wrong in so many ways and always made her feel as if she was choking.

A KC-46 was a Boeing 767 modified into a flying fuel truck —except this one had become a fuel bomb.

"How am I supposed to do this without Jeremy?" She'd come to rely on him so much in the last two years that it felt as if...as if...he wasn't there. No metaphor came to mind. As if she was missing a hand? Would that be an appropriate correlation? She simply didn't know. Metaphor failure was a common challenge for autistics, but that didn't mean she shouldn't fight against it. They seemed...useful. To others at least. Yes, she *would* keep working on them.

"Really? But you're the best there is. You've solved more crash investigations than anyone in the entire history of the NTSB." Andi Wu held a fistful of small orange flags on wires for staking out the perimeter of the debris field.

"No, Terence has done more than—"

"Not according to him."

Terence Graham had been with the NTSB for his entire career. Had she covered more ground in nineteen years than her mentor had in forty? That was hard to believe, though now he headed up the NTSB Training Academy and rarely went into the field. So, perhaps. She'd have to search the database to be sure. Actually, there was no need. Terence's word had always been good enough for her, even transmitted through a third party.

Miranda dusted the last of the snow off the airplane tire that had rolled three hundred and eleven meters past the next nearest piece of debris, then sat on it. Andi had laughed that cheery laugh of hers when Miranda had insisted that it be properly staked. *Nothing else here but the tire.* Usually her laugh made Miranda feel better, but not today.

Andi had done the staking of the debris field, Jeremy's usual task, without complaint but her laugh reminded Miranda of his excitement about every aspect of a new crash.

Worse, Andi was right. The wheel had broken free during the crash and rolled way out here. They'd photographed it in place, as well as the breakage of the axle, and were done with it. There'd been no surprises except the extreme nature of the shearing fracture in the steel of the shock tower attachment point. The pilot hadn't merely landed hard, he'd *slammed* it down.

You can't control every aspect of an investigation. Terence's admonition was a familiar one, dating back to her first investigation as a student investigator nineteen years ago. It was a concept that constantly battled with the tendencies driven by her Autism Spectrum Disorder. She wanted everything in its proper place and *hated* anything that wasn't complete. It wasn't merely unnerving. An incomplete action was a fundamentally *wrong* state of being. She needed the completion.

Yet Andi was right. A lone tire three hundred and eleven meters from the crash really left little worth marking.

"So why do I feel the need to have it staked?"

"Do you want me to try answering that?" Andi shifted briefly foot-to-foot. Perhaps she was cold, though there was little wind and the air didn't seem chilly to Miranda herself. Two inches shorter than Miranda's own five-four, Andi was a slender Chinese woman without an extra ounce of insulation on her physique but she was dressed properly for such outdoors work.

Unsure if she'd like the answer, Miranda nodded yes anyway. Andi stopped shuffling, planted her feet, and faced Miranda directly. Had her shuffling warmed her sufficiently for the moment? Or was there some other cause? Did her feet hurt? She wore the boots she always chose for site visits.

"Perhaps, Miranda, it's a need for control of something? Of anything? Jeremy and Taz climbed into their truck four days ago, turned east, and are gone. That must be a hard shock..." Andi hesitated and glanced at her carefully.

"...to my autism." Miranda knew the look. Other NTSB investigators knew she was on the Spectrum and treated her differently because of it. Maybe they thought they were helping by not directly addressing her issues, but they weren't. Instead that *help* morphed it into an annoying array of broken statements and incomplete thoughts. Unsure why, she pulled her personal notebook out of its vest pocket and made a note to think about that later. She made a second note that she especially didn't like it coming from her own team. That was enough for now, she didn't want to delay the crash investigation.

Andi nodded, shrugged, then nodded again. They'd only been dating for a few weeks—twenty-two days—and they were both being careful around each other. Weren't new beginnings supposed to be the easy part? She'd read that somewhere.

"Jeremy always..." Miranda sighed.

For two years she could simply turn and there he'd be for whatever she needed.

Then, because she hated unfinished sentences in herself as much as she did in others, continued, "...simply spoke to me as if I was a normal person."

Andi winced. "You know it was time for him to fly on his own."

"Knowing that and liking that are proving to be quite disparate thoughts in my head."

"You still have Mike, Holly, and me."

"I do." That cheered her up some.

"I promise to be less careful around you. It's only that everything between us is so new, I don't want to screw it up."

"To me, *everything* is always new, except when it's also overwhelming. That at least is familiar."

"Right. I didn't think of it that way."

And by Andi's single, simple nod, so unlike Jeremy's multiple excited nods when he grasped any new idea, Miranda understood that Andi had filed the change away and would never make that particular mistake again.

"Also, if you need it, we can request a new person."

Miranda shuddered. *New.* Such an awful word. In these last months, her autism seemed to be becoming more reactive, squeezing in harder and harder like a cherry tomato that was going to burst and spray out everywhere with no warning. She *hated* cherry tomatoes for that reason—didn't even like removing them from her salad when a restaurant included them against her instructions, in case they went off without warning.

And finding a good metaphor wasn't cheering her up either. Everything that was supposed to become easier was harder than ever. Knowing that Jeremy and Taz's departure was probably the root cause did nothing to ease the pressure that squeezed in on her.

Although...perhaps Andi was right as usual.

"Last year *you* were new."

"Last year I was a goddamn train wreck," Andi groaned in that way of hers that said she was half joking. Miranda still didn't always get why, but it was a good measure of Andi's generally positive mood.

"But now you're a good thing."

In answer, Andi leaned in and whispered so close to her ear that it tickled, "Then let's go solve a plane wreck."

"Good idea." She could either focus on her mood or on the

crash, but her ASD made it almost impossible for her to do both at once. She pulled out her notebook and entered a note.

"What was that one?" Andi asked as Miranda stood.

"My *Advantages of ASD* page: able to fully concentrate on only one thing at a time."

Andi took her hand and squeezed it tightly. "I can personally attest to the advantages of that particular ability."

Miranda assumed that was clever in some way she didn't understand.

Without staking the lone wheel, they headed back along the runway to where Mike and Holly had finished photographing the wreck and were investigating the debris field itself.

Miranda turned to see if Jeremy was following...and sighed.

Eighteen times today.

2

"SHIT!" MIKE INSPECTED THE TEAR IN HIS SLACKS THAT WAS letting in the Alaskan cold. And the blood that wouldn't stop trickling from the cut on the back of his left hand where he'd scraped it against a jagged sheet-metal edge. And the ankle he'd twisted while slip-sliding over the thin coating of snow. And...

He kicked a piece of sheet metal that looked as if it had been run through an airplane-sized trash compactor. Another typical day on a crash investigation.

Still, it beat being gunned down in his office chair. Two years ago, and he still couldn't credit his reprieve—con man to mafia target in a screwed-up FBI sting to NTSB investigator. Now *that* had been a wild seventeen hours.

Instead of being gunned down where he sat, Mike had spent the last twenty minutes in the cold, chasing around the remains of the KC-46's snow-dusted tail section in an attempt to locate the flight recorder. There were so many bits and shreds of metal that the locator signal had been reflected, refracted, bifurcated, and all sorts of screwed up when he used the detector.

The black box, which was actually painted a bright orange to make it easy to find, wasn't being easy to find. It hadn't been on its mounting pins in the tail section. Actually, it might be, but the mount was missing as well.

It took three-point-one million parts to make one Boeing 767, and he'd estimate this one had returned to the quarter-million-parts stage of disassembly. The reverse transition had been destructively abrupt.

He scraped a handful of snow from a bent piece of deck plating and made a cold compress against the back of his cut hand.

To the east, he could see Miranda and Andi returning from whatever had caught Miranda's attention so far down the expanse of the snowy runway. There was still no sign of the afternoon sun except as a dazzling brightness in one section of the ubiquitous clouds to the northwest. Anchorage was close enough to the Arctic Circle for the end-of-May sun to carve most of a full circle around the sky.

The Air Force hadn't plowed, swept, sanded, or treated the skim of snow. It had fallen after the crash. The runway was closed until Miranda authorized the cleanup crew to start work.

Landing on Runway Oh-Six meant that the aircraft had been heading sixty degrees east of north—runway names were rounded to the nearest ten degrees and the final zero was dropped for simplicity. He turned around to face the marginally warmer sunlight and look along the reverse direction. Two-Four had been the line of the aerial tanker's approach. It was probably the cleanest approach to any of Elmendorf Air Force Base's runways.

To the west there was a line of approach lights up on stands stretching twenty-four hundred feet past the runway threshold —the last three of which were missing because they'd been ripped out by the Pegasus landing short of the pavement.

Elmendorf sat at two hundred and thirteen feet above average mean sea level. In the mile past the farthest approach light, the land fell those two hundred and thirteen feet in a low roll down to the sea of Cook Inlet. The next land of any significant elevation lay a hundred miles away.

There the western end of the jagged snow-capped Alaska Range rose to seven thousand feet, well below any flight path the plane might have taken.

Courtesy of copiloting Miranda's little Citation M2 jet, Mike didn't have to think hard to work out the math. The KC-46 at a hundred miles out should still have been cruising at thirty thousand feet. A mountain wave of turbulent wind could reach the stratosphere, but was rarely of consequence past half again a mountain's height. Any turbulence had probably been below eleven thousand feet when the plane was still at thirty. And the pilot would have had another fifteen minutes of flight to recover from any problems.

So that wasn't the cause. He hadn't crashed in those mountains or into the broad gray waters of Cook Inlet. He'd augured in ninety meters shy of the runway, skidding and breaking apart across the threshold of the runway.

If he was that close, he should have *slid* onto the runway. Sure, it would still probably destroy the aircraft. But not...this. Something far more catastrophic had occurred.

Mike shook his head and scooped up some fresh snow for his hand. Weather hadn't been the issue. Reports said the runway had been dry during the landing and the winds at twenty knots out of the north-northeast. Nothing of consequence.

His specialty wasn't mechanics; it was people. He was the human-factors specialist in crash investigations, so what the hell had the pilot been thinking?

A grinding noise of metal on asphalt sounded around the

side of a crumpled aileron that stood several meters high—though it had once been five stories tall.

Holly came around the corner dragging a section of the plane like a roadkill kangaroo. Prior to his abrupt change of career to air-crash investigator, he'd been living in Denver. Holly Harper was a tall, blonde Australian who'd grown up in the Australian Outback. Yet he was the one shivering in a parka and she was the one who hadn't bothered to zip up her denim jacket.

"If you're done playing around, could you bring me a ruddy wrench?" She dropped the end of the sheet metal she was dragging with a loud bang.

"Oh good," Miranda stepped up and handed Holly a wrench. "You found the flight recorder."

Mike looked down. Holly had. The traitorous thing must have eluded him simply for the fun of it. Maybe Holly had decided to tease him and sat on it as he'd struggled through the wreckage. He wouldn't put it past her. She might share his bed, but she never let up. She insisted on calling it *his* bed, though it had been months since she'd slept in hers at the team house.

She began unmounting the bolts.

"I've got the QAR," Andi trotted over as if to prove quite how astray Mike had gone. "I spotted the avionics computer stack in a drainage ditch. The whole assembly must have been blown clear. It looks okay physically."

The Quick Access Recorder was normally mounted beneath the cockpit floor with all of the rest of the aircraft's electronics. The QAR recorded all of the data and audio feeds onto a removable drive. More comprehensive than the flight recorder, but also far more fragile. It was a superior source of information—if it survived the crash.

"I'll—" He reached for his computer, but didn't complete the gesture. Miranda already had her tablet computer out and was uncoiling an adapter cable to plug into the QAR's drive.

Normally Jeremy would be given any computer tasks to do. Except he wasn't on the team anymore. With the departure of him and Taz, the team roles were shifting but no one yet knew how. It was making for a lot of miscues in what had been a smooth-running operation.

Oh! He wanted to smack his forehead, but his hand hurt too much. Miranda, having lost the crutch of Jeremy, didn't know who to hand things off to. Being Miranda, she was taking all of the load on herself, which would account for the ever-growing number of miscues.

"Why don't you let me do that for you, Miranda?"

"Why?" She squinted at him, studying his chin. She normally focused on his left ear, because eyes were very difficult for someone on the Spectrum to look at. But his left ear was under a thick wooly hat.

"Because—" *If I let you do it, we'll all be standing here freezing our asses off for the next hour while you look at every detail.* "—it will give me something to think about other than the cold while you continue to work on the debris assessment."

She considered, nodded, and handed everything to him. Holly had finished freeing the recorder and set it on the ground. Miranda took back her wrench, pocketed it in her vest, double-checked that it was in the correct pocket, then led Holly away.

Mike perched his butt on the top of the small black box and plugged in the QAR.

Andi stayed close by. "That was very smooth. You are the master, Obi-Wan. You must teach me the ways of the Force."

"You two aren't having problems, are you?" Mike booted the tablet—but he didn't know Miranda's password. He unplugged her computer and fished his own out of the broad pocket in his tool vest.

While he waited for it to boot, he watched an Air Force C-37B land on the shorter runway. A sweet ride indeed, the newest jet in the Air Force's executive transport inventory, the sixty-million-dollar Gulfstream 550 bizjet. Moments later, a C-130 Hercules transport lumbered aloft. The far end of the field was definitely hopping, but at ten thousand feet away, it wasn't a distraction. Except at the moment of takeoff, the sounds rarely carried to them.

He booted his tablet, then tapped to load the QAR interface software.

That's when Mike realized that Andi still hadn't spoken.

A glance over said that maybe they *were* having problems. "Speak, young apprentice."

"As I'm four years older than you, I should—"

"But you know helicopters. I know people."

Andi sighed and sat down on a section of the inner refueling boom pipe as big around as her leg. Normally, when still attached to a KC-46, the long metal tube extended from the bottom of the tail section to pump fuel into other jets as they tagged along close behind the aerial tanker. The force of the crash had tried to tie it into a pretzel and had come close to succeeding. It was pinned in place by the trailing edge of a broad piece of the port-side wing—the single largest fragment to survive the crash.

He waited. Andi was a former Night Stalkers' helicopter pilot. By habit, she rarely spoke unless it was about an operation. However, as a member of Special Operations Forces for ten years, patience was not one of her strengths when the next action was hers to take.

Mike started counting.

"I keep screwing up!"

He'd made it to seven.

The second time, he made it to ten and deemed that the taciturn part of her nature had surged to the fore again.

"Andi." He liked her. A year ago when she'd joined their team, she'd still been fighting with her combat-related PTSD.

She'd let him see behind the curtain of her personal silence a couple of times. But did he like her enough to trust her with Miranda?

Not your call, Mike. Miranda chose her. He had watched for signs of Andi forcing herself on their team leader, but they simply weren't there.

"Andi, stop trying so hard." The QAR software was loaded, he asked it to graph the flight profile.

"That's it? *Stop trying so hard?* Like I'm supposed to be all Zen about this great relationship?"

Mike tried not to glance toward Holly. The back of her head had appeared momentarily around one of the two monstrous Pratt & Whitney engines that broken from the wing and tumbled along the runway, landing clear of any fire.

Like *he* was supposed to be *all Zen* about his own relationship with Holly?

A good question to ask himself later, as in after *occurrens messorem mortis*—after meeting the reaper of death. The wonders of a Catholic School education, he could consider death in a comfortably remote Latin.

"Yeah, Andi. That's about right. Don't try to peel away the mystery, because it sure as hell won't work. Be with Miranda or don't be with Miranda, there is no true understanding between people." He sure didn't understand Holly, but he *did* like having her in his world. "There is only acceptance of her as she is."

Andi didn't speak.

It sounded more wise than he'd thought it would. Maybe that would raise him from Obi-Wan status to Yoda status. And maybe he should listen to that himself. Figuring out Holly had occupied a lot of his thoughts lately, to absolutely no avail.

Andi still didn't speak. Instead she stared down at the tablet lying flat on his lap for long enough that Mike looked down himself.

Then he saw what was on the screen. A flight profile should never look like that—except when it ended like this flight's had.

In slow unison they turned to look at the section of wing that had pinned the twisted refueling pipe to the runway.

In his opinion, Andi said it perfectly.

"Well...shit."

3

"892. SEE YOU AT TEN," CRACKLED IN OVER THE RADIO.

Mini Boss Lieutenant Commander Falisha Johnson merely nodded, careful to hide her relief from the others in PriFly.

PriFly, or Primary Flight, was the air traffic control tower for the aircraft carrier run by the Air Boss and a Mini Boss like her. It sat at the highest level of the *Big Stick's* Island, the only superstructure to reach above the deck. Its windows were angled out at the top to offer the best view of both the air and the deck below.

Lieutenant Commander Gabriel "Angel" Brown, flying his F-35C Lightning II stealth fighter Number 892, had a visual sighting of their carrier from ten nautical miles out. His flight of four was returning with the rising sun to CVN-71 USS *Theodore Roosevelt*—the *Big Stick* as their boat was commonly known. He and his flight were back from an extended nighttime patrol over the South China Sea.

The sky was clear and the newly risen sun was off the starboard beam on a smooth sea. Ideal conditions.

The *Big Stick* wasn't here to be confrontational.

Yeah, sure. You go on and keep telling yourself that, Falisha.

Since when was a ship three football fields long and most of two wide, with eighty of the US military's elite aircraft aboard, ever *not* confrontational? America's aircraft carrier fleet *existed* to strike fear into the hearts of others.

The truth was that the South China Sea was one-point-three million kilometers of big fucking mess that could explode in the worst of ways at any moment. Not even the *Big Stick* would have much chance of controlling the situation if it all came apart. That didn't mean they wouldn't try.

Vietnam, Indonesia, Malaysia, Brunei, and the Philippines had long claimed various portions of the SCS, some claims overlapping and some not. Then the Chinese had taken over several islands in the middle of the sea and dredged up whole reef systems to build artificial islands. Four fighter-capable PRC military bases now dotted the SCS, as well as numerous radar, missile, and heli-bases.

Then they'd declared the entire SCS was theirs exclusively, not only for military and shipping, but also all of the fishing and mineral rights. The rights of the other five countries that surrounded three of the four sides of the South China Sea were blithely ignored.

Every now and then the People's Republic needed to be reminded that they did *not* control the world's oceans by some supreme self-declared right.

And it was the *Big Stick's* turn to do that. They were presently steaming two hundred nautical miles due east of Nha Trang, Vietnam, and the same distance northwest of the PRC-claimed Spratly Islands and the three major military airbases they'd built there in 2015 and 2016.

The Air Marshall responded to Gabe, "892, update state, go Tower."

The last part was the handoff to her. The Air Marshall handled flights from fifty to five nautical miles out. His task was to vector aircraft in an orderly flow for her to pick up.

"892, low state two." Two thousands pounds of fuel remaining, which was low but not dangerously so. That was the twenty-four minutes of fuel Gabe should have after landing, not on arrival in the pattern. But the other extreme, landing an aircraft still heavy with fuel, was significantly more dangerous. Slamming down hard with eight tons of fuel still in the jet's wing tanks could collapse the landing gear with the least error.

Gabe's next report should be when his flight reached five miles out. At his approach speed of four hundred knots, that was still forty-five seconds away.

She was glad she'd come on shift in time for his landing. The other Mini Air Boss headed below after making sure the handoff to Falisha was clean. The off-shift Air Boss remained for now, watching the show. Which meant *two* Air Bosses were watching her, but that had happened enough to not bother her —much.

Falisha kept an eye out the window of PriFly for Gabe as he headed toward the Stack—the five-mile-wide circle of the holding pattern, two thousand feet above the carrier's deck.

On the deck itself, Commander Phil Emerson, the Air Boss, had three aircraft in the launch queue, a landing bird that had snagged the number one wire—earning himself a crappy rating of two of a possible five from the landing officer—and another in-bound, already in the pattern for final approach. So she would keep Gabe's flight out of his way and circling in the Stack for the moment.

Gabe never earned less than a four for his landings, snagging the third wire of the four on the *Big Stick* and doing it dead clean every time. A five was reserved for when he nailed his landings in harsh storms or at night. LSOs weren't big on giving out fives, but Gabe always earned them when conditions warranted.

It was a precision she enjoyed greatly in her personal life as well. Mom had warned her off fighter jocks—and Dad had done nothing to disprove her warnings. His affairs and lies had created a disaster area of her childhood worse than even the South China Sea. But she finally understood why Mom had married him in the first place. Falisha was completely *gone* on *Angel* Brown, who was bound to be anything but.

The twenty-four hours she'd asked for after Gabe proposed last night—to try and wrestle her common sense to the forefront—had failed utterly. Even knowing what the future would hold, tonight she was going to say yes.

She checked for the inbounds. Gabe, with the three other birds of his flight trailing close behind, was sliding into the top of the Stack. Exactly on cue, he called it in.

"Tower, 892, overhead, angels two, low state two." And she'd bet that he was within ten feet of *angels two,* precisely two thousand feet above her deck.

"892, Tower. Roger." Dead smooth. Pure professional.

That's how she'd play it.

She wanted her Navy career as badly as he did. So, she'd solve the *creating a family issue* by not having one. And when they were sick of each other in two years or five, they could both walk away clean. Maybe after that she'd be ready for a man to settle down with for the long haul. The final crash landing from life with Gabriel "Angel" Brown would be hell, but it would also be hella-awesome while it lasted.

"Flight of four entering the Stack," she warned the Air Boss.

He didn't waste time nodding, offering only a low grunt of acknowledgment. Six more staff worked behind them, double-checking that there were no surprises and that Emerson's orders were carried out in the most efficient way. Jostling eighty aircraft around on a ship eleven hundred feet long ranked right up there with rocket science.

Today she was handling everything entering their perimeter, and Phil knew she'd keep it all under control until he was ready.

PriFly had the best view and the busiest job on the boat. The captain on the Command Bridge a story below steered the boat—at the moment to PriFly's precise direction. The admiral, another story below on the Flag Bridge, could only order it about.

From here, she and Phil commanded all flight traffic within ten miles. In the Stack, on approach, or on the deck, all orders flowed through their PriFly post high on the Island.

She checked the deck. The first of the line at the bow catapults was punching aloft, they were the patrol to pick up where Gabe's flight had left off. The trap wires at the stern were all clear and reset for landing.

"Peel 'em," Phil called out without turning his attention away from the launching aircraft. Long experience had taught her that he didn't need to look, he knew the exact state and location of everything that even *thought* about his flight deck, probably including stray seagulls.

Falisha contained her surprise and carefully double-checked the skies and the deck.

With the first launch gone, the next-up aircraft, an EA-18G Growler electronic warfare jet, was taxiing into position at the head of Cat One. The catapult's carriage raced from the bow back to midships along its slot in the deck. In a carefully orchestrated ballet, deckhands were positioned to latch the front wheel onto the carriage the moment both arrived, which fifteen seconds from now would be slinging the Growler down the deck and off the bow at flight speed.

Latched. Safety checks. The jet blast deflector swung up behind the plane to deflect its exhaust upward.

The same ballet, ten seconds behind, was happening on Cat Two.

At the proper signal from the deck, the pilot advanced the throttles to full, then saluted the deck.

She knew she was avoiding taking action. *Peel 'em?*

A carrier could manage simultaneous launch and recovery operations, but when the pressure wasn't on, the Air Boss usually ran the entire on-deck show personally, doing one task, then the other.

Phil knew exactly what she was feeling, of course, and spoke without turning. "You're ready, Falisha. Hell, you can do the whole thing as well as I can. But for the moment, only approach and landing ops are yours—but all yours. Do it."

The proper response was immediate action, but she did take one more moment to revel in the feeling. The Air Boss saying she was ready to step from Mini Air Boss to Air Boss was a dream she'd been pursuing for the last four years. *Rockin' it!*

Then she keyed the radio and swung into gear.

"892. BRC is zero-three-zero," she called up to Gabe. Gabe needed the Bearing Recovery Course to line up with the ship's runway, which was presently angled thirty degrees east of north. "Your signal is Charlie." C for Cleared to enter the landing pattern.

He dropped out of the Stack on his next circle around and began descending. He flew forward past the starboard side, turned a one-eighty in front of the bow but well above the launching aircraft. He then turned to fly sternward, well off the port side in clear view from PriFly.

With her big field glasses, Falisha double-checked as he passed directly abeam that his flaps were extended and the wheels and tailhook down. He waggled his wings in a quick wave because he knew she'd be watching. Yep, arrogant as could be, so why was she touched?

"892, in the Break," he reported exactly ninety degrees off the ship.

Gabe was guaranteed to break her heart, but she already knew that wasn't going to stop her. Her revised goal? Enjoy the hell out of it while it lasted.

Descending through eight hundred feet, he carved another hard one-eighty and approached from astern.

He entered the Groove of final approach at three-quarters of a mile off the stern.

She released Gabe's wingman from the Stack to start his own approach.

"892, call the ball," the Landing Signal Operator radioed aloft.

"892, F-35C. Roger ball. Low state one," Gabe called back.

The deck would now be verifying that the landing wires were set to react properly for an F-35C with low fuel.

Low state one. A thousand pounds. Twelve minutes. So like Gabe to push the limits. If there was some deck failure or problem with his tailhook, he'd be hard-pressed to reach any Vietnamese airport. The closest land was two hundred miles away.

She glanced forward to make sure that a tanker jet was sitting in the Corral, the area halfway between the Island and the base of the catapults. It was always there in case someone aloft needed fuel pronto.

Gabe had probably been fudging the two thousand pounds of fuel report on entering the pattern because he'd been pushing his flight limits too far—again. That scared her in a way it never had before. He was like the heavy-foot drivers who could never stand to go merely ten over the speed limit.

What if he pushed that envelope past its breaking point one day? She'd be left to live on without him. A thought that made her sick to her stomach.

Breathe, Falisha. Focus on the job.

A thousand pounds of fuel didn't leave much leeway for even a missed approach. Not that it mattered. Gabe never missed a landing, nor did the rest of his flight. They were a very tight team—the top one aboard. They were the kind of flyers that could be tapped for the Blue Angels demonstration team, they were simply that good.

Rumor was that he had *never* missed a carrier landing, not even as a trainee. A smooth operator in every way there was.

Falisha had called her Mom this morning for help talking herself out of marrying him. All her mother had done after listening to her was sigh. Then she'd said, *I know exactly how ya feel, honey. Trust me. Exactly!* Her promise to also be there when Gabe was gone—to patch Falisha back together afterward—hadn't been encouraging, but it had been thick with the voice of experience.

Paddles, as the Landing Signals Officer was commonly known, didn't have to say a word to Gabe. Not one single correction, because Gabe really *did* fly the same way he made her feel—like an angel.

The carrier was moving ahead at twenty knots, into a fifteen-knot wind, giving Gabe thirty-five knots of help in nailing the landing. Flying at a hundred and thirty-five knots, he was moving at only a hundred relative to the ship—a twenty-five percent advantage.

A US carrier's landing area was angled ten degrees to the side from the carrier's centerline so that if there was a major problem, the approaching plane could take off again without slamming into the planes launching from the bow. Or, if a worst-case scenario occurred and a plane went into the ocean, it would go off the side and not be run over by the aircraft carrier.

That was a problem with many other nation's carrier designs but not America's supercarriers. It made the landing trickier but US Navy pilots were the best in the world and proved it with every landing they made. Damn but she loved being in the service.

That angle meant that Gabe had to constantly sideslip as he simultaneously managed his angle of descent, his yaw, thrust, and a jillion other minutiae that had been trained to the point of instinct.

He flew clean all the way to the deck. So focused on that Number Three Wire that he wouldn't see anything else.

It was so damn sexy to watch him fly.

It would help if the man didn't know that.

4

GABE FLEW BEST WHEN HE DIDN'T THINK ABOUT IT TOO MUCH.
Mom had been a ballet dancer turned teacher and Dad had
been a wide receiver for the Houston Oilers for eight years back
in the day before coaching college ball. Gabe had grown up in
Mom's studio, and playing endless practice games with Dad's
Houston Cougars. He and Mom had season tickets to the
Houston Ballet, he and Dad to the Houston Texans.

As a wide receiver for the Air Force Falcons, Gabe had been
light enough afoot to play in two Bowl games himself, plus an
All-Star Bowl. The NFL had scouted him but he'd always
dreamt of flying. And the Lightning II was like the best dance
across the sky there ever was.

Instead of focusing too hard, he trusted his honed instincts
of the natural flow of the flight. And he thought of Falisha as he
let his deeply instilled flight skills stay locked into the guides of
the ball lights, and focused on that third wire on the shifting
deck of the *Big Stick*.

Departing the playing field of women wasn't something
he'd ever expected to do. Not this side of retiring anyway.

But LC Falisha Johnson was the third wire of women—the

perfect landing. Cute as hell, sure. He'd always enjoyed a bountiful supply of those. Tall too, only two inches under his six-foot height. They fit together so perfectly.

However, the best thing about Falisha was her crazy level of competence.

He'd heard the bosses talking when she wasn't around. Falisha was a shoo-in for the next time an Air Boss slot opened up on one of the nation's eleven carriers. That was sexy as it ever got, *before* she'd get started on how she loved to watch him fly. If ever there was a person in a position to judge the quality of that, it was an Air Boss. Knowing how she saw him made him an even better pilot than he'd ever dreamed was possible.

Did he make her a better Air Boss? He sure as hell hoped so because Mom and Dad had proved that's how it was supposed to work. Mom said she'd always danced for Dad even when he couldn't be there. And Dad's stats had exploded up out of average from the day they'd started dating.

Sure, Gabe had seen the train wrecks of other fliers' families. Long deployments didn't bode well for family stability —even worse than pro-ball players.

Dad hadn't been perfect by any stretch, but his lessons had reached far beyond the ball field. *You do not ever barely miss the big catch. You damn well find a way to reach those extra inches to make it. No such thing as missed it by an inch. Look at your mama. That woman is way outta this boy's league. But I went for her with everything I had and I won the big game.*

For a woman like Falisha Johnson, Gabe was damn well going to make that catch no matter how far he had to stretch.

Gabe made a last check that his aircraft was properly trimmed for landing. Normally he'd have the other three planes of his flight fully on the deck before descending to land himself.

Not this time.

Hand on the throttle, he nursed the last of the remaining

fuel. He was going to catch hell for that when Captain Levi saw his refueling load sheet. He'd fallen out of Low State One and was definitely *Bingo Fuel* now. If he had to do a go-round, he'd be deep enough into *Emergency Fuel* that he'd probably have to swim back to the ship. The Navy would not be amused if he dropped a hundred-and-twenty-million-dollar plane into the drink.

Frankly, this time he'd be lucky if they didn't hammer him with a disciplinary action. What's more, Falisha would be royally pissed at the unnecessary risk, and that wouldn't be good at all. Arguing that the Chinese J-20 Mighty Dragon that foolishly tried to intimidate them away had needed a lesson wouldn't buy ground with either the Captain or Falisha.

He should have called up the damned tanker.

Next time.

Yeah, how many times had he said that before. But it was different now. If Falisha said *Yes*, the future would be completely different and it was time to start living up to that new standard.

The landing lights of the Ball were still all centered. The electronic systems agreed. Zero drift. Not a word from Paddles.

Deck threshold in six, five...

There was a flash of heat in the cockpit.

Four...

Searing heat! No fire alarms but something was burning. His helmet and his suit would protect him long enough to land.

Three...

Raise the tailhook? If there was a fire, the safest action for the carrier would be to let the jet bolt off the deck. He could eject before it smacked water.

Two—

It was cooking him alive.

Still no alarms.

He blinked hard, but his vision was tunneling to black. No

atypical g-forces to explain that. He could still breathe—barely. It hurt.

He couldn't see anything but black with massive red spots as his vision tunneled to the Ball of the landing lights and finally zeroed out.

One!

Gabe slammed his left hand forward, driving the sidestick past full throttle and straight into afterburners for maximum thrust. He'd burn off his remaining fuel in under a minute at this rate but it was the only logical action.

He continued reaching forward to flip the switch high on the top left corner of the console to raise the arrestor tailhook. With his thousands of hours of training and flights, he didn't need to see it—which was good as his world had gone completely black.

With his right hand he hauled on the sidestick to tip the nose up in hopes that he could fly clear rather than shooting off the deck and into the sea.

It was the last mistake he ever made.

5

LIEUTENANT COMMANDER GABRIEL "ANGEL" BROWN HAD WAITED four-point-six-hundredths of a second too long to act effectively. At a hundred and thirty-five nautical miles an hour, a hundred and fifty-five mph, his actions started ten feet, seven inches too late.

The F-35C Lightning II could accelerate while climbing straight up, especially when as light on fuel as Number 892 was. But not this time.

Because LC Brown had raised the nose to a high angle of attack in his attempt to return to flight, the retracting tailhook was tipped down enough to snag the fourth wire with three inches to spare.

The inch-and-a-quarter-diameter arresting cable had a braking ability of two hundred and fifteen thousand pounds. It could stop a landing jet one hundred and twenty-five times between replacements. Wire Number Four had made a hundred and seventeen arrests since installation. Its replacement was already coiled on the deck like a giant tabletop coaster, waiting on the deck.

An empty F-35C weighed thirty-one thousand pounds.

For today's patrol, Number 892 had carried a full load of ordnance, both the load hidden inside the stealth fuselage and the load on the external hardpoints. The latter decreased the F-35C's stealth profile, but it was intended to give the Chinese something to see and think about.

The ordnance load added sixteen thousand pounds.

The pilot and the two hundred and nineteen pounds of remaining fuel were of little consequence.

At a normal landing speed of a hundred and thirty-five knots, an F-35C would apply under half of the cable's capacity as it spooled out to slow and stop the jet. In any successful landing, this *trap* required three seconds and three hundred feet of the deck.

Standard procedures dictated that the moment a pilot trapped the wire, he retracted the jet's speed brakes and advanced the throttle to max. If a plane broke a wire or tailhook, or missed all of the wires, it would become a *bolter*.

The pilot's only hope of remaining aloft, if the plane *did* bolt off the short aircraft carrier runway, lay in power.

The added load on the wire by applying *max thrust* increased from the typical twenty-eight thousand pounds to forty-three thousand as LC Gabriel Brown drove ahead on full afterburners trying to get clear of the deck before whatever was burning his plane caused a catastrophic failure.

This load was still safely within the cable's capacity.

But 892's acceleration from LC Brown's preemptive attempt to return to flight meant that he was traveling at well over two hundred knots by the time he snagged Wire Four, instead of the typical hundred and thirty-five. This increased the force on the wire by half again.

Snagged on the wire, the F-35C Lightning II jet fighter nonetheless did what it was designed to do—it drove up into the sky. The hydraulic pistons underneath the *Theodore*

Roosevelt's deck slowed the arresting cable despite the massive overload.

The cable's three-hundred-pound weight played no factor in what followed.

Caught between the forces of the arresting cable firmly snagged by the tailhook and the Pratt & Whitney F135 engine at afterburner thrust, the plane rose to hover above the deck, angled forty-five degrees upward into the sky. It bucked and swung like a caught fish fighting the line.

The downblast of the driving engines sweeping back and forth across the deck killed nineteen members of the deck crew in the first two-point-five seconds—eleven were burned alive, six were tumbled into objects hard enough to break backs or cave in helmets, and Chief Petty Officer Maria Gonzalez and Seaman Melvin Friedman were blown overboard. They tumbled into the ocean and were never found.

Still striving upward but arrested in midair above the deck, the F-35C was no longer under the control of its pilot.

Its tailhook slid to the right along the loop of the arresting wire.

On Vulture's Row, a narrow balcony directly aft of the Flag Bridge and four stories above the carrier's deck, off-duty carrier personnel are welcome to stand. There, high up the side of the Island, they can observe flight and deck operations. For many of the carrier's five thousand, six hundred and eighty crew, it is one of the few opportunities to see daylight whenever active operations are in progress. It was shortly after shift change between the two crews alternating twelve-hour shifts on the carrier. Twelve of the eighteen personnel observing LC Brown's landing attempt were the main shift's forward officer's mess culinary specialists.

The F-35C, the variant specifically modified for carrier operations, had an additional four feet of wingspan to either side that could be folded up for tighter storage. That extension was sufficient for Number 892 to ram its starboard wing tip into the crowd of observers on Vulture's Row. Six of them were cut in half as easily as slicing bread. Another nine died when the twisting flight tore the balcony off the side of the Island and dumped it to the steel deck three stories below.

At this moment, Lieutenant Commander Gabriel Brown performed the last act of his life. Still unable to see, but believing he must be clear of the aircraft carrier by now, he managed to wrap a hand around the yellow-and-black-painted half-inch-thick loop between his knees. He didn't need to see it or feel its searing heat against his palm, a thousand rehearsals and thousands of hours aloft located it with his instincts.

He yanked the ejection handle despite the fresh source of burning pain.

Det-cord cut the canopy around the edges and across the center.

The cannon under the Martin-Baker ejection seat fired and launched Lieutenant Commander Gabriel "Angel" Brown clear of the F-35C Lightning II aircraft with a force of eighteen g's.

As designed, the cracked canopy was knocked aside by the top of the seat.

Knocked sideways at high speed, it passed directly into the Captain's Bridge. The captain and the executive officer had stepped to the window to see what was amiss.

With his head severed at the chin, the captain died immediately.

The XO only lost an arm, but no one else survived there to staunch the flow before he bled out.

The canopy had sufficient momentum remaining to break through the window on the far side of the bridge.

The rocket launch permanently compressed Gabe's spine by two inches. He and Falisha Johnson were now the same height. This would remain true for several seconds.

In its proper sequence, the seat's rocket motor fired. It was designed to automatically correct his angle of flight to straight up for two hundred feet before breaking away and deploying his parachute. As the seat raced aloft, it collided with the arm of the spinning element of *Theodore Roosevelt's* long-range air-search radar mounted on the tall mast atop the Tower.

Gabriel Brown survived the collision with no new injuries.

The rocket guidance corrected for the momentary deflection. But the impact had damaged a signal wire within the ejection seat's electronics. After the lifting rockets shut down, the electronic signal sent to cut the pilot from the seat failed to reach the triggering mechanism.

With Brown still firmly harnessed to the two hundred-and-twenty-seven-pound seat, his parachute was unable to deploy. He began the long fall to the deck he hadn't yet fully landed on.

But the last flight of LC Brown's F-35C Number 892 was not quite complete.

In PriFly, Mini-Air Boss Lieutenant Commander Falisha Johnson and the on- and off-shift Air Bosses had been frozen in place by the spectacle.

It was now three-and-a-half seconds since LC Brown's belated attempt to abort the landing and return to the skies.

All three of them stared helplessly at the hard-firing plane for one-point-three seconds after LC Brown had ejected. There was no protocol for this scenario. No deeply ingrained training existed regarding the next right action for an unmanned, runaway jet held midair above an aircraft carrier's deck by its tailhook latched to an arresting wire.

At full afterburner, 892's engine consumed fuel at a prodigious rate. The last of its reserves would burn out in another eleven seconds.

They didn't have that long.

The strain on the Number Four arresting cable near the end of its rated service life stressed it far past its design limits.

It parted.

As the severed ends of the inch-and-a-quarter-thick cable lashed to the sides, the near side executed two of the three survivors from the collapse of Vulture's Row. The longer side of the cable snaked to port and sliced through the alert rescue MH-60S Seahawk helicopter kept at the ready during any active flight operations.

The crew members who weren't killed immediately were too injured to escape and drowned as the helicopter fell backward into the sea six stories below and sank beneath the waves. The USS *Theodore Roosevelt's* position placed it past where the Vietnamese continental shelf cliffed abruptly from six hundred to over four thousand meters in depth. The Seahawk helicopter rolled down the deep slope, creating a mudflow in its wake. Despite extensive search efforts, it would never be found as it and its four occupants were buried beneath two hundred and eighteen meters of silt and sand.

Freed like a Houston Oiler's wide receiver released by the hike of a football, the F-35C Lightning II climbed aloft at last.

However, its angle of flight was no longer in alignment with the USS *Theodore Roosevelt's* runway.

It flew directly into the wide windows of PriFly.

Mini-Air Boss Lieutenant Commander Falisha Johnson had a perfect view of what killed her one-point-six seconds later.

Lieutenant Commander Gabriel "Angel" Brown's ejection seat had reached an altitude of two hundred and seven feet in nine-tenths of a second. With no parachute to arrest his fall, he outlived Falisha Johnson by seven-tenths of a second before he impacted the steel deck at seventy-eight miles per hour. His spine was shortened an additional inch-and-a-half by the impact. He and Falisha were no longer the same height.

But he had outlived her.

She'd been granted her wish and wouldn't have to live on alone.

6

As a metallic blue Toyota Camry was still embedded in the armor of her SUV's passenger door, Clarissa was unsure how she'd come to be standing in the middle of the intersection of North Capitol and E Streets Northwest.

But she was.

The pale blue rayon of her Victoria Beckham dress was wilting in the heat, DC was headed for a record-breaking Memorial Day weekend. And the heat of the fire reached her a half block away with all the timidity of a sledgehammer.

She stood like any other gawker, staring up at the fiery wreckage of the George. A few laggard guests stumbled out the front door. People who had crawled out of wrecked cars stood or sat on the pavement looking upward at the burning brick building. Other cars, ones that had been too close to the falling debris, no one would ever crawl out of again.

Clarissa could see people screaming, but a strange deafness had come over her and she didn't hear them.

Police, then fire trucks, began racing onto the scene. Each flash of their strobe lights were an affront against her senses, but their sirens were no louder than a neighbor's television.

Yet it seemed she could hear every snap and crackle of the fire tearing through the remains of the eighth floor. The roof collapsed with more of a sigh than a crash, disappearing into the flames. It did so with enough force to drive parts of the eighth floor into the seventh, which began to burn in its turn.

Between one eyeblink and the next, she was standing in a sea of emergency vehicles. Ambulances, fire trucks, and police had filled the street and the intersection.

Barriers were being raised.

When an overenthusiastic cop tried to move her along, she flashed her ID. Apparently being the Director of the CIA still had power, no matter what the House Intelligence Committee thought. She was left to stand where she was.

Another eyeblink and she stood alone in a small island of relative calm among a nest of gray-white firehoses snaking across the pavement like a badly woven basket.

Her driver moved in to help evacuate the dazed and injured. When a fresh explosion blew out a section of the sixth floor, he was under the debris fall. She managed a step, but even at this distance, she could see it was too late for him and stopped.

Beyond the new collapse, the fire had spread. The Hilton had caught fire as well. Flames now towered ten, now twenty stories over the entire city block.

Due to a slight rise in the street, it was impossible to see the White House, which lay a mile and a half farther along 2nd Street. Had they sent the jet?

Or...

Clarissa turned to face the Capitol Building to the south.

...them?

The fire was now so bright that it lit the night-darkened dome a blood red that the normal nighttime floodlights couldn't wash away.

Had this attack been ordered from within those hallowed halls?

It was ludicrous that they would do any such thing, but she rubbed at her forehead to try and remove the feeling of a sniper targeting her there.

Who else had known of her monthly meetings at the George? Were they trying to take *her* out? It wasn't President Roy Cole's style, but she wouldn't put it past the members of the House Intelligence Committee who squatted beneath their cherished dome. No matter how irrational, it *felt* possible.

If she was dead, their secrets would be safe—or so they thought. She'd made a go-public-on-my-death package that would perpetrate a devastating postmortem judgment upon the committee and several others. If she went down, it wouldn't be alone.

It had taken all of her willpower in today's meetings not to mention that. But it was a threat of last resort and she hadn't yet been pushed to the edge of survival. Or so she'd thought at the time.

But...no, it wasn't their style either. It would require initiative, a realm none of those partisan saps could muster in their mistresses' beds, never mind the political arena.

No, it wasn't them.

A shout went up and she turned back in time to see the collapse as the interior floors of the historic George folded in and down. The brick shell wavered, but mostly held. No one else would ever be exiting the building except in a body bag. The neighboring Phoenix Park Hotel was now also engulfed, repeating the scenario along the block as more firetrucks arrived.

Maybe it was merely coincidence that Senator Hunter Ramson's suite had been taken out by the crash.

And...she was blowing smoke up her own ass if she was thinking that.

Being the D/CIA meant she had a far greater sense of paranoia than most. However, it also meant that her deep knowledge of domestic and international politics provided significant credence to that paranoia. Perhaps it didn't classify as paranoia—she knew for a *fact* that much of it was based in reality.

With Clark dead and the White House slipped from her grasp, was she actually a major threat to anyone who would care? There was a depressing thought.

Her remaining power was...the great unknown. She had needed—

"Clarissa?"

The ghost of Rose Ramson stood in front of her, speaking her name.

7

"YOU'RE DEAD."

"I am?"

"Up there." Clarissa nodded toward the upper story of the George, which was no longer there due to the building's collapse. Further evidence of Rose's demise was that she looked elegant and cool despite the brutal heat. Her ghost shimmered in an effortless Armani white linen skirt and jacket with a ruffled blouse of the palest green, which offset her deep red hair to perfection. Of course, Rose Ramson would look elegant even in off-the-rack Gap.

"I was afraid that you were..." Rose's remarkably realistic ghost nodded upward. "I was running late."

"Hunter?"

"I tried his phone. It goes straight to voicemail. He'll silence the ring, but he never shuts off his phone. It would only go directly to voicemail if his phone was out of a reception area," she swallowed visibly, "or it was destroyed. The George has, had excellent reception."

"Oh," was all that Clarissa could think to say. The ghost must still be an alive Rose. "Why were you late?"

Rose raised a small, gloss-white bag with no label that she'd been carrying in reply. Thick, high-gloss paper, with actual rope handles that were softer on the skin than the narrow twisted-paper ones.

Clarissa recognized it. Coup de Foudre was a very high-end and very discreet lingerie shop halfway between the George and the White House. "Cosabella?"

"Samantha Chang."

Clarissa raised an eyebrow. An interesting choice for a woman of Rose's generous curves. Though Rose at fifty could probably still fit in her Miss Utah bikini as neatly as she had thirty years ago. Clarissa herself never looked quite her best in Samantha Chang designs.

"I was—" Rose waved at the fire a little helplessly. Though they stood a block away, they had to raise their voices to be heard over the loud pumps on the nearby fire trucks and the rush of water from a dozen different nozzles and truck-mounted water cannons. "—was going to let him make it up to me. I have, *had been,* giving Hunter the cold shoulder for long enough."

There was no need to ask why. Senator Hunter Ramson's political machinations had gone terribly wrong. His actions had paved yet one more step along the path to Clark's death, and her own loss of an eventual Presidency by riding in on his coattails. Hunter also would be the only one to know exactly who had sent that plane spearing into the George—if he weren't dead.

They stood together and watched the fire in silence. The sun had set, but the street didn't lack for light. The harsh emergency lights from the trucks flooded the street. The fire splashed blood orange off the glass face of the Hall of the States across the street. Half of the states had their official DC offices in that building.

No one would have complained if the jet had hit there instead, at least no one that mattered. But it hadn't.

The states had such inflated ideas of their own importance, often undermining the very country they were part of. Someday she'd wander over to the FBI and do a little trading of good stories, tales of crazy countries in exchange for juicy tales of state psychoses.

"I guess I don't need this anymore." Rose stepped over to a small pile of flaming bedding, too unimportant for the firefighters to deal with yet, and tossed the bag of lingerie on it.

"Let's get out of here."

Rose looked at the fire and nodded. Her carefully composed features couldn't quite hide her distress. Clarissa had been with Clark for under three years, married for less than one—and she was missing him. Rose had been married to Hunter for more than thirty. Like her own mixed feelings, was it a sadness *and* a relief? Clarissa wanted to ask, but knew she wouldn't like the answer either way.

She stepped over to her car. The up-armored SUV was robust enough that it would still be drivable despite the abuse it had suffered. When she tugged on the door handle, nothing happened.

Rose tried the other side. "It's locked."

"Wait here. I'll be right back." Clarissa headed to where she'd seen her driver crushed by falling debris. The fire had been fought back from this end of the wreckage, so it was safe enough. The firefighters had moved away and the medical triage teams had already swept the area and removed the merely injured. The morgue teams wouldn't start in until the forensic people had their photos and measurements.

Being careful to keep her boots well clear of the puddled blood oozing from where his head had once been and now a marble end table lay shattered, Clarissa squatted to fish the keys out of his jacket pocket.

A voice called out from behind her, "Rifling the pockets of the dead, Clarissa? Why am I not surprised?"

Clarissa knew that voice.

Hated that voice.

It gave her a focus for everything that had gone wrong with her life in the last twenty-three days. And how close a brush she'd had with death in these last minutes.

She grabbed for the driver's gun, still there in its shoulder harness.

8

THE PIP-SIZED LATINA SHIFTED INTO SOME KIND OF FLOW STATE that Clarissa couldn't begin to follow but she knew would be the envy of any Special Ops grunt.

Taz Cortez shed her NTSB site investigation pack. By the time the hard hat clipped on the side hit the pavement, she'd bodychecked Jeremy, sending him stumbling backward over a firehose thick with water pressure. He landed heavily on his own huge site investigation pack. If Clarissa had wanted to shoot *him,* he now presented a much smaller target lying flat on the ground.

Using her deflected momentum and the distraction of the falling packs and Jeremy, Taz leapt behind Clarissa. She shook a fighting knife out of her wrist holster and into her palm.

The sharp snick as she flicked the blade release and locked it in place was in some ways the loudest sound of the whole screwed-up evening. It wasn't remote, like the jet flying overhead, or a piece of the strange silence that was the disaster.

It was close, inches from her ear—and very personal.

It became impossibly more personal half a heartbeat later.

Still squatting precariously in her Manolo Blahnik suede ankle boots, she didn't dare move. Taz had fisted one hand in Clarissa's long blonde hair. With the other, she pressed the blade against Clarissa's throat enough that she could feel how sharp the edge was.

This wasn't Taz's namesake nonlethal Taser.

A trickle of sweat slid down her throat; at least she hoped it was sweat and not blood.

"Drop it!"

Too paralyzed to move, Clarissa hesitated. She kept forgetting quite how fast Taz was with a knife.

Taz twisted her fist more tightly in Clarissa's hair.

"Fuck! Ow, already! Okay! Okay!" she set the sidearm slowly onto the pavement.

"Knock it toward Jeremy."

She did.

Jeremy, still on his butt, picked it up like a poisonous snake. He didn't appear to know how to hold it properly. At least he was no threat.

"Are you going to play nice?" Taz eased the knife a millimeter off her neck, but it was a crucial millimeter. Now Clarissa dared to breath.

"Bitch!"

"That's Colonel Bitch to you. I've been reinstated." Colonel Taz Bitch Cortez sounded completely cheerful.

"No wonder this country is so screwed up."

"Times ten to you, Director Reese. Now what are you doing here, stripping the dead at the site of a plane crash? It's not like you to get your hands dirty." With a repetition of that awful, slick-steel sound, Taz's knife was gone and once more out of sight. She stepped over to take the gun from Jeremy. The Sig Sauer P226 looked like a cannon in her small hands, and there was no question that she knew what to do with it.

First Clarissa checked her throat. Sweat, not blood.

"My driver." She fished the keys out of his pocket and wiggled them at Taz as she stood. She looked down at Taz. With the heels of her suede boots, Clarissa towered more than a foot over Taz, but that did little to improve her feeling of security.

Taz cleared the magazine and chamber, then stuffed the P226 into her vest pocket. "I'll make sure it is properly returned to the CIA at a time when I don't have to worry about you shooting me in the back with it."

"Don't tempt me."

Jeremy had clambered to his feet, but was staring at the fire.

"Not much to investigate after that inferno, young Jeremy. There was an explosion shortly after it hit, so I doubt if there was much to find before the collapse either."

"There's always something." He pulled a small notebook out of his multi-pocketed vest exactly the way Miranda Chase always did. She could see that he was noting the time and place. Then he squinted up past all of the lights toward the clear sky gone darkest blue and made another note.

But Taz was watching her. "You saw it."

Jeremy twisted to face her. "She what?"

"She saw it. Weren't going to say a word, were you? Shall I cite you for withholding information from an official US Air Force crash investigation?"

"You did?" Jeremy tripped over a fire hose, only catching his balance as he stepped between Taz and herself. As if he didn't appear to notice the *just-fucking-wither-and-die* visual daggers passing between them.

Clarissa sighed. Jeremy was always so inoffensive that she couldn't bring herself to snipe at him.

"Yes, I saw the entire event. From the moment the C-20 rounded the Capitol Dome," she pointed along North Capitol Street, "until, well, now."

Jeremy clicked on a recorder and mumbled into it for a moment about the location and the date and time. Then, "Interview with CIA Director Clarissa Reese."

"I don't have time for this, Jeremy."

"Memory accuracy has an alarming decay rate. Did you know that perception memory only lasts half a second? If it's not attached to a thought, it may be completely lost after that. Short-term memory is generally acknowledged to be efficient for only twenty-to-thirty seconds. Then the brain goes through a sorting process to determine what to move into long-term memory. Long-term memory accuracy decreases at—"

"The same rate I decide that shooting you while I had the chance increases as a good idea."

"No. No. That's completely unrelated. You're describing a conscious decision-making process requiring primary access to long-term memory for experiential factor-weighting of—"

"Jeremy," Taz said it softly, but it stopped the man before Clarissa *did* need to throttle him.

"Fine, whatever. But I didn't even get to the interesting part about new facts distorting our memories of older ones. Did you know that truly severe distortions can occur during dream states, especially if the dream content overlaps real events because our brain often considers dream and conscious experiences to have equal degrees of reality when—"

"I understand," Taz cut him off again. "But you've made you're point... Hasn't he, Clarissa?" Taz's hand rested negligently on the CIA pistol sticking out of her vest pocket. She wondered if Taz was as fast with reloading a gun as she was with her knife. Perhaps it was better to leave that question unanswered.

"Fine. Fine! Let's get out of their way." The police photographers were moving into their area with a morgue team close on their heels. How far behind would the newsies be following? She did not want her face plastered on the front pages. It might not have been a bad idea to be *dead* for a while, until she could investigate if she'd been the target. With Taz and Jeremy's arrival, that would be awkward to achieve now.

Taz shrugged as if she didn't have a care in the world. "Nothing we can do except interviews until they finish off the fire and the site cools down anyway." She might appear to be saying it to the thin air but Jeremy nodded in agreement after a quick glance at the still raging firefight.

Clarissa also noticed that neither of them had the decency to be sweating half as much as she was in the pounding DC heat. Or was it finally sinking in quite how close she'd come to dying in the George's Presidential Suite?

Jeremy carefully excised a page from the back of his notebook, wrote a note on the slip of paper, then bent down to tuck it into the driver's shoulder holster. "A receipt for the sidearm, so that the morgue teams don't think it was stolen."

Jeremy might be annoying but, like Miranda, he didn't miss any technical details.

Clarissa led them through the maze of trucks and rushing rescue workers to where Rose still waited by the car.

"They've got questions."

And there wasn't a chance that she was going to let them know that *she* might have been the target and not Senator Ramson. Better yet, let them think it was a random act. An out-of-control pilot slamming into the hotel.

At Rose's suggestion, they walked the short block into Lower Senate Park, well back from the disaster. There were benches around the Reflecting Pool there that showed off the brightly lit Capitol as neatly as the one at the other end of the Mall displayed the Washington Monument from Lincoln's steps. From the park, they'd still have a view of the outer edges of the rescue efforts without being on top of them.

As they walked along the sidewalk, friendly as could be to

all appearances, Rose made a small exclamation of surprise, "Oh!"

"What?"

"When they killed Hunter, do you think they might have been targeting you instead?"

Clarissa sighed. So much for keeping that off the table.

9

MORE OF THE ALASKAN SNOW HAD MELTED OFF THE CRASHED KC-46 Pegasus. Now it was mere patches spotted here and there across JBER's runway.

Miranda stood with the rest of her team, looking down at the wing of the crashed aerial tanker. With her much *smaller* team.

Jeremy should be making some detailed observation and then discussing it far past relevance. Taz's laugh would stop him and lighten the moment.

Instead, the four of them stood in a grim line and stared at it in silence.

"Well...shit." Holly didn't even toss in any of her broad Australian Strine.

"That's what I said," Andi commented.

"You nailed it, little sister."

"Thurman Munson," Mike said quietly.

"August 2nd, 1979," Miranda agreed.

"Who was Thurman Munson?" Andi asked.

Mike raised his tablet and the QAR like a pretend baseball bat to his shoulder and swung them. "Catcher and captain for the New York Yankees. One of the greats. Over thirty years later and he still ranks in nine different categories of statistics."

Miranda wasn't sure why Mike considered that information as pertinent to the situation.

"He," Miranda directed the conversation once more toward the relevant, "had bought a new jet, a Citation 500 I/SP, a direct predecessor to my own M2, three models and forty years earlier. He was practicing touch-and-goes. On his fourth landing, he didn't use the checklist and failed to extend the flaps. On approach he developed an excessive descent rate. His belated attempts to recover saved his two passengers except for bad burns, but he broke his neck. Unable to move himself, he burned to death before he could be rescued."

Miranda returned her attention to the wing. The flaps of the KC-46 Pegasus weren't extended. They were still tucked neatly into the trailing edges of the wing. Or rather in what was left of the wing after it had broken free, snapped in several places spilling thousands of gallons of fuel from the wing tanks, and then burned fiercely until the airport's fire crews had arrived to extinguish the conflagration.

"Only this time there were no survivors." Three duty crew, three trainees, and a senior flight instructor had all lost their lives. None of them had noted the pilot's failure to extend the landing flaps.

She pulled out her own computer and retrieved an estimated final flight profile she'd worked up for Thurman Munson's famous failure as a class exercise—it had thoroughly puzzled her eighth-grade science teacher despite several attempts to explain something so simple to her.

Holding it up next to Mike's profile of the KC-46 Pegasus aerial tanker, the profiles were nearly identical. Munson had clipped a tree short of the runway and never fully recovered. The USAF pilots had plowed through a whole line of runway threshold lights—and never fully recovered.

"There was no attempt to accelerate and no radio report of any failure of the flaps. The control to extend them was never engaged. It was a complete miss," Holly pointed to the relevant line of data.

They all stared at the wing some more. Holly's assessment was correct.

"Time to call the clean up crews?" Mike asked. "They're saying it's a matter of national security to return this runway to operation."

Miranda didn't like declaring a *fait accompli* when she still hadn't inspected the rest of the crash. But the QAR had recorded no mechanical faults. They'd have to perform a careful review of all of the cockpit communications and procedures on both the QAR and the black box's cockpit voice recorder. But they didn't need the plane for that.

She turned to Andi. "Why do I feel such a need to complete a full inspection of the wreckage?"

Andi sputtered for a moment. "How am I supposed to know that? You're the expert here, Miranda. Look, I know I've been screwing up personally, but none of us have the instincts for a crash that you do. I'd never second guess that."

"I have instincts?"

Andi laughed in her face. "Duh! Really, really good ones. What do you think you've been honing since you were thirteen? You *know* whether or not we should keep going. Unless it's your autism speaking." Then her face paled. "Sorry, I didn't mean it that way. Honestly, I never would... could... Oh God!" Andi covered her face with her hands.

Miranda had never thought of her autism as a disembodied part of herself, but neither was it an invalid proposition. She was *always* uncomfortable with incomplete actions.

But that meant she herself would be having debates between herself and her autism, which didn't make any sense.

Or perhaps the obverse of her autism arguing with her trained instincts?

No, her autism was an integral element of who she was. It was like considering an airplane as distinct from its wings—without them it wouldn't be an airplane. She rather liked that metaphor and allowed herself a moment of self-congratulation on finding a relevant one.

"I'm sorry, Miranda. I was talking about the plane when I said you would know whether or not to keep going. I mean—" Andi turned away, leaving an incomplete sentence, despite knowing how those bothered Miranda.

Before she could protest, Andi turned back.

"I mean that I wasn't talking about us, you know? When I was saying maybe we were done. You get that, right?" Her look matched *pleading* on the emoji reference page in her personal notebook. It was still the only way she could even guess other's emotions.

"You're mixing things up, Andi. I'm *me* for lack of a better word. And we were talking about the plane. Why did you insert our relationship in the middle of that?"

"Uh, because I've been thinking about it a lot."

"About stopping our relationship? But it only just started." Miranda looked down at the still open page and searched for her own emotion. Frowny face, no red cheeks or narrowed eyes—*sad.*

"No, about keeping it going. But I'm messing up again, in a new way."

Miranda tucked away her notebook, closed her eyes, covered her ears, and held her breath for a moment to think without external sensory input.

Focus on one thing at a time. That's what her personal notebook said to do.

The plane.

There was no actual question but that it was a failure in the cockpit. If the flaps had failed, they would have called the tower for a faster than normal landing, one that would have appeared otherwise normal in the rate of descent. Until the moment of attempted recovery, their approach speed was exactly where it should have been—if they'd had thirty degrees of flap extended.

She removed her hands and took a breath.

"The failure wasn't with the plane."

Andi appeared to be swallowing hard but was nodding her head as if encouraging Miranda to continue. Holly was waiting and Mike was smiling at something only he knew.

"But in the general area of the cockpit, I'd still like to look for—"

"Is one of you Miranda Chase?" A woman had driven a beige Air Force Humvee to the boundary perimeter of orange flags marking the edge of the debris field.

"I'm Miranda Chase. Investigator in Charge for the NTSB."

"Wonderful!" The woman climbed out, stepped on an orange debris-perimeter flag, and was about to kick aside a communications hatch that would have been used by ground personnel to patch in the headphones when talking to the pilots.

"Don't do that! Stop!"

The woman froze in mid-step. "Do what?"

"Kick that."

"This?" she nudged it gently with the toe of her boot. Then she looked around as if seeing the debris for the first time.

"We never know what may ultimately be important in a crash investigation."

"I'm guessing that it's not this." She nudged it again, but then stepped carefully around it.

Truthfully, Miranda estimated that it wasn't either and had to remind herself of that. When ninety-one tons of aircraft, plus an unspecified amount of fuel...

She quickly consulted the logs on the QAR.

When ninety-one tons of aircraft and seven-point-two tons of fuel hit the ground as hard as this plane had, the causal factors were far greater than a twelve-inch service hatch.

"I must conclude that you are correct in your assessment."

The woman threaded her way to them without threatening to displace any more of the debris.

She stood two inches over Miranda's five-four height, though walked as if she was a foot taller. She had Italian olive skin and lustrous brown hair with a hint of gold hanging neat to her jawline. She wore a smart uniform that had been recently pressed. Her winter jacket hid her name, but not the silver oakleaf of a Navy commander's insignia on her collar points.

"Well, how's it going? Have you about wrapped this one up?" The woman gestured as if encompassing the world as easily as Miranda might encompass a cup of tea.

"I already told the Air Force that I wasn't done seven times. I do not understand why they thought sending a Navy commander to ask their question would alter my answer. However, we were discussing that a moment ago. I know that they're eager to have this runway back in operation but—"

"Couldn't care about the runway."

Miranda wasn't sure how to complete her sentence after that.

"I've been told to deliver you to a new incident. I'm Commander Susan Piazza, by the way. You can call me Sam or Susan, I answer to both. Or Commander Piazza, I answer to that too."

"Sam?" Mike asked before she could.

"It's my nickname, Susan Ann Marie, Sam. Not like Samantha, but a lot like a surface-to-air missile." Her smile said how much she liked that idea.

"But we aren't done with the old incident, Susan." Miranda

looked at the debris field about their feet, but she could feel this
investigation slipping away and she didn't know how to stop it.

Sam... No, she'd said that was a nickname. Weren't
nicknames for usage between friends? Miranda didn't know
her, so Sam would most likely be inappropriate.

Susan shrugged. "How do I put this nicely? Hmm... Admiral
Stanislaw doesn't care. I think that about covers it. I hope that
isn't a problem."

"I work for the NTSB, the National Transportation Safety
Board, not the United States Navy. My job is to—"

"Go where you're most needed. Right?"

Miranda couldn't figure out how to argue with that either,
but it was not her sentence. It had been...hijacked, like an
airplane. That left it still incomplete by her assessment.

"Right now, you're most needed at another location. I have a
jet waiting."

"I have a jet."

"The pretty little Citation M2? I'd ask how it handles, but I
fly helicopters not jets, so your answer wouldn't mean anything.
And the helo's only for the fun of it on my own time and dime.
The Navy didn't want female jet jockeys back when I was a
young gal lieutenant—most of them still don't, truth be told.
I'm sorry, ma'am, your little puddle jumper won't do. We're
going much farther than its range. I'll make arrangements to
have it tucked into a hangar out of the weather. Shall we go?"

Without waiting for an answer, Susan turned to her vehicle.

Still stuck with two unfinished sentences, Miranda looked
at the others for guidance.

Mike tapped the edge of the tablet in Miranda's hands. "I
think that everything we need is going to be in here. We can tell
them to keep the bigger parts in a hangar for us, in case we
need to come back and look at something."

Holly patted the 3D camera she'd taken over when Jeremy

had left. "I snapped images from here to the Alice. Should be able to look at all you need to."

Miranda wasn't sure what Alice Springs in the middle of the Australian Outback had to do with images, but she supposed that Holly must or she wouldn't have said it.

Susan hadn't driven the Humvee away. She sat in her vehicle with her door closed. She was on the radio, perhaps arranging for the proper storage of Miranda's personal jet.

Lastly Miranda turned to Andi.

Andi took her time answering.

"I know helicopters. Even after a year with your team, I don't have the feel for jets. Do your instincts say that we have enough information? I don't even know who Admiral Stanislaw is, so I don't find him terribly worrying."

"He's the admiral serving on the Joint Chiefs of Staff with Drake. The top advisor on all Naval matters to Roy." Miranda answered.

Andi blushed. "Okay, maybe I should have known that. I guess if the man who advises the Chairman of the Joint Chiefs and the President says this is more important, maybe it *is* more important."

Miranda turned to look one last time at the wreck of the KC-46 Pegasus. One *last* time? Was that her instincts talking or was it the inevitability of the situation? She didn't know, but she supposed that the decision was out of her hands either way—no matter how wrong it felt.

Despite Commander Piazza's politeness, there was little doubting that she meant to have her way.

Miranda pocketed the drive from the QAR, returned Mike's tablet computer, and tucked the adapter in with the other three that she most commonly used and always kept on her person during investigations.

Holly picked up the black box recorder. It would be sent to

the NTSB Main Office for analysis. Analysis by Jeremy? He now worked in their DC lab, or he would by next week.

Did that mean he was still on her team, even if working remotely? She liked the sound of that.

As she approached the Humvee, a small furry face plastered itself to the inside of the window.

"A dog?" She stumbled to a halt. She'd never liked dogs, not since being scared by a terribly loud Chow Chow as a child. Dogs were unpredictable, noisy, dirty, and danger—

"Oh what a cutie!" Andi stepped up and tapped its nose through the glass of the driver's window. It wore pink bows and a narrow leather collar bearing tiny rhinestones.

"Cute?" Miranda couldn't catch her breath. She could hear a faint bark despite the protection of the armored glass.

Andi wiggled her finger close by the glass. "My mother keeps Shih Tzus."

"Don't ever ask me to meet your mother then."

Andi spun to look at her.

It was her sad face. Miranda was fairly sure of that, though she had no idea why.

"Okay, I won't," Andi's whisper was softer than the next muffled yip of the dog inside the vehicle.

"Good."

Now she was sure that was Andi's *very* sad face. Miranda still didn't understand why.

10

MIRANDA GENERALLY PAID LITTLE ATTENTION TO LAND VEHICLES. The interior of a Humvee surprised her each time she entered one. There was plenty of room for their packs and samples in Commander Piazza's vehicle, but not much room for people. With no weapons aboard, the cargo area was empty. But the big vehicle only had four seats.

Down the center was a rectangular hump high enough for the passengers to rest their elbows upon. It served two purposes. The first was that it allowed the drive train to be tucked up into the space underneath to increase ground clearance. The second was that it created a platform for a turret gunner to stand on, even when the vehicle, like this one, didn't have a turret gun.

Miranda was *not* going to sit up front with Sadie, Commander Piazza's Shih Tzu dog. Mike won the toss and sat up front. Holly sat in the single seat behind the driver. That left Miranda and Andi squeezed into the seat behind Mike. An airman in full armor and their weapon would normally fit comfortably. Despite being two slender women, it was still a tight squeeze.

And sitting in back hadn't done her any good as Sadie used the flat top of the central hump to trot easily between the front and the back as Susan started the engine and began the drive up the runway toward the base.

Miranda should have let Andi sit to the inside, instead she sat against the door so it was left to Miranda to confront the animal.

When it approached, Holly wrapped its entire head in her hand and gave it a brief wrestle, then let go and tickled its nose.

Sadie yipped and then waggled not only her stubby tail but her entire body.

Andi reached across Miranda to scratch it behind the ears, which sported pink bows. Then yanked her hand back as if the dog was afire and whispered, "Sorry."

"Why?"

Andi didn't explain and left it to Miranda to figure out on her own.

She stared at the dog.

It stared back at her.

Susan glanced back but then returned her attention to her driving.

She pulled out a tape measure, making sure that it was well extended so that her hand remained well above the dog. The Shih Tzu watched closely as she measured it vertically at whatever the withers were called on a dog. Miranda assumed dogs were measured much like a horse, as head height was highly variable in four-legged species.

Twenty-four centimeters, nine-point-four inches. The short-cut fur of a brown-black brindle over white made that a reasonably accurate estimate.

That didn't seem very scary, especially compared to the fifty-six centimeter Chow Chow that had weighed more than she herself did at seven years old. The roaring deep bark of her childhood nightmares had translated to the happy little bark in this animal.

Not scary.

Ridiculous might be a better word. It was as if Sadie belonged to an entirely different scientific genus, perhaps even a different family or order. Allocating the creature to the same *Canis* as the Chow Chow was absurd, except for its genus-level ability to interbreed with other *Canes*. That they even shared the order *Carnivora* seemed unlikely.

She pulled on a blue nitrile glove and rested a tentative fingertip on its back. It sat abruptly and continued to stare at her. When she tried touching the top of its head, it pushed back with pressure, as if it enjoyed the sensation.

"That's not so bad, is it?" She wasn't sure if she was asking herself or Andi.

"I always liked them," Andi replied after a long pause.

Miranda withdrew her finger, carefully plucked at the back of the glove, and rolled it inside out as she removed it to envelop the contaminated surface. Not that she suspected the animal of anything, or Commander Piazza of any ulterior motive in possessing such a creature, but it was better to be careful.

"Andi, perhaps meeting your mother wouldn't be so awful."

Her silence stretched long enough for Miranda to turn to look at her. Her expression was unreadable, then she laughed that wonderful Andi laugh. As if she'd somehow dropped all of her cares at once. Miranda was about to ask how to do that herself, as they clung to her like...cares that clung to her.

"*That's* why you said you didn't want to meet my mother?"

"Of course. You know I've never liked dogs."

"I thought it was because you didn't want to be introduced as the woman I'm dating."

"Why would I think that? You *are* the woman I'm dating."

Andi started to say something, but Miranda didn't hear it.

There was motion beyond their side window that drew her attention. The Humvee was halfway back to the hangars and they were being passed by a stream of vehicles heading in the opposite direction.

"Hey!" Miranda twisted around to watch them, lying across Andi to manage a closer look out the window.

Andi seemed to think it was an embrace and hugged her, but it wasn't.

There were flatbed trucks, several sweeper trucks, and a crane lumbering along at the rear of the progression.

Finally Andi saw where she was looking. "They must be going to clean up the wreck."

"I— Wait! Stop the car. I need to talk to them."

Commander Piazza kept driving. "Sorry, ma'am. Priorities."

"But I need them to preserve several elements of—"

"I gave them orders that if they bent, broke, or disposed of anything over one foot square, they'd have me to contend with. I also said they had to keep every scrap from the cockpit. It will all be stored in a hangar until you release it. Is that sufficient?"

"But in what order? Will it be a jumble or fully documented?"

"It will be however they place it there. Does it matter?"

Miranda considered. The flight path, the flaps, they already had the QAR and flight recorders... In the past, after scouring the debris field, she'd have focused on the cockpit and surrounding area to see if a physical checklist had been in use. While physical emergency checklists were still retained, electronic ones were more commonly used. Its use, or lack thereof, would be logged in the Quick Access Recorder.

"And you're the sort of lass they wouldn't want to contend with?" Holly asked with the broad Strine accent that indicated she was teasing. Miranda was unsure why, as the question was valid.

Miranda saw Susan look up into the rearview mirror.

Miranda looked away quickly so that she didn't have to look at her eyes.

"Yes and no," she spoke to Holly. "By chain of command I technically have no authority here beyond my rank, but I *am* the sort of person people have learned not to challenge."

Holly made a friendly humming noise, as if she was the one wagging her tail. "Works for me, mate." Well, if it worked for Holly, that was good enough for Miranda under the circumstances.

The commander turned from the main runway onto the taxiway and headed for the primary Air Force hangars where they'd parked her plane. Except her plane was gone, already towed indoors. Further support to Susan's statement of authority.

Instead, a Gulfstream G550 sat on the tarmac.

"Is that a C-37B?" Andi whispered. "I thought those were restricted to the top levels of the executive branch, like the Vice President and Cabinet members."

It had the trademark blue-and-white paint job and the long label *United States of America.*

"They are." The executive transport/command aircraft, the latter part being the key, were quite new. "Look at the additional antennas along the top of the fuselage. Satellite communications. It is also hardened against EMP attacks and is said to have several active defense capabilities." She and her entire team had the security clearances to know the details, but she hadn't had a need to know so she hadn't inquired further.

"If they sent us that plane, some bad shit must have gone down," Mike spoke from the front seat as Susan stopped the vehicle.

"That would be an understatement," Susan snapped her fingers and scooped up Sadie when she trotted forward. "You'll be briefed in flight. I was at Naval Air Station Whidbey Island in Washington State when the order came through. I was told to divert here immediately and find your team."

They delayed only long enough for Miranda to make a complete copy of the QAR from the KC-46 Pegasus crash. Then Susan arranged secure shipping of the drive and the flight recorder to NTSB headquarters and they were aboard.

Miranda had rather hoped the dog would be boxed and shipped away as well. Instead, Susan carried it to the plane.

"How is a Naval commander traveling with a pet pooch?" Mike asked as they boarded. "Can't say as I ever saw that before."

Miranda knew that it wasn't allowed except on a rare, case-by-case basis.

Then she knew. "Sadie is a registered service dog."

Susan nodded, "She is. Very useful in my line of work."

"Oh? And what's that?"

Susan merely smiled and the crew closed the plane's door and hurried them into their seats.

11

"You do know that your phone has been ringing?" Rose spoke softly.

Clarissa looked at her and then down at her favorite Hereu shoulder bag. She'd had the wits to recover it from the locked car, but all she could hear were more police sirens as they arrived to redirect the traffic disaster of Columbus Circle. Helos and jets flew overhead in constant patrol.

The four of them sat on a pair of benches by the Reflecting Pool in Union Square. Upside down in the still waters, the curve of the Capitol Dome glowed a bloody red. With the sun down, it shimmered with reflected firelight. Why couldn't the jet have targeted there and taken out the House Intelligence Committee? Apparently that was too much to ask.

Across the water, that drunken sod Ulysses S. Grant sat atop his bronze horse, facing their direction as if he was on their side, too. His reputation had been mostly rehabilitated in the last twenty years but was still far from sterling. *How many ghosts hid in your closet, Mr. President U. S. Grant? More than mine? Be glad that you didn't face the pre-election media circus of this day and age.*

Her phone rang again, and this time she heard it.

Her mind must have determined the ringing to be no more relevant than all the rest of the noise immediately after the crash. The main thing she still heard in her mind was the full throttle roar of the C-20's engines passing close overhead, then dopplering away until the Gulfstream had impacted the George —a sound she couldn't recollect at all.

"Clarissa here."

"Where the *hell* have you been?" Not exactly the sort of thing she needed at the moment. Not even from the Chairman of the Joint Chiefs of Staff General Drake Nason.

"Go fuck yourself, Drake."

Rose looked at her as if she'd lost her mind. Wouldn't surprise her one bit. Their mutual animosity went far deeper than the usual military versus clandestine services hatred. Drake had blocked so many of her initiatives and plans that...

"You can do that some other time, Drake," President Roy Cole spoke up, cutting off Drake's retort.

She was on speakerphone to the White House. Perfect. At least she now had the comfort of knowing that today had no more depths to plumb on the fast slide from bad to worst.

"I'm at the site of the attack."

"What are you doing in the South China Sea?"

"What? I'm in Union Square, looking at that ass Ulysses S. Grant. Being interviewed by the AIB because I was witness to the attack."

"Attack? What attack? All we know about is an errant jet that—"

"*Errant jet?*" Clarissa pulled away the phone to stare at it. This was too unreal. She tried to answer but nothing came out of her mouth. She'd almost died in the last half hour and...

Taz was holding out her hand for the phone.

Unwilling to trust the woman with her phone but still unable to find any words, Clarissa set it to speaker.

Only after she did so did she think to check the immediate vicinity. Union Square itself was empty. The few who might have lingered in the pleasant evening had all gone to gawk at the disaster. The Capitol Building's steps were lined with more of them.

Their small group sat in an oddly still vacuum, a block from where the city had been attacked.

"Colonel Taz Cortez here, Mr. President. Jeremy Trahn and I are presently investigating the crash of a US Air Force C-20C Gulfstream III into the George Hotel... Yes, the one off Columbus Circle. Director Reese believes that this was a deliberate attack, most likely targeting Senator Hunter Ramson. His wife, Rose, is with us and concurs that he was probably in a suite at the point of impact. The other possible—"

Clarissa waved a hand to cut her off. That she herself might have been the target was best left out of this conversation. That would start too many questions about why she'd think such a thing.

Taz smirked at her, clearly indicating that Clarissa was the who she *wished* had been in that room.

"One of ours? A suicide pilot in an Air Force jet?" Rick Danziger's deep voice, the Head of the President's Protection Detail, sounded over the phone.

"Based on the flight path identified by Director Reese—" Taz began.

"It was deliberate, Mr. President." Time for Clarissa to take back this conversation.

There was a loud noise in the background, then Danziger declared, "We're crashing the White House. Mr. President, please come with me." *Crashing the White House.* No one in or out. Full security lockdown.

Roy Cole managed to say, "We'll call you back from—" before his Secret Service detail rushed him out of the room to the PEOC. The President's Emergency Operations Center was deep under West Executive Avenue and was far safer than either the Oval or the Situation Room.

Clarissa hung up the phone and looked at the other three.

"We have under a minute before he calls back. What's the crisis if not the airplane slamming into the George?"

Jeremy's phone rang. "Hi, Miranda."

The last thing Clarissa needed was for Miranda to become a factor in this. She was the one variable that always screwed up Clarissa's plans whenever their paths crossed. Not that she had any plans at the moment to be screwed up by the annoying little woman.

"An incoming recorder for a KC-46 Pegasus crash? Sure, I can handle that."

Was that the sudden crisis? No. If Miranda's people had already arrived to investigate a crash, it was officially old news.

Taz nudged him in the ribs and then pointed toward the crash at the hotel.

"Oh, right. I might not get to it myself, but I'll make sure the lab is watching for it. We're in the middle of a launch for the AIB at the moment... Oh you, too?... Ours? Someone flew a USAF jet into the George Hotel. Killed a Senator Ramson, but they might have also been targeting D/CIA Clarissa Reese... No, she's not dead. She's right here...Yes, it *will* save the CIA the trouble of finding a new director."

"What was Miranda's launch?" Clarissa didn't care, but she didn't want Miranda, or anyone, on the topic of her near death. Someone targeting the D/CIA wasn't completely unheard of and it sounded a little too likely that way. Several of her division directors wouldn't shed so much as a crocodile tear at her demise.

A glance to Rose showed that she, too, was nearly as pale as her white Armani over the narrowness of her own escape.

"Really?" Jeremy gasped. Then whispered to Clarissa, "She

heard your question." Then turned his attention back to the phone. "Wild. Well, call if you need help from here." And he hung up.

"She didn't ask about the move?" Taz asked. "We've only been in DC for about four hours."

"Didn't need to. I texted the others as soon we arrived, so they all know we're fine."

"As if she cares," Clarissa didn't, but she knew the statement would piss off Taz—and it worked. So it was worth it.

"She cares," Taz voice was so steady it could be used to slice steel. "In ways someone like you could never understand. Though, I admit, she's not very skilled at showing it."

"Spoken like a true acolyte. Do you bow at her holy altar every night?"

"Absolutely!" Taz drew that battle line and Clarissa was very tempted to charge through and point out a few of her beloved boss' shortcomings.

Clarissa wondered how good it would feel to run Taz through with the bronze sword that the leader of the Cavalry Charge statue at Grant's Monument held aloft.

"Jeremy, what was Miranda's launch?" Rose tactfully changed the topic. She offered a look that hit Clarissa like a slap. As if she'd disappointed Rose by going after the little bitch. But Rose wasn't merely a social powerhouse, she was a top powerbroker. There was no possible way Senator Hunter Ramson could have been half the man without her working behind the scenes on his behalf.

"Oh, she said we've lost an aircraft carrier in the South China Sea. So, where did we leave off? Oh, right, your vehicle was being hit by debris. You said a chunk of brick the size of a small footstool. Let's assume a half-meter cube, that's roughly a hundred and six bricks, oh wait, the mortar. Take away a centimeter per brick, a half-cm to all sides, and add back in ten kilograms of mortar for every twelve bricks. Do you know if they were hollow red clay or solid bricks? Doesn't matter, I suppose. The building is old enough that were probably solid centers. In kilograms, that would be about..." Jeremy look at her, then Rose, then Taz. "What?"

"Are you sure you aren't autistic?" Clarissa had certainly had her fill of Miranda's weird ways.

"Are you sure you aren't a *bitch?*" Taz shot back.

Clarissa once again noticed her driver's sidearm sticking out of Taz's pocket close by her hand. Wouldn't that be perfect? Shot dead by a CIA-issued sidearm. That would make her day truly complete. Maybe Rose was right and she *shouldn't* be picking at Jeremy or his defender.

"No, I'm not. Not like Miranda." Jeremy's tone was almost wistful. "I'll never be that good."

Yet another dead-end conversation. She tried again.

"We lost an aircraft carrier in the South China Sea?"

Jeremy nodded.

"And you didn't think to ask for details?"

"Should I hav—"

Clarissa answered her phone the moment it rang, and did *not* put it on speaker. She waited for the encryption handshake tone.

"Mr. President, where did it go down?"

"You said in a hotel," Roy answered.

"I'm talking about the aircraft carrier."

"It didn't."

She was going to kill Jeremy for making her sound like an idiot to the President.

"There was a very bad accident or crash on the deck. The USS *Theodore Roosevelt* certainly won't be fully effective without a major refit but she's far from down. It happened during a shift turnover, so it caught most of the officers when the Island superstructure was destroyed. I understand that the fire is out but some areas are still too hot to enter. We've mobilized two carrier groups into the area—twenty-three and sixty hours out. If this was an attack on one of our four-and-a-half-billion-dollar carriers, this could escalate fast. We've sent Miranda Chase to find out *what* happened. We need you to find out *who* and *why*. Fast. Any resources you need. Tap anyone you have in place anywhere on this."

"Yes sir." And he was gone as someone called for his attention.

The phone rattled in her ear as someone picked up the handset. "No goddamn games on this one, Clarissa. Screw this up and you're done. Understand?"

"You're not my boss, Drake." Why couldn't the Chairman of the Joint Chiefs have been the one in the hotel suite?

"Don't test that theory, Clarissa." And then he hung up the handset with a sharp bang.

She slipped the phone once more into her purse.

Clarissa glanced once more over the water.

Rose whispered to her, "Grant was a team builder. That's how he won the Civil War. Build your team, Clarissa."

She glanced at Taz and Jeremy leaning together to discuss the pages of notes they'd taken. Clarissa barely remembered answering any questions.

"You mean...them?"

Rose had been keeping her peace. She'd become the leading lady of DC's social power politics by constantly listening and sifting information, and only then speaking.

Taz and Jeremy?

She, two decades at the Pentagon and he, Miranda's right hand. Jeremy might babble away on the strangest topics, but when he was focused, he could be very useful.

Team of opportunity? Rose's clear vote was that she could do far worse at this early stage.

Her armored SUV was not only in the midst of a record

traffic jam, even by DC standards, it was also inside the police lockdown perimeter for the incident.

She pulled out her phone and dialed a number.

"This is D/CIA Clarissa Reese. I'm at the west end of Union Square. I need immediate air transport." Because nothing on the ground was going to move again for a long time.

The underling started babbling about it being a no-fly zone.

Clarissa looked up at the sky. The alert fighters had returned to wherever they normally nested to reassess the ineffectiveness of tonight's security tactics. But the police helos continued the busy-bee buzzing overhead.

"Call the White House Military Office for priority clearance, you idiot, but waste your own time doing that—*after* you get me a bird off the pad."

"The no-fly order is *from* the WHMO, ma'am." He hung up.

12

"WHAT'S SHE DOING?"

Mike glanced over at Commander Susan Piazza, then followed her glance toward Miranda.

He, the commander, and her dog sat in three of the front-four passenger seats aboard the C-37B Gulfstream G550. VIP transport definitely worked for him—warm, luxurious, and a steward looking after their merest whims.

In the next seating section aft, Andi, Holly, and Miranda huddled together on a side-facing couch. They had their copy of the QAR data from the Alaska crash up on the big screen TV mounted on the wall. He was glad he'd given Holly and Andi the heads-up that they needed to help cover for Taz and especially Jeremy's departure. They were definitely on it.

What he really wanted to do was stretch out on one of the beds in the aft cabin, but didn't think that was about to happen.

The walnut paneling and the deep cushions of the black leather armchairs invited him to stop and relax to his heart's content. Maybe to sleep. They'd been rousted to the Pegasus crash twelve hours ago. And he and Holly might have spent too much of last night taking advantage of having the team house to themselves with Taz and Jeremy gone East and Andi staying on Miranda's island. Sleep had been their lowest priority last night, and after the Alaskan chill, it was catching up with him.

Once above the clouds, he checked his watch and saw that the sun was almost directly to starboard. They were headed southwest, and too far for Miranda's jet, which had a range limit of fifteen hundred nautical miles. That meant Japan, South Korea, or somewhere past that. At least five hours of flight time, so no need to try rushing Miranda.

"She's focusing on the KC-46 Pegasus crash." He explained the obvious to Commander Piazza to see what she did with it.

"But she won't even let me brief her on where we're going." Susan's voice was frustrated enough to have Sadie popping her head up from her blanket.

"You're spooking your dog."

She leaned forward to pat it on the head. "Can't the woman prioritize anything?"

"Nope," Mike tipped the armchair seat back and rested his feet on the one opposite.

The steward came by with a coffee pot in one hand and actual porcelain wide-based mugs. Dangling from his elbow he offered a basket of snacks. Very sweet.

"Care to explain?" Susan took her coffee black and no snack. Mike opted for sugar and left it to the steward to discover that the others would prefer hot chocolate.

"Miranda can only focus on one thing at a time without being overwhelmed."

By the slight tip of her head, Mike knew exactly what level he was going to have to start at—basics. Yet it wasn't his place to announce Miranda disorder to the world. If it was a disorder. The more time he spent with her, the more time he wondered if it wasn't the neurotypicals like the rest of them who were the screwed-up ones.

"Seriously, one thing at a time. She's only really

functional when she's doing that, and then she's an absolute genius about it. About anything. As long as it isn't people— they're a complete and utter mystery to her. Especially herself."

"Okay. And the other part?"

"What's your language, Susan? I know nothing about you."

She smiled. "My language? I speak Italian, French, Spanish, and Hebrew."

"Hebrew?"

"I wanted to read the Bible in the original, see what it really said without all of those translators getting in my way."

Mike tried to laugh, but it didn't come out very well. "Huh. Well, I guess I'm still bitter about *that*. The way they taught it at my Catholic orphanage was certainly no treat. The Bible in one hand and the whipping stick in the other, which helps me understand the Koran in one hand and the sword in the other idea. Or rather, makes me additionally annoyed by that twisting of the philosophy."

"But they are following the original. *Peace on Earth to men of good will* is the original, not *good will toward men*. Of course that's the Greek."

"Which you also speak."

Susan shrugged. "My education might have been from Catholic school as well. As to my *language*. I'm part Italian—"

"The part that shows." Out of her parka, Commander Susan Piazza was a lovely woman, perhaps a decade his senior based on her rank, but not looking a day of it. Five-six, nicely curved...

And what the hell was he thinking? He glanced at Holly, but she was thankfully too involved in the data analysis to notice him checking out their Navy liaison the night after they'd worn each other breathless. Though with Holly's training in Australian Special Operations Forces, it was always hard to tell what Holly was and wasn't noticing.

"The part that shows," Susan agreed. "The other half is English, with a direct line back to Bunker Hill."

"Traitor," he offered.

Susan laughed. "I can't say I've been called that much in my career. Yes, absolutely! A traitor to *England*. He fought on the American side. As for me, I on-boarded into the Navy at twenty-six—no idea why I waited so long. I have advanced degrees in PR, law, and communications. I was swept up by a full admiral to make sure his orders and communiques were delivered to the right people in the right tone at the right time. I haven't served anyone below an O-9 since, that's all flag officers."

"Ran an ad agency myself for a while."

Susan reached across the aisle and patted his shoulder. "An amateur. Your type are always so cute."

He knew she was teasing, but he still felt the cut. Then he rethought that. How would Holly view a trained fighter, maybe a winner of a Taekwondo tournament, versus her own deep training in hand-to-hand combat? Or a farmer who could plant his own dynamite to break up a rock versus her own ability with a wide variety of explosives against targets ranging from bridges to airplanes?

Done recalibrating his thinking in a way that *did* make him feel like an amateur for how effectively and neatly it was done —Susan had trusted his skills enough to know that he'd draw his own conclusions rapidly enough—she continued.

"You can think of me as your PIO, your Press Information Officer. I'm going to be the sole point of contact for all communications in and out of your team."

Mike wished her luck with that. She might be good, or even the best at her job. But he doubted very much that would help her. He certainly hadn't ever been able to control Miranda or Holly.

But it did give him her language.

"There's another reason that Miranda is shutting you out. Yes, first is to clear her head of the KC-46 incident. But more so, she's not going to want to hear a word that you or anyone else has to say about anything to do with a crash."

"Why the *hell* not?"

"And letting out your fiery Italian side won't help matters, Commander Piazza. That will only fluster Miranda, or she won't hear the tone at all."

He didn't need to be an expert on people to read Susan's glare.

"When we get wherever we're going, Miranda has an approach to a crash that is unique. You'll see. Any informational bias will be rejected out of hand, including a description of what happened from a third party. Again, that's her own unique approach. That's why I'm not with them. I jumped to a conclusion without crossing each and every one of the steps in between. She's now doing her own step-by-step analysis to get there. Despite her initial agreement based on the amount of immediate evidence, she may have even blocked out my solution until she has proven it to herself."

"Well, it's not going to work in this case," Susan freed her seatbelt and had leaned forward...when Miranda stepped up and sat in the seat opposite Mike as soon as he removed his feet. He noticed that she sat as far toward the window as the seat allowed before glancing cautiously at the small dog sleeping across the aisle.

He didn't have much use for cute little dogs, but he didn't question that Miranda was more terrified of dogs than he was of snakes.

13

"YOUR ASSESSMENT WAS ACCURATE, MIKE."

She noticed that he sat more upright in his seat as he nodded at her to continue. He'd been trying to teach her about reading body language. Ire or attentiveness? The latter seemed more likely. Miranda organized the data mentally before speaking.

"The flaps were never extended. Interestingly, the sterile cockpit rule that states nothing is to be discussed during a departure or landing that was not relevant to that action, technically remained intact."

"Let me guess: the trainee crew and the flight instructor."

Miranda nodded. It had been easy to overhear Mike and Susan's discussion and she appreciated Mike not forcing his conclusions upon her investigation. His instincts were good about people precisely as Andi had said her own instincts were good about planes. She still preferred to make her own final analysis, but all of the data supported Mike's hypothesis. His knowledge of aerodynamics had grown rapidly over the last two years.

"So, the cockpit voice conversation probably revealed that

they were so focused on refining some other aspect of landing technique that no one noticed the flaps weren't down or that they were experiencing an excessive descent rate as a result."

"That is precisely what we are hearing in the QAR recordings. They were discussing microbursts particular to Cook Inlet during inclement weather. They didn't react until there was a *Terrain Proximity* alert. They then wasted seven precious seconds thinking it was a test initiated by the trainer. By the time they understood that their angle of approach was too steep to be unrecoverable, it was far too late. They stalled violently into the ground. We will need to recommend to the FAA and the military that they refine the sterile cockpit rule in this matter."

"What are *they* still working on?" He nodded aft.

"Andi and Holly are going to offer a first draft of the incident report for my approval. It will only be an initial finding until Jeremy can analyze the recordings in detail."

Mike's smile said he was very pleased about something, but his tone was serious when he asked, "You're missing Jeremy in many ways, aren't you, Miranda?"

She could only study her clenched hands and nod. Jeremy had spent years studying her own reports—before they ever met—and modeled his precisely on hers. By the time he left for DC, she'd been able to submit his work with little more than a proofreading.

The disjunct of having someone new drafting the first report meant that there would be unfamiliar phrasing, the information flow might be in less-than-optimal order, and even the punctuation might stray from her standard. She considered returning and doing the work herself, but Andi had sent her away, insisting it was time for her to sit with Susan.

Except she didn't know Susan or what could be more relevant than the KC-46 Pegasus crash.

And Susan had a dog. Sadie had proven to be nonaggressive

—so far. Even less so as she was presently sleeping, though an ear twitched whenever someone spoke.

"Do dogs experience a semi-conscious state during somnambulance, allowing them to track conversations that they lack the cognitive ability to understand?"

"Never underestimate Sadie," Susan stated. "She'll surprise you every time in how much she understands about people, especially their emotions."

"How? I don't understand my own emotions most of the time."

Susan and Mike exchanged a glance that Miranda didn't understand either.

"Sadie is an empath."

Miranda considered. Had all of her own missing empathic abilities been allocated to animals like Sadie? Not the most comfortable thought. "Does she—"

Mike held up a hand to warn her off the topic.

Miranda took a pair of deep breaths to slow her heart rate and her thoughts. She was done with the KC-46 Pegasus crash until Andi and Holly had drafted the initial findings report. Mike was suggesting that she didn't want to pursue dog consciousness, or unconsciousness, at length.

The steward delivering her cup of hot chocolate reminded her of where they were.

"I've never been aboard the C-37B variant before. I'd like to meet with the pilots to discuss handling characteristics and—"

This time Susan held up her own hand in the same manner Mike had.

Which was *quite* annoying.

"Can we discuss the reason we're aboard rather than *what* we're aboard?"

Miranda closed her eyes and sat quietly for a moment. Unfinished thoughts and channels of inquiry were even more worrisome than unfinished sentences. The multiple interrupted threads each remained in her mind, drawing potential energy that should be focused upon other avenues. Like...too many power block chargers plugged into her solar-electric system at home. Even when the laptop or phone or television was off, the charger block still drew power, draining storage batteries and adding an unneeded load on the system.

That was a nice metaphor. It reminded her of home. Another reason to like it.

She pulled out her personal notebook, made a fresh page with the heading *Power Block*. On it, she noted each item that was currently *draining power* from her attention, unplugging each broken thread in succession until she felt her mind clear.

Almost clear. She noted down on her *Considerations* page to think about the peace of her island home and the changes brought about by sharing it with Andi. When she'd been seeing Jon Swift of the AIB, their schedules rarely allowed more than a night or two together.

Andi had already been on Miranda's team when they started seeing each other. That meant that she was constantly around. So, Miranda's home was always...different. *Is the island still home when Andi is there?* Thoughts for later.

When she was done, she tucked away the notebook.

"Okay. I'm ready."

Sadie had woken while she worked. Leveraging herself off the wide, padded chair arms, the dog jumped the narrow aisle between their seats to land in her lap.

Okay, she wasn't ready for that.

14

SUSAN KNEW NOT TO DRAW CONCLUSIONS BASED ON A WOMAN'S size, but she looked so...fragile. Jumping at every disturbance like she'd never been out in the world.

Now she was frozen rigid in her seat. Her arms were clamped to the chair arms as if they were flying through severe levels of turbulence, the knuckles already going white.

Susan almost scooped up Sadie, but her dog knew people. She wouldn't have chosen Miranda's lap without a good reason. Susan left Sadie where she was.

Still, it was incomprehensible that Susan had been scrambled on an elite C-37B, one that was supposed to be taking Admiral Stanislaw back to DC right now, to fetch *this* woman out of all of the possibilities.

She knew never to question the admiral's core decisions, only the ways he chose to communicate them at times. However, there was definitely something off here, far beyond Michael Munroe's explanations.

Susan had studied all of their files during the flight to Alaska and nothing about this team made sense.

Miranda Chase was autistic.

Susan hadn't told Mike that she knew that to see how he handled it: quite discreetly.

Her file said that Miranda had required a personal therapist in near-constant attendance well into college. At the same time, she was rated as the top air-crash investigator by the NTSB, the Air Force's own AIB, and Chairman of the Joint Chiefs of Staff as well as the President. She was also an only child, daughter of parents listed as working for MITRE Corporation but with no other background she could access, which practically guaranteed that they were CIA. A multi-millionairess with no clear line of where her money had come from. Chase was a recluse who owned an entire island in Washington State and a surprising array of aircraft.

She was also listed as troublesome, contrary, having no respect for any assignment, and an impressive list of other phrases that might appear on the review of a sailor who would never earn another promotion, ever. It was one step away from a dishonorable discharge.

Michael Munroe was the polar opposite. A bad boy from an orphanage. He was also remarkably handsome, though he didn't appear to be playing that card. Having a younger man checking her out didn't harm her ego at all, but he hadn't tried flirting with her at all. His own background was foggy in different ways, ways apparently hidden deep in the FBI's files that hadn't been included in the military dossier.

Captain Andrea Genji Wu, a direct lineage daughter of the legal-powerhouse San Francisco Wus. She was one of the very first female pilots to ever qualify with the 160th SOAR Night Stalkers. From which she had departed for unstated reasons shortly before joining Miranda's team. A departure marked by highest honors, including a few post-retirement ones for reasons not disclosed.

And Holly Harper, a tall blonde beauty who should be on a runway or at a bodybuilding competition, not an ex-Australian

Spec Ops operator who had no clear connection to any of the other members. Though she'd certainly noticed Holly keeping an eye on her and Mike.

Two members of the team were missing. She'd sent a current status request to the ONI. The Office of Naval Intelligence informed her that they were currently interviewing the Director of the CIA. Some kind of a miscue on the information request?

The files had described each of these people very clearly, in terms one might use in describing criminals.

Yet, *this* was the team she'd been told to oversee. A team that could stop or perhaps, based on their findings, start a war. If the events in the South China Sea were an attack on a nuclear supercarrier, that wasn't any form of a testing probe—it was a declaration of war at the highest levels.

She wanted to send Admiral Stanislaw a *Really?!* text. Probably not the best choice as he'd said the order came straight from the Chairman of the Joint Chiefs of Staff. Except the CJCS had no authority to issue orders. Did that imply that the President himself had stated this was the only team they would trust with this level of investigation?

That instruction made no sense based on the information in the files.

"The President recommends you very highly," she tested the waters. Maybe she could find out what was going on from the team itself.

"That's nice," Miranda was keeping her hands firmly on either chair arm and staring down at Sadie perched in her lap as if she might disembowel her.

But that wasn't the unusual part. Sadie was now settling down in Miranda's lap. She never did that with strangers.

"I haven't spoken to Roy in a while."

"Roy?" Susan caught Mike's smirk too late. He'd obviously

expected her to walk into the trap the moment Miranda said the name. She hated that he was right.

"You're referencing President Roy Cole, aren't you, in stating that the President recommends me? If not, you'll need to be clearer in your communication about which President you're referring to as I know several who have stated that they appreciated my services, including presidents of several corporations as well. There have also been three prime ministers and two kings." Miranda hadn't once looked up from Sadie, now curling up in her lap.

"I *was* referring to President Cole." Susan didn't know of anyone other than his wife ever calling him Roy. She'd done so consistently and effectively during the first campaign. Cancer had taken her before the second one.

"Well, I haven't spoken to him since the day after the downing of Marine Two."

After twenty-five years in the Navy, Susan could usually hide what she was thinking. But Mike's continued amusement at her surprise? Well, she wouldn't mind wiping off his face with something nasty, like a bucket of cold clam chowder.

The crash of Marine Two had broken a seventy-five-year flawless record for the Marine Corps HMX-1 Helicopter Squadron. A crash due to sabotage, which had changed the shape of the US's Middle East policies. The Middle East Realignment Plan was changing numerous alliances.

Susan also knew that it had prompted the abrupt insertion of two aircraft carrier groups into the area to contain anything that slipped out of hand with the announcement. It had certainly changed her and Sadie's lives as they'd spent two fast weeks there closing some channels of communications and opening new ones.

The Marine Two crash, she now recalled, that had been solved in an unheard of twenty-four hours. Entire defense contractors had been shut down and their key people imprisoned awaiting investigation and trial—some for treason. Only the outline of which had been in the files available to her.

Again, nothing about this little four-person team matched the information she'd been given.

Miranda Chase's achievements. Holly and Andi *attempting* to draft an initial findings report to Miranda Chase's standards. Mike's patience with Miranda, despite her oddities like sitting in silence for ten minutes—to all appearances stone deaf—while making neat notes in her little book.

Once again, Sadie, now settled happily to sleep in Miranda's lap, was probably being smarter about people than she was. Most people had learned quickly enough not question why a Naval commander always traveled with her dog. Susan had also learned, often the hard way when she didn't pay attention, to not question Sadie's judgment.

Please let Sadie be right and the files wrong.

15

THE ACCENTUATION OF THE TYPICAL DISASTER OF A FRIDAY evening DC gridlock, by the three-day weekend and the jet crash into a major hotel, had rippled across the city. Reports said the traffic was immobile from the Navy Yard to Dupont Circle and the Lincoln Memorial to the defunct RFK Stadium —the entire core was frozen. Ordering a car would do her no good; it could be midnight before it reached them. The airspace was indeed closed to non-military flights. And by the time she acted, any taxi that could escape had already been hired and left the area.

Some idiot with the imagination of a turnip had also decided to shut down the Metro *in case* the fire caved in the tunnel on the Red Line between Judiciary Square and Union Station. Except they hadn't shut down only the Red Line, they'd stopped the entire six-line system. Now all of DC was trapped in the heat. Someone was bound to go postal in the very near future.

Two hours after sunset, the temperature had climbed to a near record ninety-five degrees and a level of humidity that had nothing to do with measurable percentages. If she still had her driver's gun, Clarissa herself might be the first one to take up arms against *any* likely target.

By the time Jeremy and Taz had finished the first round of their inquisition, the fires at the George were out. Nothing left to burn there, the firefight was now centered on the Hilton.

They decided to return to the site. Any attempts to stop them at the outer barriers were quickly quashed. She was chagrined to notice that the NTSB and AIB investigator badges held more cachet with the DC cops than her own D/CIA identity.

The mortally injured were gone but the lightly injured were still being airlifted out as no ambulance could move from the scene. When she headed for one of the helos, Taz shoved her past the impromptu heliport set up in the intersection.

"The only thing injured about you, Clarissa, is your morals. And they died long ago."

Clarissa spun to strike out at fucking Taz Cortez, colonel or not. But she was simply standing there with her arms crossed, making no move to attack or defend herself.

She didn't need to.

The lone splotch on Colonel Vicki Cortez's record—of betraying her country to help her commander steal a two-hundred million plane—had been expunged by Presidential pardon. If she'd been born in the US, she could make a run for the Presidency, even have a fair chance of success. She'd never disobeyed General JJ Martinez by a single inch, except by surviving the final crash.

Yet the power she held over Clarissa was—

"Yes, I still have the picture, and so much more." Taz said it softly, then turned and followed Jeremy toward the wreckage at the George.

"What picture?" Rose asked when Clarissa didn't immediately follow.

Clarissa would rather swallow her tongue than explain. Except, with the mounting pressures of the slime molds of the House Intelligence Committee below and Chairman of the Joint Chiefs General Drake Nason above, who commanded the President's ear, her position was precarious at best.

This was Rose Ramson, and Clarissa *needed* the First Lady of DC.

"I crossed her idiot, three-star-general boss once, long ago. As a young agent, I ran a CIA site in Afghanistan. She showed up and took a photo, a horribly graphic one. Then walked away without a word."

"Who were you having sex with?"

Clarissa turned to face her. "It was a black site. I wasn't having sex." Actionable intelligence had been extracted by torture there, at least until the pansies in DC had chickened out and thrown the CIA under the bus.

"Ah," Rose didn't react beyond that.

"Okay, fine. It was neatly done, but it doesn't mean I need to like her."

"Perhaps if you didn't also act as if you feared her, it would help."

"I don't—" But this was Rose Ramson talking, the woman who missed nothing.

Clarissa sighed. Perhaps Colonel Vicki Taz Cortez *didn't* rank among her greatest worries.

Focus on the present task. Holy hell, now she was sounding like one-task-at-a-time Miranda Chase.

First, she had to convince Taz and Jeremy that there were issues at hand more critical than the crash into the George. Except to them, there weren't any. They'd believe that their *magician boss* had the other matter well in hand.

The only way to break them free was if they satisfied themselves there was nothing more here for them. And the only way that was going to happen?

She had no idea. But they clearly did.

Before she could ask, Taz and Jeremy had led them back to the remains of the George Hotel.

16

CLARISSA HAD MADE IT THROUGH THE SECURITY LAYERS surrounding the disaster of the George and the adjoining block, but was balked at the edge of the partially collapsed hotel.

After a consultation with the fire chief, Taz and Jeremy had donned hard hats and, joined by two firefighters, moved into the wreckage. She wanted to requisition a hard hat of her own, but her heeled boots would be worse than useless in the rubble and her clothes would be in ruins.

They were probably already unsalvageable from a hundred tiny injustices. The sooty handprint on her shoulder where a fireman had steadied her after she tripped over a hose. The touch of a walking wounded on her elbow as he asked her if this was where the tour started. A woman, unaware of her condition, had let a medic guide her away, but not before she'd left behind a bloody outline of her fingers on the forearm of Clarissa's blouse.

Besides, the fire chief had looked at her like she was a piece of human slime after he glanced at her ID. Obviously not a fan.

"What do you think they're doing?" Rose had stopped

beside her, without a single mark on her. "Are they searching for Hunter?"

Rose must be feeling some degree of shock if she thought that was even possible. Instead, Clarissa focused on Taz and Jeremy, then recognized the action from when she'd assisted Miranda with investigating Clark's crash.

"That device Jeremy is waving around is looking for the signal from the black box flight recorder." He looked to be happily explaining all of the details to the firefighters. They were spending all of their attention on the remains of looming walls and cave-ins of rubble into the below-ground stories.

"And it wouldn't have burned up in the fire?"

"It depends. They're very tough. The one on Clark's helicopter survived. I had to listen to his last words as part of the crash investigation." She managed to finish the sentence, though it tried to strangle her. She'd been so angry at him for dying. And hearing his voice from the grave had given her nightmares for days.

Jeremy stopped and began heaving aside bricks and shards of metal. The firefighters joined him while Taz held a portable floodlight for them. It was only a matter of minutes before Jeremy was carrying a bright orange object the size of a large handbag.

Once they reached where she and Rose waited on the sidewalk where the entrance to Bistro Bis had stood, the firefighters waved and left. They looked very relieved to be out of the guts of the hotel and shifting back to the fire, which had moved down the block.

Jeremy made quick work of disassembling the recorder until he held a section shaped like an oversized soup can.

The fire chief came by to inspect what they'd found. He nodded sagely twice before cutting off Jeremy in mid-excited explanation with a friendly pat on the shoulder. Then after a brief discussion about eventually recovering the cockpit, he returned to his fire.

Jeremy studied the orange case closely. "The chassis is fried, but exposure to temperatures over the melting point of aluminum appear to be brief. That's based on the limited deformation of the airplane's structural elements that were co-located with the black box. I anticipate a good chance of data recovery."

"That's...nice." Clarissa's attempt to sound supportive was so lame that Taz twisted to glare at her.

"It is, isn't it?" Jeremy slid the orange can into a plastic bag, then slipped it into his pack. "I'd like to get a look at the cockpit, but the fire chief says that we can't do that until a crane arrives sometime tomorrow."

Clarissa followed the direction of his upward gesture.

High above, embedded near the very pinnacle of what little structure remained, was a mostly circular imprint.

"It appears to be the broken-off nose section of the aircraft. Severely foreshortened by the impact with the building, then broken free from the rest of the airframe, which is scattered in the rubble. There probably won't be anything recoverable, but I asked him to see if he can obtain any identity information regarding the pilot or pilots once they can access the wreckage."

Clarissa should have thought of that, though air-crash investigations weren't her normal area of expertise. Maybe she could make some quick points with them, and then get them refocused on the aircraft carrier incident. She called the cyber twins.

"You found us," Heidi answered. Her voicemail sounded exactly the same as when she answered herself.

Clarissa paused for a moment to see if the message continued: *Well, you didn't really, but you found—*

It didn't; she had actually found them.

She didn't need to ask if Harry was with her, they were inseparable.

Clark would have been that way if she'd let him. He'd claimed that he was never happier than when Clarissa was at his side. It wasn't an effect she'd ever had on a man before. As annoying as she'd found it, a part of her wondered if she'd ever find that again.

Neither did she need to ask where her two tame hackers were, not even on a Friday night before a holiday. That was the advantage of giving them unlimited access to several of the most powerful computers in existence—they were rarely away from the basement lab under the CIA's New Headquarters Building.

"An Air Force jet has crashed into the George hotel in downtown."

"It's quite the spectacle on TV right now. CNN is all over it." Heidi was as cheerful as ever. "Wait! Did you say Air Force? It was one of ours?"

"Who were—"

"The pilots? Harry, get on that."

There was a blast of a keyboard so close to the speakerphone that Clarissa had to jerk her phone away from her ear.

"C'mon, Harry. C'mon. Didn't you find them yet?" Heidi's voice was a barely audible tease over the noise.

She had to wait a full thirty seconds before the roar of the keys turned to a spatter and Harry replied.

"Not exactly. Thirty-eight minutes ago, the AFOSI received a call to Joint Base Andrews regarding a pair of corpses. They're not saying anything else." Harry's keyboard continued to rattle away in the background, now more of a poking-about rate than a blast.

"The Air Force's Office of Special Investigations aren't exactly the most chatty of folks." There was the bright ding of a microwave in the background and Heidi's voice faded into the distance, but remained audible. How she stayed so slender with the amount of pizza and snack food those two consumed was a mystery. Clarissa felt as if she gained three pounds every time she so much as visited their high-tech cloister.

"I'll call Drake and have him lean on the Air Force Chief of Staff," Clarissa let them know.

"We'll call if we find anything."

"Heidi, did you hear anything about an accident on an aircraft carrier in the South China Sea?"

The next silence lasted about three seconds. Then it sounded as if *two* machine guns had fired off—the sound of Harry and Heidi both attacking their keyboards. They called out single words that must announce one's progress so that the other didn't duplicate the effort. It was also a measure of how fast they dug how deeply.

"CNN." Harry called out.

"CDN." Heidi responded about the China Daily News.

"Reddit, no. Facebook, no."

"Sina. Tencent. Renren." Chinese social media.

"NRO." "NSA." They said in unison. She didn't ask if they were going in through legal CIA access channels or through hacked back doors.

Clarissa had jerked the phone away enough to not have her eardrum pierced, then told the others about the two dead bodies at Andrews.

"The pilots." Taz's tone had no doubts. But then neither did Clarissa.

The keyboard buzz finally settled to tolerable, probably only one of them was typing now.

"Nothing surfaced on my first pass," Harry spoke up, which meant the CIA's truly big gun, Heidi, was still searching.

Though Clarissa knew that Harry's first pass was deeper than probably anyone outside the NSA could reach by their third pass, Heidi operated at yet another level again. Finally her typing too faded to a human level of key rattle.

"Two carrier groups have been mobilized into the area. That's major. Nothing else we can see from here. Not even in the US Navy command stack." That was a very bad sign and they all knew it. Heidi's voice was dead sober for a change. Clarissa's cyber twins could generally cut their way into any system. To block them, the Navy was keeping whatever had happened in a need-to-know, voice-only bubble.

"Start working it. I need answers to what happened and then we need to know who was behind it—*especially* the who. No one is off the table. You start scanning reports, I'll mobilize our embedded agents as soon as I reach a secure location." She wanted to find the *who* and then ram it up Drake's nose so hard it bled for a week.

"But it's the South China Sea." Heidi didn't need to finish that statement.

"But it's the South China Sea," Clarissa agreed. That put the People's Republic of China at the very top of the suspect list. "Unless someone is trying to frame China for us to take them out."

"Hmm," Heidi's hum was thoughtful. "I can think of some folks who would love to do that as a false flag op—ousted Hong Kongese frames the PRC for attacking our carrier, escalation, escalation, escalation, we take out the Beijing government, Hong Kong steps into power vacuum."

"And the fact that such a scenario is utterly insane?" Clarissa asked.

"Second-guessing extremist groups?" Heidi countered.

Clarissa hadn't had a moment to think about that yet. It was a possibility, but too unlikely one. "I can't imagine there are a lot of people left there who could pull off such an attack, but check it out."

"Will do. Oh, Clarissa?"

"Yes?" She'd long since stopped trying to get a *Director Reese* out of Heidi.

"Based on the timing of the order to move the two carrier groups, the crash there happened within minutes of the one at the George. We'll watch for possible links there too."

"Uh, good. Thanks." She hung up and put away her phone. Two simultaneous strikes half a world apart. Maybe if they found who ordered one, they'd find both. Wouldn't that be a coup? She could bury the House Intelligence Committee permanently with that.

And then the implications hit her.

Two simultaneous strikes half a world apart. An aircraft carrier—and the heart of the American capital.

It was ninety-five degrees in Washington, DC. Yet a sudden chill made her wish she hadn't left her jacket in the car.

17

CLARISSA'S MANOLO BLAHNIK BOOTS WERE NOT MADE FOR walking long distances across DC, not that she had any choice. Her feet rapidly escalated from aching to seriously annoying, almost as irritating as the Nancy Sinatra song itself.

No point hiking the mile and a half to the White House, the Secret Service still had the entire building on lockdown. Drake had promised to get her some answers about the investigation of the two dead bodies found at Joint Base Andrews, but he hadn't called back yet.

Out of any brilliant ideas of her own, she and Rose had followed Jeremy's desperate desire to deliver the Gulfstream's black box recorder to the NTSB headquarters. It was little farther to walk from the George than going to the White House would be, southwest across the core of DC instead of west. Perhaps the stand-still snarl of the immense traffic jam would be easing out there on the periphery of downtown.

For now, they were walking along the National Mall along with everyone else trying to hike out of the city at midnight. The droves of abandoned, fuel-starved vehicles would keep the city's impound crews busy well into tomorrow.

Groups were sitting on their car hoods with beer or wine from one of the local stores and watching the fire still visible in the distance. A thousand faces all aimed in the same direction like brainless Congressmen blindly following the party line.

Radios blared from cars in a cacophony of stations. Rock and roll, classical, and jazz mixed in the night air.

But the main theme were the news channels. Pundits discussing the: *Biggest Fire in DC Since the British Burned the White House in 1814.* She could hear them hitting every word with a punch.

The pundits also didn't know anything. Many of them were so clueless. *Kitchen fire, arson,* and *illegal cigarette smoker who fell asleep in hotel room* were only a few of the speculations. In the back of a pickup, someone had rigged a large tablet and was running the *Independence Day* movie. They had gathered quite a crowd, and a round of cheers went up when DC was destroyed by an alien laser blast.

Taz and Jeremy laughed. Rose smiled with light amusement. Clarissa wanted to take away their voter privileges...forever!

Only a few pundits were calling it an attack, but those stations were, typically for their standard fare, blaming either *foreign actors* or, on the loudest played stations, *renegade Democrats seeking to overthrow the rule of law.*

If ever there was a country in need of a little *less* freedom of speech, it was her own. They should at least have to pass an intelligence test before being allowed near a broadcast microphone.

It was a long and very annoying walk to the NTSB headquarters building.

18

COMMANDER SUSAN PIAZZA WASN'T USED TO THE KIND OF pushback she was receiving. Most of her career involved communicating with military personnel and she'd worked with her fair share of civilians—except never like these.

What did she have to do to get through to these people?

Most civilian contractors fell into one of two categories: cowed by her military rank, or self-important jackasses who she had no compunction about running over as needed.

In all fairness, there was a third category that she'd done her level best to cultivate over the years: the competent. She remembered something Richard had explained to her long ago. He was a JAG lawyer she'd dated whenever they'd chanced to land on the same base, until he'd settled down for some unknown reason. It was an urge she'd never shared. Life was far too much fun as a single woman. With no strings affecting her travel or career choices, it was a total win.

Besides, she'd tried the whole tie-the-knot trip briefly— complete fiasco.

Richard had said, *They give a secret test in first-year law. If you're incredibly smart and competent, you get a waiver. If you aren't, you have to take twenty credits of ego.*

Richard had no ego at all about his competence. Richard's assistant, however, had clearly failed both the test and the ego courses, been required to take *forty* credits worth, and would have been filed under PIA, for Pain in the Ass, if he hadn't been so skilled in the courtroom. His win/loss record was the envy of JAG. Richard's cases rarely reached court because he managed to work out solutions long before it went that sour.

Miranda's team landed in the competent category...maybe.

Holly and Mike appeared to have plenty of ego, but *appeared* was the key word there. The only people they were particularly on their guards with were each other, so much so that she couldn't tell if they were a couple or not.

Captain Andi Wu, a top pilot for the 160th SOAR (a *very* top pilot if her record was to be believed), had absolutely no ego at all.

Susan always needed a calming breath before she could speak to Andi. She herself was qualified in several small helos, the Robinson R44 and the Bell LongRanger being her two best.

Captain Wu had flown Sikorsky Black Hawks, MH-6 Little Birds, and one highly classified report hinted that she'd been a lead test pilot on the S-97 Raider helicopter—*the* lead. If the R44 was a Ford Focus and the LongRanger a Honda Civic, the Raider was pure Formula 1, maybe even land-speed-record rocket car. The F-35 Lightning II of the helicopter world.

And nothing in Susan's past repertoire aided communication with Miranda.

It was a nine-hour flight from JBER to Nha Trang. A C-37B had never been designed to land on an aircraft carrier, not even one that was still fully operational. Vietnam had granted them clearance to land, refuel, and transfer passengers between aircraft. Very careful of the delicate balance of the situation, the government had allowed only a fifteen-minute window for any US aircraft or personnel to be on the ground.

The pilots had informed her that they'd even been requested to declare a fuel emergency offshore, reporting they were en route to Singapore a thousand miles farther southwest. She wondered what excuse the C-2 Greyhound had been asked to use for happening to be at the airport for the same fifteen minutes.

The C-2 was a stout little plane that filled the COD— Carrier Onboard Delivery—niche. And it did look rather like a squarish Greyhound bus with wings. It was being replaced by the MV-22 Osprey tiltrotor in the next few years and the thought made her sad. The old plane had been servicing aircraft carriers since Vietnam, and every trip she'd ever made to a carrier at sea had been aboard one. Soon it would be gone.

Not long after that, her own career would be ending when she reached mandatory retirement. She'd always been willing to let the Navy call the shots, except when she hadn't, and then had to convince someone to change their orders. But she didn't think that would work this time.

She'd miss the adventure and travel. Besides, there was still so much to be done, including here and now.

"Miranda," Susan risked interrupting Miranda's discussion with Mike regarding the possible causes of the species variations among *Canis familiarus*.

Miranda continued as if she couldn't even hear the midsentence interruption.

"—with a hundred and seventy recognized dog breeds you would think that the genetic variation would be at the genus or perhaps family levels, but they aren't. There are surprisingly few genes that are changed to make this," she nodded down at Sadie in her lap, whom she still hadn't touched, "into a Saint Bernard. That might actually be an interesting experiment, to see how little was required."

She started to reach for her little notebook, which woke up Sadie to look at her. Miranda instantly returned her hands to either chair arm and stared fixedly at the little dog until it had curled once more into a nap.

Susan tried again, leveraging off the momentary distraction. "Miranda."

"Yes, Susan?" She didn't look up, though Sadie had begun to snore gently.

"May we discuss the accident we're flying to investigate?"

"What makes you so sure that it is an accident? And also, what do you mean by accident? Pilot error, maintenance failure, equipment breakage, outside actions like a bird strike, or something else? There are navigational errors, operational, command, design, and many other types within each category. As many variations as there are types of dogs?" She asked the question of herself. "Perhaps, though I can't see any direct corollary that might constitute an enlightening application of such a concept."

"It's my first plane crash, I was unsure what to call it."

When Miranda didn't answer, Mike answered for her. "It's an incident until determined otherwise."

"An incident," Susan prompted.

"Yes, that's what he said," Miranda agreed.

And there it was again. Repetition appeared to annoy Miranda Chase. But annoy was too strong a word. It was as if she...had no use for repetition? Instead she continued to stare at Sadie.

Before Susan could test that theory, Holly came forward and scooped Sadie out of Miranda's lap and dropped into the fourth seat.

Sadie squeaked in surprise at the rude awakening. Holly was holding her around the middle, leaving her hindquarters to dangle. Her little doggie kicks had nothing to push against.

"Have you been terrorizing our Miranda?"

"Hey," Andi handed her tablet computer to Miranda, then scooped Sadie out of Holly's grasp. Making a cradle of her arms, she sat on Miranda's chair arm. Miranda held the tablet in one hand and began picking individual dog hairs off her jeans with the other. A Shih Tzu didn't shed much, but she picked up each hair individually and dropped it into the remaining ice of Mike's ginger ale glass.

Susan noticed that Miranda didn't move away to give Andi more room to sit, nor did Andi attempt to hold herself clear of Miranda. Was Miranda that comfortable with all of her team, or were they a couple? If the latter, they hadn't given a single prior sign of it. Though they had shared that seat on the Humvee, that had struck her as expediency, as neither woman could weigh a hundred and ten.

Sadie snuggled down in Andi's arms with a happy wiggle. At least until Holly reached across the aisle to place a fingertip atop Sadie's nose. Sadie tried to free her nose, but Holly's touch followed her every motion. Sadie became annoyed enough to try and nip Holly's finger but couldn't manage it.

"Ms. Harper," Susan offered her best displeased command tone.

Holly continued the game for several more seconds before Andi raised an elbow to block her.

"You may," Miranda said without looking up from checking to see if she'd missed any hairs.

"I may what?" These people were confusing the crap out of her.

Miranda almost looked directly at her, but not quite.

Mike came to Susan's rescue, "Explain why we're being whisked to Southeast Asia with an Air Force Commander riding herd on us."

Finally. "I—"

"We're not a pack of sheep or cows," Miranda noted. "Why would she be riding herd on us?"

"It's a—"

"Because we're an unruly mob." Holly signaled someone out of sight behind Susan and the steward came up beside her. "Any chance of a quick pint in this flying pub?"

"No, ma'am," the steward replied. "We're a military craft and don't stock alcohol."

"You're joshing me, mate. This is a top-brass bird. Nothing set aside for the VIPs? I find that a fair stretch." Her accent was shifting from light to broad Australian. "How about a spider?"

"Ew!" Mike and Andi said in unison.

"A spider, ma'am?" The steward was unflappable.

"Do you have root beer?"

"Yes, ma'am."

"And vanilla ice cream?"

"Ice cream sandwiches."

"Ace! Scoop the middle of the latter into a glass of the former and you've got a spider."

"Ma'am would like a root beer float?"

"That's what I've been sayin', mate. Do your worst."

"Yes, ma'am," he departed with a smile after clearing up some of the detritus, including Mike's dog-haired ginger ale glass.

Miranda held aloft one final dog hair, but couldn't find anywhere to place it. Finally Mike took it from her, then surreptitiously dropped it to the floor when Miranda stopped looking.

Susan turned to try again with Miranda...who was now studying Andi's tablet computer. Her motions said that she was editing something.

Mike caught Susan's attention and winked. "You've lost her for a bit while she reads over what Andi and Holly wrote up about the JBER crash."

She reached across and snatched away Andi's tablet.

Miranda squeaked in surprise, sounding enough like Sadie to almost be funny.

The transition was instantaneous, but not in the way she expected.

Mike snapped out a sharp, "No! Don't!"

Miranda didn't look up or protest. Instead she placed her hands over her ears, shut her eyes, and bent down her head.

Andi shoved to her feet, tossing Sadie down on the seat behind Miranda's and appeared ready to do battle.

Holly's voice was very soft, chillingly so. "You'll want to be handing that to Mike very slowly." There was no hint of any accent at all.

"No," Susan matched her tone for tone. "I have a major crisis awaiting us and I need your team's attention to be focused exclusively on that."

"You got our attention, mate. Now if you don't want to make an abrupt exit of the aircraft at fifty thousand feet, you'll hand that back."

"I've faced down plenty worse than you over the years...*mate.*"

"No," Holly almost smiled. "No, you haven't."

Susan was never able to fully reconstruct what happened next.

One moment she was in control of the situation— marginally, but in control.

The next, her head was spinning from where it had been slammed against the window. The tablet was gone from her hands. She was out of her seat and being walked toward the rear of the plane with an arm twisted painfully high behind her back.

They passed the couch, into the rear cabin, and into the small bathroom.

"You're about to be sick as hell," Holly's voice sounded solicitous. "Not that I give a rat's ass. Now lean forward."

Susan had no idea how she came to be on her knees, but she puked violently into the bowl.

19

CLARISSA WAS GOING QUIETLY MAD.

She'd go noisily mad if it would do any good, but a glare from Taz had informed her how inadvisable that would be. Clarissa could still feel where that blade had rested against her throat as if it was a line of embers that continued to burn there. A discreet peek in a hand mirror hadn't revealed any mark but she could feel it nonetheless.

When they'd arrived at the NTSB headquarters, the offices were all dark, no surprise in the middle of the night. The gaudy facade of the International Spy Museum spread most of its red glow toward the street and did little to light the NTSB's offices across the square. This far from the core, traffic had been breaking up and starting to move by the time they arrived.

But Jeremy and Taz wouldn't leave headquarters, not to circle the city and go out to Langley. They had immersed themselves in the NTSB recorder lab.

She'd been here only once before, to help interpret the recovered voice recorder audio for Clark's final flight three weeks ago.

Hearing his few words captured by the cockpit voice

recorder had haunted her dreams on and off since. Often she sat up alone in the darkness on the verge of calling out his name. It was becoming quite annoying and she wished that her dreams or subconscious or whatever would shut up and go away.

Walking the shadowed halls of the NTSB less than a month later echoed with ghosts and her own spiked heels.

Jeremy dove into the black box data recovery process. She hadn't seen the early, mechanical part of the process before. What should have been exciting, or of at least consuming interest, wasn't. It was slow, tedious, and infinitely boring to watch.

She considered heading out to Langley, but it was no better than here for what she needed to do. Also, they were less than a half mile from the White House if she was called in. Yes, this would do nicely for now.

"Where's the nearest conference room with secure comms?"

Once she finally had enough of Jeremy's attention to receive an answer, she turned to Taz.

"You call me the minute you goddamn find anything, Cortez, or I'll string your boyfriend up by the balls and you by your tiny ears."

Taz gave her the finger. At least they knew where they stood with each other.

Clarissa left Rose to keep an eye on them because she didn't have the clearance for what came next.

For the next several hours, Clarissa escalated every operative she could. Instructions began filtering out to agents in China, Russia, India, and Iran. She also woke them up in *friendly* countries: France, the UK, Japan, and Israel.

The challenge? She didn't know what she was looking for. Had the aircraft carrier suffered a terrible accident or been attacked? Had the man who killed Ramson been a solo psychotic, a religious fanatic, or being blackmailed so they had no other option?

Without knowing anything, it was hard to know how wide to cast the nets. And some of them were one-time nets, embedded sleeper agents who, once they'd broken cover, would have to be extracted. It took years to replace those kinds of assets.

It was a risk, but she cast as wide as she could except for the sleeper agents.

But to the local informers she dangled the ultimate prize: a US passport and a lifetime income.

By the time she was done reaching out, the first influx of return reports had begun—revealing nothing of interest.

20

SUSAN STARED AT HERSELF IN THE MIRROR OF THE C-37B's lavatory. No lump on her head, though one of her temples was distinctly sore where it had hit the airplane's window. No real pain in her gut. She knew how the latter had been done, though she'd never actually seen it—or experienced it. The gut punch had been abrupt rather than deep. Just enough for her stomach to decide something very bad was going on and it was time to abandon ship. The lingering soreness reminded her of aching stomach muscles after a case of food poisoning rather than of playing punching bag to an Australian Special Operations soldier.

She rearranged her clothes as well as she could with the aid of the tiny mirror before stepping once more into the cabin.

The rear cabin of the aircraft had two couches that could be converted into beds.

Holly sat on one, elbows on knees, fingers interlaced.

The privacy door to the rest of the plane was closed.

Susan didn't need an invitation to know what happened next; she sat down across from Holly.

"Nice punch," she rubbed her stomach.

"Thanks. I'm sorry, but I had to stop you on two accounts."

"Care to explain before I have you arrested for assaulting an officer?"

Holly's smile barely touch her lips. "Good luck with that: Australian forces, retired. Besides, you really want my help, trust me."

"Okay, I'll at least listen."

That, oddly, earned her Holly's nod of approval and she sat back in her seat.

"First, you were on the verge of throwing Andi Wu into a military mindset with your misguided target of her girlfriend."

"It would be nice if *someone* was of a military mindset here." At least *girlfriend* explained some of the dynamic between Andi and Miranda, though not all of it.

Holly finally leaned back at ease, just as she had the instant before Susan had lost track of what happened and been *escorted* out of the forward cabin.

Susan tried to mirror Holly's casual posture but there was still a tightness in her gut. "So, educate me already."

Holly stared at her so long that she became aware of every single noise in the plane. The well-insulated engines, the occasional creak of the interior fixtures, the minor sliding tone shifts from being airborne rather than parked on the ground. The windows showed the aching depth of stratosphere-blue above a hazy sea lost in the lower troposphere. If there were voices beyond the closed door, she couldn't pick them out.

"How much of our files did you read?"

"All of them."

"Including Captain Wu's attacks of PTSD?"

No, she hadn't seen anything about that, at least not in the crappy files provided by the AIB. Or quite why she'd left the 160th SOAR.

"That was the piece of her military mode I really didn't

want you triggering. Setting her off can deep-six Miranda badly and we need her to function right now."

Susan was horrified. She'd seen men and women, damned fine ones, knocked out of the service with PTSD. Done enough volunteer work with such disabled vets when she was on leave that she knew some would never again be able to toe the line properly, not even in civilian life.

"No, that would never be my intent." That Andi was out on an active team at all was a huge statement of strength.

"So, you read the *Air Force's* files on us." Holly didn't ask.

The Navy's files were very sparse regarding this team, so she'd asked for the AIB's. The US Air Force's Accident Investigation Board had been the most likely to have interactions with civilian air-crash investigators.

"I won't ask how many of those were compiled by a waste of space named Major Jonathan Swift. I *will* suggest that you never mention his name around this team. Just a friendly word of advice."

That was certainly news. Major Swift was the one who had personally transmitted the files to her. Oh! This team obviously knew him, which meant he *had* been a field investigator. Yet he was now the one flying a desk and this was the team sent to crash-site investigations, at least tacitly, by the President himself.

"Yes, that was my source." She nodded for Holly to continue. Susan wanted to see where this led before she made any decisions.

"Shit! Next time I see him, I'm gonna fold that asshole into a tiny ball, stuff him down a dunny, and invite all me mates over for a right proper piss up. His report describes Miranda as dangerously unstable and me as a psychopath?"

Susan again nodded.

"Maybe I can convince Drake to flush his ass."

"Drake? I still can't believe you folks call the Chairman of the Joint Chiefs and the President by their first names."

"Only Miranda does in person. He's Jon's uncle. No nepotism. He's the one who grounded Jon's ass after the last fiasco that nearly got the lot of us killed, followed by his fuckups at the Vice President's crash investigation." Holly rubbed at her face. "Okay, I'll lay this out once. You're clearly smart enough to get it."

She'd been so ineffective over the last several hours as she tried to find some handle to understand and control this team that she'd begun to doubt her skills. It wasn't an ability she'd doubted very often in her career.

"I'm only a psychopath if you're an asshole, otherwise I'm as sweet as a brown desert mouse."

Susan couldn't stop her laugh at that.

Holly shrugged her guilt. "Okay, sweet and me aren't real mates, but as long as you don't mess with Miranda or Andi, I couldn't care a mouse's hind end."

That seemed unlikely. "What about Mike?"

"He's a grown boyo, can tend to himself. Always a little too cocksure, though I do my best to keep him in the place such men belong."

"You and I may match there. Men are wonderful, but mostly at arm's length."

Holly looked out the window over Susan's shoulder long enough for her to turn and look as well, but there was nothing there except the sky darkening toward sunset. It didn't take a genius to see that Mike was a topic that was causing Holly some discomfort.

"Miranda?" she prompted when the silence continued to drag out.

Holly's attention snapped back fast. Yet she waited for Susan to speak first.

"If she's not Major Swift's *unstable to the verge of psychotic,* then what is she?"

"Thought that would have been obvious to someone like you long ago."

"She's autistic. I get that. I don't have much experience with the disorder, not enough to judge how disabled she is."

"Wipe that fucking word from your vocabulary. On the autism spectrum. *Fuck* disorder! Miranda is *not* disabled. She's an absolute genius at a level folks like you and me will never understand. But the world-at-large and people-in-specific? They're a complete mystery to her. No, they're a swamp of infinitely variable sucking mud that she constantly struggles to forge a path through. And she does that by applying an awesome hyperfocus."

"So when I snatched her tablet..."

"...you dumped her straight into the deep end of the swamp."

"Is she going to be okay?"

Holly shrugged. "Mike and Andi are good for her. Better than me. My role is more..." she flexed her hands in and out of fists.

"...physical."

"Aye." And once again she leaned forward, elbows on knees, and stared down at her hands.

Susan's chagrin ran deep. She'd been treating this team's peculiarities using Major Swift's reports as a guide. No wonder nothing she'd done had worked with them.

But it wasn't that simple. She'd tried to speak with Miranda several times only to have—

"You bitch! You've been managing me the whole time."

Holly offered that shrug again without looking up.

"That's why you sat down across from me. After I waited patiently through that analysis of the KC-46 crash at JBER, you balked me every time I tried to talk to Miranda."

Yet another shrug.

"You do that again and I'll—" Susan certainly wouldn't be challenging a Spec Ops warrior herself, "—sic Sadie on you. She has very sharp teeth."

"I'll keep that in mind, Commander." But Holly's mood didn't lighten for even a moment.

"Okay, why?"

Holly started that shrug, caught herself, but didn't look up from her hands. "Nothing in those reports about how I transitioned from SASR (Special Air Service Regiment down in Australia) operator to NTSB, was there."

No point in denying it. There wasn't.

"Not a whole lot of folks know this outside of the regiment." Holly again stared out the empty window as she spoke. "I lost my team. Sole survivor. Not my fault—I know that now—but my commanders weren't impressed at the time." Then she made a face somewhere between a grimace and half smile. "Especially as I gave them little choice in the matter. I also probably shouldn't have attacked the unit commander at the funeral in an attempt to take all of the guilt on myself. At least that's how Mike explained it to me. Mostly fits."

"So you jab at authority every chance you get." Susan would be angry if Holly's pain wasn't so clear to see. She wondered if Holly could see it herself. "No matter how stupid that is?"

"Well, a girl's got to have *some* fun." She didn't sound as if she was having much.

There was one more piece, and now that she could see through the chaff, she could make a good guess at what it was.

"Mike Munroe getting too close?"

Holly studied her hands again, flexing them, not in fists, but more as if she didn't recognize them.

"I'll keep my hands off him, though he is very pretty." Susan tried to make it funny, but Holly didn't react to that.

"He is." She kept flexing her hands as if they hurt.

21

Miranda had known that she didn't have to wait long.

By the time she'd uncovered her ears and opened her eyes, Commander Piazza and Holly were gone from the cabin. She'd managed to miss all of the chaos that ensued whenever anyone triggered one of her team into protective mode. She'd deemed that problem would spike the moment Commander Piazza had taken her tablet.

She'd been right.

By focusing on avoiding exposure to the results of that action, she also managed to *not* focus on the abrupt interruption to her own mental processes.

"They're in back," Mike nodded toward the stern of the aircraft when she looked his way. Which was better than Holly preparing to eject Susan at fifty thousand feet. That would be a remarkably dangerous action, as the C-37B had no airlock that would allow the retention of cabin pressure. She'd been able to hear Holly's threat despite covering her ears.

Actually, as they were headed west of south, they were cruising at fifty-*one* thousand feet. Holly frequently rounded off numbers when she was upset. Now that she considered the matter, she understood that most people did, even when they weren't upset, which struck Miranda as a decidedly lazy way of thinking.

So many things were changing so fast, but some were staying very much the same. Miranda had known what Holly was about to do. Not because she had understood what was happening when the commander grabbed her computer, but because she'd felt the internal slide down to places she'd never wanted to experience again.

Holly reliably rose to her defense when someone acted against Miranda herself. But she didn't like the accompanying violence or chaos either. At least with Holly, it would be over quickly.

Andi was hovering. *Her* face was now familiar enough that Miranda could look at it for several seconds at a time. She could see the...wrongness?

"Are you upset?"

"I'm worried about you," Andi rested a hand firmly on her shoulder. She'd always paid attention to Miranda's aversion to light contact.

"I'm okay." And she was, which was a pleasant surprise after any altercation or pending altercation. However, Andi's face hadn't changed. "But you still look worried."

"I'm trying to do what is right. I'm..." Then she turned away to look at Mike. "...being stupid."

Mike nodded firmly.

Before Miranda could ask why, Andi had wrapped her into a hug and held her tightly.

Miranda let herself be held, "You have great hugs."

"Thanks," Andi's voice sounded shaky by her ear. She held on a moment longer, then released Miranda and turned to face away toward the rear of the cabin.

Miranda leaned out to glance aft, but the rear door was closed. Andi didn't appear to be looking in quite that direction.

"Should I now be asking if you're okay?"

"I'm fine," Andi's voice was...not a good indicator for Miranda. So she took Andi at her word.

Andi eventually scooped up the dog and sat in Holly's chair. Andi kept her face buried in Sadie's fur.

Mike returned her tablet, actually Andi's tablet. She tapped the screen awake and continued her editing. The text was far cleaner than she'd expected. The layout followed her preferred analysis methodology. There were a minimum of extraneous words that she always found so annoying in most other investigator's reports.

It was...familiar.

That was illogical, because it was completely about the crash of the KC-46 Pegasus aerial tanker at JBER. Yet it was...

"You copied my report on the crash of the Embraer ERJ jet in Atlanta."

"The format, not the details. Is it okay?" Andi finally looked up.

Miranda finished it with fewer edits than she might have made to one of Jeremy's early reports. "I agree with your conclusions. Forward it to NTSB headquarters for Jeremy to verify against the data recorders."

"High praise indeed," Mike spoke up.

"Oh, was I supposed to praise her? I didn't know." She turned to Andi. "Well done." Then back to Mike. "Was that appropriate?"

"It was very...appropriate, Miranda," he had that smile she could never interpret.

"Good." Now she could cross that off her mental list. Prior to that they'd been discussing the high diversity of dog species.

She looked down at her lap in surprise. When she'd handed the tablet to Andi, Andi's arms had been full of the dog. So they'd exchanged the tablet for Sadie across the aisle.

Without thinking, Miranda had left a hand resting on the

dog's back after she had set it in her lap. Directly against her palm, its fur was so soft. The warmth, rapid heartbeat, and each breathing motion were not as alien as she'd anticipated. Perhaps classifying all dogs as dangerous carnivore attack animals had been overly generalized.

"Sadie definitely likes you," Susan stopped by her seat to pet Sadie's head before returning to her seat.

"I am...unconvinced as to whether or not I like it."

"Her."

"Is a dog always referred to by its gender? What am I supposed to do if I don't know the animal's gender?"

"Miranda," Susan leaned forward after buckling her seatbelt and running a hand over her midriff. "The dog doesn't understand human speech. And if the owner is offended, they're an idiot."

"In the qualitative sense of the word? How do you measure that without inquiring as to their IQ? I've never been comfortable with such classifications. And if they haven't been tested, then—"

Holly, who stood in the aisle between herself and Andi, rested a hand on her shoulder.

"I'm doing it again, aren't I?"

Holly squeezed her shoulder as Mike nodded. "But don't worry about it, Miranda. Let's see why Commander Piazza is escorting us to the opposite corner of the Pacific Ocean."

For travel from the Gulf of Alaska to the South China Sea, that was a sufficiently accurate description.

Holly nodded to Susan, "You're up, Squid"

Susan smiled at Holly, who was still standing in the aisle as all of the seats in the group were taken, "You're still a bitch, boot."

"Proud to be."

Which was odd as Miranda understood the first to be an

insult to all Navy personnel and the latter to imply Holly was fresh out of boot camp, which was wholly inaccurate.

Neither made any other comment, which Miranda took as good advice and kept her own mouth shut.

Susan then looked at her watch before turning to Miranda.

"Approximately thirteen hours ago there was an *incident* on CVN-71, the aircraft carrier USS *Theodore Roosevelt*. An F-35C crashed badly during landing. The present casualty count is fifty-seven killed, another forty-seven injured, and fifty-two still unaccounted for."

"Unaccounted for? How the hell did that happen?" Miranda needed no emoji chart to identify Holly's fury.

Miranda didn't want to listen, but couldn't help herself. The snippets of information and conjecture that had been sent to Susan were often conflicting. What was clear was that something had gone terribly wrong during the landing of the nation's most advanced jet on one of the world's largest warships.

She heard the change in the C-37B's engines, the descent had begun. Thirty minutes to landing. Another thirty to sixty minutes after that to reach the ship.

Susan had been right, she did need to be briefed prior to arriving on the scene of this accident. She needed six months notice, not sixty to ninety minutes.

She interrupted Susan but refused to feel bad about it. "I need everything you have on the design, construction, and performance characteristics of the F-35C Lightning II."

"But that's classified," Susan protested.

Miranda lifted Sadie out of her lap and passed her to Holly. "I also will need operations manuals for Nimitz-class carriers, especially landing and deck procedures."

"Also classified."

Miranda pulled out her ID wallet, flipped past the NTSB

identification to the CAC—military Common Access Card—
and held it out.

Susan inspected it carefully. "Okay, I believe you, but I don't
have ready access to—"

Miranda pulled out her phone and dialed as Susan's voice
petered off.

"Miranda."

"Drake," she always appreciated that Drake didn't waste
time on frivolous niceties when there were important issues at
hand. She quickly listed the documents she needed loaded
immediately to her secure server.

"I'm glad you're on this incident, Miranda. You'll receive it
all in ten minutes if I have to cut off someone's head."

"Won't that make it harder for them to do the task?"

"Yes, but it will motivate whoever replaces them. Bye,
Miranda."

"Bye, Drake."

Susan handed back her ID very slowly. "Why did you call
the Chairman of the Joint Chiefs of Staff to expedite the
delivery of technical manuals?"

Miranda took her ID, tucked it into its proper pocket, then
made sure none of the cards had been knocked askew by
extracting the CAC for Susan's inspection.

She pulled out her computer, tapped it awake, and opened
her secure mail link.

"It seemed the most expeditious. Besides, I didn't want to
bother Roy."

"Roy? You would have called the President about this?"

She didn't bother answering as the first document
appeared, *F-35C Lightning II Pilot's Operating Manual, Volume I.*
She opened it and began reading quickly.

22

"I THOUGHT WE HAD CONTROL OF THE AREA."

Zhang Ru let Liú Zuocheng's comment rest lightly on the warm evening breeze. He had to be careful in how he answered. He and Zuocheng might bear the same title, Vice Chairman of the Central Military Commission, but General Liú had held the post for years. It was only Ru's second year on the CMC and less than a year since he'd discredited General Chen Hua and ripped the co-Vice Chairman position from his dying clutches.

Ru had uncovered Hua's weakness shortly after his own ascension to the CMC—a taste for brutally raping lesbian couples. He'd set a trap, using his wife Daiyu and the delectable young mistress he'd recently acquired. Hua had rammed his dick into the trap with absolute abandon.

Ru's timing had been bad. By the time he'd *unexpectedly* returned, planning to catch Hua in the act, Hua had choked his mistress to death even as he'd taken her. Daiyu lay on the floor.

Grabbing the heavy scissor tongs from the fireplace, he'd clamped them around Hua's neck and crushed his windpipe. He'd held it so until long after the girl's eyes had bulged in death and Hua's matched them.

Cào but he still missed driving himself into the girl's exquisite ass.

The dead girl, Daiyu's teary testimony, and a dead general had proved most efficient in opening up his seat for Ru's ascendency to replace Hua as co-Vice Chairman. He'd also managed to choose his own man to take the vacated seventh seat on the CMC, now guaranteeing him four of the seven votes.

In retribution, he'd utterly destroyed General Chen Hua's family, shredding it to the last soul. Hua's ancestral burial grounds had been razed, his image had been purged from all state media present and past, and his fortune was now in Ru's hidden accounts.

He had considered keeping a particularly comely granddaughter, a recent pageant winner, to replace his mistress, but decided it was best not to wake up some night with a knife in his heart. So he'd enjoyed her thoroughly, then altered her records to say she was an Uyghur terrorist and had her incarcerated in a Xinjiang reeducation camp. She hadn't lasted long among the guards.

Ru and Zuocheng sat on the veranda of his new apartment in Opus Hong Kong. Ru appreciated General Chen Hua's taste, the penthouse suite was remarkably luxurious. The exotic woods, the plush furniture, and the wall hangings of rare art created a mix of ancient wealth and modern perfection.

Well up the side of The Peak on Hong Kong Island, it commanded a sweeping view of the entire width of Victoria Harbour, Kowloon, and most of the New Territories. The air was fresh here. It didn't smell of the city but rather of the dry oak and myrtle stonewall trees—so called because they were planted to stabilize the retaining walls and steep slopes of The Peak.

It also smelled of money. The wealth here was obscene, and it had been well past time for these people to be brought into line from their little democratic games. It had been his and Zuocheng's first collaboration on the CMC.

Yet it was not so luxurious that Zuocheng might envy him the location, as he had acquired a house on Peak Road during the suppression of those misguided uprisings. That was an unimaginable luxury worth twenty times Ru's apartment.

"Not bad for a pair of old pilots. Hard to believe that we started out flying Chengdu J-7s against Vietnam." They'd been young jet jockeys who'd cut their teeth on the 1979 Sino-Vietnamese War. A propaganda triumph...and a loss in every other measurable way. Over forty years later and the Vietnamese were still a tricky problem. Their alignment with Russia and growing alignment with the West would have to be dealt with someday.

Zuocheng nodded his agreement and sipped his glass of Crown Royal 18—General Chen Hua had excellent taste in whiskey, which Ru could now afford to continue at four hundred US a bottle. The man had stashed away *immense* symbols of wealth over the years.

Daiyu was overseeing the preparation of an elegant meal. She had learned to enjoy her power over the household and would often provide him with particularly delectable treats in his bed, joining in herself only when he requested her. Tonight she had promised him twins. She'd known how the anticipation would arouse him pleasantly all through the evening. But he'd have to wait until Liú Zuocheng was gone as he insisted on being true to his one wife.

Two serving women arrived with a plate of delicate *har gao*. The steamed shrimp dumplings looked perfect, as did the two women.

The twins! Daiyu was delightfully teasing him. So identical he couldn't tell them apart.

Their semi-sheer high-neck white blouses hinted at their equally white underclothes and pale skin. One blouse was buttoned to the left and one to the right, the only discernable difference between them. A small nicety that added to the intrigue. Their unusual height, within centimeters of his own, and slender faces made them slightly exotic to his Beijing eyes. Yes, Daiyu had chosen very well.

Liú Zuocheng accepted the engraved narwhal-ivory chopsticks from the tray one held and selected the second-best *har gao* from the platter the other offered. Zhang Ru was careful to select the third best dumpling. *I will not question your position, but don't forget how closely I lurk.*

Apparently lulled into believing that Ru was wholly his puppet, Zuocheng selected the most perfect one next. Yet he was sufficiently distracted by the twins' beauty that he didn't notice when he dribbled a spot of the dipping sauce on his pant leg. He then applied so much pressure to the *har gao* with his chopsticks that it burst even as he placed it in his teeth.

Ah, not so pure as you would have me think. Perhaps Zuocheng would be with the twins before the night was out, seeing as his wife had remained in Beijing after all—no one here to see. There was always Daiyu for his own satisfaction if needed.

Time to distract his superior and let the anticipation simmer within. He returned to Zuocheng's prior comment.

"We *do* control the South China Sea. The surrounding countries barely dare contest this anymore. It is only the Americans who ignore our sovereign claim."

"And the accident on their aircraft carrier?"

It was hard to know. Within minutes of it, the Americans had put up a no-fly zone. Any ship or plane approaching closer than a hundred kilometers had been sternly warned aside.

Two pilots, ordered to test the Americans' resolve, had actual gunfire shot close by their aircraft at ninety-six kilometers out. Very close by.

It was terrifying how quickly the Americans had protected

the zone. They had locked down thirty thousand square kilometers within minutes. And they'd done it over ten thousand kilometers from their own shores, yet only seven hundred from China's mainland. Despite all of the PLAN's boasting, he knew their own navy couldn't do that more than a few hundred kilometers off their own shores. Past the reach of their own land bases, they would be easily overwhelmed. The effort required for the Americans to enforce such a large no-fly zone in unfriendly waters was beyond imagining.

The twins had moved to a discreet distance, preparing the veranda table for the meal in graceful unison. Zuocheng's attention was most focused, watching their every move with a distracted half smile. Ru might well have to arrange a later night with them for himself.

"The Americans are like angry hornets at the moment. It is best not to stir the nest. Our satellites show that the ship's damage is very significant. We don't have images of the event, but we do of the aftermath."

"They are sending two more carrier groups into the region," Zuocheng sounded almost lazy.

Mā de! Shit! How had he not heard of this himself? He turned away to hide his emotions. Pretended to look south beyond the Peak of Hong Kong Island as if contemplating the distant wounded ship; his new apartment faced north and east. A mere nine months as co-Vice Chairman had simply not given him the time to make all of the connections he needed.

If the twins proved effective with Liú Zuocheng, he might have to requisition them on a permanent basis to see what information they could glean about the general's intelligence network. That would have other advantages as well. He'd have Daiyu look into doing that if tonight was a success.

Two carrier groups, and a crippled third one. There was still life in it, as it had proven when brushing off their surveillance flights. Three carriers, over two hundred state-of-the-art, fifth-generation fighter jets—a quarter of their entire carrier fleet all focused on the South China Sea.

It was a time of great care.

Calmer now, Ru returned to watching Zuocheng watch the twins. Their delicate motions, their slim linen skirts that reached to their ankles but hid none of their pleasing fitness, their long black hair worn in neat ponytails down their backs.

This might also be a time of great opportunity. Chaos often was.

23

"I DON'T HAVE TIME FOR THIS SHIT!" LIEUTENANT COMMANDER Penny Brightman glared at the returning C-2 cargo plane.

The *Theodore Roosevelt* was still held together with no more than duct tape and spit. She hadn't woken for the accident itself —that she'd only been asleep an hour after a double twelve-hour training shift was the only excuse she had—but the alarms had taken care of that. First the seven short and one long of the General Alarm, followed by the continuous ring of the fire alarm, followed by a too-abrupt silence.

It wasn't in her training to question whether or not it was an aborted drill. She dressed quickly and attempted to climb the ladders into the base of the Island.

But she couldn't. It hadn't been a drill.

Stairwells were blocked with fallen steel. Sealed hatches, hot to the touch, warned of fire on the opposite side.

Upon finally reaching the deck, she'd taken the requisite fifteen-second-maximum allowable time to stare at the destruction in dumb shock.

The towering Island superstructure was a blazing ruin. Bodies and wreckage were scattered about the base. Her boots crunched on the debris scattered down the flight line though she'd finally emerged onto the deck well away from the disaster itself. Fire had blackened the paint around every hatch and air vent for the first three stories.

Fire crews were battling their way into the deck-level hatches.

The aft half of the three upper stories had no glass in the windows and flames still boiled out into the air. The forward half was no more than the outlines of a structure. A massive blast had blown out walls, PriFly had collapsed down onto the Command Bridge, and both of those onto the Flag Bridge below.

The giant mast that rose ten stories above the Island, covered with radar and communications antenna, was tilted outboard at a crazy angle, but still clung to the carrier.

At sixteen seconds, Penny's training kicked into gear.

Find who was in command and step in wherever needed.

It had taken under three minutes to determine that *she* was the senior ship's officer remaining on the boat—in any department, not only Command. Flying officers didn't count because they knew shit about ships. Penny knew that, because just like every carrier commander, she'd been a pilot first. The learning curve required to operate a carrier was ungodly.

She tracked down Paddles, the Landing Signals Officer, whose position at the port-side rear of the carrier had saved his life. When he began to describe what had happened, she'd shut him down.

Accident, not attack. All I need to know for now.

More fire teams in their red vests were joining the battle of what had once been the Island.

The foredeck had remained untouched, though debris was scattered down its length from some explosion. A glance upward at the destruction wrought on the Island saved her having to guess the *where* and she didn't have time for the *why*.

Spotting the jets circling overhead, she'd taken a gamble and launched a tanker without first doing an FOD—Foreign Object Debris—walk. She'd sent it from the farthest-to-port Number Four catapult, hoping for the best. It had worked.

The moment the tanker was safely aloft to refuel the circling aircraft, she'd sent a line of fifty crew armed with buckets and brooms to clear all four of her launch catapults down to the last stray screw and piece of broken glass. One missed piece sucked into a jet engine could down the plane before it had a chance to fly.

Penny had the off-watch launch crew, who were now the *only* launch crew, prioritize replacing all four landing wires and then perform their own FOD of the after deck.

Thirty-eight minutes after they were supposed to land, the rest of LC Gabe Brown's flight were on the deck.

The radar still spun at a skewed angle on the wounded mast. However, all of the access to its data had been within the destroyed superstructure, as was everything else she needed. Time to go Old School.

Her engine controls quickly became shouting to a nearby helmsman over the roar the noise of departing and landing jets. He, in turn, called the engine room using one of the unpowered speaking tubes that threaded throughout the ship. Neither of them could recall the last time they'd seen the tube system in any use other than ceremonial, but they depended on it now.

A Special Ops team, which she hadn't known was aboard, stepped forward to volunteer their services. It included a combat air controller from the Air Force's 24th STS. As both air marshals had apparently been in the Island, he took over the outer airspace with a pair of handheld radios. A radioman was soon giving him verbals from the USS *Antietam's* radar, a Ticonderoga-class guided-missile cruiser that was part of the carrier strike group. She paired the controller with the surviving off-shift Mini Air Boss. Together they had sweated bullets throughout the long day, but no one new had died in air operations.

That wasn't a victory, it was a triumph.

The next big problem was parking. The electronic Ouija Board had died along with its operators. Fitting eighty jets and ten helos aboard an aircraft carrier required an entire department of professionals, constantly redistributing aircraft. If two jets came up out of the hangar in the wrong order, that was the way they had to launch. If the C-2 Greyhound cargo plane was parked on the Hangar Deck in front of an F/A-18 Super Hornet, the fighter jet wouldn't be flying anytime soon.

Two long folding tables were set up at the base of the Island, then weighted in place with an AGM-114 Hellfire missile each. With outlines of the two decks spraypainted on the table surfaces, they set up a physical board. A 20 mm round, hijacked from the Phalanx auto-gun and rubber-banded across a popsicle stick, became an F-35, with the bird's number on the stick. Twin-engine F/A-18s were two rounds on a stick, and helicopters were crisscrossed popsicle sticks. Jokes about shit-on-a-stick had eased some of the tension.

Blue-vested runners were dispatched to make notes on where everything was parked at the moment. Each role on deck had a different color vest, and she wanted to give a medal to every damn one for not panicking.

It was only then that the search-and-rescue helo was missed. She released a frigate from the strike group to chase back along the *Big Stick's* path, with no luck. Though they did pick up the bodies of several of the deck crew that had been blown overboard and left in the carrier's wake.

She asked, but there were no officers with carrier experience anywhere else in the strike group, so she off-loaded tasks onto her lower rankers, better to have some experience than risk a no-experience know-it-all coming aboard who outranked her.

It was over an hour before the Ouija Board Handler called out to no one in particular, "We're missing 892. Where the hell is 892?"

Well, Penny decided, that answered one thing at least. She pointed upward at the ruin of the Island superstructure. How the hell Gabe Brown had landed in PriFly after killing everyone in the Captain's and Admiral's Bridges was still a mystery.

The explosion of 892 and the fire had killed everyone from PriFly at the top, down through the command decks, through radar and flight control, and into the pilot's ready room at deck level. Four times she'd called for a plane, only to be told that its pilot couldn't be found. She made a point of personally adding each name to the Presumed Dead list as those and other callouts couldn't find the person. The second double-column sheet was almost full. A hundred and sixty souls and the count was still climbing. That didn't include the injured that were strewn about sick bay and the ship's operating theaters.

Fourteen hours since the incident, they were holding on by their fingernails with no rest in sight. The accident had occurred at shift change, so that lost both command teams. Only she and a few others had been on a special training schedule so that they weren't in the Island when this happened, which meant she was in hell with no relief in sight.

And now what?

As Acting Captain, she'd spoken several times to the Admiral at CINCPACFLT, the four-star Commander in Chief of the entire Pacific Fleet. He'd agreed she'd made the right decision to take over the ship herself.

Then, to really piss her off, she'd received a call from Admiral Stanislaw of the Joint Chiefs that she was to show all due courtesy to a civilian investigation team and would she please send a Greyhound to pick them up. Fishing out the plane from the Hangar Deck had grossly disrupted the shipboard traffic and had forced the Handler to fully reset his Ouija Board—again. He'd had to do that every two to three hours, but that didn't make it any easier.

Stanislaw was so far removed from reality that he didn't understand what she needed was a ship's captain, not a useless flock of goddamned tourists. She'd never been more than a watch stander.

But CINCPACFLT had said she was in charge until further notice. The carrier's B-crew was on shore leave after six months at sea and it would take days to pull them back together and deliver a qualified command team to the *Big Stick*.

When it was determined that they were still flight and navigation operational, she'd been ordered to remain on station. Pushing so many patrol aircraft aloft had been her decision, which doubled down the load on every team from air traffic control to deck operations, but it couldn't be helped.

The Air Boss slid the C-2 Greyhound in between two flights of returning F/A-18 Super Hornet jets. Then he shuffled it to park on Elevator 4 at the portside-rear of the deck and left it there. It would take another feat of magic to restow it anywhere else. They wouldn't need that elevator for another fifteen minutes, which made it a problem for some other time.

Five people deplaned. Four civilians and—*Thank God above!* —an unexpected Navy Commander come to take charge. The Admiral wouldn't have sent her if she didn't have carrier experience.

Penny dispatched a white-vested safety observer to escort them across the active flightline. The four civilians could be blown overboard for all she cared, but she needed that commander.

24

THE CROSSING OF THE BUSY FLIGHTLINE OF THE USS *THEODORE Roosevelt* from the C-2 Greyhound hadn't been long enough for Susan to process the damage.

US aircraft carriers were supposed to be inviolable. No fleet carrier had been sunk since 1942. And the worst damage in modern times had been a couple of aircraft accidents. The carriers themselves had been almost untouched.

But the Island!

The front half of the upper three of seven stories was mostly missing. The back half a burned-out wreck—the fire must have been intense as she could see warping in the remaining steel. The hundred-foot-tall main radar mast mounted atop the superstructure tilted at an unnerving angle, thankfully to outboard rather than overhead, making the ship appear drunk. Wreckage was everywhere, shoved out of the way but everywhere except the flightlines.

The safety officer had given them all heavy earmuffs on landing and then escorted them to a rag-tag group of card tables close by the Island's base.

"Commander Susan Piazza, requesting permission to come

aboard." She saluted the group as well as she could, but the shock was still too great. Her voice stumbled.

"Permission granted."

There were no flights at the moment, so everyone's earmuffs were shifted aside, but the noise was still horrendous. Broken planes, damaged with debris from above, were having fuel and ordnance removed. Others, already stripped, were being dragged toward an elevator to be shifted down to the Hangar Deck. Everything was in a barely controlled state of orchestrated chaos. And this was fourteen hours *after* the incident. What had it been like half a day ago?

Susan hadn't really focused on the group she'd been led to. The woman who had responded to her salute had brunette hair to her jaw, wore camo khakis and a Navy-blue t-shirt with no insignia.

"Aren't we already aboard?" Miranda asked. "Should we have asked permission before stepping on the deck? I don't like to be rude."

"It's how we do it in the Navy, Miranda. You're fine."

The woman at the table glanced at Sadie in her usual cross-shoulder pouch so that Susan could have her hands free. Dogs were strictly against regulations on ships, without special permission by the captain, but no one argued with Susan for long about her Shih Tzu. A dog on board didn't appear to bother the woman.

"Would you like a briefing before or after I relinquish command?" the woman asked her.

"Relinquish command? Why would you do that?" Susan was missing something.

"You're now senior officer on the boat."

Susan brushed at the silver oakleaf on her collar points. "I am?"

"Yes, ma'am."

"I'm only a commander, Captain." Susan again looked at

the Island and wondered quite how many had died up there to make this woman the ranking officer.

"I'm only a *lieutenant* commander, Commander. I'm LC Penny Brightman."

"I work in communications, *Acting* Captain Brightman."

"Shit! Sorry, Commander Piazza. I didn't mean to say that out loud."

"I've heard worse. Where are the rest of the command crew?" Then Susan glanced up and behind Brightman, but turned away quickly. So wrong! Is that where the captain had been? Perhaps still was?

Acting Captain Brightman's deadpan look answered that question.

"No one?" There should be twenty or more officers above a lieutenant commander.

"Not that we've found."

Susan looked down at the array of tables. Actual missiles and sections of steel weighting them in place against the wind blasts of jets maneuvering about the deck. Rough drawings of the ship covered with ammunition and popsicle sticks. Another table of radios. And the one in front of the captain had pages of scrawled notes and sketches, bearing numerous cross-outs for changing situations. Amazing.

"Are you operational?"

In response, one of the radiomen shouted, "Guard your ears."

Susan turned to make sure that everyone had their earmuffs in place. They did.

Except someone was missing.

"Miranda!" she shouted but couldn't hear herself.

But Andi must have heard as she spun around to look.

Miranda had wandered down the flightline. She was walking along the Number Four wire out onto the deck.

Andi started to move, but Susan grabbed her shoulder. The

woman was, or had been, a Night Stalker and should know carrier operations.

With her other hand, she slapped her hand on the arm of a white-vested safety officer and pointed to Miranda.

She couldn't hear his curse, but she could see him shout, *Shit!*

Andi tried to surge forward again. Susan would have lost her if Holly hadn't grabbed her in a two-armed bear hug. Still she struggled to get to Miranda.

The white checked the sky aft, then sprinted toward Miranda. He tackled her and kept right on going until they were on the far side of the line.

Two seconds later, an F/A-18 Super Hornet slammed down and caught the Number One wire. Its engines roared to life until the wire had halted it almost exactly where Miranda had been standing moments before.

The pilot looked pissed as hell as he cut the engine, then raised the hook to drop the wire. In all of the confusion, he hadn't been given a wave-off to abort the landing. The wire slid back toward reset.

A hand spun Susan around.

The Acting Captain was right up in her face. "I want these people off my ship. Now!"

"That's not going to happen, Lieutenant Commander." They'd each shoved back one ear of their muffs.

"You don't get to—"

"By order of Admiral Stanislaw and the President of the United States, this team is not leaving the ship until we know what happened."

"We know what the hell happened. Your civilian almost got one of my people killed saving her stupid ass. No one crosses the deck without an escort."

"I know that, Acting Captain," Susan took a breath and did her best to make her voice calm and professional. "I apologize in my oversight of assuming they, too, would know that protocol. I will make sure it doesn't happen again."

The jet had taxied away and the arresting wires were all reset. The pilot still looked pissed as hell.

The white had Miranda halfway back but she stopped him in the middle of the landing area. After a brief argument, one of the radios on the table squawked.

"Landing officer. White Seven. Time to next landing?"

"LO to White Seven, you have ninety seconds."

"Roger."

Susan could feel Captain Brightman steaming beside her.

Miranda was walking back and forth across the deck. She looked up and waved to the others to come join her. Holly turned to look toward the LC as if asking permission. Now that Miranda was safe, Andi had stopped fighting. Mike was smart, watching Holly for his cues.

Brightman waved them all forward in clear disgust with a shouted, "Hurry!"

Andi raced over and embraced Miranda hard, then began yelling at her. Good. Someone had to and Susan was glad it wasn't her.

By the time Mike and Holly had trotted over, Andi had calmed down.

Within seconds, Miranda had them all studying the deck. Then, with a gesture from Miranda, they scattered, each in a different direction.

The white looked toward Brightman as if asking what the hell he should do. Every untrained person on an operational flight deck was supposed to have a white at their side. There was only one of him and four on Miranda's team.

Before Susan could think of what to do, they each came to a halt, then turned to look up from the deck and faced Miranda.

She made some notes in a notebook, then waved toward the stern. Mike walked one side of the line, Holly on the other, and

Andi stayed close to Miranda down the middle. The white was hustling after Miranda's unexpected change of direction.

"What is this, synchronized swimming?" Brightman snarled at her.

"I have no idea. I was told to pick them up in Alaska ten hours ago from a KC-46 Pegasus crash site and deliver them here with all due speed. All I know is that they have the kind of access swabbies like you and I only dream about."

"Dazzle me."

"Miranda, that's the brunette in the middle, called the Chairman of the Joint Chiefs to get copies of all of the technical manuals for F-35s and the *Theodore Roosevelt*."

"General Drake Nason?"

"Direct line. No operator. And the kicker?"

Brightman waited.

"She said that she'd called him because she didn't want to bother Roy."

"Roy, as in..." Brightman started in disbelief but appeared to choke when she tried to finish the sentence.

"As in President Roy Cole. First name basis?" Susan had only seen the President in person once, from the twenty-seventh row during a speech attended by three thousand other sailors.

They shared a look and Susan knew that, for once, they were both out of their depths here. One thing was clear, it was probably best not to mess with Miranda.

25

AT SEVENTY-FIVE SECONDS, THE WHITE HAULED MIRANDA AND Andi off the flight line and waved the others aside.

Susan did her best to appear patient through it all to keep the Acting Captain in check. Was that her role now? Smoothing the world for the strange Miranda Chase was *not* how she'd expected to be spending this day. Of course, neither had she expected to end up in the South China Sea aboard an aircraft carrier, in whatever condition.

It was actually her single favorite aspect of her job, she never knew what came next or where she and Sadie would be spending the night. Sadie was currently snoozing happily in her pouch, oblivious to all of the deck noise.

There were three more landings before Miranda and her team completed whatever they were doing. Twice, Miranda knelt and inspected the deck through a magnifying glass. She took a number of pictures.

Two more jets and a helo were aloft in the time it took the group to walk the football field length from the stern to the... command bridge. Susan didn't know what else to call Brightman's setup.

"What was that?" Brightman demanded the moment Miranda arrived. "We know what the hell happened. A pilot botched his landing, then tried to take off again, but botched that too."

"Oh, then did *you* fire the laser?" Miranda asked.

"What laser?"

Without answering, Miranda pushed aside a clipboard on Brightman's center command table. Susan saw that it was a list of names and grabbed it before the clipboard could fall to the deck. She recognized a name near the top of the list. She'd known Admiral Jenkins quite well. They'd had a brief affair after his wife left him. They still traded birthday and Christmas calls. Or they *had.*

Some of the names had a single slash in front of them. His, like many others, had an X.

She turned the list to Brightman and pointed at the markings.

"One slash is missing, two is confirmed dead."

Susan inspected the length of the list, recognized a few other names she'd met at conferences or trainings over the years.

In the meantime, Miranda had set up a computer on Brightman's table. The others were tapping on their phones, sending her data. In moments, a diagram of the deck appeared. It showed the exact path each person had walked.

What had seemed random while watching their progress, now showed up as a clear shape on the screen. Two clear shapes.

Miranda spoke up as she kept typing. "The additional landings have blurred some of the features, but for the most part we can see two patterns. The more obvious marks are out here around the Number Four arresting wire. Hot jet exhaust washing across the deck at a thirty- to sixty-degree downward angle, I'm sorry I can't be more specific. I hate to estimate, but it appears to be in keeping with a single Pratt & Whitney F135-PW-100 engine. I will have to make several tests on afterburner thrust profiles before I can confirm this."

Brightman was staring at Miranda as if she'd been speaking Greek, or perhaps perfect English but had been an alien transported down from on high.

"The more intriguing pattern is the shape I've marked with the green line. I'd like to send a section of your deck back to the lab to be sure but—"

"You are *not* cutting a hole in my deck."

"I don't need much, a half meter square should be more than sufficient. Right about here." She marked an X several meters forward of the stern landing threshold on her diagram. "I'd also like a similar section of the deck, but forward of this line." She placed a mark that ran from where they were standing at the Island, directly to the other side of the deck.

"Again, not going to happen," Brightman spoke slowly. "But why don't you tell me why you want them."

"I don't like to repeat myself. Are you having memory problems?" Miranda squinted at Brightman's shoulder. "The laser."

"And now I'm the one having to repeat myself. *What* laser?"

Miranda looked to Susan, but she had no idea what was going on.

Miranda pointed up, straight up. "That one. Whichever one burned this section of your deck plating. It is lighter close to either side of the runway's centerline and almost non-existent under the longer fuselage."

"Why would that be?" Susan decided to take the hit for Brightman. She still didn't know what Miranda was talking about.

An airborne laser? Unlikely that one could get within a hundred kilometers of an aircraft carrier group. Unless it was domestic. A terrorist attack from a US plane in the South China Sea? That didn't fit.

A—

No! The next thought was too ridiculous. Or perhaps terrifying.

Looking around, Miranda plucked the clipboard from Susan's hands. Before she could protest, Miranda had opened the clip, twisted the pages to either side, and released it, crumpling their corners.

Before Brightman could explode, Miranda began talking.

"Imagine this is an F-35C." The pages did stick out past the clipboard's edges like wings. "I'm assuming by the fact that we're on an aircraft carrier and the pattern of the exhaust marks that it wasn't an F-35B."

"It was a C," Brightman managed, though Susan swore she could hear the woman's teeth grinding over the sound of the jet now taxiing to the forward catapult.

Miranda appeared to ignore the interruptions of the flight operations as if they never happened. They were simply non-moments of time when all conversation ceased, Brightman issued a few commands regarding ship heading or tactical patrols, conferred with one of her other officers about operations, and earmuffs were replaced then removed after launches and recoveries. Miranda always restarted at exactly the same place in the sentence she'd left off.

"So, the clipboard I'm holding—" she dropped it on the table. "Oh, never mind, the scale is all wrong." She stepped over to the Ouija Board and picked up a round with a popsicle stick. "This scale is much better. It's within eighteen percent anyway."

The Handler tried to grab it back, but Holly rested a hand on his shoulder and he flinched aside as if he'd been punched. Others wouldn't know that the tall, beautiful blonde had also been a top Aussie Spec Ops operator, though

Susan herself now had no trouble remembering. Holly had probably squeezed a nerve cluster as neatly as a Vulcan nerve pinch.

"How do you figure *eighteen* percent?" Susan still couldn't tell if what Miranda Chase was saying was fact or some fantasy in her head.

Holly rolled her eyes at her and Mike was smiling. Andi was...shifting herself to always be between Miranda and the flightline. Her arms were slightly spread as if to grab Miranda at the least misstep. So Andi understood air carrier deck operations, she'd simply been willing to sprint into harm's way to protect Miranda.

For about the twentieth time, Susan wondered who the hell these people were.

Miranda continued, unaware of all of the dynamics around her. That was about the only thing at the moment that made perfect sense.

"A six-foot card table to represent the USS *Theodore Roosevelt*. The painting of the deck outline on the table isn't quite to scale, but it does reach end-to-end. A three-hundred-and-thirty-two-point-eight-meter-long ship reduced to a six-foot table. The F-35C Lightning II's length is fifty-one-point-five feet. This round," she held up the model for the plane, "is a hundred-and-two-millimeter round. That makes it eighteen-point-four percent too long for this scale. A .30-06 round would be closer, it's only two percent too short, but I didn't see any available. I could wait if you'd like to fetch some but I don't really see the point."

"Why not?"

"The four-and-a-half-inch popsicle stick is completely out of proportion. It's almost fifty-nine percent too long to properly represent the wingspan. I'd have to cut off the identifying number you've written on the wing to correct that."

Susan hadn't seen her look at a calculator once, nor a look-up table for any lengths. Maybe she really was that good. "Why don't you proceed with the tools at hand?"

Miranda looked at down at the Ouija Board diagram and pointed. "Why is that one parked in the Island?"

The Handler reached for the plane Miranda held.

Susan waved him off. She didn't want a repeat of the events on the flight here.

"That," the Handler pointed at the bullet-popsicle stick combo parked on the drawing of the Island, "was Number 892. It's still up there, or at least some of it." He pointed toward the wreckage above them.

"Oh," Miranda put down the plane she'd picked up, Susan would now bet to within a millimeter of its original location, then selected the one with 892 written across its popsicle stick.

This time Acting Captain Brightman had to wave off the Handler's protest.

If Miranda noticed, she gave no sign.

26

MIRANDA HELD NUMBER 892 AND DID HER BEST TO ESTIMATE THE correct approach. In the past, she would have used her tape measure. But speed was of the essence here. Not only had Susan said so, but the constant interruptions of the flight operations were very trying. She had to freeze and mentally hold her thoughts still—each time a plane arrived or departed —to not lose her place.

She walked until she was four and a half table-lengths away —ten and two-thirds carefully measured paces—and held it nineteen inches above the table's surface. There was a permissible degree-and-a-half of variation in the approach glideslope, so that should be enough to cover any errors.

No, it wasn't.

A standard folding table was thirty inches tall. She pulled a tape measure from its pocket in her vest and checked her estimate. Forty-five inches from the deck. Unacceptably low. She raised the plane model four inches and tucked away the tape measure.

"If your pilot was on an accurate approach, he would have

been three-and-a-half degrees up at three-quarters of a nautical mile out."

The Acting Captain spoke up, "That's exactly where he would have been. LC Gabriel Brown was *always* clean in the Groove."

"Good. That makes this easier. So...a normal approach," she walked up to the table, slowly lowering the disproportionate plane.

She could only hope that she was doing it accurately. Portraying the relative speed properly in proportion to the reduced ratio of the models was quite complex to maintain accurately.

"Mike, we'll need to talk to the Landing Signals Officer to see if he was erratic on this flight."

"He was," the Handler reported. "I talked to the LSO earlier. Five to seven seconds out, he began to drift. One second out, he fired his engine to full afterburners without saying a word why."

"Okay, Andi, I'll want you to verify that on the ship's data recorder if it's still operational."

"Got it!"

Miranda held the *aircraft* clear of the edge of the table and wobbled it, though she didn't like stopping the time-scale portion of the simulation. "We can assume this is the moment when the laser first impacted his aircraft and he began to react."

"What—"

But Susan silenced the Acting Captain before she could interrupt. Miranda appreciated it, though the open question was quite annoying.

"Our first *concrete* evidence of the laser," she made a guess at the question, then hurried on in case she was wrong, "is on the stern of the landing area." She pulled a small flashlight out of her vest and shone it down upon the aircraft.

The light shone brighter than she'd anticipated, which had her looking upward. Night was falling. She'd missed that transition. She looked back down.

"It etched the decking to either side of the aircraft without interruption. Where the narrower wings passed, the deck was partly shaded from the laser. Almost no etchings appear along the centerline because the fuselage shadowed the deck from the tip to the tail during its passage. The laser was sufficiently focused that it spilled very little before or behind the plane. The laser wasn't bathing the deck but was rather actively tracking the flight of Number 892."

"Gives a whole new meaning to the old pick-up line: *Want to come in and see my etchings?*" Holly asked in her thicker Strine, indicating it was a humorous statement.

Others laughed, confirming that.

Miranda didn't know what the *old* meaning would be, unless it was the logical juxtaposition of viewing art versus viewing the carrier's metal decking. She still failed to see the humor in the situation.

"The wavering of the edge and the width of the beam could definitely be explained by atmospheric scattering. I need to call Jeremy regarding—"

"No calls off this ship without my specific authorization," the captain said quickly.

"—laser scattering as—"

"Permission denied."

"—he's fired those and I've only studied them."

"Sorry. No. Not at this time."

Miranda pulled out a notebook and made a notation.

"What was that?"

"I didn't want to forget that I need to talk to Jeremy."

"Do you often forget things?"

"Never," Mike and Andi said in unison.

Miranda admitted that was true but she liked to be sure and tucked the notebook away.

She set the 892 model back on the Island at exactly the angle the Handler had originally placed it. Then she looked aloft and tried to assess the damage path of both the laser and the jet's exhaust on the deck. She corrected the angle and shifted the plane aft several centimeters. The Handler made no comment so she didn't either.

"I'd like to see the plane now."

The Acting Captain waved toward the debris swept up against the base of the Island. "There. And more up above. The fires have been out for a while, so it may be cool enough to inspect. Portions of it were blown out to sea, I'm sure."

"How soon are you recovering those?"

"Probably never. It's four thousand meters underwater, and the force of the explosion of all of its ordnance and the resulting fire probably left few pieces bigger than my hand."

"Still, I'd like to see them." She was glad she'd kept her flashlight out as there were no lights showing from the open hatch at the base of the Island. She needed to find the plane's skin.

Then she spotted an ejection seat in the pile of debris.

"Was that the seat from 892?" She hurried over to it. "Where's the pilot?"

"He's dead."

"I had rather assumed that based on the dents and blood on the seat. I need to see his body. And especially his helmet and flightsuit."

Miranda had a hard time ignoring the Acting Captain's next question, "Is she for real?"

Miranda hated that question, and she never knew what to do with it.

Then she heard Andi's voice, barely audible despite the brief lull of activity on the Flight Deck.

"More real than you, me, or anyone else on this boat. You'd do well to remember that, Acting Captain."

Andi was always the calm one. And it worked as it always did, Miranda felt calmer after Andi had spoken.

Miranda pulled out her personal notebook to check. She'd started a page to try and catalog voice tones. They were very hard to quantify, but she had several pictures that helped.

Andi's tone somehow matched the picture of ice. Deep, arctic ice. But she still didn't know what that *indicated*.

27

ACTING CAPTAIN PENNY BRIGHTMAN STOOD RIVETED TO THE deck as this Miranda Chase person led her team away to study the wreckage. They began working the line as methodically as they had walked the deck: one step at a time.

The woman claimed that Number 892's crash hadn't been an accident but rather an attack.

And then walked away as if that revelation was of no consequence?

A direct attack on a US aircraft carrier? It was incomprehensible.

It did make her feel bad for all of the foul thoughts she'd been heaping on Gabriel Brown's memory throughout the day as she'd struggled to keep her ship together without losing her shit. Or was it the other way, keeping her own personal shit together to keep from losing her ship?

But now...

She picked up her secure satellite phone and waved for her Number Two to take over operations. He was a four-year lieutenant who definitely deserved a promotion to LC after this.

Circling wide of the wreckage swept up against the base of

the Island, where Miranda's team was currently uncovering who knew what scary-as-hell revelation, she stepped onto the narrow walkway that ran along the outboard side of the Island.

There was scattered debris underfoot, twists of steel, an instrument panel that might well have been one she'd used during every watch she'd ever stood, and glass that crunched underfoot. There was also a large panel of curved acrylic that might have once been part of 892's cockpit canopy.

One hour's sleep in the last two days. She'd been trained regarding how deeply that could distort any decision-making process, but she was out of options.

Standing here, she leaned on the railing because she wasn't sure she could trust her knees. The sun had set and now it was the running lights of the destroyer USS *John S. McCain* patrolling a thousand yards out that shone brightest. It was but one of the ten ships, two submarines, satellites, and aircraft that were supposed to keep this carrier safe.

She wondered what Captain John "Wayne" McCain would have done. Five-and-a-half years he'd been prisoner of the North Vietnamese less than three hundred kilometers from here. He'd survived horrors she couldn't begin to imagine.

This? This was nothing by comparison and he'd found his way through it.

Taking strength from that, she pulled out the card that she was never without since the day she'd been cleared as a watch stander on the ship.

Running her thumb down to highlight *Pinnacle Report*, she noticed that her hand was shaking.

Exhaustion and low blood sugar. That's what she'd believe it was. Nothing she could do about the former until the next carrier group arrived. She'd definitely get some food—after this call.

She punched in the associated phone number before she could conjure any more doubts, and hit dial.

"Authorization code."

Penny gave the operator the code that she'd been told to memorize then destroy.

"Verified. Proceed."

"Pinnacle – Front Burner." Highest level of national security interest, a pre-conflict attack.

"Understood. Please hold."

Hold?

The world was ending, at least the one she knew, and she was on hold.

Someone had deliberately attacked an aircraft carrier.

And she was on hold.

She needed some goddamn hold music for distraction. Maybe a recording of the US Marine Corps Band playing "Louie, Louie" or Lady Gaga's "Million Reasons". Because she could think of an easy million reasons to walk away from this mess. The woman knew what she was singing about. If not for having sworn the loyalty oath—Penny's one good reason to stay —she wasn't sure she could see this through.

"Identify," a deep male voice came on the line without introduction.

"Lieutenant Commander and Acting Captain of CVN-71 USS *Theodore Roosevelt* Penny Brightman."

"Aw, hell."

It was soft, and it wasn't the response she'd been expecting.

"How long was she aboard before she figured it out?"

Penny was about to ask who, then realized that was pointless. Miranda Chase. "Under twenty minutes, sir."

"What did she find?" Still no identity, but there was no mistaking a voice so used to command.

"To whom am I speaking, sir? If I may ask?"

"Sorry. I must be tired—about a tenth as tired as you, I imagine. Drake Nason and I'm here with the President."

"Sir! Mr. President!" She jolted to attention so fast that her tired grip almost lost the phone overboard. That would teach her to doubt Miranda Chase's credentials.

"At ease, Brightman. Accident or attack? Dumb question. You wouldn't be calling in a Pinnacle report if it was the former. What did she find?"

"Laser, sir. Aerial."

"Someone flew a laser-equipped plane over one of our carriers without us knowing?"

"No sir. Ms. Chase said something about the dispersion of the beam and atmospheric scattering that I couldn't quite follow."

"You'll find that happens a lot around her."

Which didn't make Penny feel any better. "It makes her think it was fired from orbit. Someone deliberately attacked a pilot during landing using a big-ass laser." Penny flinched. "Sorry for the language, sir. As you stated, I've been awake a long while. The pilot's actions as he was attacked is what caused the damage to the carrier."

The Chairman of the Joint Chiefs of Staff sounded unrealistically human as he sighed unhappily. "Going to be awake a while longer. At least until the *Vinson* gets close enough to send you some serious coverage."

"So I surmised, sir."

"Smart girl. Okay, run down your status for us in language that a 75th Ranger and a mere Green Beret can understand." How anyone could call a President with Roy Cole's battle record *mere* was beyond her. Ranger teasing Green Beret? Well, the Navy was better than either of those.

"For a pair of grunts? I don't know. I can try, sir."

There was a bark of laughter before she could bite her own tongue off. Penny forged ahead rather than thinking about whether or not they would lock her up for insulting the Commander in Chief.

Over the next fifteen minutes, the Chairman and the

President listened and asked detailed questions. Good questions, hard ones that made her think. The logistical ones she was generally able to tell them the work was already done or in progress. The tactical ones were much more difficult. Thank gods above and below that the strategic questions were all above her pay grade.

By the end of their questions, she had a lot more work to do tonight than she'd started with.

"I'm looking at your file here, Lieutenant Commander Brightman."

"Sir." And what exciting revelations was he reading there?

"Sterling recommendations for your promotion to commander. Only awaiting your captain's signature." She hadn't known that a promotion was even in process. Just like the captain to want to surprise her.

"The captain is dead, sir." Penny closed her eyes against the darkness, but it didn't shut it out. Damn but she was going to miss serving under him.

"Yes, so I have signed it in his stead. Congratulations, Commander Brightman."

"Thank you, sir." As if that mattered right now.

"The *Carl Vinson* is now close enough that we're going to fly their executive officer over. Sorry, we couldn't do it sooner. There were other logistical concerns that distracted our attentions."

He didn't elaborate.

She didn't ask.

"It will be good to relinquish command, sir." Penny leaned her back against the outside of the Island. She would have sagged onto the starboard walkway in relief but she didn't want to sit on broken glass.

"I'm sorry about that, Brightman," the President's voice was far gentler than the chairman's.

"I'm not."

"No, I'm sorry that you won't be relinquishing command. He will be there to assist and train *you*. By Presidential order for meritorious service above and beyond the call of duty, and a damn sharp view of the situation even when exhausted past reason, you are hereby bumped one grade to Captain. I couldn't do that until Drake had signed your promotion. The vessel is yours, Captain Brightman. Take care of her for us as you have been and she'll be in good hands. Again, congratulations."

"You're fucking kidding me."

Both men laughed, but General Nason was the one who replied. "Not for a minute, Captain. CINCPACFLT fully concurs as does your Flight Wing commander. And do please remind Miranda to call us when she figures out who just declared war on the United States of America. Best of luck."

And Penny was standing alone in the dark holding a disconnected phone.

She leaned there with her back against the steel Island. It had probably been blazing hot with the internal fire this morning. Now it was still warm from facing west into the sunset but she couldn't move away. All she could do was lean there, facing the night for several minutes as she reviewed the conversation.

Then she remembered the last question that the chairman of the Joint Chiefs had asked before the whole promotion aberration had been dropped on her head.

Is the carrier's mechanism to arm and load the special weapons functional?

Command called them *special* because they didn't like to call them what they really were. Those who lived with them in the secure hold aboard ship called them by name—the B61-12 nuclear bombs.

28

At the knock on the conference room door, Clarissa collapsed back into her chair. She'd lost all track of time and had nothing more to report to the White House now than after the crash.

Everything was a dead end.

"Come in." Clarissa checked her watch.

Seven hours?

Seven hours, and all she knew was that a plane had crashed into Ramson's suite at the George and someone had crippled a US aircraft carrier. She still had no lead on who for either one.

Rose opened the door and slipped into the room. She looked as she always did, at ease and elegant. Clarissa felt like a rumpled mess.

"Sorry. I had to get that moving."

Rose nodded. Then she shook her head. Then nodded again.

Her coif was still immaculate. Her clothes had none of the odd soot stains that her own bore. Nor did they look as if she'd walked across half of DC in the midst of a heat wave.

"Are you okay?"

Rose opened her mouth, then closed it again.

Clarissa remembered how she'd felt after Clark had died when his Marine Two helicopter was sabotaged. The anger had suffused every thought, every moment, until she'd felt so brittle she thought she'd break.

And it was Rose who had hauled her back from the edge. Had given her a path back to sanity.

How had she done it?

Even if Clarissa could remember, it would probably be irrelevant. She had shattered on the outside, whereas Rose was showing nothing but, perhaps, shattering on the inside. The only sign that anything was wrong was her *lack* of vivacity through the night's events. Rose was inevitably the center of any group she was a part of. Everyone wanted to be next to her, to be part of the social glow of the First Lady of DC.

Not now. She was painfully quiet.

"All I could feel at first was the anger," Clarissa offered. "Clark took so many of my plans to the grave with him, it was all I could feel for the longest time."

"I remember," Rose's voice was little more than a whisper.

Clarissa spotted a small fridge. All it had were bottles of water. These NTSB people were hopeless. She set one in front of Rose and returned to her kitty-corner seat at the head of the conference table. For the first time since entering, she looked at the walls.

Six large pictures were in a line. A plane taking off, a ship throwing up a bow wake, and a train blurred with its speed. There were also pictures of highways, pipelines, and bridges. The six types of accidents the National Transportation Safety Board inspected. It was actually a powerful message as the only adornment in the otherwise plain conference room of white walls, beige floor, and Formica wood-patterned table.

The NTSB were incredibly good at finding the causes of accidents. But they were also very good at moving past them because it was their job to develop answers on how to avoid accidents in the future. Or even anticipate them and recommend preventative measures.

"Maybe I don't need to go anywhere."

"What was that?" Rose looked up at her for the first time since she'd entered.

"Remember the day I offered you the Vice Presidency?"

"The same day that Hunter destroyed it for both of us. Thank you so much for that memory of my murdered husband."

Rose had used some tough-love tactics to snap Clarissa out of her funk. Maybe she'd try returning the favor.

"Yep, that was Senator Hunter Ramson all over." She ignored Rose's glare. "But while he may have cost me the Presidency and my husband, he didn't destroy me as well. Close, but not quite. You saw to that. I was just thinking, what's the one thing I'm really good at, Rose?"

"Running the CIA. What's your point, Clarissa?" It was the most life she'd shown the whole evening. She cracked open the water bottle and took a delicate sip. It was also the first time she'd ever heard a caustic tone from Rose directed at anyone. She'd take it as a sign of life.

"I *am* really good at running the CIA. Even Drake and the President couldn't deny that. I'm not even forty yet, the youngest D/CIA in history. Think of what I could still do."

"You're right. Though you will need to be more careful to curry the favor of each administration. Of both parties, if you want to survive. You must become politically neutral and indispensable."

Clarissa nodded to herself. Rose was usually right about such things. Her policy to date had been mutually assured destruction of her political adversaries. To shift away from *If you ruin me, I'll destroy you* was going to take serious rethinking.

"Whereas me, without Hunter," Rose sighed. "How long until I fade away?"

Clarissa laughed at her.

Even at that, Rose did little more than scowl. She was too much the perfect hostess to ever show her true inner reactions.

"Rose, my friend, you aren't at the end, you're at the beginning."

"The beginning of what?"

Clarissa could see it all laid out. Some of which she couldn't tell Rose yet. Having promised her the Vice Presidency, only to have it ripped away hours later... No, she wouldn't do that to her friend again.

"First, we're going to get you out of Armani and Dior summer clothes."

"If you make me wear black, I'll—"

"McQueen black dress. Last month *you* put *me* in a black pantsuit because you said every woman looks powerful in McQueen. You will look amazing in a suit-dress."

"But who do I have that I would want to look powerful for? I had everything invested in my husband's image. He was my political voice. I've spent my entire life investing in him."

Clarissa smiled. "Yes, and in the process you also made yourself the First Lady of the DC social scene."

"How long will that last without Hunter?" She twisted off her diamond ring. "This doesn't help me anymore." She stared at it for a moment, then tucked it carefully into her purse.

"Without Hunter, you are about to become the most power social consultant that DC has ever seen. Your horizon is no longer limited to one man. For your first job, I'm hiring you to make me look good to both parties as the top choice for the long-term Director of the CIA."

Rose studied her for a long moment, then offered the first slight smile of the night, though it was day now. And brighter than it had been since Hunter's mistake a month ago that had ripped away their shot at the White House.

"And your second job?" Clarissa teased.

Rose tipped her head slightly in question.

"There are too many kingmakers in the political arena. You're going to become the most powerful *queenmaker* in history. You're going to start at the very top with Clark's replacement."

"Clark's replacement? But the President hasn't announced his choice for his Vice President."

"Not publicly. However, I was in the room when he told the National Security Advisor Sarah Feldman that she was his choice. We're going to start you with her."

After a far briefer moment of consideration, Rose's smile showed exactly how she'd won Miss Utah at eighteen, snagged Hunter Ramson and made him one of the most powerful senators in Congress, and how she'd wowed Washington for all of the years since.

Yes, she was going to serve Clarissa's future plans very well, and they both knew it.

"Together we—"

29

T AZ SLAMMED OPEN THE CONFERENCE DOOR WITHOUT KNOCKING. "You done playing your little games yet, Clarissa?"

Games? She'd been busting her ass, expending valuable resources around the world to try and find information on who had attacked the *Theodore Roosevelt.* She'd—

Rose's single raised eyebrow was all that kept Clarissa from verbally attacking the little bitch.

Even her? She couldn't help asking with an eyeroll.

Rose nodded.

Shit! This was going to be much harder than she'd thought.

"What's up, Taz?" Clarissa couldn't repress the snarl, but it was probably more productive than an otherwise satisfying attack.

"Do you want to know our progress or can I please get away from your field of contamination? They must have an emergency shower somewhere here."

"What have you got so far? I really need some answers."

Taz sighed and sat across from Rose, "Not much."

"Well, give me what you've got."

"Between the heat of the fire and being pummeled with

several tons of concrete, the recovery from the flight recorders took time. Jeremy managed to access the flight data first, which proved it was no accident. There is almost no voice data from the pilot. Taxiing and tower clearance, nothing more. He's combing the data now to see what else he can find, if anything. Any actions by the pilot that might have created another sound and so on. But we're not betting on anything constructive." Taz slumped in the chair.

Just as exhausted as she was?

Or perhaps equally frustrated.

Clarissa offered a piece of her own frustration. "Nothing from the Office of Special Investigations either. At least not that they're willing to release to the CIA. Do you want to take a run at them?"

Taz shook her head. "Those folks were always a pain in the ass. Far harder to leverage than you were back in the day. You folded at the first threat. They wouldn't even talk to my—" Taz's voice stumbled "—my former commander until they were done with an investigation."

Clarissa hadn't connected before that they were three women who had each lost so much. She and Rose had lost their husbands and their shots at the White House, Taz had followed her commanding general for nineteen years only to have him betray his oath in the end. Maybe they were more alike than she'd thought...or would ever admit to Taz Cortez.

"Anything else?" Clarissa needed to prove the CIA's usefulness. She had to prove to Drake and the President that they'd been underutilizing the agency for too long. But they approached their precious Miranda before calling the CIA. They treated her as if she was a rabid dog, not the director of the world's most-feared spy agency. The CIA had *earned* that reputation and she was not being allowed to leverage it to the max.

"We received a call from Miranda a few minutes ago."

When Clarissa stood, her feet immediately set in to throbbing. Her boots might look stylish, but they hadn't been made for hiking. She'd have taken them off, but she'd been afraid that her feet would swell and she'd never get them back on.

Taz patted her hands downward, indicating Clarissa should sit down. "She's done. Apparently there was a delay, something about the Acting Captain not giving her permission to call earlier."

"Acting Captain." Clarissa absorbed that. She'd used her credentials to obtain access to the satellite imagery. But seeing a destroyed command superstructure on her phone's screen and hearing it confirmed were two quite different sensations. Someone had managed to kill an aircraft carrier commander.

"What did she have to say?" Clarissa sat once more, then rubbed her forehead. She could feel the previous day and night's sludge coating her the way fire char had coated everything at the George.

"Miranda and Jeremy had an intense discussion that was very difficult to follow. Even for me. She was being very cagey."

"Can she *be* cagey?"

"Not in my past experience. I assume that she's under a high security lockdown of some sort."

"No surprise there. Someone crippled a four-billion-dollar aircraft carrier. Even my teams can't get more information about that."

"Perhaps," Taz conceded as if it was physically painful to admit Clarissa was right about anything. "Anyway, they discussed something that I think you should be aware of, which is why I'm here."

"And?" It was like pulling teeth.

"They discussed the atmosphere at length."

"The atmosphere?"

"Temperature, pressure, and particularly humidity—at various altitudes."

Clarissa couldn't imagine what they were discussing that for, unless it was a piece of space debris that had fallen on the ship.

"And they discussed lasers." Taz appeared to be enjoying her slow dribble of information.

Clarissa again had to resist the urge to slash at her. "Lasers?" she managed in a reasonable voice. "Someone shot a laser from where, from orbit?"

Taz shrugged this time. As if she truly didn't know.

"Seriously?" She'd meant it as a joke. "One big enough to shatter an aircraft carrier?"

She shrugged again. "Miranda was being *very* cautious about what she said. If she hadn't asked about laser etching of aircraft carrier deck plating, we wouldn't have known where she was at all."

Clarissa could feel the blood draining from her face.

Who had anything like that? Space-capable countries were few and far between. And most of the list was painfully aggressive.

30

"THANK YOU FOR LETTING ME CALL JEREMY EARLIER. THAT WAS most helpful as we've continued our investigation." Miranda was pleased that she was no longer forbidden to use him as a resource.

"It would have helped if you'd mentioned the true level of your team's clearance sooner." Captain Brightman was leading the team belowdecks.

Miranda must remember to be more careful in her own future self-education though. There were whole segments of knowledge that Jeremy had pursued recreationally that she'd never expected to be relevant. But he was no longer at her side. She hesitated long enough to pull out her notebook and make a note to brush up her knowledge of high-power lasers.

She was almost run over.

The ship was almost as busy belowdecks as it was above. And as confusing. Miranda hurried after the captain because, if she was swept aside, she feared she might never be found again.

"I had thought that was obvious by the fact that we were

assigned to this investigation. Do you often have uncleared guests boarding a recently attacked ship of war?"

"No. I don't think so. But I'm new to this." The captain opened a door and led them inside the compartment. "I've been in this compartment twice in my life, and now it's mine. That's more than a little scary."

"Scarier than an attack on your ship?"

Captain Brightman laughed briefly but it seemed as if it was a rough sound, like the way coarse sandpaper would feel against her hand. A very unpleasant sensation.

"No, not that scary. But I was trained for that. I wasn't for this," she waved a hand.

The captain's in-port cabin was quite sumptuous. Captain Brightman had said that when they were at sea, this cabin was primarily used for entertaining. While at sea, the ship's captain typically resided in the small cabin directly behind the bridge. At the moment, that no longer existed.

The big cabin was decorated in a style befitting the ship's namesake. The highly polished dark wood flooring and wainscot paneling provided a lushness that her own home's rough Douglas fir paneling didn't. The oriental rug and brocade armchairs made a properly commanding setting. The captain's desk stood before a large portrait of the twenty-sixth President.

"Doesn't he look oh-so-ready to beat someone with a big stick for hurting his ship?" Andi whispered to her.

Painted in browns, he stood with a hand on a stairwell newel post and a fist on his hip holding back his jacket. He stared out of the portrait. She found his gaze unnerving, despite knowing he'd been dead for over a century. She slipped out her personal notebook and inspected the emoji page.

"I think it is more *determined* than *angry*." She turned the page to Andi. "See, the straight line of the mouth. The forward-focused eyes without any eyebrow motion."

"Could be. Could be."

Captain Brightman waved them to sit around a long mahogany table. The Executive Officer flown over from the *Carl Vinson* had taken over deck operations and they were downstairs for a meal and a meeting.

"We now have limited video satcon available, Captain," an orderly told her.

Miranda's team, the captain, and Susan with Sadie beside her filled less than half of the table.

The table hadn't been preset, the servers had to reach awkwardly between people to do so. Everyone sat in exhausted silence. Their postures of sagging shoulders and drooping eyes confirmed Miranda's assessment by matching her emoji page.

Several minutes passed before they were served individual tureens of French onion soup accompanied by fresh-baked garlic bread. The massive impact of flight operations had apparently had little effect in the operations belowdecks.

"Sorry for the delay, Captain," the head server bowed slightly. "We lost an entire shift from the main galley during the attack."

"Carry on, sailor."

"Yes, ma'am."

Miranda was cutting an arc in the crisped Parmesan and Swiss cheese crust with her spoon when the large television screen at the head of the table lit up with Drake's and Roy's faces.

Captain Brightman pushed to her feet and saluted, as did Susan and Andi. There was a loud clatter of dropped silverware.

Unsure of her own correct action, Miranda noted that Holly stayed seated and simply waved, so she did the same. It felt awkward to do it with her off hand, so she switched her grasp and waved with the other hand.

"At ease, everyone." The President hadn't stood, though he

had saluted back. "I know you're pressed for time, so feel free to eat while we talk."

"Yes sir." Captain Brightman sat far straighter than she had moments earlier.

"What can you tell us?"

"Miranda has found..." the captain turned to look at her, then looked away, "...I don't know what, sir. All I know is that we're running at over eighty percent capacity for flight operations. We've managed to clear all of the dead from the Island below the PriFly and Captain's levels. We have six missing overboard, we think. We're patrolling the area for potential recovery operations, but it seems unlikely at this time. Four of those were our best search-and-rescue team and their helo. Our BARCAP—Carrier Combat Air Patrol—has successfully maintained the hundred-kilometer radius no-fly zone. The Chinese have made three tests of our perimeter, but none in the last four hours and none penetrated past ninety-six kilometers."

"Well done, Captain." Roy spoke up.

Drake took over. "We didn't want to bother you while you were dealing with getting the Roosevelt operational, but we have been in touch with your escort submarines. They're reporting nothing bigger than a UUV—Unmanned Undersea Vehicle—probing your area, which they deep-sixed. You'll have two additional Australian subs around you within the next two hours. But CINCPACFLT is managing them so that you don't have to."

"Good to know, General. I'd sleep better, except I'm still a long way from getting any sleep."

"Roger that. What do you have for us, Miranda?"

Miranda looked over at Susan.

"What?"

"You said I wasn't allowed to speak to anyone about this investigation. You said you would do all of the communication.

Other than the call to Jeremy that you and Captain Brightman authorized, I have not done so. I was also careful about limiting the content I discussed with Jeremy as I was unsure who was working with him."

Susan coughed and looked to the screens.

Drake was looking at her with raised eyebrows.

Miranda checked her notebook. *Surprise? Disbelief? Shock? Humorous pause before a joke's punchline?* She couldn't be sure.

"I'm sorry, sir. It seemed an advisable instruction at the time." Susan faced her. "Please speak freely."

"To Drake and Roy, or to anyone?"

"For the moment to the General and the President. Ask me about others as it comes up."

"Thank you for the specificity."

Mike gave Miranda a thumbs-up as Holly laughed at Susan.

Andi tipped her head toward the screen where Drake and Roy were still waiting.

"Oh, yes." Miranda had finished her soup, so she set down her spoon. "Based upon the etching of the decking and selected parts recovered from the aircraft, it was struck by an orbital laser in the three-hundred-kilowatt range, which was fired upon—"

"Can you put that in relative terms for me?" Roy asked.

"—the plane. Do you recall the damage caused by the AC-130J Ghostrider laser in—" Miranda glanced around the room and was unsure of Susan's or Captain Brightman's clearance in the matter, "—that incident last year?"

"All too well," Roy groaned as if the remembered pain was still visceral.

Miranda concurred. Mike and Jeremy had almost died during that operation. It had been a very upsetting time.

"This had approximately twice the delivery power, and that's delivery, not origin. After passing through the entire atmosphere, rather than a mere fifteen-hundred meters like before. The atmosphere is presently unusually dry for this time of year, therefore its delivery power was maximized. That is only a rough estimate. Captain Brightman has declined my request to have a section of her deck removed and sent to the lab."

"They burned one of my ships with an orbital laser?" Roy sounded... Miranda reached for her notebook.

"Aghast," Andi whispered.

"Oh," Miranda nodded as the waiter served a course of chicken in lemon sauce with asparagus and fingerling potatoes. Then she shook her head. "The ship was only burned a little. I wouldn't have noticed if I hadn't seen the setting sun reflecting differently off the exposed section of the landing runway."

"Then what happened to the ship?"

"Oh, that was completely because of the pilot's actions. I thought that was clear. I inspected his canopy, helmet, flightsuit, and seat. Then I had the medical staff rush an autopsy. I don't think they were pleased."

She'd had to have Susan go to the captain and order it. It was far more important than broken bones and people's various remaining burns remaining from the firefight. All of the critical patients had already been treated.

"They're asking what you found out, Miranda." Andi whispered.

"Oh. He'd been cooked."

31

SUSAN DROPPED HER FORK ONTO HER PLATE WITH A CLATTER THAT seemed to shake the suddenly silent cabin. She wasn't the only one.

"Cooked?" the President barely choked out the word.

"Yes, only partially, but yes. He'd been superheated inside his cockpit."

"Cooked?" The President repeated. Hard to blame him; it was too unreal.

"Did you wish me to repeat that, Roy? The word is accurate. Verifiable by simple observation without any conjectural inaccuracies. His flightsuit and seat showed significant signs of burning. As did his face protected only by his visor." And Miranda began cutting into her roast chicken. "Internally he was—"

"I don't need any more details on that." The President looked positively ill.

"If you like. It may not be directly connected to the cause, however it is relevant to the crash and the damage to the USS *Theodore Roosevelt*...herself." Miranda paused her chewing for a moment and appeared to actually look directly at the screen. "Is *that* accurate?"

"Is what accurate? You're the investigator on site."

"Like the majority of US Navy ships, the USS *Theodore Roosevelt* is named for a male. Yet in colloquial English, we refer to a ship as she. The Russians call their ships by the masculine-gendered pronoun, which seems far more consistent with both their and our own ship-naming practices. Perhaps you should change either the common pronoun usage or how you name your ships, Roy."

What would have completely flummoxed Susan six hours ago now had her laughing along with the other members of her team. The captain looked unamused but Susan noticed that General Nason and President Cole were smiling.

"I'll give it some thought, Miranda," the President nodded.

"I'd be glad to send you a list of some truly exceptional women who have served in the military and government, sir." Susan couldn't quite believe her own cheek.

"Yes, the naming is disproportionately male," Miranda observed. "Especially when compared to modern forces. Including historical forces skews that of course, because of the bias of the military against inclusion. Roy, was that in violation of the law, discrimination based upon sex?"

"We've fixed that rule, Miranda."

"Oh, good." Miranda appeared mollified and returned to her meal.

"Sir," unready to turn to her own meal, Susan turned to the President. "Has there been any progress on the *who*? I have done limited research from here, enough to know about the prior, ah, harassment of allied aircraft by Chinese ship-based lasers. They were mostly low-powered dazzlers intended to temporarily blind rather than..." she nudged her plate of roast chicken farther away, "...severely injure. Could this be an escalation of those practices?"

"Nothing more concrete than such a conjecture at this time."

"Miranda," Susan was having a hard time looking at her enjoying her meal. Was that why Miranda never looked directly at someone, she found it too upsetting? "Would there be anything to distinguish one country's laser from another?"

"No. Coherent light, or in this case infrared light...hmm. It seems unlikely that anyone has developed such a powerful maser, doesn't it?"

"Maser?" Susan hadn't heard of that one.

"A microwave laser. No, I think they're still in the testing stages for weaponization. It must have been a laser tuned to the infrared—an iaser perhaps, though that is an awkward vowel construction. As I was saying, coherent light, whether or not it lies within the visible spectrum, is still coherent light no matter whose equipment generated it."

Susan had always thought she herself was tough and that nothing could forge past her guard. But watching Miranda eat roast chicken while discussing how the pilot was burned out of the sky was more than she could manage. A quick glance around the table showed that Miranda was the only one immune to the metaphor. Could she not see it?

Miranda waved a fork as if indicating the flight deck above them. "All of the rest of what happened was due to his actions during the landing operation. It was really a fascinating sequence of events that we don't have fully mapped yet. The Landing Signal Officer noticed the first atypical flight action between five and six seconds ahead of the landing itself; that was probably the initiation of the laser strike. I haven't had access to the PLAT cameras yet."

"The...what?" The President had been a soldier, not a Navy pilot.

"It's the Pilot Landing Aid Television, Mr. President," Captain Brightman answered. "It records every aircraft's approach as an aid to the LSO—the Landing Signals Officer. It hasn't been our highest priority."

Susan swallowed hard and carefully nudged her plate completely aside. "Miranda, is there anything on the PLAT that will tell you more about the attack itself?"

"Beyond the precise moment of initiation of the attack, no. All the rest was a straightforward series of events. An unlikely sequence, but Mike's witness interviews have corroborated the observed results to date. The pilot's actions were commensurate with attempting to protect the ship as he was dying, though he achieved quite the opposite result."

The President and the Chairman of the Joint Chiefs exchanged looks that Susan could easily read.

She spoke up, "We'll get back to you if we have any new developments. We await your further instruction."

"Right," the President faced the screen. "Captain Brightman, no, we weren't mistaken in your promotion. Carry on, Commander Piazza. Your instincts were good, but I need no protection from Ms. Chase. Miranda, thank you, you have our numbers if you find anything else. For future reference, you have my permission to call either of us under any circumstances, even when someone tries to order you not to. I'm sure that Ms. Harper can convince any reluctant parties to comply." He offered a wry smile at the last.

"Aw, Mr. President," Holly replied. "You're just making this girl a happy little vegemite."

But Susan knew that no matter what she said, Holly was not as random or as carefree as she'd have everyone think.

The screens blanked.

Still, no one was eating. Sadie sat up in her chair and sniffed toward Susan's chicken. She cut a few pieces onto a tea saucer and placed them on the seat cushion beside the dog.

But she still wasn't ready to eat any herself.

32

DRAKE CLOSED HIS EYES, THOUGH THE SITUATION ROOM SCREENS had blanked.

Escalation.

The world wasn't going out in one massive nuclear roman candle as so many had feared in his youth. Instead, global security was being chipped away one little piece at a time. Governmental suppression of its citizens, countered by trade tariff, countered in turn by dangerous military fly-bys, followed by this or that dictator climbing to power, then proceeding to...

Christ, where was it all going to end?

This slow erosion was the old story of the frog in the pot of heating water turned into global reality. Would they find a way to jump out before it was too late? Were they already past that point?

"Thoughts?"

Drake looked up at the President's question, but Roy was turned to face the third occupant of the Situation Room. National Security Advisor Sarah Feldman had taken a seat out of the camera's eye view per the President's request.

She was a neat and striking brunette almost as slim as his

wife. She was also a brilliant strategist with an encyclopedic knowledge of military capabilities both domestic and foreign.

"How reliable do you consider Miranda Chase's assessments?"

"Platinum," Drake answered. "I don't think she can physically say something that she doesn't *know* is true. Not feel, but *know*."

"I was afraid of that." Sarah rose from the seat she'd occupied along the side wall. She stepped up to the chair at the President's right hand, then hesitated.

"It should be yours soon enough, Sarah. Sit." Drake knew the President had planned to announce her as his nominee for Vice President during his Memorial Day address in forty-eight hours. She was a good choice to replace Clark. And it would also put her in direct line for the Presidency at the next election. He could think of many worse choices.

"Who has that kind of weaponry?"

"Not us," Drake knew they were developing it in the labs, but space-based? Not that he'd heard of. "The problem, Mr. President, is power. My understanding is that it requires a robust nuclear reactor to generate that level of power, a surveillance-quality telescope to direct it, and the rocketry to push that big a payload into space. And that's only the beginning. I remember Miranda's assistant Jeremy talking about the immense amount of math to punch a focused beam through that much atmosphere is enormous. All combined, that means: India, Russia, China, the EU, and us. I don't think Japan, Iran, or North Korea, for all of their braggadocio, are there yet."

"I will assume, for the moment, that we have not declared war on ourselves today."

"I would second that with the unlikelihood of the EU doing something similar." Sarah was not to be outdone for a disaffected tone of light sarcasm.

"That leaves: India, Russia, China? Who isn't mad at us today?"

"I'd tentatively set India aside," Sarah spoke less confidently. "They're very focused on their first human spaceflight program and are not looking to be distracted from that. They have the launch capability, but I'm not sure that they have the capacity to pursue, uh, extracurricular projects like large, space-based lasers."

Drake's head was hurting again. He knew what that meant.

First, he needed to call Clarissa and ask for the CIA's help. She always made an annoyingly big deal about it when he needed something from her.

Second? The second call was going to be much, much worse.

33

For the first few hours after their languid meal, Zhang Ru had been intrigued by Liú Zuocheng's perseverance. The twins had been most attentive servants throughout the ten-course meal. Their service was elegant: from the most delicate shrimp spring roll to the flaky, succulent meat of the steamed whole red grouper. The final exquisitely simple almond cookies with Hennessey XO French cognac served by candlelight should have done it.

Yet Zuocheng continued to linger at the table past midnight when he should be off bedding the twins.

There had to be a way past the man's guard. Of course, like himself, Zuocheng had survived many leadership changes and continued his climb to power. Would he be the next President and Chairman of Central Military Commission? Once he had that power, it would become very difficult for Ru to replace him. He would need leverage, but the man continued resisting the temptation of the twins beyond tracking them with that damned half smile.

Now they had been relegated to the background, only

occasionally putting in an appearance on the verandah to freshen drinks or offer small digestives.

The conversation had not been particularly illuminating either. If Ru didn't know better, he would say that the man was simply enjoying a quiet evening. But at their level, nothing was as simple as it appeared on the surface. Even the silence hid a move and countermove.

Zuocheng's refusal to bed the twins was a statement of control against temptation. Ru's own peaceable silence declared his unending patience in achieving his goals. The aching need to release that silent tension into an available woman threatened to overwhelm him, but that was not how the game worked.

Instead, he watched. And waited.

The constellation of the White Tiger of the West had climbed high in the night sky and was now plunging down to devour the annoying little countries of Southeast Asia. The hour was so late now that the Black Tortoise of the North had clambered from his bed to tell of the coming winter, though it lay an entire summer and fall away.

And still the silence stretched between them. The city below had mostly ceased its flashy Western nightlife. including its utter disregard for common sense. To teach them reason, they would have to behave for a long time before they were allowed even the minor liberties of neighboring Shenzhen. It had fallen silent with the night. The only sounds, for the twins moved as quietly as the night breeze, were the occasional late-night jets climbing out of Hong Kong International.

The harsh buzz of his personal phone seemed to split the night.

He had been the one to disrupt the perfect, delicate balance that had been building since dinner. With his own bare hands, he was going to murder whoever had called him. Slowly and very painfully.

He pulled out the phone and saw that the number was hidden. Only one bastard had this most private number who had dared to hide his own. Of course, his own was also masked from this caller.

"You had best answer it," Zuocheng spoke for the first time in an hour.

"My apologies, my friend." But when he started to rise, Zuocheng rested a hand lightly on his arm.

"Don't keep your American friend waiting."

The statement chilled Ru to the core. No one, absolutely no one could possibly know of this contact, yet Zuocheng was absolutely right. How? The man was masterful. Perhaps Ru did have more to learn from him.

He accepted the call on the last ring, but he did not set it to speaker. *I am still in control here, Zuocheng.*

"*Wéi.*"

"Was it you?" Drake Nason was never one for the niceties.

Normally Ru would drag it out to irritate the man, but he needed to get him off the phone quickly. How in all creation had General Liú Zuocheng known of this connection?

"What are you talking about?"

"Don't fucking play games with me."

For once, Ru wasn't. "Enlighten me?"

"At 0513 hours your time this morning, did the PRC attack the aircraft carrier USS *Theodore Roosevelt?* Be very careful how you answer."

"Attack your carrier?"

Zuocheng twisted to stare at him. He never should have said that aloud.

"I swear to God, if I trace this back to you, I'll see that your president finds out and has you executed in the slowest and most painful way possible."

"I..." It was impossible that he was having this conversation. "I know nothing of this. I am promising."

"As if that means anything." But Drake sounded calmer. "Tell me who there could command a satellite-launched attack."

Ru tried not to turn, but he couldn't help himself. He had spent his entire career in the PLAAF. The Air Force had been his path to power.

General Liú Zuocheng had commanded the CNSA for years before his ascension to the CMC. The Chinese National Space Agency would certainly oversee any space-based weapon development. And twenty years ago, Zuocheng had made his reputation with the complete reorganization of all of the space defense contractors into a far more effective—and profitable— structure. Gods, the *power* this man held was staggering.

"Well?" Drake was at least still honoring their agreement to not mention either one's name.

"Attack?" Zuocheng asked softly.

"What was that?" Drake snapped out.

It was forced upon him. Ru had hoped to dodge this pivotal moment until he had surpassed, or perhaps buried, Zuocheng. Now he must decide in a single instant. Was he Zuocheng's servant...or his enemy?

"I...have a friend who may be able to help." His choice was made. He was handing over utterly damning proof to Zuocheng if the man one day decided to erase Ru on a whim.

Ru pulled the phone from his ear to tap it to speaker, but Zuocheng plucked it from his hand and held it up to his own ear.

"*Wéi?*"

34

DRAKE HESITATED. HIS AND RU'S DEAL HAD BEEN THAT THEY would contact each other only in moments of international crisis and that no one must ever know. They had agreed to not so much as answer the phone if anyone else was present.

Now Ru had handed off his phone as if this was a party call. Not that Drake himself was in any position to protest. He had cut off the Situation Room microphones to the Marines of the National Security Council who managed any data requests from the room. But the President and National Security Advisor sat silently by him, listening in on the speakerphone.

He now had a choice. Hang up or trust the one person on the planet he trusted least. President Cole nodded but Roy didn't understand who they were dealing with. And now that the phone was in another's hands, Drake didn't understand either.

"You may speak to me or I can have General Zhang Ru tortured for all of the details that can be extracted from his mind, then executed—and this connection will never be available again." The man's English was better than Ru's and had a slight British accent.

At least Ru was finally in over his head, which made Drake feel a little better. He repeated himself regarding the attack.

"Satellite-launched? You think that we are like your Cold War movies of evil Russians with missiles parked in orbit ready to rain them down upon you." Drake could hear the *pitiful* judgment but the man had the decency not to voice it.

"A," Drake looked down at his notes from Miranda, "nuclear-powered, micro-pulsed laser with a three-hundred-kilowatt delivery capability, operating in the infrared or near-infrared range."

There was a distinct pause.

"That would not explain the damage our satellites observe on your carrier." The man spoke far more carefully. He was no fool, he knew what all of that description meant, including what damage it could cause.

He also hadn't denied such a laser's existence, which should have been his first action. Of course, he would realize that Drake wouldn't believe a word of it, so perhaps he'd chosen to not waste their time.

A glance showed that neither Sarah Feldman nor Roy Cole had failed to note that as well.

"The attack killed one of our pilots on landing. His final dying action, in an apparent attempt to abort the landing and save the carrier, inadvertently caused the damage."

Again a long silence, before the unknown person continued. "That is an honorable pilot."

"Yes, he *was*. Now, was it you who attacked our pilot? As I informed your colleague, answer very carefully."

"I am not a child."

Drake couldn't stop the laugh. He knew that Ru had to be still standing there, though apparently only hearing half of the conversation. Whoever was on the phone would know that and was using it.

That's when he connected who that meant he was talking to. He scrabbled for a pad and pen.

Sarah shoved hers across the table at him.

He wrote down a name, followed it with a question mark. Then, on consideration, crossed out the mark and spun it for the others to see.

Liú Zuocheng, co-Vice Chairman of the CMC. The second most powerful man in all of China.

Sarah looked aghast. President Cole looked thoughtful.

"Is your President sitting there, listening with you?" Zuocheng was neither a child nor stupid.

Cole sent him a questioning look that asked *Consequences?*

Drake could only shrug.

Cole tapped his finger three times on the table then answered, "He is."

In the background, there was a faint shifting of sound. A slight breeze across the microphone? As if Zuocheng was walking. Pacing? Or walking away from Ru?

"Let us be frank with each other then."

"Yes," Cole answered.

"I firmly disavow your right to intrude in our territorial waters of the South China Sea with your warships."

Roy prepared himself to protest, but Zuocheng continued before he had a chance.

"Dazzling some Australian pilots in flight is only what they deserved for invading our, *our* territorial waters. They belong to us. However, I know the consequences if we were to directly attack one of your United States warships during one of your so-called Right of Innocent Passage showing-off exercises."

"A law to which China was a signatory." Cole countered.

"Yes. But to the point, am I not witnessing the consequences of such a misguided attack with the approach of your two additional carrier groups. I envy that capability to project so much power at such a great distance from your shores. Until we have it fully developed ourselves, we will continue to remain very cautious. Provided we are not unduly provoked. You would be advised to be cautious of your actions now as they will guide our actions in the future when *we* can do the same in *your* territorial waters."

Drake was glad he didn't have command of the US military. He'd be sorely tempted to wipe the Chinese off the face of the planet. How he managed to keep calm enough to ask the next question impressed even himself.

"Are you stating that we provoked your response?"

"No, I am stating that the People's Republic of China did not attack your aircraft."

"Then was it India or Russia?" Drake snapped out, hoping to jar him.

But the man was unflappable. "I consider, based upon the excellent and growing relations of both of those countries with our great Republic, that either would be an unlikely aggressor."

"Then?" Drake pushed.

Zuocheng cleared his throat carefully. "How certain are you that the origin was space-based?"

"One hundred percent." *Please be right, Miranda.*

"That is...unusual. I would ask that you give me a day to consider this."

Sarah wrote something furiously on her pad and shoved it toward the President. He read it and turned it to Drake with a nod of agreement.

"I personally," Drake swallowed hard, "will meet you or someone who can speak for you in eight hours in..." he looked at Sarah but she nodded emphatically, "...Brunei. Until then, keep your jets, boats, and subs way the hell away from our carrier or we'll deep-six them like the UAVs you sent in earlier and damn the consequences. Understood?"

"Brunei?" Zuocheng seemed to spend a moment

considering. "Yes, that is sufficiently neutral. It will be an interesting event. I look forward to meeting you."

The phone clicked off.

Neutral? He supposed it was. The Chinese wouldn't be welcome in Taiwan, Japan, Vietnam, or the Philippines. He wouldn't be welcome in Russia or half a dozen other countries in the region. In the past, Hong Kong would have been possible, but no longer.

Drake turned to Sarah, "I appreciate you keeping the time pressure up on him, but how the hell am I getting halfway around the world in under eight hours? Are you planning to put me on a sub-orbital launch aboard a rocket?" It was a concept that the military was researching, but it was far from ready for such usage.

"I thought about it. There is a launch today, but I think it would be a little obvious—even if we could scrub their launch and fit a passenger capsule in time—to have you splashing down in the South China Sea. And I don't trust the Chinese to not interfere, then claim that that wasn't them either."

"You're going to stuff me in the back of an F/A-18 Super Hornet for an ungodly number of hours with...what...six midair refuelings. I'm getting way too old for this shit, Mr. President."

Sarah didn't give Roy a chance to speak. "Nope. You have *one hour* to get to Andrews. Figure out who else you want to take with you, not including me. If my attendance was uncovered, it would reflect badly on the President when he nominates me for the Vice Presidency."

"So, if this leaks, it's on me."

"Only too right," Sarah didn't slow down. "Two-seat limit, total. Now excuse me, as I'm still the National Security Advisor, I have to go call the Sultan and beg his indulgence," and she stepped out of the room.

Drake turned to the President. "Well, she's got the giving

cryptic orders part of being a future Commander in Chief down."

Roy nodded. "Yes she does. Remember, her parents were both Jarheads."

"It shows."

"It does." Then Roy leaned forward, suddenly serious. "Look, Drake. Defuse this any way you can. That's why I'm sending you and not some ambassador or pissed off regional commander. If Clark was still alive, I would send him, but I seem to be between Vice Presidents at the moment. My NSA needs to be here for her own nomination to VP. Without that, she doesn't carry the kind of weight you can. All that puts you in the hot seat. Fix this, but make it clear that I'm going to have a second carrier group in the South China Sea by the time the meeting begins. And they have a deadline to solve this, when the third group arrives thirty-seven hours later."

Then Roy Cole was gone as well and Drake was left to stew in his own juices.

One hour?

Who the hell was the one person he would need from DC for this meeting?

35

TAZ AND ROSE SAT WITH HER IN THE NTSB CONFERENCE ROOM. Clarissa didn't know if either of them spoke Russian but that couldn't be helped. Besides, they would only hear her side of the conversation.

But Gregor hadn't taken Clarissa's call.

She supposed that was hardly surprising. He must suspect that she'd been instrumental in the disastrous loss of a major spy satellite that he'd mentioned the last time they'd spoken. That a top FSB agent had been implicated would have spooked him badly. What he, hopefully, still didn't know was that it had been stolen in midair rather than destroyed, and the FSB agent had become an elite guest at a highly secure CIA black site.

As a department head at the Progress Rocket Space Centre in Samara, it was no surprise that Gregor was gun-shy about taking her call.

However, Clarissa knew his weak spot.

Or she had a year ago.

The cyber twins had bounced her call off a server farm in Turkey, which they still controlled access to after last year's hacker war, to reach around the new Iron Curtain.

Taz, Jeremy, and Rose all watched her. She'd prefer to do this in private, but she might need these people in the future. A bridge would be better than a firewall.

The twins needed less than thirty seconds to place her call to Gregor's woman. It paid to hire the best.

"Vesna, are you still with the same man you were fifteen months ago?" Clarissa opened the conversation in Russian without any preamble.

The woman's gasp of surprise, tinged with fear, confirmed her identity and her answer.

"Is he still at the same job?" She didn't have to wait long for the woman to regain her composure.

"*Da.*" The offer Clarissa had once made to the woman—to report Gregor to the FSB as a foreign agent, as Clarissa's *personal* foreign agent—hadn't been forgotten. If he went down, there was no doubt that his lover would go down with him. Vesna had been very motivated to cooperate after that.

"Let him know that he has a single hour to contact me regarding Russia's space-based laser program." She didn't need to repeat the threat.

The silence stretched long enough for her to become aware of some rhythmic, thumping sound in the background but she couldn't quite identify it.

Jeremy entered the room, but Taz shushed him with a quick "*Tijo!*", followed by a finger to her lips when Jeremy looked puzzled. Well, that answered that question. Jeremy didn't speak Russian. And Taz could do more than speak it, she could think in it.

"He does not works with the lasers," Vesna finally spoke. She tried to sound resolute, but failed miserably. Protecting her man or herself? Probably both.

"Then he has fifty-nine minutes to determine who does and call me back."

"Holding on please." The woman didn't mute the phone.

Instead, there was noise of motion, a door, and then a growing thump of American rock and roll. It was a sound Clarissa had heard on prior calls with Gregor. Vesna worked at his favorite sex club in Samara, Russia.

The volume grew until ABBA's "Dancing Queen" was painfully loud. She hated disco. It also muffled the whispers and the hand-off of the phone.

"*Da.*" Gregor did not offer his usual greeting referencing their affair some years ago. Long before she'd married Clark and eventually become the Director of the CIA, they'd had a delightful dalliance. He remained the most robustly equipped man she'd ever been with. Typically, also a common point of their flirting calls since. Not this time.

Nor did she offer any tease in return. "A satellite-based laser assaulted one of our aircraft carriers seventeen hours ago. Vesna says that you don't work with lasers."

"I don't." But he didn't sound surprised. So he too had heard of the attack.

"Was it Russian?"

"How am I supposed to know?"

"A question that perhaps the FSB could be asking if I tip them off."

"Now, Cla—"

"*Don't* say my name."

"Right. Sorry." They'd always used nicknames: Monster for how nature had blessed him and Beastmaster for her efforts to tame it.

Jeremy showed a piece of paper to Taz. After a single glance, she shoved it in front of Clarissa. A meaningless hodgepodge of numbers and scattered words. The only part she understood was Miranda's name at the top.

Taz waved for her phone.

Having no way to interpret what was so urgently relevant about Jeremy's scribblings, Clarissa switched to speakerphone.

"Do your satellite-based lasers have the ability to deliver three hundred kilowatts to a sea-level target, with active tracking?" Taz asked.

Clarissa saw the words *300kW* and *tracking* on the note, along with a daunting amount of math. How was she supposed to have picked out those as the pertinent details?

Gregor hummed thoughtfully as ABBA gave way to AC/DC. Perhaps their DJ played music alphabetically. It made her wonder what was happening onstage at the sex club. But that only reminded her that the last time she'd had sex with Clark had been in the Camp David sauna a mere twelve hours before his death. That took all of the fun out of it.

"We are challenged to deliver one kilowatt from orbit. But you didn't hear that from me."

Taz stared at her across the table.

Rose and Jeremy looked back and forth between them, obviously not understanding Russian.

"Would he even know?" Taz asked softly in rough Arabic. A safe choice as Gregor spoke only Russian and English, and the latter was mostly what he'd needed to help understand stolen US designs.

Clarissa could only nod. She wouldn't call off the other agents she had mobilized in Russia, but Gregor was a major department head at Samara. If the Russians built any secret satellite weaponry, it would be done there and he would know.

She asked him a few more questions to be sure, but it was clear that, as always, Gregor knew everything that happened at Russia's premier satellite factory.

"I'm sorry for the scare, Monster." And Rose wanted her to be nicer to people. "Also apologize to your lady as well. I had to know."

"Um," Gregor didn't sound convinced. "If you find out how it was done, you will be telling me?"

"*Nyet!*" They said in unison and both laughed weakly.

It was a joke they had traded many times since their first sexual bout, when it had been a question of if the other was worn out yet. The contest had remained undecided as they'd eventually passed out together from sheer exhaustion. The scorching lust between them was no more, losing the last dregs of any residual heat.

With nothing more to say, all that remained was listening to "You Shook Me All Night Long" giving way to Aerosmith telling them to "Dream On."

"Goodbye, Monster."

"Goodbye, Beast."

She wondered if she'd ever talk to him again. Another piece of her past, of simpler times, burned away and gone to ash.

36

"VERY TOUCHING," DRAKE HAD ONLY HEARD THE LAST OF THE conversation as he'd stepped into the room. D/CIA Clarissa Reese always brought out the worst in him.

Seeing Clarissa look anything other than conniving or viciously angry was so unusual he almost didn't recognize her. Seeing her displaying human signs of sadness was a first. At Clark Winston's death, she'd alternated between *I'm-fine, business-as-usual steel-eyed-bitch,* and her viciously angry-at-the-world mode.

If something happened to Lizzy, he might be angry for her being taken from him, but it would be far more about the sadness.

Clarissa looked up at him, then gave him the finger.

"Missed you, too."

Taz Cortez jolted to her feet, snapped to attention, and saluted when he'd stepped in.

He returned it. "At ease, Colonel Cortez. Hey, Taz, Jeremy, welcome to DC. Ms. Ramson, so sorry for your loss." Rose did indeed look distraught. Perfectly dressed, utterly exhausted, and as elegant as the one other time he'd met her. Once met, there was no forgetting Rose Ramson.

She offered him a nod that bordered that strange land between regal and charming.

"What did you learn, Clarissa?" He looked at his watch. Not because he didn't know how pressed for time he was, but it made his point. The aftermath of last night's traffic jam was still ugly out there though it was almost lunch time. Even his police escort had struggled to open a passage for the mile-long drive from the White House.

"The Russians say it wasn't them and I believe them," Clarissa stated.

"How high up is your contact?"

"To quote the song, 'Dream On,' Drake. I don't give up my sources, especially not to you."

He spotted a small headshake from Rose and a silent curse from Clarissa.

"Fine! High. Progress Rocket Space Centre in Samara, department head."

Drake couldn't stop his whistle of surprise. Damn but the woman *was* connected in strange and interesting ways.

Taz spoke up, "He claimed that they couldn't deliver over a kilowatt to the ground from orbit."

"Miranda said the strike was in the two-fifty to three hundred range," Jeremy followed up seamlessly. "That's not some simple multiplication factor. For a trans-atmospheric event, the complexity of power delivery escalates with...hmm... I'll have to think about that. It could be the square of the increase in power. Or perhaps the log-base-ten would be a better model... Integrated through a medium—that would be the atmosphere—varying with elevation, temperature, and humidity to—"

"Jeremy." Taz didn't make it awkward or nasty. She simply said it in a simple conversational tone.

"Oh, sorry." Jeremy blushed, but he wasn't completely stopped that easily. "I'll let you know if I can work it out more specifically. In summary, I'm actually not surprised that the Russians can't do it. Their claims typically far exceed their actual capabilities. And this attack would be a significant leap beyond any of the leaked research I've read."

Drake nodded his thanks. The boy was practically a technology savant...and young enough to be his grandson. It would be humbling, except that at Jeremy's age he'd already been commanding an entire company of 75th Rangers in very unsavory places.

"Anything on China or India?"

Clarissa shook her head. "The silence is deafening from India. They're still in the comm and weather satellite phase, plus every observation sat they can arrange over Pakistan. Then they've piled a human spaceflight goal on top of that. Space Force style capabilities appear to be nonexistent. I have no reports from China yet beyond a few educated guesses that say if they aren't there yet, they're close as far as capability. Iran and North Korea are focused on warheads. I'm assuming, mostly, that the EU isn't the one shooting at us."

Her summary was a confirmation Drake had expected rather than the out-of-hand dismissal that he'd been hoping for. His life would be easier if China couldn't have done it. Then he'd know that General Liú Zuocheng was playing some move-countermove game by agreeing to come to the meeting. What he'd really expected to happen on the call was flat denial followed by Zuocheng hanging up the phone.

However, if they had the capability, the stakes would be much higher. That alone perhaps explained his willingness to come...if he did.

"Regrettably, that matches my wife's assessment as well." What did surprise him was Rose Ramson's presence. He hadn't known of her having any ties with the CIA or the NTSB, yet she was sitting in the NTSB headquarters during a highly sensitive call by the CIA.

"I," Rose noted his attention, "would take some explaining, General Nason. However, you are acting as if time is not your friend at the moment."

"I would be interested to hear it, but you're right. Some other time. Let's go, Clarissa. You and I are on the move."

"Not until I shower and change my clothes."

Drake actually looked at his watch. "Nope, sorry. Nothing personal. We'll try to have something for you at the other end."

"What about us, sir?" Taz had remained at parade rest. Did he need the tough warrior? If he had the room aboard whatever Sarah was arranging, he might take her along. But his safety would be the least of their worries. If it came to that, there was probably only one *next step*—war.

"Keep focused on what happened to Ms. Ramson's husband."

When Jeremy started to protest, Taz rested a hand on his shoulder. "You'll have Miranda's team with you, I assume, sir." She offered it as close to an order as a colonel could make to a four-star general.

"Maybe not all five of them, but yes." He should have thought of that sooner himself, but finding Clarissa had been his first priority when she didn't answer her phone. Apparently she'd been busy speaking on it.

"Five?" She and Jeremy looked at each other in some distress.

He didn't have time to explain Commander Piazza's role with the four regular members of Miranda's team. He'd sent her to grease the Navy wheels for whoever Miranda ran up against, which she'd done better than most.

Thinking of buffers...he eyed Clarissa, then turned to Rose.

"Ms. Ramson, what is your security clearance?"

"The same as my husband's was, General Nason. He

confided in me...much of the time." And that pause was the first flash of anger he'd ever seen on her face. Her glance at Clarissa said that the two women shared that anger at a dead man. Interesting...again for another time.

He would keep that in mind for any future meetings he was forced to have with Clarissa. He was half tempted to take Rose with him instead. Partly to spite Clarissa and partly because she would probably be a dynamo in smoothing out any diplomatic ruffled feathers. But there was only the one other seat and, whatever else Clarissa might be, she was damned effective.

"When and where is this meeting?" Clarissa asked as they headed for the door.

"In seven and a quarter hours, and—you wouldn't believe me if I told you."

37

"How can we *not* be going?" Jeremy begged for an answer the moment the conference room door had closed behind Clarissa and General Nason.

Taz didn't know what to say. She could feel the pain of being left behind herself, and *she* hadn't been Miranda's right hand for the last two years. The move *had* been the right next step for her, and for Jeremy. She knew that, but he still had doubts and she didn't know what to do about them.

"And the *fifth* person. Who's that? Can he help Miranda? Or is he going to be a problem like Major Jon Swift? Or maybe someone who won't understand what she's like? Who replaced us so quickly? We only left four days ago. I don't understand what's happening. If she still needed us, why did she let us go?"

"What is she like?" Rose asked in a soft voice when Jeremy finally paused to take a breath.

"She's the best person—ever!" Jeremy declared.

"Yes," Taz agreed, and not solely to mollify Jeremy. "You'll meet few people like her. She's also one of the strangest."

"In what way? I've never heard of her before tonight."

And Taz could feel it. The room was calming down.

Jeremy's breathing, which had been coming short, was easing. Even she herself felt calmer. Rose's simple question was *precisely* the right thing to ask Jeremy to calm him down. That was a little spooky.

"She's the best air-crash investigator in history." Jeremy would be loyal to her until his dying day. Taz wondered if she'd ever live up to Miranda's image. How was she supposed to do that? She could live with Jeremy but she'd never be the most important woman in his life. An awful revelation that she'd prefer not to have had.

Rose raised her eyebrows. But it wasn't a challenge, nor pretend surprise. She communicated interest.

Taz latched onto that to keep from drowning in her own thoughts. Since when did she need anyone other than herself, anyway?

"She is mechanically brilliant. If you're an airplane—"

"Or a helicopter," Jeremy put in.

"—or a helicopter."

"Or—"

She rested a hand lightly on his arm and resisted the urge to dig her fingertips into the radial nerve to silence him.

"However," Taz continued before Jeremy could list every mechanical conveyance ever conceived, "she has a massive blind spot. Emotions are very elusive to her. Sudden noises, arguments, even actively chaotic situations throw her badly. Though a chaotic-looking yet static-in-reality airplane...or helicopter wreck, she can stroll into and see patterns no one else can."

"You're describing someone on the autism spectrum."

"I am."

Rose Ramson folded her hands neatly on the table. "A curious mix of competence and incompetence then."

"She's *not*—"

Taz applied just the slightest pressure on where the radial

nerve passed over the bone close below Jeremy's elbow. Only enough to gain his attention, not enough that he'd even be aware of any pain.

"Exactly." Then she turned to Jeremy. She wasn't comfortable having him around Rose Ramson until she understood more of what was going on here. "Did the black box from Miranda's Alaskan KC-46 crash arrive yet?"

"Oh. Yes. Almost an hour ago. Oh my God. I have to get started on that." Halfway to the door, he stopped, then returned to kiss her on top of the head. For never needing anyone, Taz felt ridiculously better for his gesture.

"He's sweet," Rose said after Jeremy left.

"He is."

Rose contemplated her own hands for a while before speaking into the silence. "I should like to meet his Miranda one day. I have the opposite affliction."

"You're autistic? You don't fit anywhere on the Spectrum as I understand it."

"No. I understand people, I always have. People are...easy. Not necessarily simple, but easy for me. Mechanics? Airplanes? Each time my computer updates, I'm at a complete loss. If my car breaks, I'm likely to faint. Hunter was little better than I was, so at least he could empathize with my woes. I think it would be interesting to meet my polar opposite."

"I'll let you know the next time she's in town." *And I'll stay an inch from your side so that I can take you down if you mess with one single neuron in Miranda's head.*

"Ah, the warrior."

Taz wasn't used to people seeing that in her. At a single inch over the military minimum of four-ten and often in danger of falling below the ninety-four-pound weight limit if she didn't train rigorously to maintain muscle mass, no one saw that in her.

No...Jeremy did. In fact, no one on Miranda's team had

questioned her skills. Outside of the team everyone did, until they crossed her.

But not Rose Ramson. Yet another red-flag warning.

"What's your role here?"

"My role?" But Rose wasn't playing coy. She looked perplexed by the question. "I'm rather unsure myself."

"Here to spy for Clarissa?"

Rose actually laughed. "A spy for the master of spies? I've rarely felt as useless as I have these past hours. My place was always to make my husband appear in the best light. I have used him as my entry into DC society. Now? I have no idea about what I am supposed to do. If you don't mind my asking, how much of what you do is keeping Jeremy focused and on task?"

The image of herself in twenty years having no purpose other than keeping Jeremy on track had her shifting in her seat. Was that what Andi would be doing for Miranda, her sole purpose in life limited to keeping Miranda functioning in modern society?

"You see the problem," Rose nodded. "Yet Clarissa would—"

"Please tell me you don't trust that bitch." And Taz the warrior had now screwed up. Of course the woman was allied with Clarissa, it was obvious to anyone who watched them together. And she'd just now put herself square in Rose Ramson's sights as an enemy. How powerful was the leader of DC society without her husband at her side? *Pretty damn* was Taz's guess.

"Trust? You, me, and even Clarissa trust no one; it is the only way we feel safe. Am I right, Colonel Vicki *Taser* Cortez? I did not recognize you until General Nason mentioned your rank and name. I've only known you by rumor, which is far larger than life but perhaps deserved. You trusted your General Martinez?"

"Until I didn't." She had outlived her commanding general, barely. After trusting him for all those years, she'd broken that trust and lived when she was supposed to die with him.

"Just so."

"Are you planning to *redeem* Clarissa somehow? I need to warn you, it won't work."

"You show little faith, Colonel Cortez." Then Rose sighed lightly. "Not that your lack of faith is necessarily misplaced. She has plans. I am not yet in a place to judge them."

"And until you are?" Taz couldn't tell if they were forming an alliance or if they were simply two women both caught on a knife edge with no safe way off.

"Until then, what is the next step in trying to figure out who killed my husband?"

"That's going to take some doing, but something Jeremy said has given me an idea about where to begin."

38

It was high noon when Drake and Clarissa were cleared onto Joint Base Andrews with two minutes to spare. The driver dropped them by one of the 89th Airlift Wings' secure hangars. This one was across a wide taxiway from where the President's 747s were kept.

Inside were the two C-32s that were most commonly used by the Vice President as Air Force Two...when there *was* a Vice President. He'd ridden in them several times himself enroute to critical meetings. But the modified 757 would require eighteen hours to reach Brunei, not counting a refueling along the way.

With the big doors open, inside the shadowed hangar was still hot. The Memorial Day weekend heat wave was showing no sign of relenting.

"Next time, give me a little more warning," Clarissa brushed at her clothes, which did indeed look the worse for wear.

"I would have, if I'd had it myself. I only had fifteen more minutes than you did and spent most of that getting to you. I tried calling, but you were on that secure call."

Then silence fell between them. Clarissa might rate as the one person he was *least* likely to be chums with...outside of the murdering bastard Zhang Ru. Maybe if he came to the meeting, he could unleash Clarissa on Ru, then stand back to watch the show.

They didn't have to wait long in the sweltering hangar. Within minutes of the appointed time, a long, sleek jet rolled in.

Sarah Feldman had been as good as her word. But Drake had to blink several times and the aircraft still didn't seem to come into focus as it eased to a stop close in front of them.

The engines cycled down, and a lone pilot stepped out as a fuel truck rolled up to it.

"Oh, I do love that look on people's faces. Captain Conklin at your service, sir and ma'am." He wore slacks and a button-down shirt, but his salute was pure military. "If they'd told me who I was meeting, I might have dressed up a tad. My apologies, General. I work mostly with civilians now and it's easier when I blend in a bit."

"At ease, Captain," Drake returned the salute, but couldn't take his eyes off the aircraft.

It had more relation to an arrow than a jet. Half of its length was in a tapered nose that stretched an unlikely distance ahead of the front landing gear. It was as if a sleek Gulfstream had told a lie until its nose would put Pinocchio to shame. The wide delta wing was so thin that it seemed to disappear when viewed edge on.

On the side was painted, *X-54B Gulfstream.*

"That long nose," the captain began doing knee bends, "splits the air almost silently at supersonic speeds. Think of the pointy tip on supersonic fighters or the Concorde."

"I didn't think it would be ready for testing of the A version until later this year."

"I know. Private sector, right? Never ones to waste time. Need to make it profitable as fast as possible so they can actually get to work. Hustle, hustle, hustle. The A and B are in testing simultaneously. Military insisted on their own test pilot and I pulled the lucky straw." Conklin patted the low wing as if it was a puppy dog, then began a series of loosening stretches.

"Is it really boomless?"

"Supersonic to Mach 1.5, on the ground they'll hear a thump around seventy-five decibels. That's quieter than a telephone ring tone, probably little more than a big truck clunking over a sewer grate. At Mach 2.5, which we only do over water, it will be closer to an alarm clock. The old cannon-crack? We've got that one completely licked."

"And it's ready for prime time?"

"Well, sir, that's news to me. An hour ago, I was in Georgia, planning a test flight and a dinner after with this sultry brunette. Now we're scheduled for two hours to cross the country—never been cleared by the FAA to do that At Speed before except in a narrow test corridor across Kansas. Someone has a serious bit of pull."

Drake didn't mention that it was the future Vice President.

"Then an hour and a bit more at full boogie to our refueling stop at Hawaii. About the same again to reach your meeting. Never flown transoceanic before either. Could be very exciting." Then the fueler called him over to sign the loading sheet.

"Wonderful," Drake muttered to himself.

The interior was as long and lean as the exterior implied. The cockpit forward had windows around the single pilot, but they faced sideways or upward at a steep angle more akin to a skylight. With no bulbous cockpit dome to interrupt the plane's intense streamlining, there would be no clear view forward. Large computer screens placed before the pilot, but above the instruments, must be linked to forward cameras.

"Production bird is planned to carry ten to twelve folk," Conklin told them happily as they hunched over to head aft. "They'll eventually be expanding to about twenty, or so they tell me. Only have the pilot in the X-54A. Could be five of us here in the X-54B if it wasn't for all of the test gear. Also, truth be told, your two passenger seats are all they have built so far."

Their seats were arranged facing forward to either side of an aisle so narrow they were practically rubbing elbows. Across from them stood two racks of equipment filled with gear he didn't begin to understand.

"Water bottles and some candy bars in the bag there. Let's get going. There's a..." Conklin waved a hand vaguely toward the rear before he latched the door and turned for the front of the aircraft.

Drake twisted to look behind him, barely missing clunking heads with Clarissa as she did the same. A tiny commode, with no curtain, was placed close behind the passenger seats.

Just perfect.

39

"I HAVEN'T SLEPT IN DAYS," COMMANDER SUSAN PIAZZA STOOD
beside Mike on the Hangar Deck of the USS *Theodore Roosevelt.*
They'd arrived from Alaska at sunset and she'd been in the
dark ever since. Midnight had drifted by three hours ago. Other
than the scattered lights of the circling carrier groups, there
was nothing to see beyond the floodlights directed at the
wreckage. Miranda, Andi, and Holly were reassembling the
crashed F-35C one scrap at a time.

"It certainly feels that way," Mike seemed utterly
complacent, glad to stand and watch the other three at work.
They'd been at it for hours. She didn't understand most of what
they were doing, but neither could she tear her eyes away and
go beg a few hours in a bunk.

"No," Susan massaged the back of her neck. "I mean that
literally. I started this *day* in Washington, DC. Early morning
flight to JBLM in Washington State with Admiral Stanislaw.
From there I was rerouted to track down you lot, and now I'm in
the South China Sea. My watch says that it's 1500 hours back in
DC. But I'm too tired to figure out which day that is."

"Well, it's three a.m. local now, so you haven't been awake

all that long." Mike showed her his watch as if she hadn't just
looked at hers.

"And how do you figure that, Mr. Munroe?"

"Easy, the International Date Line. We crossed it going west.
It's still yesterday."

Susan would have laughed if she could find the energy. She
couldn't. "Mike, when you cross east to west, it goes the other
way. I've been awake twenty-four hours longer than I was
minutes ago."

"Oh, yep. That's harsh then. No wonder I'm so tired." His
smile said that he knew that and was merely teasing her. Or
testing her. Or maybe he was simply being Mike, enjoying his
head games.

"Why aren't you helping them?"

Miranda had taken over a corner of the Hangar Deck from
the very reluctant deck chief.

In some ways, it was even louder here than on the Flight
Deck. Up there, only the landings and departures were
particularly loud. In between, there was a lot of noise—the
retraction of arresting wires and release of steam catapults, the
lowering and raising of jet blast deflectors, or the heavy whine
of starting jet engines. It was a mechanical orchestra in
constant motion, but heavy earmuffs over earplugs blocked
most of it.

Down here on the Hangar Deck, *everything* was loud. The
bang of forty thousand pounds of returning aircraft slamming
down on the deck that was their ceiling. The roar of seventy
thousand pounds of jet, heavy with fuel, headed aloft on full
afterburners. Those were only somewhat muffled by the
decking.

But every single sound here was trapped, and echoed about
the steel cave like a gong struck with a sledgehammer. The
pealing bells of Easter morning service in the church next door
to her family home back in Massachusetts had nothing on this

place. They were both sounding hoarse from raising their voices over the din.

The hangar was a steel box two football fields long, including the endzones, thirty meters wide, and two-and-a-half stories tall. With fifty planes and helicopters crammed into it, the vast space was so crowded that it was less navigable and louder than when she'd attended the Woodstock Festival as a young child. The three days of the concert were her first memories.

She'd transitioned from being an insipient flower child hanging out with hippies to serving thirty years in her country's military. She, for one, had always appreciated the irony of that progression, but the service had fit her down to her socks. No two days were ever the same and the different places *were* fascinating. Perhaps she understood some of Mike's complacency. Or perhaps contentment.

Though Miranda's team were children by comparison. Not a one of them had been alive when she'd been dancing in the mud to Richie Havens and singing along with Arlo Guthrie and Joplin in her own way. She still remembered much that hadn't been in the movie.

But when had she become old enough to think of people in their thirties as youngsters? Retirement loomed ahead, but far enough off that she could still ignore it by focusing on what was happening around her. Time really needed to slow down rather than accelerate, at least once in a while.

The Hangar Deck added its own cacophony to the clamor from above.

The four massive elevators, which could each shift a pair of jets to and from the Flight Deck, didn't exactly move in the same gentle silence as a glassed-in mall elevator carrying six eager shoppers.

Aircraft repairs, of which there were still many to do since the incident, seemed to be mainly comprised of smashing sheets of metal together like banging pots and pans, sharply punctuated by the high whine of power tools.

Squat tow tractors imposed deep diesel roars as they shifted jets, planes, and helos in the tight space. The wind of the carrier's forward motion blew through the giant gaps made by the elevators and funneled out the open fantail, dragging the sultry tropical air, lightly tossed with the stench of jet fuel and hydraulic fluid, over them.

It was even noisy visually. Jets with folded up wings were packed tightly beside the origami project that was a folded-up MV-22 Osprey tiltrotor. Every square inch that wasn't taken up by aircraft was filled with supplies and spare parts. Forklifts and mobile cranes shuffled back and forth with a terrible intentness of purpose. Nothing stayed still for long here.

And every sound on the Hangar Deck was trapped, repeated, and amplified by the underside of the Flight Deck and the steel walls until it gathered in their corner by the Number Three elevator. Only Sadie, asleep at her feet, gave no indication of anything amiss.

Miranda had built an island of floodlights. Thousands of pieces of aircraft had been spread out—the found remains of F-35C Lightning II Number 892. Each had been excised with the care of an archeologist, or would have been if Miranda had her way. Susan had worked with her to allow the carrier's crew to deliver all of the pieces. Some, like the engine, were hauled below by heavy cranes. Others had arrived in large buckets and been dumped on the deck plating with a loud clatter and bang of a hundred parts.

Miranda arranged the pieces almost as fast as they arrived. Holly and Andi appeared to be mere extensions of her consciousness, placing each scrap properly with only the least indication from Miranda.

Surprisingly few were allocated to the *Unknown* section. A large number were allocated to the *Ship Parts* section as the gatherers were either erring on the side of caution in what they collected, or they simply wanted all of the wreckage off their deck and were dumping it on Miranda.

Despite the bewildering array of metal and carbon fiber, Gabriel Brown's F-35C was taking shape once again.

Susan turned to Mike standing beside her, "Did she really memorize all of those manuals on the way here?"

He shrugged a maybe and kept watching. It *was* mesmerizing.

"How does she know where every single piece goes?"

Miranda happened to be nearby when she asked her question. She pointed over Susan's shoulder, then Mike's.

Susan turned and was face-to-face with a pair of F-35C Lightning IIs parked close by in the crowded Hangar Deck. One had suffered only minor damage from the incident on deck, the other had been severely damaged by falling debris and much of its inner workings were visible.

Susan laughed. *Not* magical, scary-level memory.

By the time she turned back, Miranda was once more reassembling the plane. However, even though Susan now watched for it, she didn't see Miranda look at either plane behind them. The plane map truly was in her head.

And it was working.

Some sections were blanks. The right wing was believed to have been blown overboard when his ordnance had exploded in the fire after his final landing in PriFly. The tail had been spotted, dangling precariously by the mount for the perilously damaged ten-story-tall radar mast atop the Island.

Miranda had blithely ignored the captain's *No Trespassing* caution signs. Holly had cursed and followed as Mike had explained, *She does that. Nothing is more important than the crash, not even her own safety.*

Susan had noted that Mike had also been on the move to

follow Miranda into the hazard before Holly had waved him back.

She looked again at the three people doing the sorting.

"Why aren't you helping them reassemble the plane?"

"I'm not allowed." That's when she picked up on Mike's stance, arms tightly crossed and incredibly intent on each piece they lifted and place—even though they'd been at it for hours. "There's no question that I slow down their process during a reassembly. Like you, my specialty is human factors."

Susan had never seen herself as lesser for those skills, yet Mike clearly did.

"You do understand that they value you for the exact skills you have."

"Sure. They piss off someone enough to want our team dead. *Send in Mike. He'll fix it.*"

"There," Miranda pointed into the middle of the mess. "That's what we were looking for."

A glance at Mike showed that he had no clue.

"What—" Susan was startled.

But Mike cut her off with a sharp gesture. She'd thought they were reassembling the plane as some sort of an exercise. She hadn't understood that they were looking for something specific.

Miranda stared down at where she'd just indicated, suddenly as frozen as a statue. As if the least motion might make the whole thing explode all over again.

"What?" Susan whispered to Mike, but he simply shook his head tightly. Everyone was watching Miranda standing completely still in the middle of a hundred-million-dollar scrap heap, not counting the cost of the damage to the aircraft carrier.

Three minutes by her watch, no one so much as wiggled their toes except Sadie, who yawned, stretched, rolled onto her back, and fell asleep again with all four paws up in the air.

40

CAPTAIN BRIGHTMAN STRODE UP AND LOOKED AT THE FROZEN tableau. "What's the status? Can we clean this up yet?"

No one answered. Susan wasn't sure what to say.

"What the hell is going on here?"

Mike shushed her.

She prepared to argue, but Mike shushed the captain again.

"I need that tail section," Miranda came back to life so abruptly that they all twitched in surprise.

"Miranda, where it broke off and snagged in the superstructure? It's probably too dangerous to recover outside of a naval shipyard." Susan still couldn't believe that Miranda and Holly had crawled into that precarious area to inspect the damage.

"Andi?" Miranda asked.

Andi Wu turned, not to Miranda, but to look upward toward the damaged Island above as if she could see it through the steel of the Flight Deck's underside.

Did this team have some kind of telepathy? Susan was used to smoothly coordinated teams, and fixing deeply dysfunctional ones, but these people were something else again.

"Yes," Andi nodded at the ceiling, "I can do that. The MH-60S Seahawk has a long enough winch cable. I'll need someone to go into the wreckage to attach it though."

"No worries," Holly straightened up from placing a three-foot section of wing strut just-so amongst the wreck.

"What? No!" Brightman snapped. "I'm not risking it. The downblast of the helo's rotor blades could knock over that mast. I won't risk losing my flight line again."

Andi held her arm out sideways, dangling her forearm from her elbow. "I'll fly off to the side and then set up an oscillation to swing the cable where Holly needs it without bothering anything." She waved her hand back and forth as if it was dangling from a scarecrow's elbow, flapping in the wind.

"No one can be that accurate."

Susan actually laughed. "Sorry, Captain. If Andi says she can do it, believe me, she can. I've seen her military file."

Brightman stared at them for a long moment then hid her face in her hands. "I can't believe this. Fine! Go!"

"Mike?" was all Holly said before jogging out of sight with Andi. The slap of their feet blended rapidly into the carrier deck noise and they were gone.

Miranda's whim apparently wasn't a whim, it was an absolute command.

"Any idea what she saw?" Susan asked him.

Mike shook his head. Then he stepped forward to help Miranda slip the next piece into place.

"I do wish we had the canopy." Miranda turned back to sorting through the latest collection of debris to be delivered.

Brightman had narrowed her eyes and was staring hard at an unremarkable half-meter square of carbon fiber in the *Unknown* pile.

"Captain?" Susan could see that something was bothering her.

"I saw...somewhere...where was it?" Brightman scrubbed at her face. "C'mon, Penny. C'mon..."

"What were you doing or holding when you saw it?"

The Captain pulled out her phone, then stared at her hand as if she didn't recognize it. She jolted and looked over at Susan, "Oh, well done, Commander."

Susan loved that memory trick every time. So simple yet effective.

"You, what's your name?"

"Mike Munroe, ma'am."

"Good, go up to the command bridge...tables...whatever it is. Ask them to give you a couple of airmen. There's a walkway along the starboard, seaward side of the Island. That canopy, at least I think it might be, is lying close to the forward end of the walkway."

"On it, ma'am."

And now it was only the three of them, Captain Brightman and herself, watching Miranda sort through the scraps.

"Miranda," Susan called out, hoping to draw her out. "You'll have the canopy shortly."

"That would be helpful," Miranda didn't look up. When her phone rang, she placed another piece before she answered.

41

"HI, MIRANDA."

Drake had made the call on speakerphone, which Clarissa appreciated, though it was hard to hear. The Gulfstream X-54B was a military test plane and not much effort had gone into sound insulation. It wasn't as loud as a C-130 Hercules—but it wasn't some nicely muted jetliner either.

"Hello, Drake." It sounded as if she stood in the middle of a Jamaican steel drum band competition, with each band playing a different tune.

"I was afraid that I'd wake you up."

"No."

Clarissa, at least, knew better. She'd been shoulder-to-shoulder with Miranda through the night of the investigation into Clark's death. And all last night with an equally driven Jeremy. Until the crash was solved, there would be no rest for her.

"Oh, good. Well, I need your team in Brunei in three hours."

"Why?"

"We have a meeting with the Chinese."

"But we don't know if it was their satellite yet."

"Still, I need you at the meeting," Drake used a much gentler hand with the woman than Clarissa ever had.

Maybe they were having an affair. No, that couldn't be right. Clarissa couldn't imagine who would actually want the annoying little woman. And Drake was clearly enamored of his new wife. It had only been a year. He'd find out soon enough how fast that wore off, even if Clark hadn't *worn off* her yet. Damn the man for dying.

Then she thought about Rose's final instructions before Taz had burst into the conference room. Being nicer to everyone around her, whether they deserved it or not—mostly not—was going to be hell.

"But I still have work to do here," Miranda kept protesting.

Clarissa opened her mouth but then bit her tongue to avoid cutting the woman off.

"We still need to—"

"—be ready to support your findings at this meeting. Presidential order. You found out it was a satellite attack and only on one pilot. That's, sadly, far better news than I'd feared." Drake had slid into the middle of Miranda's sentence as if they were speaking with the same voice.

"Rather than a strike against the carrier itself. Yes."

It had worked! Damn but that was slick. Clarissa would have to remember that tactic the next time Miranda—

"I need you there in case the discussion requires an eyewitness of the technical details."

"But—"

Or maybe it hadn't worked.

"—how are we supposed to get there in time?"

"Miranda," Clarissa leaned in and explained, because sometimes it was too obvious. "You're on an aircraft carrier. Ask the captain for a helicopter or something."

"And if she says no?"

"She won't." She imagined that after having Miranda

aboard for seven hours, the captain would be thrilled to be rid of the NTSB team. "Have that Commander Piazza ask for you."

"Okay," and Miranda hung up without any further comment.

"Why didn't you call her earlier?" Clarissa asked. "And *I* for one am not going to buy any crock about you being afraid she was sleeping."

"It's 0300 their time—"

"You didn't think it would be the best scenario for foreign relations if you unleashed Miranda on the Sultan before we arrived."

Drake nodded his acquiescence. Then he studied her through narrowed eyes. "What's up with you?"

"Why?"

"You've been tolerable and helpful for the entire flight. What are you up to, Clarissa?"

"I'm not up to anything." Not now that she was in decent clothes.

Thankfully the pilot had insisted that they stop for longer than a simple refuel and bathroom break at Hickam Air Force Base.

She had requisitioned a ride across the airfield to the Daniel K. Inouye International Airport. There she'd made a strategic strike at Hermès, which had been tricky as it was mostly Hawaii-appropriate leisure wear when she needed power suits. But Kate Spade's and Prada's airport shops stocked only handbags and shoes—useless under the circumstances.

The softly draping chocolate silk slacks and blazer over a white blouse would work nicely. Though Kate Spade had partially redeemed themselves with the perfectly matching pumps in the right size. She'd felt even better about spending four thousand dollars on the outfit after she'd charged it to her government account.

"Why don't I believe you?" Drake was scowling at her across

the narrow aisle. He didn't have Clark's warm vitality that had destined him for the eventual presidency, but the man was damned handsome in that rugged-soldierly way.

Here she was, attempting to be decent and Drake was still crapping all over her. Well, she'd show him that he was being an utter shit by ignoring him completely. But it took the memory of Rose's words to keep from giving him the finger first.

She pulled up the latest reports from her field agents, which she'd been studying before Drake had called Miranda. They mostly revealed nothing about this case, but there were some interesting trends and a few very specific threads that she'd have to think about tugging to see where they led.

Several of the Russian reports supported Jeremy's assessment of Russian military and space readiness, or rather the lack of it. Perhaps the boy's move to DC would be more useful than Clarissa had thought.

And then she groaned to herself. That meant she'd have to start being nice to Colonel Taz Cortez too—*intolerable.*

42

After she hung up the phone, Miranda returned to her sorting of crumpled bits of aircraft.

"Miranda," Susan called out.

"Yes?" She didn't stop.

"Was that General Nason on the phone?" Susan took a guess as they'd spoken a surprising number of times in the last twelve hours.

"Yes."

"And he wants the team somewhere else?"

"Yes."

"Where?"

"Brunei." She looked as if it caused her physical pain to say that.

"When?"

"Not for a while. Three hours."

Susan sighed and turned to the captain. "It appears that we have a request from the Chairman of the Joint Chiefs to move this team to Brunei for a meeting. What transport can you spare?"

"A C-2 Greyhound or a Seahawk could have you there in time. Spare? Christ, you people are going to make me nuts. I'm short on C-2s because they're moving bodies out and emergency supplies in. And I'm short on Seahawks because I'm working an anti-submarine perimeter six hundred kilometers in circumference."

"We need something to—"

"Yes. Yes. I understand, I just don't have to like it. Okay, as soon as they're done with the tail section recovery, I'll break loose a C-2. That's assuming they don't drop that radar mast across my flightline. And no, you can't keep it. I want my plane refueled and turned back around immediately."

"Yes, ma'am." Susan saluted. "And, ma'am, if I may say that, based on what I've seen, I agree that your promotion is fully deserved."

"Promotion into hell."

" 'It's not just a job, it's an adventure!' " Susan offered the Navy Recruiting slogan with a grin. It was the one that had been used when she herself was in college.

"Christ, Commander, please tell me I'm not that old."

"Only some of us, Captain." They traded smiles.

"So, what has she learned?" Brightman nodded toward Miranda.

"Who knows? She never states anything until she's absolutely positive of the facts."

"Possibilities?"

Susan waited, knowing that Miranda often heard without showing she was paying attention.

Nothing.

Susan shook her head. "Guess not."

"Perfect. Just perfect." Brightman held out her phone, with the number showing on the screen.

Susan snapped a photo with her own phone. Her nod

promised that she'd call the moment she learned anything concrete.

The captain turned away, headed for the aircraft maintenance shop.

43

"DIDN'T SEE YOU AT THE CRASH LAST NIGHT."

Major Jon Swift jolted back from his desk so hard that he'd have fallen off his chair if he hadn't slammed into the filing cabinets first. It wasn't much of an office but at least it was in the Pentagon and not some remote, back-forty posting.

However, there was enough space for him to tilt too far. The chair legs slid out from beneath him. Three-quarters of the way to the floor, the legs caught against the desk drawers and the chairback against the cabinet handles. He lay suspended a foot in the air and for a moment couldn't figure out how to extract himself.

Looking over the top of his desk, only her head showing from his low angle, was Taz Cortez, with Jeremy and a lovely woman he didn't recognize but who now must think him an utter fool.

"You could have waited until I Tasered your ass again before falling down." Taz's smirk was acid-laced as usual.

He struggled half out of the chair, which then slipped off the last file cabinet handle and jarred him to the floor—hard—crunching his elevated shin on the underside of the desk.

Jeremy came around the desk and helped him to his feet.

He pulled up a pant leg. No blood, but it was going to hurt for a while.

Then he clearly saw the third person, a statuesque redhead of uncommon beauty in a very high-end white dress. All of the beauty and class that Miranda Chase had lacked. He had no idea what he'd ever seen in Miranda to begin with. The woman was batshit crazy for sure. Unlike Taz Cortez, who was just fucking nasty.

"What are you people doing here?" Jon attempted to wrestle his chair free, but it was still jammed between the desk and the filing cabinet. He tried shoving the desk aside with his hip, and received a sore hip for his trouble.

Then he spotted Taz's smile. She probably had a foot jammed against the front so that it wouldn't move.

"Fine. What do you want?"

"The complete status of the Air Force's investigation into the crash of the C-20C Gulfstream III into the Kimpton George Hotel yesterday evening."

"I can't give you that, you little witch. So why don't you go back to being dead?"

Taz sighed. She reached to her side.

Jon slammed himself back against the file cabinets so hard that he briefly wondered if he'd cracked his own spine on the drawer handles.

Rather than pulling out her Taser, which she'd shot him with several times in the past, she pulled out her ID. She held it out at arm's length until he dared shuffle forward enough to read it.

"Colonel Vicki Cortez of— Oh shit! No way!"

"Of the Accident Investigation Board. Which makes me your superior officer. So, salute, Major," she snapped out. "Unless you want your ass busted all of the way back down to a slick sleeve."

"You couldn't!" Only E-1 raw recruits had no insignia on their uniform sleeve. He was an officer, goddamn her.

"Go ahead. Try me. No need to bother your Uncle Drake, I already have you on falsifying reports about Miranda. A little bird told me. By the way, the next time you see Captain Andi Wu, I'd suggest running in the other direction—fast. She's some kind of pissed at you."

Jon looked in Taz's eyes and all he saw was cold death. No heat, no anger. She'd squash him like a bug without caring one way or the other.

He pushed himself to attention, ignoring the twinges in his shin and back, and saluted.

"Yeah, yeah." Taz gave him an insultingly lame salute in return. "Now tell me everything you have on the dead pilots and who did it to them. I can already assume that they were murdered and their plane was stolen to crash into the George Hotel. I need the details."

Jeremy was up on his toes in anticipation. All he'd ever cared about was the crash.

The lovely, ageless redhead watched him with...curiosity. No way to tell whose side she was on. Then he noticed the ring line, with no ring. A good sign. Who had arrived with Taz Cortez. A very bad sign.

Once he had his chair upright again, he called up the two pilots' files on his computer screen, then turned it so that they could all see it.

"The two bodies we found at Joint Base Andrews were easily identified. Nothing had been taken: clothes, wallets, phones, insignia. Everything accounted for. The plane in question was assigned to a transport mission. After the crash, replacement pilots were brought in to prep another bird in the same hangar to service that mission. They found the two dead pilots in the luggage compartment as part of their preflight. Knife to the heart, slim blade so not much blood. Nothing

M. L. BUCHMAN

unusual about them. Good service records, families, everything normal."

"Okay."

The redhead moved to the one guest chair his office boasted and settled into it slowly as if she was suddenly far older than she looked.

"We have one man who came through base security last night but is still unaccounted for. A Captain Justin O'Dowd. The pilot who we presume killed them, stole the plane, and crashed it into the hotel. His record is also clean."

"Do you have any audio of his voice?" Jeremy asked.

Jon tracked down the file and hit play.

"No. No. Send it to me."

"Are you cleared to—"

Jeremy held out a CAC. The Common Access Card listed him as a consultant to the AIB with a clearance significantly higher than his own. Right, he'd forgotten that Miranda's whole team was cleared to the heavens themselves.

"Fine!" He sent the stupid file, a lift of O'Dowd's voicemail greeting. Taz and Jeremy didn't acknowledge his thinking of that. They were both so damned insulting. Taz had been raised from the grave and dodged the prison sentence they probably all deserved. All because of Miranda cozying up to Uncle Drake in ways she'd never done with himself in the entire year they'd been dating.

Within moments, Jeremy was loading the audio file on his tablet. He played a recording of a plane taxiing, and the tower's clearance. Then he played the segment Jon had provided. Not much there to tell if it was the same person, less than a dozen words.

They all waited in silence while Jeremy worked for several minutes.

Jon spent most of that time wishing they'd all go away. He spent the rest wondering if his career was over because he'd been stupid enough to sleep with Miranda Chase and now her team members were going to hound his heels until the day he died.

"It's a voice match," Jeremy announced. "That's our bad-guy pilot."

"His record is immaculate." Jon pointed at the history.

"A sleeper agent," the redhead said in a voice that was simultaneously bedroom deep and infinitely refined. "A sleeper agent killed my husband."

"Killed...*who?*"

Taz rolled her eyes at him. "Major Swift. Report this man immediately to the FBI and Homeland Security. We need a full re-check of his background. I can't believe you were sitting on this."

"I wasn't sitting on—"

"Now!"

His survival instinct grabbed the phone and had him dialing.

Killed who? He knew there were a lot of dead at the George crash. But who was this woman connected to? Someone so important that Taz had cleared her through Pentagon security. Or had she cleared herself?

The implications of that were very, *very* bad.

44

"BUT THIS IS IMPOSSIBLE."

"Miranda," Susan tried her most calming voice. "That was the Chairman of the Joint Chiefs of Staff requesting your presence at the meeting. You can't say no to that."

"No."

"Which *no*? You can't refuse or you can't go?"

"This investigation is incomplete. There is more information that is essential to fully understand what occurred." Miranda's protest still hadn't answered the question.

This is what Susan was paid to do, make sure that her superior's communication occurred clearly *and* was listened to.

"I'm sure that General Nason has taken that all into consideration before pulling you from the investigation."

"I should be investigating the KC-46 Pegasus crash," her voice was almost dreamy. "That's what should have been done next. I haven't finished my review of the preliminary report."

"Yes you did," Susan assured her. Miranda had, hadn't she? "And..." she searched her memory through the confusion of the last nineteen hours since she'd reached the team. Or negative forty-three hours for crossing the International Date Line. She did her best to clear her head and tried again. "And...yes, you told Andi to send it."

"But did she? I didn't follow up. So much has happened. What if I missed something when you grabbed the report from me? I don't know. I simply don't know." She pulled her tablet computer out of its vest pocket but seemed to lose focus and didn't turn it on.

Before Susan could think of a new tactic to convince Miranda they were going to Brunei, Elevator 4 engaged loudly on the other side of the hangar. It whined its way down from the Flight Deck level. As big as a basketball court and capable of moving sixty tons of aircraft, it took fifteen long seconds to descend the three stories.

Once it lowered into view, she could see the Seahawk helicopter parked in the exact center. Andi and the other pilot were still going through shutdown procedures. Beside it, Holly sat at the controls of a mobile crane, from which dangled the crumpled tail section of an F-35. Mike stood by two airmen carrying a battered and scuffed acrylic canopy.

When Susan turned back to look at her, Miranda didn't move an inch.

Mike scanned between the two of them, but didn't seem to notice anything out of the ordinary to cause more than a concerned second look at Miranda's unmoving figure.

No one disturbed her, though it added more complication and delay doing tight maneuvering to place the pieces in their proper locations around her, especially the awkward and badly battered tail.

Everyone backed off once the tail and canopy were in place to Holly's specs.

Miranda continued her statue thing.

Four long minutes this time by Susan's watch.

"It's still not enough," Miranda's voice started as a whisper but fast rose to a wail of pain. "It's here, it must be here. But I can't see it. I can't do this alone. I—" She went to her knees in the midst of all the wreckage.

Susan went to move forward, but Andi brushed by and wrapped Miranda in her arms.

Miranda's phone rang.

Miranda shrieked, scrabbling at her pocket.

Andi snagged it and heaved it to Susan. She caught it against her chest.

Taz.

With Miranda's shrieks climbing louder than the echoing power tools as somewhere forward the crew continued their efforts to keep the *Theodore Roosevelt* running, Susan couldn't remember who Taz was.

Mike, too, had surged forward, but Holly had grabbed him, finally knocking him to the deck.

"Commander Piazza here."

"Where's Miranda?" Taz was a woman. "What the *hell* is that noise?"

Miranda had impossibly folded up even smaller. Sadie scampered forward and disappeared into the huddle somewhere.

"Fuck! I know that sound. Are you the one who did that to her? I'll fucking hunt you down and kill you, slowly and just as painfully." That's when the memory connected. US Air Force Colonel Vicki Taser Cortez, a war criminal according to Major Jon Swift's files. A former member of Miranda's team.

Another call tried to beep into the background.

Susan made several attempts to get in a word edgewise, but couldn't think of what to say between the torrent of abuse, the noisy beeps of the incoming call, and Miranda's undiminished howls.

An instant after the second phone call stopped trying to get through, Susan's own phone began to ring.

At a loss for what to do, she tossed Miranda's phone still connected with Taz to Holly, then answered her own.

"Commander Piazza here."

"Are you airborne yet?" She recognized the voice this time.

"No sir, General Nason."

"What the hell is that noise?" The Chairman of the Joint Chiefs sounded almost as annoyed as Taz had.

How the hell was she supposed to explain this?

"*Piazza?*" Drake's voice ground out.

"I'm...not sure, sir. Miranda appears to have reached her limits."

"Fuck! What did you do to her?"

"Nothing, sir." *Christ in heaven,* who wasn't on this woman's side?

"Ask her—*Shit!* No, that won't work, will it? Piazza, fix this. You have less than two hours to deliver her to Brunei. And she does no one any goddamn good in..." he paused as if listening to the sounds of Miranda's pain, "...this state."

Then he hung up, clearly pissed as hell.

Holly hung up on Taz at about the same moment. Then she stalked over until they stood inches apart.

"I was gone under fifteen minutes, Piazza, what the fuck did you do to her?"

Susan took the one step that placed them toe-to-toe and shouted in Holly's face.

"I. Didn't. Do. *Any!* Fucking. Thing."

Holly studied her long enough for Susan to wonder if she was about to die. Then her shoulders sagged.

Though they stood so close, Susan could barely hear Holly's whisper.

"Well...shit."

45

DRAKE LOOKED LIVID AFTER THE ABORTED CALL.

The X-54's cabin didn't offer a great deal of privacy. Their close proximity engendered a level of togetherness that Clarissa had never desired with Drake Nason. Yet for the last six hours, they had debated their differing perspectives of global tensions—military versus clandestine operations—and it had been fascinating.

"Who put the bee in your bonnet?" Clarissa couldn't begrudge him not having his phone on speaker, it was *his* phone, but she'd dearly love to know what had happened on the other end of that call.

"Miranda's having a meltdown. Someone pushed her too hard."

"General Drake Nason, perhaps."

He spun to glare at her. For an instant she was facing the pure soldier. *That* she understood.

Clarissa began counting on her fingers. "She lost a third of her team four days ago when Taz and Jeremy came East. And you had to know that Taz and Jeremy would have contacted her for advice about doing their first investigation on their own at the George in DC. *I* know because I was there. Second, she's on an Alaskan crash investigation and you have her shipped off to the South Seas before she's done. You *know* how much she hates that. Except, third, you don't let her finish that one either and you're now ripping her ass off to Brunei. Why? To meet with people. *Strangers.* Shit, Drake, how did you think that was going to turn out?"

His face had shifted from fury to horror...and then back to fury. "If you saw all this, why didn't you say anything? You've been sitting a foot away for six hours and you don't say a damned word?"

Clarissa wanted to unload it all on him. *Because you've made it so abundantly clear that you'd rather be dunked in boiling oil than ask for my or the CIA's advice.*

Wanted to make him suffer for every time he'd put her down, cut her off, blocked her initiatives—all of it.

But he had chosen her for *this* meeting. There was only one of this type of plane anywhere in the world, and there were only the two seats. Out of all of the possibilities, when the shit truly hit the fan, he'd chosen her.

She tried to argue herself out of it, but couldn't.

So—she told him the truth.

"The wonders of twenty-twenty hindsight. I wasn't the one pushing her buttons, but I didn't see it coming either."

Drake grunted.

After a while, he spoke morosely. "Why doesn't that make me feel any better?"

"Welcome to the human race."

"Okay, if you're suddenly so brilliant—"

"I've always been brilliant, you simply refused to notice. I may have slept with Clark. But no matter how many times you implied or thought it, I wasn't sleeping my way to the top. I'm *damned* good at my job. And I *miss* Clark!" Against all likely possibility, she *did*. He hadn't been a brilliant man, but he'd been a damn good one. She hadn't had much experience with that. And the way he'd always seen her as beyond beautiful and sexy and brilliant… Holy hell! She really *did* miss him. That was a nasty irony to discover after he was dead.

He'd been poisoned, then burned to death. Somehow that fire kept eating away inside her. What happened when there was nothing left to burn?

"If you're so *always* brilliant, how do I go about mitigating this?"

Drake was finally asking her advice and she didn't have any handy recommendations.

"Okay, thinking aloud here…"

He nodded for her to continue.

"I… No. We… Oh, crap. I don't have anything. Either her team gets her back on her feet or they don't. It's beyond our control. All we can do is hope for the former."

They sat in silence for many miles before she thought of a question.

"Why were you calling her? What was your question for her?"

Drake tipped his head to crick his neck. "For Roy. I hate not being there for him. He insisted that without Clark to send, it was up to me to go to Brunei."

It was perhaps the first time in the whole flight she felt on top of it.

"I know exactly who to call."

46

TAZ'S PHONE RANG. *"WHAT?"*

"Hold please." A female operator dropped her into hold-music hell before she could finish saying, "You're the one who called me..." *Bitch!*

Worse, it was her former general's favorite piece of music, "Bésame Mucho". His wife's favorite love song—until some druggies needing their next fix had burned her down for her ATM cash. General Martinez had listened to it as if he had *enjoyed* driving the dagger of memory into his own chest. Maybe he had. His wife's death had eventually killed him and everyone near him—except herself.

Was she doing the same goddamn thing to herself, embracing the pain? Someone please tell her she wasn't being that stupid.

Her palm was already sweaty on the slippery phone case because of the call with Miranda, or the attempted one. Holly had said she'd take care of it. If anyone could, it would be her. But Taz's hands still shook with the adrenaline.

When she'd asked who had answered Miranda's phone,

Holly had said some Navy puke of an officer who was about to die a bloody death. Fine by her.

"Is this Colonel Taz Cortez?"

Taz straightened up so fast she almost broke her knee against the front of Jon's desk. Everyone in the room jolted at the loud clang. She barely managed to suppress a curse of pain.

"Yes sir."

"How are you doing, Colonel?" Why was the President asking her that? Oh!

"We've confirmed who killed the two pilots and Senator Ramson, sir."

Jon startled and twisted to look at Rose. Taz couldn't believe that he was dumb enough to think he had a chance with a woman who had that much class. Apparently he was. So not gonna happen.

"And you've let her know?"

"She's been with us, Jeremy and me, since our first arrival at the incident. We have a hypothesis that the attack specifically targeted him, rather than some form of domestic terrorism. We've asked the FBI and Homeland Security to continue pursuing that angle."

"Well done, and good news," he cleared his throat, "in a horrible way. I wanted to talk to you about Jeremy."

"Yes sir." She tried to think of what they might have done wrong.

"As both Miranda and Drake are overseas and headed into a crucial meeting..."

News to her.

"...Drake has suggested that you could be of service to me. I was hoping that one or both of you could come here to the White House. I may need information or technical advice very rapidly as the meeting develops. It starts in an hour. Are you in the area?"

"At the Pentagon, sir." Taz looked around the room. She

needed to get Rose out of here before Jon Swift drooled all over her. "May I ask Ms. Ramson to join us?"

Rose glanced up at her with curiosity.

"I've found her insights into personnel and motivations to be highly useful." Taz told both her and the President.

"Yes, please do. Then I can also offer my condolences in person."

"We'll be there shortly, sir."

"You'll be cleared through the West Entrance. We'll be setting up in the Situation Room."

"Yes sir. Thank you, sir."

Taz hung up and tried to take a calming breath, but Jon interrupted even that.

"Who were you talking to?"

"Above your clearance level, *Major* Swift." God it felt good to mess with *someone's* head. "Contact me the moment you hear anything on the perpetrator. The very second. And yes, that's a direct order." Then without giving him time to respond, she waved Rose and Jeremy out of the room.

Half out the door herself, she turned back.

"And if I don't answer my phone, call the White House Situation Room."

47

THE FIRST THING MIRANDA WAS AWARE OF WAS THE LOW DRONE of one...no, two Allison T-56 turboprop engines. So, she was on a C-2 Greyhound. The sound of four T-56s on a C-130 Hercules would be completely different. Even through the heavy earmuffs.

The second thing was that she was leaning on Andi's shoulder. She had no trouble identifying that. They'd been together for less than a month, but its shape against her cheek was so distinctive that she could easily recreate it in 3D mapping software.

The third thing was a warm lump in her lap.

The dog!

She jolted upright and looked around.

She, Andi, and Sadie were in the front row seats to the starboard side of the Greyhound's cabin. The two pilots sat only a few feet in front of them. To the port side sat Commander Susan Piazza. And behind her was—nothing! No more seats, simply an empty cargo bay.

"Where are they?"

Andi reached across to flick on the intercom on Miranda's

headset. She repeated her question. The C-2 was too loud to comfortably converse without the headsets.

"Holly and Mike are continuing to work the F-35. You said there was something important, so we decided that they would stay and keep working on it. We all hope that was the right decision."

Miranda would much rather have them here with her. Her team was now broken into little pairs spread across the globe. It felt fragile and tenuous, as if she'd lost pieces of herself. *Knowing* intellectually that she'd get at least two of them back... didn't *feel* any better.

She hated the aftermath of an episode. They were so rare now that each one was like...sticky glue dragging her back to her childhood. Even coming up with the metaphor didn't make her feel any better.

Andi handed her a bottle of orange juice and a plastic-wrapped roast beef sandwich. The last meal she could recall had been in the captain's cabin, but she had no idea when that had been. Maybe crashed blood sugar had been part of the problem.

She knew it wasn't but it sounded better that way.

And she was hungry.

After glancing to Susan for permission, she fed a sliver of the roast beef to Sadie. Rather than begging for more, Sadie licked her nose several times before walking out of her lap, across Andi's, and jumped across the narrow aisle into Susan's.

After Miranda finished the sandwich, she felt a little better. The comfort of doing something routine, no matter how unusual the environment. Outside the window, the predawn light was finally erasing the last of the stars. They were still racing over the unending water of the South China Sea. Daybreak.

She hoped that today would be a better day.

Then she remembered where they were headed and doubted it would be.

"A meeting." It was pointless to ask if she had to attend. That decision had been taken out of her hands. Next time she'd have to fight back harder against the darkness so that she could maintain some say in her own future.

"Yes, in Brunei. Have you ever been there?"

"No. Their worst helicopter crashes were all before my time except for two rather obvious military crashes. Their only significant airplane crash was a German Dornier that killed ten while I was still in high school."

Andi laughed that friendly laugh of hers. "I haven't been there either."

The humor eluded Miranda as usual, but the feeling of inclusion didn't. It was a curious paradox that she was only now learning to accept about Andi: Miranda didn't need to understand her to like being around her.

"What is happening with the KC-46 crash?"

"We sent in the report. And they've reported back that the black box concurs with our initial findings. The training flight crews were too busy discussing possible emergency procedures at each step of the landing process to understand that they were actually entering into one. When the proximity alarms kicked in, the pilots assumed it was done by the trainer. They wasted too much time determining that the alarms were real, not simulated."

"Oh, that's a relief."

Susan looked at her with narrowed eyes. "It's a relief that they screwed up and crashed a three-hundred-million-dollar plane?"

"No. It's a relief that we are now relatively certain of the cause." Miranda wasn't sure why she had to explain that.

Thankfully Andi did. "You aren't a flier, Commander Piazza, so perhaps you wouldn't know. The Sterile Cockpit rule is supposed to apply at a level that neither of the crews nor the onboard trainer managed properly. During critical flight stages, the only discussions allowed in the cockpit relate to that stage of flight—that *specific* stage. We will have to recommend to the Air Force that their training be amended to clarify that during a landing, they may *only* discuss that specific landing, and not any hypothetical problems about a *generalized* landing."

At least Miranda could stop worrying about that crash for the moment. She made a note to recommend review of all FAA and military Sterile Cockpit training language.

Then she made a second note to retrieve her own plane from the hangar at JBER. She didn't like this scattered feeling at all.

Before Susan could ask anything else distracting, she asked about the crash in Washington, DC.

Andi shrugged. "I haven't heard from Taz or Jeremy in a while."

Miranda flipped over to the pilot's intercom and asked for permission to place an air-to-shore call. They gave her the code to synchronize with the onboard systems.

48

Taz's phone rang the moment before she handed it over to the Situation Room security team. No cell phones were allowed past the outer security door.

She glanced behind her, but the West Wing lobby was a crush of people hurrying from task to task.

There wasn't much of a corner to step to in the small security foyer, but she did so. Jeremy and Rose also stepped aside with her, offering some buffer before she answered—more carefully this time.

"Hello?"

"Hi, it's me, not a recording of me."

"Hi yourself, Miranda. Are you okay?"

"I seem to be."

"I'm so glad. Did Holly 'kill the bitch' like she promised?" There was a long silence that Taz had learned meant puzzlement. "There was some Navy puke of an officer that Holly was going to kill for me."

"Oh."

"Not literally." They'd left the team less than a week ago and already she was forgetting the rules.

"Figuratively kill someone?"

Taz felt herself smiling, "Close enough."

"Andi," Miranda asked Andi as an aside, "what 'Navy puke of an officer' was Holly going to figuratively kill? Taz wants to know did she do it and keep her promise?"

Taz couldn't hear Andi's response.

"Oh, you mean Commander Susan Piazza. No, she's here with us. But why would you kill her figuratively? And if you did, literally, I think it would greatly upset her dog."

"Don't worry about it, Miranda. I'll talk to Holly when we're done and straighten it out." And she'd find out why the hell Holly hadn't done as she'd promised.

"She's not here."

Taz listened to the sound in the background. Inside an airplane, military by how loud it was. And Holly hadn't stuck by her side like glue? Now Taz had a new target, a tall blonde named Holly Harper was gonna get her ass kicked the next time they met.

She took a calming breath, it seemed to be the day for that. It helped the same amount all of the others hadn't.

"What was your question, Miranda?"

"Which question?"

"The one you called me about?"

"Oh, that. Yes. What is the status of your DC crash investigation?"

Taz should have known. "It wasn't an accident. It was an intentional crash. So the NTSB is done. We'll stay involved, but it's Homeland Security's problem now. A kamikaze flight with an Air Force Gulfstream as the bomb."

"Oh, that's a relief. No, wait. I'm not supposed to say that, am I?"

Taz had no idea why not. "Whatever you say, Miranda."

"Oh, okay. I guess I'll ask Andi... Oh, she says it *is* okay to be relieved that it was murder and not an accident... Wait, maybe it wasn't. Or..." Miranda collapsed into confusion.

Taz knew to pick up the pieces quickly. "The possible target appears to be a Senator Ramson, head of the Senate Armed Services Committee. I have his wife Rose with me."

"And Jeremy?"

"And Jeremy is here too," Taz confirmed.

"Tell him... Uh, tell him...I said...*Hi.*" And she was gone.

Taz stared at the silent phone, then looked up at Jeremy. "She says, *Hi.*"

Jeremy laughed aloud. "Well, it's nice to know she's back to normal."

Taz thought about it and decided that *was* good news.

Now she could return to worrying about what the hell was going on. Why was she walking into the Situation Room for the first time in nineteen years of service?

49

THE FLIGHT TO BRUNEI WAS ALMOST ON THE GROUND BEFORE Susan woke up. Figuratively, not literally. The latter would have required that she'd been asleep, by now a luxury past imagining.

No, what she woke up to was that she should have made different choices on the aircraft carrier. She looked across the C-2 Greyhound's aisle at Andi and Miranda.

They sat with their heads close together. She was in the same intercom loop they were but she might as well not have been. They were discussing the remains of the F-35C and its crash on the carrier in terms she didn't begin to understand.

"A stress factor analysis along these shear lines in the shock pistons should provide an accurate method of calculating the force of impact."

"No, we have to integrate the rate of shock absorption across time, though probably only to the millisecond scale for this scenario. We then would factor that like this." And Miranda tapped a few quick notes into her computer.

"Right. Okay. Then we can start estimating..."

Susan tuned them out.

It was a language as unique as her own. If she began speaking with them about sociometric analysis of group cognition, their eyes would probably cross as badly as hers were now. Of course, after more than thirty years of hands-on training, she rarely had to reach back into her formal education.

But was it safe to interrupt them?

Normally such a question was easy to consider. A simple estimation of present-tense irritability compared with the message's relative priority. But Andi and Miranda appeared perfectly calm. Except in this case, that wasn't any measure of the kinds of reactions an interruption might engender.

So she settled on a bit of subterfuge.

Susan nudged Sadie awake, gave her a good scritch in apology for interrupting her nap, then waved her across the aisle. Sadie leapt the aisle and landed in Andi's lap, who placed a free hand lightly on her back without looking up. Her mother had kept Shih Tzus so, of course, she was completely comfortable with one.

Sadie looked back and Susan signaled her to keep going.

Sadie clambered out from under Andi's hand, walked over Miranda's left arm, sat in her lap, then stared up at Miranda's face and began to wag her tail furiously.

Miranda's initial action was to withdraw her hands completely. That broke her connection with the keyboard. Which was a good start.

But neither did she pet Sadie.

Instead, she stared straight down, her face mirroring Sadie's in some way Susan couldn't identify.

She waited another fifteen seconds to ensure Miranda's break from her structural calculations.

"I've truly never seen her like someone as much as she likes you, Miranda."

"I do find it rather surprising...and not nearly as upsetting as I'd initially imagined."

"Well, I'm glad, but I still get my dog back when all of this is over. Don't forget."

"I won't," Miranda still hadn't looked aside.

"There are a few things we need to discuss before we land."

"I'm not looking forward to this," Miranda appeared to tell the dog.

"I know. There are a few rules we need to discuss."

"That's good, I like rules. It would make life so much easier if there was a practical, standard set of rules."

"It would, but then getting people to adhere to them becomes the next challenge. We have laws at global, national, state, county, and city levels, yet we have a large number of rulebreakers."

"Like the man who flew the C-20C Gulfstream III into the George Hotel and killed a senior member of Congress."

"Umm, yes." Susan had heard only a few mentions of something happening in DC. How or who had... Didn't matter. She didn't need to know.

And here she was off track already. Or maybe not.

"There are numerous rules regarding behavior in Brunei. We will need to be very careful about not breaking any of them while we are guests there."

"Do you have a list?"

"I do. I think that most of them you won't break by your very nature. It isn't near Christmas, so it's illegality in public is of little consequence. Nor would pornography or alcohol be an issue."

"It isn't."

"Drugs, even some prescription drugs, can be problematic as some are—"

"No. I don't do drugs."

"Not even when...?" Susan was unsure how to ask tactfully

about the collapse Miranda had gone through.

"No, not even then," she offered the smile of a rare sense of humor. "Prior to the hiring of my therapist, my parents kept me dosed on a variety of therapeutics. Tante Daniels threw them all away and taught me how to be myself."

Andi looked horrified and squeezed Miranda's hand tightly. So, they were a new couple to not have covered such ground yet.

"I suppose then that there are only two others. The first is that you two can not show any affection for each other."

"Wait. *What?*" Andi twisted to stare at her. "Please tell me that doesn't mean what I think it does."

"No, it means *exactly* what you think it does. The Sultan has declared that LGBTQ, etc., is punishable with death by stoning."

"Why that God damn—"

"And that's the second one. Saying anything, and I do mean *anything* negative about the Sultan is incredibly illegal. Not even when you think you're alone. Not even by yourself standing on a beach even though you think no one can overhear you."

Andi continued muttering imprecations upon the Sultan's head.

"No, Andi, don't!" Miranda practically shouted. "We're well within the waters of Brunei's exclusive economic zone. I don't want them to do anything to you."

Susan had expected that Miranda would be the problem on this one. Instead it was Andi Wu who was livid at being told she was less than normal.

Andi blew out a hard breath, then patted Miranda's hand. "For you, Miranda. I'll do it for you." Then she turned to Susan. "Just make sure that I don't meet this Sultan. It won't go well."

Susan offered her a grim smile. She could definitely grow to like Andi Wu.

50

"ARE YOU READY FOR THIS?"

Zhang Ru nodded. "Though I never thought I'd travel somewhere that made our own leader appear benevolent."

"Each is strict in his own ways," Liú Zuocheng appeared philosophical as their Boeing 737-800 taxied toward the terminal at Rimba Air Force Base. This plane had been outfitted as a strategic command center as well as a VIP transport. They could start a war from here if they had to. And they could do it in luxury.

"We have free education and—"

"Don't try to lecture me, Ru. After secondary school, our higher education scholarships are terribly limiting—soon to be nonexistent. And free medical is almost fully abolished because it is our economic growth that must rule all. Here in Brunei, both are free for life. Their Gross Domestic Product per capita is four times ours and they live longer than we do. Do your homework before you speak again."

Ru did his best to show no outward sign, but he would not soon forget the insult.

Instead, he stared out the window.

One of those American carrier airplanes was pulling up at the same moment they were.

They and the Americans both deplaned at the same time. A small royal guard was awaiting them by the terminal, but on the tarmac there were only themselves and the two planes.

He recognized two of the three people who deplaned.

Their fancy crash investigator and her Chinese assistant. Their clothes were smeared with oils and dirt as if they'd come directly from the crash investigation. He didn't know the third woman, though he liked her looks. She wore a military uniform that showed sharp packing creases. If it weren't for Zuocheng's presence, perhaps he'd have a chance to find out how she looked out of it. The first two had knapsacks and the third had a small roll-on suitcase—and a dog.

A fuel truck rolled up to the old American plane and began spooling out a hose.

He wondered how many hours they'd have to wait for Drake to come from DC. Would they have a hotel room waiting? And would any of those three women—well, not the strange investigator—be interested in waiting with him?

He was about to approach when a third plane arrived.

It was like nothing he'd ever seen...outside of a few *Artist Concepts*. It looked as if its nose had been caught in the antique rollers of his grandmother's washing machine mangle that had pressed it flat and long. It looked fast standing still, in a way that no jet in the PLAAF fleet ever did.

Gulfstream X-54B, he read on the side.

He'd never heard of the B variant. His latest report said that the A was still in development. Experience had taught him that could be years.

The door opened and Drake climbed out followed by a stunning blonde. She stood as tall as he did with her pumps' heels. The shimmer of her deep brown silk attire invited the eye to admire the woman. And there was a great deal to admire, from long legs to proud breasts a man could happily die in. But even she couldn't outshine the plane.

"Do we have anything like that?" Zuocheng asked softly.

"Not even on the drawing boards." Though they damn well would once he returned to China. Gulfstream. A private company. It would be much more difficult to steal their plans than the military and government combined—there he could always buy the engineers he needed. Though none more useful than Su Bin. He had been most useful in stealing the plans to vastly accelerate the design of the new Xi'an Y-20 super transport. It was almost a pity when Ru had to throw him away and let the Americans lock him up.

The Gulfstream would be a very different challenge.

He stepped into the fray.

"Drake, old friend. I haven't seen you since—"

"You blackmailed one of my staff sergeants so badly that he killed himself—after condemning you, I might add—*and* did your best to murder an entire helicopter flight crew."

He opened his mouth, but Drake offered the slightest tip of his head toward Liú Zuocheng. Without a word he made it clear that he would next reveal how Ru had thrown away a J-20 Mighty Dragon jet fighter, letting it fall into American hands. The way Ru had planned it, it should have worked. If it had, then Taiwan would already be folded into submission under Beijing's control just as Hong Kong had been.

"Yes," he managed through gritted teeth, "that seems about right."

"I thought so." Drake turned from him without shaking his hand as if he was a worm, and faced Zuocheng. "General Drake Nason at your service."

"General Liú Zuocheng at yours. Who are the rest of your team?"

Drake introduced... *Mā de!* This woman built for sexual

fantasies was the Director of the CIA? It made his balls shrivel to be this close to her. She stared at him with those fathomless pale blue eyes as if she could see his soul. A devil witch.

Miranda walked past Liú Zuocheng's extended hand. *See how you like it!*

The odd little woman stopped close in front of him. She did have truly daunting powers. And research had revealed that they weren't only in crash investigation but also extended into research and development as well. She could be very useful.

"Hello, Miranda."

She stared at the center of his chest. "You are a *very* bad man."

Please, ancestors, keep her mouth away from the J-20 crash. "If you say so, Ms. Chase."

She responded, but the ancestors had been listening.

While she spoke, the two American aircraft restarted their engines and began taxiing for departure. There was no chance of Zuocheng hearing her accusations, which ran out before anyone could hear again. Perhaps ancestors, perhaps luck, but he'd make more than a paper sacrifice upon their graves at the next festival.

Having had her say, whether or not anyone could hear her, she stepped away to meet Zuocheng. But it didn't stop the glare from the small ABC who accompanied her. American Born Chinese weren't fit to soil the dirt under their shoes. So few felt the pride of their ancestors. They were far harder to buy or recruit than any average American.

"US Navy Commander Susan Piazza," the attractive brunette was the first to offer to shake his hand. "I see that you are the pariah of this outfit."

"Pa—" He didn't know this word.

"The unwanted and perhaps evil second cousin." She offered a companionable smile. Not sexual, at least not that he could see, but perhaps friendly.

"Are you too the pari..."

"Pa-ri-ah." She shrugged in a way that said perhaps.

Then the sleek American jet, the X-54B, reached the runway. Unlike a fighter jet, it didn't run three hundred meters and jump aloft. Instead it moved down most of the runway on the ground. Then it didn't merely climb aloft. It leapt like a krait snake.

By the time it had climbed out of the pattern and circled to once more point northeast across the Pacific, a thump as loud as a handclap rolled down from the sky.

It had gone supersonic? That quickly? And no real supersonic boom. Impossible!

"How fa—"

"Classified!" The ABC snapped at him. Drake's smile backed her up.

Drake had crossed the seventeen thousand kilometers from Washington, DC, in the last eight hours. It was a terrifying ability.

The leader of the honor guard, who had stood to the side during the introductions, now stepped forward. He was dressed in a white jacket with black slacks bearing twin side stripes of white. His company were dressed in white uniforms, with a curious knee-length bright blue kilt. The leader carried a sword, the others bore rifles.

"Greetings from His Majesty the Sultan and Yang di-Pertuan of Brunei, Darussalam Hassanal Bolkiah ibni Omar Ali Saifuddien III. He regrets that he is unable to meet with you personally but he is pleased to offer you his country's hospitality for your conference. Should you require a moderator, he or his son will make themselves available. *Always in service with Allah's guidance.* That is our country's motto and we hope that Allah leads you well."

"Meaning he is smart enough to not tangle himself up in our mess unless we're making it worse," Drake nodded to the leader of the guard before turning to Zuocheng. "Let us take his guidance and do our best to not disturb his majesty."

"Yes," Zuocheng nodded.

"Perhaps, to impose as little as possible, we can all make a meeting upon our aircraft?" Ru indicated the 737. "It is quite comfortable inside."

Zuocheng looked at him in surprise but then nodded at the sense of it. The advantage of home turf.

Besides, the chance to create ties with the Chase woman and find out how tightly the little Chinese girl was bonded to her country was too good to pass up.

"I would sooner burn in hell," Drake said politely. "Knowing you, Ru, you'd try to poison us." He turned to the guard. "I hope that his majesty has deigned to give a moment of thought of where we might find a place to meet that is appropriate, discreet, and *neutral.*"

The leader nodded, did a snap turn, and walked away. They all turned to follow him.

Ru wished he could interpret Zuocheng's half smile, so similar to when he was watching the twins last night.

This was going to be a very long day.

51

THE FIVE MILES FROM THE RIMBA AIR FORCE BASE TO THE OMAR Ali Saifuddien Mosque was executed in matching current-model black-and-gold Mercedes-Maybach S 580 Coupes. Each came with its own driver and escort—the latter literally riding shotgun.

With only two back seats each, Susan was alone for the brief ride. The luxury was...fantastic! Over the top, but that's what she needed in her current state of exhaustion. There was even a refrigerator and a built-in drawer for a pair of champagne flutes for the rear-seat passengers. Though, being Muslim, it was a *dry* country and there was Evian to pour into the flutes—in four different sparkling flavors as well as plain. They had even provided a small bowl of water on the floor for Sadie.

It was too bad that being wrapped in her own private quarter-million-dollar cocoon of luxury would last so briefly. But the motorcycle police escort assured them of a very fast passage through the capital city of Bandar Seri Begawan.

The low sunlight of early morning made the city shine. It

wasn't a tall city, few buildings rose over five or six stories. Coconut palms were fewer than she'd expected and patches of dense trees more common. It was also a very flat and very clean city. In many places the empty two-lane roads were the highest elevation, raised to not interrupt the communities below.

With only twenty percent of the country's half-million people living here in the capital, the city had an open, casual feel. It also had none of the odors she'd come to expect from crowded third-world cities, or first-world for that matter.

It smelled like...

Oh, now there was a good memory.

Early in her career, she'd been serving in Scott Air Force Base, way too far from an ocean for a Navy gal and twice too far for a Massachusetts one. In a bar she'd overheard that someone had lost her housemate. The woman in the bar was transferring to Hickam AFB in Hawaii, but her housemate had fallen for that fatal sickness: marriage and kids—fatal to a proper military career, especially back then. Susan had butted in and they'd hit it off. She'd put in for a transfer to the adjoining naval base at Pearl Harbor and spent two glorious years working and lounging in the Hawaiian sunshine, about the longest she'd been in any one spot.

Brunei was like that. It smelled of ocean, tropical jungle, sunbaked beaches...and oil. At Pearl it had been from the busy Navy and Air Force bases, here it permeated the land with the aroma of money. The economy of Brunei was oil, oil, and more oil. The tiny country sat astride such massive reserves that it was one of the first places Japan had invaded in World War II despite how far it lay from their home islands.

Brunei had also adopted a no-cut policy in their jungles years before to foster eco-tourism.

It felt both sanitized and comfortable. Susan preferred her life a little more rough-and-ready, but there was something to be said for living here. She could probably walk any street at three in the morning in safety. Though sex trafficking at the highest levels of government was a problem, despite the brutal punishments if caught, the streets themselves were incredibly safe.

Of course, she could also receive death by stoning if she ever had an abortion, even used the abortion pill, or was stupid enough to have an affair with a married man.

Overall, she'd take the much messier nature of the US. A place where Andi and Miranda were free to be together simply because they wanted to be.

They still puzzled her, though there was no way to see into someone else's relationship. Miranda was problematic at best, yet her team worshipped her, especially Captain Andi Wu. She requested an update file on the latter, and received back a whole lot of *redacted* and *classified* responses. However, one thing was clear, she'd been one of the top helicopter pilots ever created by the US Army, before leaving abruptly and joining Miranda's team. Susan knew that was not the sort of woman who gave her loyalty lightly.

And maybe that worship wasn't wholly misplaced. Miranda had certainly spotted the laser attack fast enough, within minutes of boarding the *Roosevelt*. Something no one aboard had noted in the prior twelve hours.

The car rolled to a stop in a tight convoy with the other three.

She checked on Andi and Miranda, but they were standing farther apart than even Director Reese and General Nason. Each acting as if the other was infectious. Good. Horrid that they had to, but they had listened.

Their group was escorted to the national mosque. A dazzling structure of white marble and what might be bronze paneling that glowed in the morning sun. The massive golden, at least she hoped it was golden and not actual gold, onion-shaped dome atop the structure was brilliant and perhaps the tallest structure in the city. A dozen smaller but equally golden minarets sprang from the structure.

Then she considered the wealth of this tiny nation and decided that it probably *was* real gold.

The honor guard provided lovely silk scarves for each of the women to cover their hair. She hoped that she would be allowed to keep hers, it was an artisan's work in a vivid pattern of gold on dark green that was closely related to paisley.

They were led through a small park and around the building on immaculate paving inlaid in geometric patterns. The mosque itself was wrapped on three sides by an artificial lake crossed by several wide marble walkways. A sinuous one led to the middle of the lake at the end of which stood a massive golden barge half a football field long.

The honor guard addressed them again in his oddly stilted way. "His Majesty the Sultan offers you the *Mahligai Barge*. It was modeled on the ship of Sultan Bolkiah, who ruled during the Golden Age of 1485 to 1524 by your reckoning. It is considered a particularly holy spot. He offers it for your exclusive use as long as you have need of it."

Once they were seated in one of the peak-roofed gazebos on the stone barge, they were quickly served with a massive breakfast.

"What's this?" Miranda peered at it closely.

"Nasi lemak," a waiter answered. He began describing the rice, spicy sauce, and dried fish dish dressed with a hard-boiled egg. There were also bowls of fresh-sliced guava and mango.

All Susan cared about was the coffee, which was strong enough that she was surprised it wasn't on the prohibited drugs list. Exactly what she needed.

There was the easy silence of weary travelers enjoying a fine meal. The setting on a barge *floating* upon an artificial but lovely lake, reflecting a magnificent mosque in the middle of Brunei's capital, created a lovely ambience.

However, it soon shifted to the awkward silence of two nations who despised and didn't trust each other.

Finally, Susan knew why she was here.

52

"MIRANDA, WHY DON'T YOU TELL US WHAT YOU KNOW SO FAR?"

Miranda continued to inspect her meal. It looked...strange. She preferred brown rice, but her plate bore a cup of such perfectly formed white sticky rice that not a single grain had fallen from the freestanding mound arched into a perfect hemisphere. The sauce, she tested it carefully with the tip of a chopstick, was indeed very spicy. But Andi was eating it by mixing it with little bits of the rice and fish.

Perhaps it was okay.

However, Drake and Clarissa were using their forks and spoons. Should she not have used her chopsticks to match them? Andi was using hers, so she would accept that as a guide.

"Miranda?" Susan asked again. Commander Piazza wasn't a useful indicator as she hadn't touched her meal yet, keeping both hands around her coffee cup as if someone might take it.

Miranda considered the best way to evenly excise sections from the rice ball without damaging the perfection of the symmetry, but was unsure how to begin. Explaining the crash she still didn't understand would be easier. She set her chopsticks down on the edge of her plate, focused on the line of the sun sliding along the minarets, and cursed—very softly so that the guards wouldn't hear or be offended.

How had she not seen that?

She pulled out her phone and dialed quickly.

53

"Ms. Ramson. I'm so terribly sorry for your loss."

"Thank you, Mr. President." He had come directly to her first upon entering the Situation Room.

Rose had never been in this part of the White House and was unsure how to react. She'd attended any number of state dinners with Hunter, but those were always in one of the grand rooms in the Residence's ground floor.

The President and Hunter had despised each other despite her best efforts, so invitations to the smaller, more elite parties in the private areas above had been rare. Only when Hunter's power in the Senate had finally mandated an invitation had she climbed to those stratospheric social levels.

"But I'm quite sure that you will not miss him."

His wry smile was also kind. "We never did see eye-to-eye."

"Especially not lately." Rose thought it best to have everything on the table between them. Having now stepped this close to power, the Situation Room, she didn't want to be brushed back out to the lobby.

His nod acknowledged Senator Hunter Ramson's bitter battle to block the President's Mid-East Realignment Plan.

She looked at this man in this particular room. His entry had changed it, without changing anything. The world clocks were still on the wood paneled wall. The screens beyond the end of the conference table remained blank. The comfortable chairs still circled the oak conference table. She'd been warned how small the real Situation Room was in reality, which was true.

Yet the focus of power had shifted with the President's arrival, tracking him like an all-seeing eye. The eight Marines, sitting out in the main area of the Situation Room in their two-tiered semicircular desk, were now poised to answer his slightest request. With President Cole's entry, this was no longer another well-equipped conference room—it was the seat of American political and military power.

This was where the strategic implications of the MERP had been hashed out.

Rose had little doubt of the result when Taz and Jeremy finished their investigation. Hunter's inability to block the passage of MERP had infuriated the Saudis and several other OPEC nations.

And yet... "Mr. President, though it may prove to have cost my husband his life, personally, I believe that your plan in the Middle East is sound and well-considered."

In that instant, she had his full attention.

No longer the gracious politician at state functions, which was Rose's only real exposure to the President outside of television and the papers, he now embodied the soldier as well. Such a contrast to Hunter, who had always been soft. There was nothing soft about President Roy Cole.

"Thank you. That means more than I expected." And his simple nod brought an unlikely warmth to her cheeks.

"The truth, Mr. President. This seems a place where anything else would be inadvisable."

"Indeed, Ms. Ramson." Then he turned to take his chair as he thanked Taz and Jeremy for coming.

The shift of attention was so abrupt that she practically stumbled into the void the President left in his wake.

She managed to find her seat as a disembodied voice announced a call for Mr. Jeremy Trahn. As it was patched through, Rose tried to understand what had happened.

In truth? Nothing.

And yet it felt as if she was telling herself a bald-face lie while sitting in the nation's Situation Room.

54

"Jeremy, Miranda called from Brunei. We've made the observations, but we need some math run. We don't want to distract her with the calculations. Besides, she'll appreciate your confirmation on it." Holly spilled it out fast.

"I'm in the Situation Room." Jeremy had been here before. No, he hadn't. But he'd talked to Miranda on conference calls when she was here. And Mike. But he'd never been here himself. Had he? This must be how Miranda felt when the world whipsawed her back and forth. He wanted to ask her, but it didn't seem like the appropriate time.

He'd never been in the Pentagon before today either. Yet Taz had entered as if it was the most normal thing ever.

He wished there'd been time to test the rumor that it was possible to walk from any office to any other office in under seven minutes across the seven floors of the world's largest office building. Instead, Taz had breezed them from the underground parking to Jon's office in under two minutes, like the twenty-eight kilometers of corridors were simply in her blood.

"You can't do calculations in the Situation Room? Snap to, mate."

"Right. Go ahead!" He opened the laptop he'd been allowed to bring into the room.

"Okay, we have an F-35C that was burned by an orbital laser during landing on an aircraft carrier. It's—"

"You *what?*" But then he noticed the President's unhappy scowl. Well, that explained where Miranda had been. "Okay."

"I'm sending you a large number of images and a landing camera video. Miranda estimated that the laser was focused on the plane beginning six-and-a-half seconds before the landing went seriously wrong. I'm sending you three sets of images. One is closeups of the laser etchings on the carrier's flight deck. The second is the reconstructed wreckage and the last is shadowing angles where one part of the aircraft shielded another due to the angle of the attack. We need you to compare the flight path and landing angles with the damage on the deck. Then back it up with the burn versus shadow angles on the plane. Miranda wants us to locate the angular area of Earth orbit from which the laser fired."

"Like James Bond *Moonraker, Diamonds Are Forever,* and *GoldenEye* all combined. I'm sooo all over this."

"Go get 'em, Q."

And the breath caught in his throat. He'd thought that coming East would cut him off from Miranda and Holly, but they were all still in it together. He glanced at Taz...they all were.

But there was no magic moment about it, because Taz was explaining Holly's request to Rose and the President.

Didn't matter. They *were* in it together.

He opened a window to the secure server he'd set up exclusively for Miranda's government work and there it all was.

He plugged the aircraft carrier's heading and GPS data into his mapping software, then watched the landing video as the

President was called out of the room. By the time he returned, Jeremy had layered the observed Flight Deck etching on the carrier, recognizing Miranda's characteristic measurements. It felt as if he was looking over her shoulder as he positioned it properly.

Jeremy hummed the theme for *GoldenEye*. It wasn't one of the greats like *Goldfinger* or the overrated *Live or Let Die*, but it *was* Tina Turner and she was awesome.

Rather than shifting the object side-to-side—the plane over the decking—to discover the most accurate shadowing, he kept the plane looping over the deck from seven seconds out until it snagged the Number Four wire.

Then he shifted the light source trying to match the results to the observed markings on the deck.

Variations in altitude of firing the laser and the angle of attack offered several solutions.

He stored the most likely result but it wasn't accurate enough. Nine degrees of possible east-west shift wasn't *too* awful for a first approximation. But the north-south axis was far less indicative and covered thirty degrees of sky.

"*And it's a big-ass sky.*"

"What was that?"

Jeremy was suddenly sitting in his seat again rather than floating at varying angles over the South China Sea. "What is what?"

"What you said," the President was squinting at him. Rose appeared to have been in the middle of saying something.

"What did I say? Oh, *And it's a big-ass sky*. That's from the movie *Armageddon*. The head of NASA is telling the President that the reason they didn't spot the planet-killing comet was because..."

Taz rolled her eyes at him. Jeremy finally clued into what he was saying and stopped. Presidents probably didn't like hearing about Armageddons.

"Sorry, sir. I have a first estimate, but it covers too broad an area of sky. My first look narrows the attack area to less than two-tenths of a percent of the sky. However, if the firing range is from an orbit of two hundred and fifty kilometers, that's MSL (above Mean Sea Level), there is still three-quarters of a million square kilometers of orbital area that was occupied by the satellite for the crucial six to eight seconds. But we don't know the height of the orbit and I don't have a sufficiently accurate analysis of the data yet to estimate the orbital altitude. If it's a thousand-kilometer-high orbit, that would be, uh, twelve-point-six, that's rounded off a bit, million square kilometers."

The President's expression was absolutely deadpan.

Jeremy could feel himself shrink. Soon he'd be so small he could hide inside his computer case as they tossed him out of the room and never let him in again. Here, in the Situation Room, like the coolest setting on the planet and he was screwing up so much that—

"Jeremy?"

He looked up at Rose's soft call.

"I didn't understand most of that."

"Sorry." No one had. No one *ever* did except Miranda. He stared down at the keyboard.

"But," Rose continued, "the part I think I understood, correct me if I'm wrong, is that you found a *section* of the sky from which the attack probably originated."

"Oh no, it was absolutely from there. But it's a big..., uh, sorry about the language. It's just that space is really, really big. And now I'm quoting *The Hitchhiker's Guide to the Galaxy*. Sorry."

"I'm merely wondering, what satellites were in that really, really big area, that's smaller than all of space, at the right time to make the attack?"

The President was studying Rose intently.

"I don't know. The ones we're interested in would be

classified, so I don't know them. We'd have to ask—" He slapped his own forehead. Then he turned to Taz.

She didn't even hesitate. She tapped a button on the intercom. "Please get me in touch with General Elizabeth Gray, the head of the NRO."

Yes, Drake's wife, the head of the National Reconnaissance Office was in charge of the nation's satellites—as well as knowing all about the foreign ones.

55

Miranda's phone buzzed with a message from Jeremy. *Check the server. First-order approximations. Still working.* And a smiley emoji that Miranda smiled back at. Emojis helped so much in understanding messages, she wished that people came with equipped with them.

Then she opened her computer and logged into the system. The *Mahligai Barge* had excellent connectivity. That struck her as curious, the original fifteenth-century barge wouldn't have had wi-fi. Of course, it also wouldn't have been made of stone.

On the server was a list forwarded from Lizzy at the NRO.

"I've got something from your wife, Drake."

The conversation, which had been hard to follow, collapsed. She only knew enough to know that it hadn't been going well—mostly in ways that Susan Piazza seemed able to follow but utterly flummoxed Miranda.

Instead, she'd spent her time trying to draw conclusions from too little data. The shifting angle of sunlight on the mosque's dome had made her realize that the laser-light attack hadn't merely come from *above*. It had shone down from a specific point which should be identifiable if they could calculate the specific angle of attack. They already knew the precise time.

The list was long.

She dismissed all of the new internet constellation satellites that were being pushed into low-Earth orbit by the hundreds. They were too small and underpowered to deliver such a powerful laser strike.

The ones in high geosynchronous orbits were equally unlikely. Those were primarily communications satellites intended to remain over a specific point for television broadcasting and the like.

No, a weapon of this kind would be terribly expensive. It would be in an orbit where it could be constantly on the move.

"Miranda?" Drake asked, but thankfully Andi shushed him.

At the bottom of the list, Lizzy had listed six birds.

Four were American, though one was the Hubble telescope so she dismissed that.

One was Canadian, a known weather satellite.

None were Russian.

The last one was Chinese.

Lizzy had also attached a full write-up on the last one.

Miranda looked up, "You are a very bad man, General Zhang Ru."

56

RU STARED AT THE LITTLE HORROR OF A WOMAN.

Rather than either he or Zuocheng bedding the twins—and one of them damn well should have—they had spent the night proving to themselves that PRC forces had *not* been responsible for the attack. It was one of the reasons they had requisitioned the 737 command post for the flight down, so that they could continue their research during the two-hour flight.

And now this Chase woman was pointing her ghoulish finger of death in his direction.

"I do not care what you are saying. None of our satellites fired a laser in the South China Sea yesterday. And we have no planes in the sky above you. We do not break maritime law. It is America that does this in *our* waters." Which was a useless rehash of their last hour of conversation. This meeting was achieving nothing.

"Could you then please tell me the purpose of your Ziyuan-2B satellite? We know that it is not the weather satellite you claim, just as twenty-two years ago your Ziyuan-2A weather satellite was actually a Jianbing-3 high-resolution imaging mission."

"The ZY-2B is a paired satellite for *imaging*. Nothing more." Which was all he really knew about it until last night. Zuocheng had revealed that it was in truth a fantastic weapon. But saying it existed at all proved to be too much of a clue as she continued pushing.

"A narrow-aperture, high-resolution telescope can also be easily adapted for use as a focusing mechanism for delivery of a burst of coherent light. Why did you use it to kill one of our planes?"

"We didn't use it for—" Then Ru knew what he'd done. He'd admitted to the existence of the weapon. Zuocheng regarded him from that place of deep silence he so often used. Ru would have kept his mouth shut if that Chase woman hadn't kept poking at him.

Everything she said came out like a voice of the gods. No one questioned it. No one doubted her word. It was ludicrous and—

The silence around the table seemed to reach from the barge to the Islamic heavens in this awful place. He needed a drink and a woman. And not some narrow-hipped little bitch.

He needed something like that blonde with the magnificent breasts. That was a woman worth the time to bed. That was *if* a man could stay hard when being watched by those devil blue eyes. They seemed to bore into him, each time he faced them. He could resist her easily.

But the little Chase woman? She knew his secrets, and didn't care if she revealed them. She knew of lost jets and showed no emotion. And now she'd tricked him in front of Zuocheng. He couldn't begin to calculate the danger of that mistake.

What would it take to make her change that righteous expression? A flaming sword rammed where a man belonged?

Her eyes weren't blue, but she was the true devil.

"*Cào nǐ zǔzōng shíbā dài,*" Ru spat out. *Fuck her ancestors back to the eighteenth generation* indeed. He'd like to do every one of them personally. Fuck them with hot steel up the ass.

He never saw the blow coming.

It came from the side—and was so fast.

It lit his throat on fire.

The next one to his temple catapulted him backward out of his chair.

He could dredge up no more than a groan after a kick impacted his crotch as if on its way to his brain.

He managed to roll away, but the next kick hammered his temple again.

It was the last thing he remembered.

57

"WHAT DID HE SAY?" MIRANDA WHISPERED TO ANDI WHEN SHE was finally released and returned to her chair.

The Brunei honor guard had appeared within seconds of Andi's attack, but she'd stopped before they had restrained her. Miranda was surprised that Ru wasn't dead after what Andi had unleashed on him.

Medics were called and had wheeled Zhang Ru away, much the worse for wear.

After that, half the honor guard continued to face outward along the walkway, to keep tourists away. However, the other half now faced inward and kept a careful eye on where Andi sat.

Andi shook her head and wouldn't meet her eyes.

When Miranda leaned in to ask again, Susan stopped her.

"You're in Brunei," she whispered.

Andi looked upset.

Which Miranda's mother had taught her meant that comforting was appropriate. An arm around the shoulders and a kiss on the temple. It was a gesture her mother had made often enough. But she did remember the rules, no displays of public affection between same-sex persons. They were lovers. That didn't make them subhuman. The rules were most unfair. And by having *that* thought, she was breaking the other rule of not disparaging the Sultan. This was so hard.

"My colleague," General Liú Zuocheng spoke softly to her, "was somewhat intemperate. Some other time I should like to hear why you anger him so. He is known for his, how do you say, ice-cold temperament during confrontations. The curse he uttered is exceedingly foul in our language, denigrating the last eighteen generations of your ancestors. I apologize on his behalf."

"Oh," Miranda wasn't sure what else she was supposed to say. "Okay." Perhaps that was sufficient. Eighteen generations would typically range from three hundred and sixty to five hundred and forty years ago. She didn't even know who her grandparents were. To the best of her knowledge, her family tree included two people other than herself—and they were both dead.

The general squirmed briefly in his chair, as if it was made of the same stone as the rest of the barge, before turning to Drake. "You have no reason to take my word for it, General Nason, but neither did I shoot at your plane nor can I find evidence that anyone else did with our satellite."

"Drake," Clarissa spoke up. "Based on what I know of their command structure, it is possible that a firing could be made without General Liú's knowledge, but it's unlikely that he would not uncover it in a dedicated search. Such an action would require multiple control log entries and the like."

"Very astute," the general nodded.

"So, where does that leave us?" Drake asked. "I'm inclined to believe you, though I don't trust you any more than you trust me."

"Oh, but I trust you a great deal. One does not rise to our level, or even his," Zuocheng nodded at Ru's empty chair, "without a certain level of commitment and integrity. Precisely to what goal may vary, but it makes us predictable in many ways."

Predictable?

Miranda looked again at the orbital mechanics of the ZY-2B. After thinking about it for a few moments, she leaned out from beneath the gazebo's roof enough to look directly aloft.

The sky was a crystalline blue, atypical for a tropical country that would more typically be a hazy blue. She didn't know if that was normal for Brunei or not, but it was existent now, which was all that mattered.

"What are you looking at?" Susan asked her quietly.

Miranda pointed upward. "Ideal conditions."

"For what?"

She'd thought that was rather obvious.

"In twenty-seven minutes, the Ziyuan-2B will be passing directly overhead. It will be in the best position since our arrival if someone wants to cook us alive the same way they did the pilot."

Everyone looked up except Andi, who still looked down.

"But we have a stone roof over our heads," Susan nodded upward.

Miranda glanced at her watch, corrected for their relative position in the fifteen-degree width of an idealized Time Zone, and then pointed over General Liú's shoulder.

"The sides of this stone gazebo, sorry, I don't know the proper religious name for this hut-shaped structure, are open. In twenty-three minutes it could cook General Liú from behind. In, now twenty-six minutes," she swung her hand up, past the roofline, and continued until she was pointing upward over her own shoulder, "it could cook us without harming him. The dark blue of the sky indicates low humidity at the moment. There are no clouds. It is an ideal shooting scenario for a high-power orbital laser."

Susan stared at her blankly. Others were staring at her as well.

Perhaps she understood why Andi sat with her head down. Miranda didn't want to look at anyone either.

"Simply an observation. Not a prediction."

They kept staring.

58

"HOW LONG HAVE WE BEEN DOING THIS?" HOLLY TRIED TO straighten up, but her back was hurting her worse than after a 20K hike with a full ruck.

"Since birth," Mike groaned.

She grabbed Mike's wrist and looked at his watch. "We landed on this bucket of bolts carrier twelve hours ago. Twenty hours puts us back to Alaska. Twenty-seven to arriving there. Thirty to Tacoma. Bed was—"

"Forever ago."

She dropped to sit on the hangar's deck and Mike collapsed beside her.

"What are we doing now anyway?"

Holly looked at the wreck but couldn't remember. She simply kept picking up pieces and trying to turn them back into the airplane. The pickings were now so meager that they were scrounging through the *Unknown* pile again. Placing a piece earned a high-five no matter how small.

Mike flopped onto his back, then rolled up a shoulder. She reached under it, pulled out a three-inch section of hydraulic line, that curiously she could picture exactly where it belonged.

It couldn't, it simply *couldn't* be important enough to stand up to place it. Closing it in her fist, she lay her head on Mike's shoulder and closed her eyes.

"You feel mighty good, Hol."

"You always say that."

"Because it's always true. I could make a habit of this."

"If that's a proposal, I'm going to have to hurt you."

"Why would it be so awful?"

"Because!" It was the only answer she had. They'd been sleeping together for over a year. A several-fold new record for her. Even while lying exhausted past breathing, on the steel deck of a battered aircraft carrier, Mike felt good.

She was almost asleep when she heard the captain approaching. Her gait had shifted since being promoted, it was quite distinct.

"You two need to take a bunk. You've earned some shuteye."

"Can't," Mike mumbled against her ear.

She patted his chest in thanks for saving her the energy of responding.

"And if I make it an order?"

"No authority." Mike muttered.

"We don't work for you," Holly agreed, then hated herself. So tired, and she'd wasted a slice of her slim reserves to repeat the sentiment. Miranda wouldn't have approved of such waste.

Her phone rang. It was impossibly far away, in her vest pocket. And her vest was hanging way over by the engine air intake housing.

"You answer it," Holly said to Mike.

"It's your phone."

"And to think I was falling for your protestations of taking care of me for an eternity."

"I'm more a one-lifetime-at-a-time kind of guy."

"Welsher. Con artist."

"Sure. At least I used to be," Mike sighed for good times long gone when he actually had been a stooge for the FBI.

"Are either of you going to answer that?"

Holly waved a hand at the captain to help herself.

"Captain Brightman here."

...

"She's lying on my Hangar Deck and feeding me some line of Spec Ops crock. Personally I think she's one of those lazy Australian types, sir."

...

"No, he's no better."

...

"Yes sir. I managed a few hours shuteye. Which looks as if it was a few more than they've had."

Show off, Holly thought as loudly as she could. Since when did ship captain's get to sleep while poor crash investigators toiled on and on without complaint?

Holly could get to like this. It was a very low energy scenario. And Mike was very comfortable.

"You aren't talking about the M-word, are you, Mike?" There was a horrid thought.

"No. No. I don't think I was. Maybe agreeing to live together in sin for the rest of our lives. That kind of thing."

They were already sleeping together. She hadn't been in her own bed at the team house in...a long damn time.

"You're thinking pretty quietly there, Hol."

"Are you shitting me, sir?" Captain Brightman was no longer enjoying her conversation.

Holly wasn't sure yet if she was enjoying this one. Mike was asking her in a weak moment. His chest was a very nice place to lay her head, very warm and cuddly. "Maybe I'll get back to you on that later, Mike."

"In person? Really?" Brightman was going on with far too

much energy. It must come from that few hours of cushy sleep she'd treated herself with.

Maybe Holly should try that herself.

"Uh-oh," Mike whispered.

"What?"

"Listen."

Holly forced herself to listen to the captain's conversation on her phone.

"Well, with the *Carl Vinson* pulling in, I suppose I can spare them."

"CVN-70," Holly felt pretty good about knowing that. "That means it's an aircraft carrier with N, nuclear propulsion. Very fancy."

"Smartypants. Do we want to be spared?"

"Spare tires. Spare parts."

"Spareribs," Mike countered.

"That sounds good. If you loved me, you'd go get me a big plate of spareribs and serve them to me one by one."

"I might eat them myself and only give you the bones to gnaw."

"Cheapskate."

"Are you two done?" Captain Brightman was looking down at them once again.

"Done for."

"Done in."

"Done with my ship," Brightman corrected. "I'm giving you notice that I might throw a party once you're airborne."

Holly eyed the captain, but she looked as if she might be serious. "Um, perhaps you were right, Mike."

"About what? Living together happily ever after?"

"No, about we should have been listening."

59

HOLLY DIDN'T KNOW WHAT THE NUMBERS MEANT. OR QUITE WHY she was hand-carrying them to Brunei. Something about no other way to insert military personnel without pissing off the Sultan.

She did know that she was going to do it quickly though.

She'd done this before, once, a year ago, but Mike never had. So she paid more attention to him paying attention to the briefing than she paid to the briefing itself.

It lasted three minutes flat. The pilots' ready room was still a burned-out husk at the base of the USS *Theodore Roosevelt's* Island. So instead, they were meeting in a small tent set up in an area called the Junkyard, against the Island's aft wall. There were no longer any broken planes parked there. A mobile crane, a forklift, and two spare arresting wires in great circular coils were parked there—much more the Junkyard's normal fare.

In fact, if one didn't look at the Island itself, or the Command Bridge made of tables along its side, the *Big Stick* looked ready to kick ass. A helo and two volunteer welders, dangling on winch lines from the cargo bay, were in the process of adding new safety cables to the tilted mast. Too big to straighten, they were pinning it in place until it could reach a Naval shipyard for repairs. It should be okay if they hit no rough seas on the way.

She and Mike were lectured on how to use their survival suits, what to do if the pilot said they were ejecting, and how their best chance of survival after that was keeping together.

"And try not to think about the sharks," the briefer said with a nasty smile.

After that, all she could think about was sharks, of course.

Holly slid back into her Special Operations Forces training. Mike stayed cool through pure willpower and it looked good on him.

Helmets secure, hands shaken by the captain, they were each led to the backseats of two F/A-18F Super Hornet jet fighters that had been brought on deck by the same elevator they'd ridden up on. The flight crew buckled their seatbelts for them.

A quick glance left and she could see Mike's plane lined up on the Number Two catapult.

The instant the crew were clear, the long canopy swung down and the jets rolled forward.

In less than twenty seconds, the pilot came on the intercom, "Hang on!"

She hadn't even promised that she'd see him on the other side.

Nor could she now. And she *did* want to.

The dual jet engines roared to life, barely muffled by her heavy helmet.

Then she spotted her pilot's salute around the edge of his tall ejection seat and braced herself.

A second later she was slammed back into the seat's padding.

Between the steam catapult and the jet engines, they

accelerated from zero to a hundred and sixty in two seconds flat.

Once the weight of acceleration had climbed off her chest and she could breathe again, she checked. Mike's plane was less than a hundred feet away. His helmet was turned to face her. When she waved, he waved back.

Now she had nothing to do for the next thirty minutes while they flew five hundred miles at twice the speed of sound. Nothing except worry about Miranda's numbers. That, and debating whether Mike was teasing her or being serious about wanting more from her than sharing his bed.

60

"Hɪ, Mɪʀᴀɴᴅᴀ."

She spun around.

Holly!

And Mike!

Holly and Mike!

Standing here on the *Mahligai Barge.*

Miranda didn't care about what rules might or might not apply, she pushed out of her chair and threw herself at them.

Together they held her tightly and she could feel the *edge* creeping back toward the darkness it lived in. Andi was still acting strangely since she'd beaten up Zhang Ru. Drake, Zuocheng, and Clarissa were still in some sparring match she didn't understand.

Susan stepped in when...she was needed?

Miranda didn't know how she chose when to intervene but she appeared to know. That had left Miranda with nothing to do but sit and cringe as the Chinese satellite had crossed overhead. She'd felt the target creeping to a flatter and flatter angle on her back until it had finally sunk low enough that the atmosphere would be too thick to shoot through reliably.

"I think she missed us," Holly kept the hug tight.

All Miranda could do was hold on and nod.

"Makes you feel all warm and fuzzy inside, doesn't it?" Mike asked.

"It does, matey. It definitely does."

Again, all Miranda could manage to do was nod as the weight dropped off her in layers.

When she finally felt she could stand tall again—though not too tall as Holly and Mike were both six inches taller than she was—she started thinking again. It was as if her brain had shut down the more her team was scattered about. Now that they were coming back, so could she.

"We were asked to bring you this personally." Holly pulled out her phone and turned it for Miranda to see. "Any idea what it means?"

Miranda knew exactly what it meant. But it was too unlikely.

She went to her own computer, and keyed in the information.

Checking the numbers didn't change anything.

"Everything okay, Miranda?" Susan asked. The others were watching her.

"I'm not sure." She didn't like to lie but it was the safest path at the moment. She was sure about what the data showed, but really hoped that she was wrong anyway.

She shut down her computer, picked up her phone and walked out into the direct sunlight. Nine-fifteen in the morning and it was already punching down hard. She'd be happier if she was in Alaska or at the team house. No, not the team house with its empty bedroom where Jeremy was supposed to be. Nor the hangar office with the long empty workbench.

Her house, her island home. With or without Andi. She hoped it was with, but she didn't understand what had happened to Andi. She wasn't the one who'd been hit yet she was acting as if Zhang Ru had beaten her.

Miranda dialed her phone.

61

"Hey," Mike called to her as if they stood yards apart not inches.

"Hey, yourself." Holly was still trying to figure out what the numbers meant. Miranda clearly knew. Maybe it was some sort of a secret code.

"No, Holly. Look around."

She did. They were in the lap of an obscene amount of luxury and religious fervor. None of which surprised her. Well, maybe a little. She'd spent too many years in battle zones where the religious fervor was highest where abject poverty ruled.

Bitch Clarissa, Drake, and a Chinese general who she didn't recognize were nattering away like they were old friends. The four stars on the jacket draped over the back of the elderly Chinese man's chair matched Drake's, so that was fine. Let the four-stars do whatever it was that four-stars did.

Susan and Sadie sat at the edge, a part but not at the center.

And Andi sat at the far end, hunched into herself.

"What the hell happened to her?"

Susan looked over. "Andi hospitalized the other Chinese general. Barehanded. The reactions were...mixed."

Holly should have noticed the vacant seat next to the other Chinese. It was askew. All of the other unoccupied chairs around the table were in perfect alignment.

Christ, she was too tired to be walking into an unknown situation. She slapped her face to try and clear her thoughts.

The back of the misplaced chair was scuffed, the others all so perfectly finished as she'd expect for visiting dignitaries of this level. One, two, three spots of blood on the white marble. A half-meter area still miscolored with dampness.

Holly pictured the fall of the chair in her head based on the scuff. A wet spot off to the side where something had been cleaned up, blood or vomit, but not quite dry yet. In the present humidity and temperature, that meant it had happed within the last hour.

"Zhang Ru."

"What, really?" Mike twisted to look at her.

"Oh yeah." She went over to Andi, but the reaction was wrong. She wasn't rubbing her knuckles as if to remove blood that wasn't there or as if they hurt. Her hands were clenched white. So white that it was going to hurt like hell when she finally unclenched them and released the blood flow.

Holly dragged over a seat, spun it to face the other way and dropped into it so they were thigh-to-thigh but facing in opposite directions.

"So, Wu, you finally beat the shit out of Zhang Ru."

She nodded.

"About fucking time someone did it."

She nodded again.

"If you look up, I'll give you a high-five. We've all wanted a piece of him for a while."

Andi shook her head.

"Okay, so that wasn't it. You gonna run a guessing game.

Gotta warn you, I still haven't slept since we launched to Alaska, so my guesses will be stupid as shit."

Andi shrugged.

What the hell was going on with this girl? Holly looked around and spotted Miranda out in the sunshine having an earnest phone conversation with someone.

Well, sometimes you had to test a lever to see quite how big it was.

"You know that you're really worrying Miranda."

Andi knocked the chair over backward as she bolted to her feet. Her legs had turned to such Jell-O that she'd have faceplanted into the next chair over if Holly hadn't grabbed her. Keeping a firm hold, she kicked Andi's chair upright once more, then shoved her into the seat.

"That's a little better." Damn big lever. She'd be sure to use it more carefully next time. Thank God she didn't have a lever like that. She barely managed to not turn to look at Mike. But she didn't, so it wasn't any big thing for her. Right?

"Don't you get it, Holly?" Andi's voice was begging her from somewhere down deep. Deep in pain. It was a place that Special Operations people were trained to believe didn't exist, but Andi was there now.

"Nope. Exhausted. Suck at guessing games. You know, all that sort of excuses."

"I beat the shit out of General Zhang Ru."

"Good."

"No, I should have killed the bastard. Instead I gave him a real reason to hunt us. To hunt Miranda. I went after him because of how badly he insulted Miranda—like a life threat. That's when I attacked him. But no matter what I come up with, I can't see how to get her out of that trap. By God, I should have murdered the bastard right there in front of everyone."

"Why didn't you?"

Andi looked at her, really looked at her for the first time. "Did you see who else is sitting at that table?"

She'd seen but...

"He's co-Vice Chairman of the Central Military Commission. Ru did it. Wormed his way to Number Three in all of China. And I just beat the shit out of him in front of Mr. Number Two. If I'd killed Ru outright, would he have had any choice but to launch a war? Great headline: *American Spec Ops Soldier Murders Senior Chinese Leader.* Just perfect, huh?"

"Maybe. You always were the smart one, Andi."

"Me?"

"Sure, Mike and me? We're a comedy routine. Conman and Supergirl—not the sharpest Jake and Sheila, just jaded as hell survivors. Taz the loyal warrior, Jeremy the next generation. You rang the damn prize bell, don't lose sight of that."

"Ru was the prize bell?"

Holly rolled her eyes at her.

"Don't lose sight of what then?"

Holly nodded toward Miranda. Andi turned to look and went quiet.

62

"THERE'S NO QUESTION ABOUT YOUR NUMBERS?"

"That's the third time you've asked me, Miranda. That's not like you."

It wasn't, but she didn't know what to do about it. "You accounted for the nine-degree cross angle of the landing strip on an aircraft carrier?"

"Miranda, I didn't like the numbers either, none of us did. I even tried to factor in diffractions off adjacent thermal layers. Particle scattering, volcanic dust from last year's blast in Tonga, pollen counts. Nothing changed the numbers more than a few tenths of a degree. What I sent you is the only window that fits all of the criteria that you and Holly gathered. I even called the aircraft carrier and had the captain retake several of the images after Holly headed your way, but the numbers didn't change."

"What am I supposed to do?"

There was a long silence. She knew the President and Taz were there, but neither spoke.

Then a woman's voice spoke so softly that Miranda would have missed it if there were even a single seagull calling overhead at the moment, "May I make a suggestion?"

"Yes, Rose, please do. Personally, I'm stumped." She'd never heard Roy admit that before.

Rose. Rose Ramson. Taz had mentioned her yesterday when they'd started the DC crash investigation. Was she also an advisor to the President?

"I would suggest getting the Chinese general out of there as fast as convenient. I believe that Admiral Stanislaw mentioned a Commander Piazza. She has a reputation for efficiency in such situations."

"Then?" Miranda asked.

"Then," Roy said heavily, "we'll figure out what the hell happens next."

63

When Miranda waved her over, Susan didn't want to move. With General Zhang Ru gone, the conversation had improved —marginally, but better. She'd been working all morning to find a way to bridge the gap between the two men, to nurse along the flickers of hope.

Director Reese was doing a fine job of offering information and insights, some uncomfortable to China but others uncomfortable to the US. But she was helping the situation less than she thought. Calling Liú Zuocheng an idiot one more time, no matter how creatively, wasn't helping in the slightest. Yet she seemed unable to stop herself.

In some curious ways, Clarissa Reese shared attributes with Miranda Chase. Her focus to task and dismissal of everything else as irrelevant. And her severe lack of tact. With Miranda, it was a part of her autism. With Director Reese, it became clear that she simply didn't care much for people. Similar but different. An observation Susan was sure Clarissa would *not* appreciate.

Miranda waved again.

Susan excused herself, signaled Sadie to stay in her chair,

and strode out onto the prow of the barge. It rose proudly in a great tapering curve that mimicked the reflection of the mosque's onion dome to the side. Only the slightest breeze rippled the surface and offset the heat. This would be such a fine beach day. Yes, she and Sadie deserved some serious beach time when this was done. Bikini, sunscreen, a sunshade for Sadie, and stretch out with a good book. Who knew what interesting male might be walking by.

"What's up, Miranda?"

In answer, Miranda handed over her phone.

There was no active call on the screen. Instead, there was an image of a satellite. Susan didn't know anything about those.

"Scroll down," Miranda said softly.

Technical specs. Orbital angle and period. Purpose: surveillance. Owner / operator:...

"Really?" she looked at Miranda.

Miranda nodded. "Roy wants you to make the Chinese man go away."

"Roy? As in..." No point in asking. "Me?" She couldn't imagine how the President knew she even existed. "And then?"

"He doesn't know. But he wants you to make the Chinese man go away."

Susan knew that Miranda hated repeating herself. Were her nerves climbing toward that edge again?

"I'm not questioning your math," Susan said with great care, watching Miranda's eyes. They were skittering about, looking for something safe to focus on, much faster than she'd seen before.

"Or Jeremy's," Miranda whispered.

"Or Jeremy's, but are you both absolutely sure? This is huge, Miranda."

She nodded tightly.

Well, everyone up to President Roy Cole himself depended

on this woman. Her confirmation would have to be good enough.

In the background, she heard another spate of sharp voice tones at the table. At a nervous whine from Sadie, there was a sudden silence followed by a moment of brittle laughter.

"May I borrow this for a minute?"

Miranda barely managed a nod this time. By the sharpness of the tiny motion, Susan knew she couldn't leave Miranda alone no matter how major the problem was at the table.

She caught Mike watching them, and waved him over. Then she crossed and met him halfway.

"Miranda needs all of the help she can get at the moment."

He didn't even nod, just kept on walking. But she could hear him ask aloud, "I have a question for you, Miranda. How do you think they clean those crazy onion-shaped domes after the gulls poop all over them?"

As Susan passed behind Andi, she looked at Holly and raised a hand as if saluting, but instead shaded her eyes and squinted. The military sign for *Watch Out*.

Holly swiveled her head once—and didn't need more. "C'mon, Andi, let's go see what's ringing the prize bell."

Susan had no idea what that meant, but they rose together and headed toward Miranda. She'd done all she could there and continued toward the conference.

The three at the table had fallen once more into silence. Sadie's head was raised and watching them closely. Uncomfortable silence.

She had five more steps until she reached them and would have to act.

In her hand was proof that General Liú Zuocheng was not lying. It had *not* been an attack by the Chinese.

But if he was somehow dismissed, he would wonder if she had held proof that it *had* been of Chinese origin. In which case the shaky sliver of trust built here would be shattered.

The question was, did Susan trust the word of the Director of the CIA?

General Nason had selected Reese for this meeting. And her lack of tact spoke of a forthrightness surprising in a former CIA field agent.

At her last step, Susan remembered something Clarissa had said about the logistics of firing the laser of the Chinese satellite.

That's when she smiled.

64

IN A STRANGE WAY, ZUOCHENG WAS ENJOYING HIMSELF.

Only those who had risen to such heights could understand the view that climb created. It formed a common language shared with no more than a few dozen people around the globe. He didn't know how Zhang Ru had become connected to the American Chairman of the Joint Chiefs of Staff, but General Drake Nason was one of the few who spoke his own language.

Of course, the Americans honored their greatest soldiers by stripping them of all power when they achieved their membership of the Joint Chiefs of Staff. They became advisors only.

Foolishness!

The great generals of the CMC were active leaders. They commanded the greatest combined military in the world. They even had the Falcon Commando Unit, their own personal elite Special Operations Forces who reported only to the CMC. If the Americans had a similar unit, Zuocheng had never heard of it. It was a thought to engender nightmares, until each time he remembered how crass the Americans were and how public. They'd never be able to hide something like China's Falcons for long.

Yes, these talks were like walking through a verbal minefield, even without having Ru to aim as a weapon. However, to talk man-to-man, though he might be the enemy, with such a fellow warrior of such an elevated rank was a pleasure of its own.

The woman Clarissa was curiously the one at the table who held the actual power. Her power lay in leading the most feared spy agency in the world.

Mossad and MI-6 were shadows in comparison. The Russian FSB was festering from the inside and would soon eat itself like the snake Ouroboros who bites his own tail. India's Research and Analysis Wing certainly had the scale, but they cared about little beyond Pakistan's borders.

Their own Ministry of State Security still couldn't challenge the tentacled global reach of the CIA.

It was humbling, and it was run by a woman. Not an attractive one either. She was too oversized in a Western way, too blowsy, though there was no doubting Director Reese's mind or inner drive. He preferred his wife's delicate features and manners. Her elegant hands the first time she had poured tea for him—the memory was still perfectly clear five decades later.

Of course, Zuocheng had seen many powerful women this day. The knowledge of the crash investigator and the hair-trigger warrior hidden within the American-Chinese soldier. He even appreciated the woman with the dog. Though her role was undefined and her officer's rank far below their own, she had several times proved herself as the voice of reason.

Now she returned carrying a phone she had not left the table with.

"If I may interrupt?"

Zuocheng nodded. They weren't saying anything constructive anyway. As interesting as he'd found the personalities, the meeting had achieved nothing of substance. Unless he counted the humiliation of Zhang Ru.

Yet he counseled himself to patience with Sun Tzu's words: *If you know your enemy and know yourself, you need not fear the result of a hundred battles.* The day had been *very* educational in experience if not in facts.

The commander sat and rested a hand on her little dog. He hadn't dismissed the dog's presence as the others had. His wife preferred the Pekingese, a proper Chinese breed. Personally, he favored the Chow Chow. One of the oldest dog breeds in the world, a great warlord had once fielded five thousand Chow Chow as hunters and guards. Zuocheng knew a dog's abilities in the drawing room as well as in the field. The Shih Tzu might be Tibetan, but it was no less perceptive for that handicap and Zuocheng had kept a weather eye on the small animal.

"Ms. Reese made an interesting comment earlier with which you agreed, General Liú. I would like to return to that observation."

She had a nicety of speech. While not as carefully circumspect as Chinese, it was a relief from Drake's warrior mode and Clarissa's open aggression. He nodded his head to invite her to continue.

"She noted that it would be very difficult to hide the records regarding the firing of a weapon like an orbital laser, after the fact."

"It would indeed." And when he found out who had prematurely revealed the abilities of the ZY-2B satellite, they would be sent to the Ladakh region to fight battles with India and live out the miserable remains of their short lives in the bitter Himalayan cold above five thousand meters.

"Then I would like to suggest that we look once more."

"But I have already—"

She lifted a hand to stop him. "I would suggest that we have been looking with the right question...but in the wrong location."

65

SUSAN TOOK ONE LAST DEEP BREATH, AND HOPED IT WASN'T HER last breath of freedom. The President had asked Miranda to ask her to make General Liú go away. But it wasn't the right choice to create more rather than less stability.

The President had asked, through a civilian, so she would *not* think of it as an order but rather a recommendation. She was the one on the scene, she only hoped that it wouldn't end her career.

Susan set Miranda's phone in the middle of the table.

The others leaned in to look at the small screen.

Exactly as Miranda had done, she started at the image and scrolled slowly downward.

When the all-important owner / operator notation showed, Susan closely watched their reactions.

Drake Nason's face went brilliant red with barely suppressed fury.

General Liú Zuocheng raised a single eyebrow in interest—the man's control was immense.

Director Clarissa Reese was a study in emotions: shock, disbelief, a quick questioning glance that Susan answered with a nod worthy of Miranda's surety, and then a fury as deep as Nason's own.

"So," Susan spoke into the stunned silence. "While the Chinese are in the clear, other than pushing the boundaries of international treaties against space-based weapons, it would appear that someone has hijacked the CIA's own marginally legal weapon. How do we find out who did it?"

"What?" Nason twisted to look at her, then again to face Clarissa. "You didn't do this?"

"Jesus, Drake." Clarissa rolled her eyes. "What kind of a psycho do you think I am?"

"The kind who launches a space-based laser against all—"

Clarissa cut him off by waving a hand at Zuocheng.

"Hey, I'm not the only one. Jesus but you're such a pansy, Drake."

66

Heidi and Harry had been most of the way home when Clarissa had called them back to work. It was after ten at night. Last night they hadn't made it home at all, catnapping in turns on the office floor as they'd fielded reports from various CIA agents and done as much investigation of their own as they could from their computers about who might have attacked both DC and the USS *Theodore Roosevelt*. Worse, they had depressingly little to show for it.

"We really need to get a life," Heidi spoke up as they reentered their office in the basement of the CIA's New Headquarters Building less than twenty minutes after they'd finally left it.

"Other than this one?" Harry dropped into his chair and began unlocking his computer systems. The screens lighting up one after another.

When had their office begun to smell of stale pizza and salty chips? When had it all begun to look so...mundane? It was a vast improvement over the nest she'd built in the corner of an abandoned warehouse back in her hacker days, but it felt as if it was compressing down on her.

"Yes, other than this life."

Rather than a Red Bull, she grabbed a water bottle from the small fridge. Her security badge, granting her Top Secret access, flapped and fluttered on its neck lanyard.

She punched in Clarissa's number from memory on the CIA's secure phone by her desk.

"Seriously, Harry."

He stopped and looked at her while the satellite tracked down Clarissa so her phone began to ring. "Okay," and he turned back to his computers.

Harry was always open to what was needed, but his nature was more head down than hers, though she'd never really noted it before. But he was right. For the moment they had access to some of the world's most powerful computers— legally. This wasn't a bad gig at all. But it was aging out fast.

"Harry?" Clarissa answered the phone.

"Heidi. With Harry."

"Good. I want to you to trace all actions relating to a satellite."

Heidi and Harry frowned at each other. "Are you sure you don't want the NRO? We don't do anything with actual satellite control."

"Call whoever you fucking have to. Wake them up. Call your pal Jeremy, I think he's in the Situation Room. I don't care. I want to know who hacked the Defender II. They fired it yesterday at 6:04 a.m. Chinese time over the South China Sea."

"Got it." Defender had been the name of President Eisenhower's failed attempt to create a nuclear weapon emplacement in space over Russia. Heidi really hoped this wasn't related to that.

There was a long pause, then Clarissa spoke softly. "The Defender II is one of ours." Then she hung up.

Again they looked at each other.

Harry brought up an image, one they'd been looking at yesterday. An aircraft carrier. On fire. The time stamp had been 0615 as it came into the surveillance satellite's view.

"Oh shit."

67

"IT WAS A HACK."

Clarissa almost wept with relief as the pressure inside her chest let go all at once. For the half hour since she called the Cyber Twins, she hadn't dared to breathe.

She set her phone to speaker. Miranda's team had rejoined the table, so everyone would hear her vindication at the same time.

"You're on speaker. Please repeat that."

"It was a hack, not an inside job." Only then did Clarissa pay attention to the voice.

"Do we have a point of origin yet, Mr. President?" Clarissa prayed that it wasn't inside her own organization.

"Jeremy is working on that with your people. He says—"

"We have some good leads," Jeremy interrupted the President in his excitement. "Homeland Security brought on the NSA to trace Captain O'Dowd's background and contacts, too. Harry and Heidi have, of course, already patched the security hole the hacker used. Or rather, made it look as if they hadn't but left a trap if the hacker tries coming back in."

"Captain O'Dowd?" Clarissa managed edgewise.

"He's the missing pilot. The Air Force officer who stole that plane from Andrews and killed Senator Ramson. An alias, of course, or maybe a name change. He was a sleeper agent, you know. Anyway, we're tracing an overseas contact that may have been his mission launch signal. It occurred within minutes of the hack on the Defender II's command stack to fire the laser. The command was sent when the satellite's orbit passed over the Middle East. The timing's right for the *same* person to do one task and then the other. And there's a common footprint to the two channels. The NSA thinks that may be a coincidence but Heidi doesn't." He finally wound down.

"The footprint?" And Clarissa regretted it the moment she asked.

"Their digital footprint. Every coder at our level has a style, a set of mannerisms. A juxtaposition of habit and a collection of techniques to address different interface issues. She and Harry think the footprint is familiar, a freelancer known to work for the highest bidder. Right now they're spoofing a contract with an embedded tracer. They'll have him the moment he responds and they'll call you, Director Reese, when they do. Then you can mobilize—"

"Thank you, Jeremy," the President's heavy voice rumbled over the phone.

"Oh right. We'll let you know what we find. It could take a while, but the coding techniques to mask their signal definitely let us surmise a common point of origin. Uh...shutting up now."

And he finally did.

"Oh, and if Miranda's there, tell her I said, *Hi!*" Then he was finally quiet.

Clarissa looked down the table and saw that Miranda was smiling. Some kind of nerd code?

"Well," Drake said slowly, "General Liú. It would appear that unless Chinese hackers were involved in this, we owe you an apology. We greatly appreciate your attendance here. I believe we are done."

"Not quite, Drake," the President spoke up.

68

Zuocheng watched the status screens running on side-by-side monitors.

After long negotiations with the President, they had reconvened the meeting aboard his 737 still parked at Rimba Air Force Base in Brunei. He didn't lead them through the command-and-control section, of course, only admitting them into the luxury suite at the front of the plane.

Of them all, only the woman Susan Piazza had looked twice at the fine furnishings. How spoiled these Americans were.

"Not quite a poker plane," Mike had told him as if that meant something, "but that's not what we're here for."

Zuocheng hadn't asked for an explanation.

Instead, he'd sat and watched the left-hand screen.

Neither satellite was technically against the 1967 Outer Space Treaty as neither was a weapon of mass destruction. There had been a brief debate about whether nuclear-*powered* classified the lasers as nuclear weapons, which were explicitly prohibited. But it was ultimately agreed that was too much of a stretch.

Yet the two 2014 UN General Assembly Resolutions to not

allow a space-based arms race definitely included the ZY-2B and the Defender II. Both China and the United States were parties to that agreement.

And their President's recommendation had come down to insisting that be honored.

"Deorbit burn complete on Ziyuan-2B," a voice announced. The left-hand screen began flashing a red message: *Orbital failure.*

The silence in the room was palpable. He should be able to do something with the seven Americans seated in what might be legally construed as Chinese territory aboard his aircraft— what could they do if he ordered an immediate departure? Nothing. But he couldn't think of what might be achieved without considerable backlash.

Instead they all watched the right-hand screen. It was down counting seconds of remaining burn. Forty became thirty. Which became twenty, then ten.

After nine minutes and forty-three seconds, it cut off.

There was a long silence before a different voice, one based in some American bunker, reported, "Deorbit burn confirmed complete on Defender II. Tracking on planned profile."

They shared tea and silence for the twenty-six minutes it took the two satellites to fall through the atmosphere, burn, and sink together into the sea near Point Nemo. It was the spacecraft graveyard, the farthest point from land in any ocean —halfway between Chile and New Zealand.

As a mutual gesture of good faith, their naive President had said.

Liú Zuocheng took comfort from Sun Tzu's wisdom: *Never interrupt your enemy when he is making a mistake.*

None of them appeared to have remembered that Ziyuan-2B had been designed as a twinned observation satellite, the two craft supposedly allowing coordinated, high-resolution 3D imaging. In reality, they were two sides of a single new weapon.

The second one still remained in orbit.

He was patience itself until they had deplaned.

They all made noises about a happier, more cooperative future.

Once they were gone, a subordinate informed him that Zhang Ru was out of surgery and in recovery.

"Get him aboard, in a stretcher if you can, in a coffin if you have to. Then get us back home. Make sure I do not see the bastard."

Alone in his private office, he contemplated the Americans' next action. Every one of their actions were always so public. Every decision reviewed by so many. It is what made them such an easy target for theft of their technology—so many saw every plan that it offered many opportunities to insert or buy an agent. Their *oversight committees* and transparent methods would also hamper any future actions by the CIA in space operations. If they managed to launch another satellite of their own within a decade, it would be a miracle.

For him, the next action was simple.

He picked up the phone and called the director of the China Academy of Space Technology. "General Liú Zuocheng here. I need a replacement for one of the Ziyuan-2B satellites. Begin manufacture immediately."

Zuocheng had greatly enjoyed watching first-hand as the CIA Director writhed during the unjustified destruction of their magnificent weapon.

Next, he sent a *Job well done!* message to the Chinese hacker's drop box. He was the highest paid military specialist in China, and worth every yuan. That also meant that he was dangerous as could be. But Zuocheng had uncovered his real identity and made sure that a special unit tracked him constantly through the nation's facial ID systems.

For now, Zuocheng had proven that the satellite laser design, which he'd had stolen from the Americans in the first place, worked magnificently against a real-world target. Laying the blame on Saudi Arabia—and a fictional defense contractor who the Americans would never be able to track down because none had been involved—was perfect.

At the next meeting with the Crown Prince of Saudi Arabia, Zuocheng would have to consider telling him that the death of the American Senator had been laid at his door as the price for not offering a better deal for oil to China. No, he would keep that for himself. It was sufficient to know that nothing could now heal the prince's relations with America.

After that, he began considering his next move.

69

Ru woke slowly.

He was no longer in a hospital. That was good. His last few wakings had been little more than foggy dreams and fluorescent lights.

Some memory from...last time? The time before? A doctor reading out a litany.

"I don't know if he'll ever speak properly without an electronic voice box. His larynx was badly crushed. The blow to his temple was so severe that we had to remove the eye. Both of his testes were burst, but there was no lasting harm to his urinary tract." He'd droned on about other fractures and breaks, but they were of little consequence.

Now that the drugs were clearing out of his system, Ru had no trouble remembering what had happened. That little ABC bitch had attacked him.

She was going to pay. She and the Chase woman. He would take them both and make them suffer. How many times could he fuck the ABC in front of her precious girlfriend before she died? Maybe he'd whittle her down one joint for each time he

315

took her until all that was left was a torso and a destroyed mind.

Then he'd start in on Chase. For her, he'd think up something worse. He'd take her with a red-hot poker and see how the little lesbian liked that.

He blinked his eye, his *one* eye. They were going to pay for that too, personally—an eye for an eye.

He didn't recognize the room. It was rustic, little more than a hunting cabin. A fireplace burned hot, flooding the room with its heat. An unlit gas lamp, a table, and the bed he lay on. The one window let in a dull red glow. Sunrise? Sunset? Didn't matter.

The pain had been so immense that he'd been positive the old bastard Death awaited him. Yet he'd survived. That would show them he wasn't so easy to kill.

Pushing up— He couldn't! Straps pinned him to the bed.

Couldn't even turn his head enough to see the door when it creaked open.

Liú Zuocheng stepped in.

"My old friend," Ru called out. Or tried to. All he managed was a croak—one that caused an excruciating slice of pain. Shattered larynx, right. He'd have to remember to return that favor as well once he had his hands on those two women.

Zuocheng picked up one of the chairs and set it by the foot of the bed so that they were facing each other. He wore outdoorsman clothes as if this was a hunting cabin.

"I wouldn't try speaking again, Ru. Captain Wu caused quite a bit of damage with that first blow. The straps are to keep you from hurting yourself further, for now."

Ru grunted but even that hurt.

"Yes, you have many questions. I shall answer a few for you. Though perhaps not the ones you expect."

Zuocheng settled himself more comfortably.

"Where are you? I grew up here. My sister and I had

bedrolls by the fire. Father was a trapper. We're quite remote here is all you really need to know; the nearest neighbor was three kilometers away but they moved to the city long ago. I didn't come from privilege as you did. I succeeded because of my skill and drive."

He recrossed his legs as if they were having a friendly chat after a good day trekking together in the forest. Ru had never liked the forest.

"Now to the answers. First, I must thank you for removing your predecessor. General Chen Hua was becoming a serious impediment, but I couldn't remove him myself. My hands had to remain clean there."

Ru had enjoyed removing the bastard. It still didn't replace the death of Ru's young mistress, she'd had such a perfect ass. Well, he would have those exquisite twins soon. And maybe he would find himself a blue-eyed Westerner with magnificent breasts.

"Your various plots against me were foolish, of course. Sun Tzu states one should keep one's friends close and one's enemies closer. You have studied Sun Tzu, haven't you, Ru?"

Not since Zuocheng had practically forced the book upon him while they were serving in Vietnam and he'd used it to level his barracks bunk.

"Ah, an opportunity missed. I recruited your prior mistress very early on, the lovely Chen Mei-li. I knew of my granddaughter's preferences for women, of course. I was quite pleased how they took to each other after I introduced them. Those two girls do make such a beautiful couple. Everything you said in their presence came directly to me, of course. But I knew they were going to grow beyond either of us as they are very impressive in their own way. Therefore, I needed other solutions."

Mei-li. He should have seen that somehow. He'd thought that the whore and her lesbian lover were his window into

General Liú Zuocheng's operations, not the other way around.

Zuocheng rose, but returned to the foot of the bed after replacing the chair by the desk.

"Oh, and the first two people you thought you owned on the Central Military Commission have always belonged to me. Your latest addition, well, the crash of his personal helicopter last night was most regrettable."

When Ru recovered from this, and he had no doubt he would, he would kill Zuocheng so slowly. Ru would make sure that his *old friend* took months to die and spent every minute of it in exquisite agony.

"Your usefulness to me has ended. But there is someone else who wishes to see you. Goodbye, Ru." Zuocheng walked out, leaving the door open.

By straining against the straps, Ru could see the edge of the door.

His one good eye was watering badly with the strain by the time someone came in.

"Daiyu!" He managed a painful croak. His wife. She would free him from this. Then together, they would destroy Liú Zuocheng. Without Zuocheng's protection his granddaughter and Mei-li would become easy targets—followed by Chase and her bitch lover.

Daiyu stopped at the foot of the bed and stared down at him with her arms crossed under her breasts. When unclothed, they weren't her best feature. Perhaps he'd have her change them, at least the shape of the left one. Its asymmetry was distracting.

He couldn't read her expression as she spoke. Always so perfectly neutral.

"Had I known what you really were, I never would have married you last year when General Liú asked me to. But I owed him a family debt. You may recall that he was the one who suggested you marry me."

Daiyu? Daiyu had betrayed him as well? He'd have to burn her with all the others who had betrayed him.

"Oh, don't worry about me, not that you ever would. I'm very good at what I do. General Liú has asked me to run his extensive Hong Kong properties—including the gift of your apartment for myself. Thank you, I like it very much. I'm also the one who suggested inserting the twins into your household. Though they were ultimately unnecessary. Your loss. As agents, they are exceptionally skilled at what they do to extract a man's secrets."

Ru fought against the straps, but they had less give than a five-point ejection seat harness. Was that why Zuocheng had watched them so closely that night with a half smile dancing upon his lips? Not lusting for them himself, but thinking of how they were set as a trap for Ru himself. They too would—

"You always had a favorite threat when you spoke of wanting revenge on a woman."

Daiyu turned to the roaring fire. She pulled a heavy iron poker out of the coals. The lower third glowed a brilliant red with the heat.

"Ca-at?" He managed.

"Castrate you? Oh, no, my dear *husband*. I'm not going to stop until we're far, far past that. My only remaining question is how slowly can I insert it and how far up can you survive it. Maybe you'll live long enough to feel your black heart burn."

Returning to the foot of the bed, she yanked aside the scratchy sheet.

That was when Ru realized that he was naked, and his legs were strapped well apart.

70

"You know what we missed, don't you, Drake?"

"What makes you think I missed it?"

Clarissa leaned back in her seat. Eighteen hours Brunei to London, eight more to DC. She was going to be dead in business class by the time they landed. And sitting next to Drake the whole way, she'd be a certifiable basket case as well.

"Can we not fight? Just for once. We're stuck with each other for twenty-six hours—"

"Don't forget the two layovers. That makes it thirty-one."

"How would you like to be the one who ends up dead when we get there, Drake?"

"Well, if you put it that way, I think my showing up dead might upset my wife. I should warn you that Lizzy can be quite a handful when she gets riled."

Maybe Clarissa could find a pill that would let her sleep from here to DC. Let Drake shuffle her from one plane to another like an oversized piece of carry-on luggage.

"But to your point, Clarissa, I didn't forget that Zuocheng said the ZY-2B was designed to operate in pairs."

"So what are you going to do about it?"

"Absolutely nothing."

"*What?*"

"Easy. You don't want to upset the flight attendants."

Clarissa accepted her glass of champagne from the attendant, who did indeed eye her carefully. Thank God they were airborne and away from Brunei. She needed this and needed it badly. The bright fizz and gentle sweetness did make her feel better. Now she simply needed a good soak in the tub, fresh clothes, and a foot massage—yet another thing Clark had been skilled at. Yet another thing she'd lost when he burned to death.

She couldn't suppress the shiver. Clark, Ramson, all of those people on the *Theodore Roosevelt*. Her husband, the White House... How much had she lost to fire? When she found a new apartment, if it had a fireplace, she'd have it bricked up *before* moving in.

Drake accepted his ginger ale can and glass of ice with grace and received a pleasant smile from the pretty attendant. They always did like men in uniform.

Clarissa was about to tease him over being so lame, when the attendant placed a miniature of Johnnie Walker Black beside his glass. He quickly mixed a highball and sighed.

"Oh my God, that's so much better."

"That's almost human of you, Drake. Now what the hell do you mean you aren't going to do anything about that satellite?"

"Oh, that's easy. I'm not going to do a thing because you're going to take care of it."

If her jaw could drop, it would, but it was clenched too tight to let go. "Oh, and how am I going to do that?"

He set aside his drink and pulled out his tablet computer. He searched for a moment, selected a folder, then dropped it in front of her before picking up his drink once more.

The folder had a list of PDFs.

The first was titled, "Monarch Butterfly Wing Study."

"Are you shitting me?"

"Keep going," Drake had leaned back and closed his eyes, though he continued to sip his drink.

Further titles were: "Low-Visibility Satellites" and "An Evaluation of Space Tugs for Deorbiting Space Debris."

"I still don't get the butterflies."

"Fascinating creatures actually. Did you know that one of the most light absorbent materials in the entire world is the black areas of a Monarch butterfly's wing? DARPA has developed a material based on that. One that is over ninety-eight percent light absorbent across the visible spectrum. You know what that means?"

"That it will look like a black hole."

"Precisely. Now imagine a space tug coated with this material. As long as it approaches from a parallel or higher orbit, so that space rather than the bright Earth is the background..."

"It will be fucking invisible. A black hole in black space. Have we tested this?"

"You're aware of the X-37 spaceplane that the US Space Force flies?"

"Sure, the mini space shuttle."

"That's the one. Our space tug fits very nicely inside its payload bay. Space Force will loft it. It is up to the CIA to determine exactly which satellites are space weapons—not space surveillance, only the weapons. Then you will coordinate with Space Force for their clandestine deorbiting."

"No one will ever see what caused their weapon to fall out of the sky." Clarissa could barely catch her breath. It was beautiful.

"Precisely. Are you interested?"

Interested? Was she *interested*?

"You know," she scrolled down to the next section, which

showed a whole series of flight tests she'd never caught a hint of, "if I didn't hate your stinking guts, Drake, I could kiss you."

"Oh, then please remember that you hate my stinking guts."

"Deal." They shook on it. Then she opened the article on Monarch butterflies and began reading, completely forgetting about her champagne.

71

Susan was in heaven. Well, close to it, if Brunei's tourist literature was to be believed.

She was at least in *personal* heaven.

Tanjung Batu Beach had been made to order. It had fine snorkeling when she needed to get wet, food stalls and nonalcoholic bars lined the landward side when she needed sustenance. Mostly what she wanted to do was lie in the sun and watch the waves roll in. Sadie was perfectly content under a small sunshade that offered a view of everything happening on the long expanse of pale sand.

Her bikini earned her the usual admiring looks, despite many of the Westerners on the beach also wearing as little. But most foreigners who came to Brunei's beaches were a subset of the backpacker breed: all fresh out of school and jaunting from one place to the next. Brunei attracted the adventure and ecotourist types. The party crowd would be in Indonesia, Thailand, or Australia.

It didn't matter, they were all too young for her to even consider as a friendly distraction.

That was okay. After these last few days working with

Miranda, Susan simply needed to stop, be quiet, and enjoy the beach.

She'd ridden out plenty of crises during her career, ones that had permitted far too little sleep. She might not bounce back as she had in her twenties, but she still could. However, for the first time in her entire career, she felt as weary inside as her body did on the outside.

Such baby steps. Two satellites downed today, four more quietly launched tomorrow.

Chinese-American relationships were going to hell. Russian-American ones weren't merely *headed* back into a Cold War, they were already there. How long until the next big war? How many small ones were running even now?

"I've got a choice, Sadie."

Sadie turned to look at her from her little shadowed hutch, resting her chin on her outstretched paws.

"I know. I didn't think I'd get here so quickly. But once I started thinking about it…"

She'd spent over thirty years chasing fires for the military. She'd successfully dowsed more than most and had the accolades to prove it. Both the Military Women's Memorial and the US Naval Memorial Museum had featured her. Her hometown museum in Lawrence, Massachusetts, had done an entire exhibit on her once, and again in an Honoring Servicewomen of Lawrence exhibit.

"But after a lifetime of chasing fires, it might be nice to go back home and sit by one." She'd left behind a dozen hobbies. There were languages to learn, she missed her garden like an ache in her heart, she still had a whole stack of unfinished quilts and needlepoint stashed in a trunk in the family home.

"When was the last time we hit a good old pool hall, not some place packed with fellow squids on the prowl, but hometown locals? Decent New England accents as glad to drink a beer as take the next shot? I ask you."

Sadie didn't have an answer.

Susan tickled her muzzle. "You've got some gray showing."

Sadie probably still had a few years in her, but she'd spent her life on the road as well. No roots.

Susan thought back to the crap apartment she'd shared way back when in Honolulu. Coming back to the same place each night had been a joy, not a burden. For decades her life had been hotels or TDY, temporary duty, base accommodations—she was never still.

Four weeks a year leave. And where did she go every time?

It used to be places like this, well, with a little more action. But this wasn't really leave. This was the twenty-four hours before she could catch a flight headed in the right direction.

For a while now, whenever she hit leave, she went home.

"After all these years, that thread is still tugging me there."

Sadie yawned as if this was old news.

"I'd need to keep busy." But she knew the answer to that, too. How many hours had she sat at the American Legion trading old stories? Or at the DAV, helping disabled vets file insurance paperwork? A lot. Back in the day it had all been about the convoluted paperwork for Vietnam Vets to get coverage for Agent Orange exposure. Now it was about PTSD and TBI—traumatic brain injuries. But she liked working with them, helping them. And there were always more veterans to help than she could ever assist during her brief trips home.

Susan looked out at the clouds scudding along the distant skyline, a few spilling dark rain showers on the ocean as they passed.

Above, the sky was shifting toward the hazy blue of incoming weather. Not blocking her sun yet, but it would by tomorrow.

"Not a good day for firing orbital lasers."

Sadie shook her head, scattering sand and making her ears flap.

God, the things she'd never wanted to know.

Tomorrow was Memorial Day. A day for remembering the dead. How many would remember her when that day came? How many more if she went home to where she could help and live with the same people from one day to the next? Her itinerant lifestyle had been glorious, but was it time to move on?

"Fight the small fires of home?"

She liked the idea of slowing down and helping people. Not massive geopolitical maneuverings that mobilized entire carrier groups. But helping people who she could sit with and they'd remember each other's names.

"Would you like to have a garden you could play in every day?"

Sadie didn't look as if she'd mind that at all.

72

MIRANDA AND ANDI STOOD SIDE BY SIDE ON A CLEAR-SPAN wooden footbridge, staring down at the flowing river. The Temburong was fifty meters wide here, active along the banks but in smooth flow down the middle.

The Sultan had, again through intermediaries, offered a refuge to celebrate the success of their meeting. Across the longest bridge in Southeast Asia, stretching thirty kilometers from the capital city across the Brunei Bay, they had transitioned from quiet urban to jungle primeval. Their cabins were tucked under the canopy at the border of the Ulu Temburong National Park—the Green Jewel of Brunei.

It was *intensely* green. Their innovative no-cut policies, and having enough money that there weren't peasant farmers in need of the farmland or wood, meant that the tropical jungle grew lush all around them.

Over the burbling of the river, the sounds of the jungle echoed back and forth. Frogs croaked from the trees. Large black hornbill birds, sporting enormous, curved bills of white and orange—one a male by the orange horn above its beak like a mad rhinoceros—perched farther along the bridge's rope railing and ignored them completely. A brilliant blue butterfly landed on Andi's shoulder, then fluttered away without her noticing.

"Well, that was a fun one." Andi nudged a stray leaf on the wood decking out through a gap at the base of the railing.

"I can't say that I found it to be much fun."

"I was joking."

"Oh, right."

Miranda let her shoulder rub against Andi's. *Don't mind us. We're just two friends leaning together and watching the river go by.*

There was no one around to notice anyway. Adventurers were off adventuring. Mike and Holly were sleeping together in a lounge chair on the shadowed veranda of their hut. Their hosts were so discreet that she couldn't even remember what they looked like.

"I don't get how they tied together."

"They who?"

"Senator Ramson, the attack on the *Roosevelt,* the South China Sea. It's like the Chinese were part of it, but then Ramson's death doesn't fit. If it was the defense contractors trying to start a war, Ramson still doesn't fit. He was their friend. Either way, you stopped them cold."

"You know I'm not good at this?" Miranda had so much trouble seeing the field when it was wider than a crash investigation.

"I know, sorry." Andi bumped their shoulders together. "Crap, I'll be glad when we get out of this country."

"Me too. Mostly I want to go home."

Andi didn't say anything. Was this one of her uncomfortable silences, or one of the comfortable ones? Not knowing how to tell, Miranda decided that she'd assume the latter until it was proved otherwise.

"I did talk to Roy and Rose about this though."

"What did they have to say?"

"They weren't sure."

Andi's laugh was loud enough to make the rhinoceros hornbills look their way, then return to ignoring them. "So, they were of absolutely no help."

"I guess not. But they tentatively agreed with Sarah, the new nominee for Vice President."

"Who you're already on a first-name basis with." Her smile was soft as Andi looked at her. "And what did *she* have to say?"

Miranda tried to remember. It was as if she lacked the baseline concepts upon which to attach their words. "The MERP, the Mid-East Realignment Plan..."

"Which got the Vice President killed for even thinking it up." Andi's interruptions never bothered her. They were more like accents to her own thoughts.

"...cancelled a huge number of weapons sales because the oil-rich countries of OPEC were among the largest buyers of American military exports."

"Oh no!" Andi was shaking her head.

"What?"

"Let me guess what she said, and then please tell me I'm wrong."

"Okay."

Andi took a deep breath. "Someone, probably the Saudis, mobilized a sleeper agent to collude with the defense contractors and take out Hunter Ramson for not stopping MERP. Then the contractors, and perhaps other weapon suppliers, decided that—as long as they had that hacker on board already financed by someone else—they could start a Chinese-American war. It would be very good for business. Both the oil business for the Saudis because it takes a lot of oil to run a war, and for the defense contractor business. It would also help distract from the attack on Ramson. So they could continue to collude even if one could no longer sell weapons to the other." Andi paused. "You're not telling me that I'm wrong."

"I know you asked me to." Miranda looked for help, but it was only the two of them on a bridge high over a river. "But that's exactly what Sarah said."

"Well...shit!"

"You never curse."

"Sometimes I do. Holly said I used it dead-on."

"Oh, okay. As long as you're good at it, that's fine."

Andi's soft laugh seemed to float out over the river and be carried gently toward the sea.

Under cover of where their elbows were touching on the rail, Andi slipped her fingers into Miranda's.

A long time later, as the setting sun changed the sound of the forest calls and the hornbills had flown away to their nest, Holly and Mike called out over the soft burbling of the river.

"Dinner will be ready soon."

Still they stood, watching the sky darken until the first stars punched through the light haze.

"It will be good to get home," Andi whispered and squeezed her fingertips.

Miranda freed her hand to pull out her notebook. She flipped to the *Considerations* page and showed it to Andi.

"*Is the island still home when Andi is there?*" Andi read aloud, though she seemed to have trouble pronouncing the last few words clearly.

Miranda then struck out the line and wrote a capital Y beside the entry.

When she looked to Andi, there were silent tears sliding down her cheek.

Not wanting to break any national rules, Miranda replaced her notebook and once more crossed her arms on the railing.

As they stared down at the placidly flowing river again, Miranda slipped her hidden fingers into Andi's and squeezed back.

EPILOGUE

"YOU'RE MAGNIFICENT," JEREMY MANAGED. HE LAY ONCE MORE IN the sea, or forest, of boxes that was their living room.

"Me? Why?" Taz, finally worn down, lay in another aisle among the cardboard...towers? Maybe they were towers. Only their feet touched from where they'd each collapsed.

"You had the energy to order dinner delivery. I don't think I could have done that," he told her. "I love that about you."

"Well, guess what, Jeremy, that means that you get to answer the door."

"When?"

The doorbell rang.

"Oh. You're spooky, Taz. You know that, right?"

"I do."

He managed to attain a standing position, leaned on a box for support, and almost fell into it. It was the oversized one— open and empty—that their field packs had been in.

Taz lay on the carpet, her eyes closed, and smiled at her triumph of not having to move.

He staggered to the door, caught the driver halfway to his car, and beckoned him back. The cartop sign showed that dinner was from Hong Kong Kitchen. Jeremy had missed even that. The delivery driver's look left no doubt that he'd rather be playing video games than dealing with people too exhausted to answer their door in under ten seconds.

Jeremy received a grunt for the tip, then the boy slouched his way back to his car.

Returning inside, he sat down next to Taz among the boxes.

She sat up, slipped out her knife, then slit two flaps off the box and set them on the carpet as placemats.

He set out Szechuan Spicy Baby Shrimp and General Tso's Chicken. "Good choices."

Taz had already split apart her bamboo chopsticks and snagged a piece of chicken. She answered with a loud, "Yum!" around a full mouth as she sucked in cool air against the heat.

Jeremy was reaching for his first taste of shrimp when he noticed the angle of his chopsticks and stopped. He slowly shifted the chopsticks back along the same trajectory, though he wasn't sure why.

Taz had stopped eating and was now watching him intently.

Was it the angle? Or the spacing? Or that they were chopsticks?

He was so tired that the image blurred and he saw...the line of the F-35C Lightning II's last flight crashing onto the aircraft carrier's deck. Just like the hack on the laser satellite. It had come in sideways. Just like his chopsticks sliding in over the edge of the container. His *Chinese* chopsticks sliding over the edge of—

"Taz! Taz!"

"What? I'm right here, you don't need to shout."

"Quick! We need to call."

"Who? The restaurant? Why?"

"No! No!" Jeremy couldn't believe that he'd missed it. "We need to call everyone else: Harry and Heidi, Drake and Clarissa, Miranda, the President...everyone! The hack didn't come from Saudi Arabia, it came *through* them! The—" he waved the chopsticks in the slicing motion. "—it came out of China!"

Taz's eyes shot wide. "That means—"

"The Chinese really *did* attack the USS *Theodore Roosevelt,* with one of *our* laser weapons! That general they were meeting with was probably all wrapped up in it."

Taz was shaking her head, but the motion was slow and uncertain.

"Trust me," Jeremy pleaded. It made sense, everything fit, but it wasn't the sort of thing he could prove. At least not quickly.

Taz's headshake turned to a firm nod. *She trusted!*

"God but I love the way your brain works, Jeremy." She kissed him quickly, then they both grabbed their phones. Their dinner would be long cold by the time they returned to it.

AFTERWORD

It is startling or perhaps, as in this case, sad when real world events overtake fictional ones.

A month after the crisis in this book was conceived and written, an F-35C Lightning II did, in reality, crash while landing on the aircraft carrier CVN-70, USS *Carl Vinson* in the South China Sea. After the pilot ejected, the jet fell overboard into the ocean, sank, and was finally recovered from over three thousand meters of water. Seven, including the pilot, were injured in this event.

The aircraft carrier was operational in under thirty minutes and the plane was recovered five weeks later, an amazing technical achievement of its own, from twelve thousand feet of water. The cause of the fair-weather, daylight ramp strike (a landing so low that the pilot clipped the tail-end of the ship) is still under investigation.

The *day* after I finally decided on and wrote the cause of my fictional crash, a People's Republic of China warship aimed a military-grade laser at an Australian military airplane in flight —an escalation of prior, lower-grade actions. Their attack occurred well beyond the bounds of the South China Sea. It happened in the Arafura Sea close by the north coast of Australia, well within the Australian Exclusive Economic Zone. The pilots landed safely and are reported to have fully recovered.

I decided to retain these elements of my own story, but can't help wishing this was a cautionary tale, not one *ripped from the headlines.* Even though I did write this story before these events occurred, I can't help but be saddened by the rapidity with which they became reality.

Hoping for a brighter, safer future.

M. L. Buchman

North Shore, MA

March 2022 (the first days of the Russian-Ukraine War)

ABOUT THE GUEST CHARACTER

Susan Piazza backed *The Great Chase* tabletop strategy game based on this novel series for a Kickstarter fundraiser at the reward level of *Join the Team for One Novel* (Thank you so much, Susan.) This afforded me the opportunity to sit with her for several hours, share cheesecake and discuss knitting, quilting, and the curious twists and turns of her life.

Due to circumstances beyond her control, Susan was unable to continue the career she so loved in the US Navy past her first eight years. The decades since have done nothing to diminish her passion for the service or the continued joy it has brought her.

During her service, she was indeed the communications expert for an Admiral. In fact, most of her character's past throughout this work is lifted from fact, not fiction. The fiction? I did my best to give her the career that she didn't have the opportunity to fulfill. In the ending scene I created for her character, I also attempted to capture her joy of home that pulled so hard against her joy of travel and the challenges of the Navy.

Over the years, she has volunteered thousands of hours

helping disabled vets, especially bringing her legal skills to their aid (she became an expert in navigating the complex paperwork for proving claims for veterans and their families). She is an active member of the DAR (Daughters of the American Revolution) and a past Commander of both the Disabled American Veterans and the American Legion, her favorite charity. (You may donate to this amazing non-profit at: https://mylegion.org. *Tip:* local donations work locally, so contact your local chapter).

I gave her that same impressive rank in her fictional service. Any missteps her character makes in this book are the manufacture of the author. Everything she does right, came straight from the real-life Commander Susan Piazza.

To meet her was a joy. To know her, even a little, a pure pleasure.

MIRANDA CHASE SO FAR

AVAILABLE IN EBOOK, PRINT, AND AUDIO

MC#11 - SKIBIRD (EXCERPT)

IF YOU ENJOYED THAT, HERE'S A TASTE OF
WHAT'S COMING IN SUMMER 2022

SKIBIRD (EXCERPT)

Altitude: 48,000 feet
Off the coast of Antarctica
69°22'25" S 76°22'18" E
approximately

"Kolya, I am going to rip out your eyes and crap in your skull!"

"This is not my doing, Captain."

Captain Fyodor Novikov knew it wasn't his navigator's fault, but he needed someone to blame. The cargo jet was creaking worse than his grandfather's knees as the storm slammed the Ilyushin-76 one way and then another across the Antarctic Sky.

When they had departed Cape Town International Airport, the report had been for clear weather all the way to Progress Station in Antarctica. And it had been...for the first four thousand kilometers of the flight.

But then Antarctica had decided to have a fit worse than his mother had when he'd brought home Aloysha. The shouts, the pounding of fists on the armchair...even in his bedroom that night they'd lain together listening to Mama's foul mutterings through the thin walls.

In retaliation, he had married the gorgeous Tatar blonde from Kazan—and regretted it ever since. She'd had an extended affair with his commander, which had caused one type of problem. Major Zubov had made sure that Fyodor was always assigned the most distant, longest lasting assignments, keeping him far from Moscow.

Then she'd moved on to *his* commander in turn, which had caused Fyodor an entirely different type of problem. Major Zubov now assigned him the worst flights and the oldest aircraft in retribution.

It wasn't his navigator, it was *Aloysha* who should have her eyes ripped out. Little status-climbing *Sterva!* Whose bed would she find next, the Russian President's?

At least that's what he'd expected, but he'd checked his messages shortly before takeoff. Aloysha's low voice had left a long, rambling apology of how he'd been the only man to ever treat her properly and how could she make it up to him? She made several very explicit recommendations that, as always with her, had left him aching with anticipation.

He was actually thankful for this long flight. It would place him out of reach for several days while he somehow convinced himself to say *Nyet!*—when he knew full well he'd say *Da!*

A new vibration made the control yoke rattle and buzz against his palms.

The massive Ilyushin IL-76 cargo jet had been modified for long range and could fly over nine thousand kilometers when traveling empty. Even with a full load of sixty thousand kilograms, his range would be eight thousand. It would have left him more than enough fuel reserve to return to South Africa when the storm notice had reached them as they crossed the sixtieth latitude south.

However, the damned administrators of the Arctic and Antarctic Research Institute were cutting corners. In fact, the ARRI were cutting off whole sides trying to keep Russia's five Antarctic stations operational, down from the Soviet Union's twenty-three.

One of his grandfather's favorite topics, while consuming an excess of vodka, was discussing the collapse of the Motherland in a voice far too loud. Grandfather had helped build the Pole of Inaccessibility Station in 1958. Occupied for twelve days, it was the farthest point in Antarctica from the ocean in all directions. The last time it was visited—which happened about once a decade—all that remained of the original two-story hut was the bust of Lenin that had perched at the top and the tip of a radio antenna. The rest had been buried beneath the drifting snow.

The Geographic South Pole, where the Americans squatted in their deluxe super-station, was eight hundred kilometers from the center of the continent. *That had taken Russian know-how,* Grandfather would pound the table with the bottom of his empty glass, making his point as well as fresh dents in the old wood.

It was Russian *stupidity* as far as Fyodor was concerned. The traverse in each direction had taken longer than the occupation of the place had lasted.

The question now was, how long would *they* last?

The freak, mid-December storm was worthy of the dead of winter, not the height of summer.

His four-engine IL-76 "Candid" was one of the largest cargo planes in the world. Which gave the winds buffeting them about something to truly grab a hold of.

It rattled like a tin can of old bolts and screws being shaken by Baba Yaga herself as she strove to raise the demons of the wind. If so, she was depressing good at it.

The IL-76 was so old, thanks to Aloysha dumping Major

M. L. BUCHMAN

Zubov, that it didn't even have a glass cockpit. Fyodor had to fly using all dial instruments. His GLONASS receiver had been mounted on a spindly arm, which had snapped and shattered the receiver two months ago during a rough landing. Maintenance was still *waiting for parts,* which probably meant the repair order was stalled in Major Zubov's inbox.

To carry a backup GPS receiver to position himself by using the American satellite system was forbidden.

So it was up to Kolya, seated in the IL-76's navigation station directly below their feet, to keep them on course. He always managed, and Fyodor was careful not to ask how. Kolya probably used his personal iPhone for GPS positioning.

However, his copilot was a party fanatic—who Major Zubov also wanted as far away as possible—so care was needed not to use American technology in his presence. Fyodor always warned Kolya when his copilot left his seat in case he decided to visit the navigator below.

The IL-76 Candid had a two-story cockpit. Fyodor, his copilot, the engineer, and the loadmaster all had seats in the upper level. There wasn't much chatter, they were each approaching dead-ends in their careers and only Party-man-copilot didn't know it. Below them, seated before the curve of the down-and-forward-looking windows and surrounded by his instruments, Kolya sat alone with the best view in the plane.

Somewhere, out in the blinding whiteness below, Kolya would find their landing strip. In mid-December, the snow-and-ice around Progress Station would have melted away enough to expose the hard earth. He hoped they had done a better job of grading since their last landing. He'd thought that it *would be* their last landing at Progress. How the landing gear remained attached was both a miracle and a testament of old Soviet engineering.

The days of threatening underlings with a trip to the Gulag were gone, again much of grandfather's disappointment.

However, Fyodor had offered the men responsible for the runway maintenance an assignment to the Navy's *pride and joy* if they didn't take better care of the runway. The country's sole aircraft carrier, the *Admiral Kuznetsov*, was little better than a slave ship. It had to be towed to sea and anchored there for flight operations. It definitely offered crew members a shortened lifespan from hazardous materials, fires, accidents, and numerous other failures. And every person in the Russian military knew it.

The runway had better be perfect this time or he might pass on a dose of Major Zubov's revenge.

With a gut-churning plunge, and a raucous protest from the wings' joints, he began his descent from a hundred and fifty kilometers away.

Down into the maelstrom. Which was precisely the descent he already knew he'd be making with the sultry Aloysha when he returned to Moscow.

Because of Major Zubov's various assignments, Fyodor was exceptionally well practiced at flying old equipment through horrid weather. It was likely that he could have made a safe landing and simply had another bad-weather-flying story to tell.

However, a pair of objects impacted his plane while still at forty-one thousand feet. They hit so close together that they sounded like a single event.

The first piece, a long needle shape the width of a soccer ball, was moving at hypersonic speeds. It drove a shockwave of air ahead of it. The air was so intensely compressed that it burned at twenty-four-hundred degrees.

The object barely slowed as it passed through the copilot from his right shoulder to his left hip. Next, it punched through the floor and vaporized a thirty-centimeter-long section of Navigator Kolya's thigh before blasting out the bottom of the airplane and continuing on its way. It also destroyed Kolya's phone, which had been monitoring the American's GPS system.

The second piece hit at effectively the same instant and speed but ten meters aft.

It was this piece that sealed the IL-76's fate. It punched a hole through the central fuel tank, and the last of the jet's fuel began to dump out the hole. All four engines would flame-out from fuel-starvation long before the big plane reached the ground.

The bang of impact and the scorching passage of the first object left Fyodor deaf, blind in his right eye, and covered in second- and third-degree burns from the heat of the object's passage. He couldn't feel the copilot's hot blood sprayed over his right side. He couldn't hear Kolya's screams as his femoral artery pumped out his life's blood, spraying red all over the navigator's cabin.

In agony, Captain Fyodor Novikin fought the controls all of the way down.

It wasn't enough to save the plane or any of its crew.

———

"CERTAINLY DIDN'T SEE MUCH OF THIS STUFF GROWING UP." Holly Harper was busy ignoring Mike Munroe's suggestions that she leave her cozy nest to go out in it.

Hit by a rare snowstorm, Miranda's personal, private island had been coated a foot deep with fluffy white stuff—a rare event in Washington State's San Juan Islands. Even rarer, it had happened mere days before Christmas and it was predicted to be cold all week. They were going to have a white Christmas. She'd never had one of those and was looking forward to it. As long as she didn't have to go out in it.

"You do understand that's snow, right, Mike? Frozen water. As in cold."

"Brisk! Besides, compared with where I used to live—"

"Blah. Blah. Denver. Blah. Blah. Skiing. Blah. Blah. I remain one unconvinced Aussie. Where I grew up a cold winter's day was thirteen degrees—"

"Then you're fine, it's only down to twenty-seven this morning." He waved out the big picture window where the late sunrise glinted off the brilliant snow.

"Centigrade, you Yank. That fifty-five degrees to you. I'm staying here. Besides, my toes are all warm and cozy."

Mike began making chicken noises. Thankfully, he wised up before she had to hurt him.

Coming this summer.

ABOUT THE AUTHOR

USA Today and Amazon #1 Bestseller M. L. "Matt" Buchman started writing on a flight from Japan to ride his bicycle across the Australian Outback. Just part of a solo around-the-world trip that ultimately launched his writing career.

From the very beginning, his powerful female heroines insisted on putting character first, *then* a great adventure. He's since written over 70 action-adventure thrillers and military romantic suspense novels. And just for the fun of it: 100 short stories, and a fast-growing pile of read-by-author audiobooks.

Booklist says: "3X Top 10 of the Year." PW says: "Tom Clancy fans open to a strong female lead will clamor for more." His fans say: "I want more now...of everything." That his characters are even more insistent than his fans is a hoot.

As a 30-year project manager with a geophysics degree who has designed and built houses, flown and jumped out of planes, and solo-sailed a 50' ketch, he is awed by what is possible. More at: www.mlbuchman.com.

Other works by M. L. Buchman: *(* - also in audio)*

Action-Adventure Thrillers

Dead Chef
One Chef!
Two Chef!

Miranda Chase
Drone*
Thunderbolt*
Condor*
Ghostrider*
Raider*
Chinook*
Havoc*
White Top*
Start the Chase*
Lightning*

Science Fiction / Fantasy

Deities Anonymous
Cookbook from Hell: Reheated
Saviors 101

Single Titles
Monk's Maze
the Me and Elsie Chronicles

Contemporary Romance

Eagle Cove
Return to Eagle Cove
Recipe for Eagle Cove
Longing for Eagle Cove
Keepsake for Eagle Cove

Love Abroad
Heart of the Cotswolds: England
Path of Love: Cinque Terre, Italy

Where Dreams
Where Dreams are Born
Where Dreams Reside
Where Dreams Are of Christmas*
Where Dreams Unfold
Where Dreams Are Written
Where Dreams Continue

Non-Fiction

Strategies for Success
Managing Your Inner Artist/Writer
Estate Planning for Authors*
Character Voice
*Narrate and Record Your Own
Audiobook**

Short Story Series by M. L. Buchman:

Action-Adventure Thrillers

Dead Chef

Miranda Chase Origin Stories

Romantic Suspense

Antarctic Ice Fliers

US Coast Guard

Contemporary Romance

Eagle Cove

Other

Deities Anonymous (fantasy)

Single Titles

The Emily Beale Universe
(military romantic suspense)

The Night Stalkers
MAIN FLIGHT
The Night Is Mine
I Own the Dawn
Wait Until Dark
Take Over at Midnight
Light Up the Night
Bring On the Dusk
By Break of Day
Target of the Heart
Target Lock on Love
Target of Mine
Target of One's Own
NIGHT STALKERS HOLIDAYS
*Daniel's Christmas**
*Frank's Independence Day**
*Peter's Christmas**
Christmas at Steel Beach
*Zachary's Christmas**
*Roy's Independence Day**
*Damien's Christmas**
Christmas at Peleliu Cove

Henderson's Ranch
*Nathan's Big Sky**
*Big Sky, Loyal Heart**
*Big Sky Dog Whisperer**
*Tales of Henderson's Ranch**

Shadow Force: Psi
*At the Slightest Sound**
*At the Quietest Word**
*At the Merest Glance**
*At the Clearest Sensation**

White House Protection Force
*Off the Leash**
*On Your Mark**
*In the Weeds**

Firehawks
Pure Heat
Full Blaze
*Hot Point**
*Flash of Fire**
Wild Fire
SMOKEJUMPERS
*Wildfire at Dawn**
*Wildfire at Larch Creek**
*Wildfire on the Skagit**

Delta Force
*Target Engaged**
*Heart Strike**
*Wild Justice**
*Midnight Trust**

Emily Beale Universe Short Story Series
The Night Stalkers
The Night Stalkers Stories
The Night Stalkers CSAR
The Night Stalkers Wedding Stories
The Future Night Stalkers

Delta Force
Th Delta Force Shooters
The Delta Force Warriors

Firehawks
The Firehawks Lookouts
The Firehawks Hotshots
The Firebirds

White House Protection Force
Stories

Future Night Stalkers
Stories (Science Fiction)

SIGN UP FOR M. L. BUCHMAN'S NEWSLETTER TODAY

and receive:
Release News
Free Short Stories
a Free Book

Get your free book today. Do it now.
free-book.mlbuchman.com